Critical Praise for Cor

Nightfall
Minnesota Author Project Best Indie Adult Novel Award
(Runner-Up)

"Some readers might think the term 'corporate thriller' is an oxymoron. That's because they haven't read former trial and corporate attorney Lutterman's Pen Wilkinson thrillers."

—*St. Paul Pioneer Press*

"It's a great read, with plenty of scary moments that will push you to race through it. Don't count on getting any sleep if you read it at night."

—Sandy Penny, *Sweet Mystery Books* (5 stars)

"*Nightfall* is a gripping political thriller, a serious page turner. I was totally hooked and I highly recommend reading it. And if you liked it as much as I, then the whole series might be for you too."

—Kerstin, *Whispering Stories*

Freefall

"The story is fast-paced and the suspense doesn't let go until the final rewarding conclusion."

—*Mystery Sequels*

"[T]he pace is fast and Pen is an interesting character. Her injury is part of her life but doesn't define her. And yes, she has a rich, handsome boyfriend. One thread running through the excitement is Pen and Marsha's relationship, as they finally come to terms with the accident."

—*St. Paul Pioneer Press*

"[A] significant step forward for the series . . . readers will eagerly anticipate Lutterman's fourth adventure starring Pen Wilkinson."

—*Cedar Rapids Gazette*

"Pen must go in search of her missing nephew, a computer prodigy who may be able to prevent a cyber catastrophe that could destroy a major bank and send the world economy into, yes, freefall."

—*Crime Fiction Lover*

Windfall

"Pen Wilkinson is one of the most intriguing new characters on the Minnesota crime scene."

—*St. Paul Pioneer Press*

"A nicely written and taut book, *Windfall* would be a welcome addition to any library for fans of corporate thrillers . . . a fun read."

—*Reading Other People*

"With a fast-moving action-packed plot, this thriller has you jumping at shadows and considering keeping a gun on your nightstand, or better yet, under your pillow. Character driven and well written, you feel like you're in the middle of the action."

—*Sweet Mystery Books*

Downfall

"*Downfall* is an exhilarating, action-packed financial thriller . . ."

—Harriet Klausner, *Mystery Gazette*

"[A] fantastic read . . . an entertaining and engrossing book."

—*Charline Ratcliff Reviews*

"*Downfall* by Brian Lutterman is a well-constructed thriller . . . an excellent read."

—Larry Krantz, *Readers' Favorite Reviews*

"[R]eplete with suspense made even more dramatic by the protagonist being confined to a wheelchair."

—John A. Broussard, *I Love a Mystery*

Bound to Die
Minnesota Book Award Runner-Up

"[A] taut, swift-paced and well-plotted debut thriller by a Minnesota author."

—*St. Paul Pioneer Press*

"[A] gripping, twisted, lethal saga, and one that quickly captures the reader's total attention and won't let go until the shocking climax…"

—*Midwest Book Review*

"An inexplicable quadruple murder, a duplicitous presidential adviser and a mysterious and deadly cult called the Bound bear mysterious connections to each other in lawyer Brian Lutterman's debut mystery, *Bound to Die*. Widow Tori McMillan wanders jungles, mountains and the nation's capital as she tries to find her best friend and a group of missing children, as well as to determine what actually happened to her husband."

—*Publishers Weekly*

"[B]ound to entertain…gets your interest from the get-go."

—Kristofer Upjohn, *Pine Bluff Commercial*

"With the help of an infatuated police officer and the hindrance of an FBI agent, Tori finds herself traveling from the Yucatan jungle into the mountains of Denver to the steps of the White House. Before it is over, Tori will question all that she believes to be good. Tori also puts her life on the line in order to solve the mystery that now threatens her sanity."

—Susan Johnson, *All About Murder*

Poised to Kill

"Author Brian Lutterman has proven himself to be a master story-teller in this masterfully woven tale of tycoons and terrorists. *Poised to Kill* is highly recommended reading, especially for en-thusiasts of contemporary action/adventure thrillers."

—*Midwest Book Review*

"Lutterman keeps his readers on the edge of their chairs until the last page. The twists, chases, and shootings by professional ter-rorists keep occurring with increasing tension. Written in the first person, Lutterman draws his readers into the thriller. Lut-terman is the author of *Bound to Die*, another taut, top quality thriller. This is a suspenseful, must read book."

—Marion Cason, *I Love a Mystery*

"[A] good, enjoyable read, with satisfying links to today's soci-ety. Lutterman should garner wide audiences for this story, and for those to come."

—Carl Brookins, *Reviewing the Evidence*

"Lawyer and author Brian P. Lutterman's latest novel, *Poised to Kill*, is an action-packed suspense thriller that's just simply en-joyable. Lutterman, who packed a punch with his debut novel, *Bound to Die*, proves that he is not just a flash in the pan or a one-book wonder with *Poised to Kill*... Highly recommended."

—*New Mystery Reader Review*

Deadfall

Brian Lutterman

Conquill Press
St. Paul, Minnesota

This book is a work of fiction. Names, characters, places and incidents either are products of the author's imagination or are used fictitiously. Certain liberties have been taken in portraying actual law enforcement and prosecutorial agencies. This is wholly intentional. Any resemblance to actual events, or to actual persons living or dead, is entirely coincidental. For information about special discounts for bulk purchases, contact conquillpress@comcast.net.

DEADFALL

Copyright © 2020 by Brian Lutterman

Cover Design: Rebecca Treadway

Library of Congress Control Number: 2020934289

Lutterman, Brian

Deadfall: a novel / by Brian Lutterman – 1st edition

ISBN: 978-0-9995385-3-1

Conquill Press/September 2020

Printed in the United States of America

10 9 8 7 6 5 4 3 2 1

Dedicated to the millions of people worldwide who live their lives with purpose, courage, and dignity . . . and a disability.

Also by Brian Lutterman

The Pen Wilkinson Series

Downfall

Windfall

Freefall

Nightfall

Other Books

Bound to Die

Poised to Kill

dead·fall

/ˈdedfôl/

noun

: a trap arranged so that a heavy weight is dropped on the prey, killing or disabling it

My wheelchair jerked back and forth as we struggled for the gun, her face contorted into a wild grimace. She let go with one hand and tried to hit me in the head. I managed to turn my head but still took a glancing blow. Somehow, I still held onto her gun hand, which she pushed downward, once again aided by her other hand, trying to point the weapon at me.

The light was right on us now. I heard another shot from the woods, but I paid no attention to what was going on. I was busy trying to keep from being shot in the face.

I twisted desperately with both hands, but I could see it was a battle I wasn't going to win. I'm not weak; I have strong arms from propelling myself in a wheelchair all day. And she wasn't a big woman. But standing over me, using her lower body, she had too much leverage.

She leaned forward, putting her weight into the effort, and the gun slowly moved to within inches of my face.

I let go with my left hand, reached down and grabbed the left wheel of my chair, and yanked it sharply. Now leaning forward, she lost her balance, firing the gun as she stumbled. I yanked on the wheel again as I pulled her forward. She tripped over the footrests, landing on her hands and knees, then rolled over, pointing the gun at me.

She had me, point blank.

"Now eat this," she said.

PART ONE

The Dead

Los Angeles

Chapter 1

When you have a run-in with your employer, you usually figure the worst they can do is fire you. But when your employer is the US Department of Justice, you know your fate could be a lot worse than just being canned. Federal prosecutors have a lot of power, and if they decide to bring it to bear on an individual, well, that's an individual you really don't want to be. I inched north on the I-710 toward downtown LA, wondering if I was on my way to becoming that person.

Phase One of the process had been completed half a year ago, when I had been quietly eased out of my job as an assistant US attorney for the central district of California. The reason? It depended on whom you asked. If you looked at the official record, my departure was deemed advisable for medical reasons. Like most lies, that one contained a kernel of truth; I was in fact beginning to suffer from post-traumatic stress disorder. If you asked one of the bigwigs, off the record, they'd say I was insubordinate and not a team player. That, too, was false, unless you considered showing unusual initiative to be insubordination. If you asked me, my real offense had been showing up the aforesaid male bigwigs. They simply couldn't abide a good outcome resulting from ideas that did not at least look like theirs, produced by people who didn't at least appear to be them. I'd tried my best to stay out of the limelight and deflect credit, but it hadn't worked.

One of the most perturbed officials had, unfortunately, been the biggest bigwig, US attorney Dave O'Shea, who had been all set to nail a political rival for running a bid-rigging scheme. That operation, however, had been proven to be minor, receiving little publicity, compared to another massive, illegal scheme I'd uncovered at the same time. The resulting embarrassment had greased the skids for my exit. And the call this morning from Susan Hecht, O'Shea's assistant, had chilled me.

"Ms. Wilkinson? Mr. O'Shea would like to see you this afternoon."

As I drove, I was still racking my brain, trying to think of anything I could have done to get on O'Shea's bad side again. I had been involved in solving a murder in Minnesota but had successfully kept my role out of the media. The experience, however, had been traumatic, and I'd nearly been killed. I'd spent most of the time since my termination recovering from the resulting PTSD and had been largely successful. Thanks to intensive therapy, medication, rest, and the passage of time, I now considered myself healed. More than that, my relationship with my boyfriend, James Carter, had been mended. I'd been fortunate. The last thing I needed now was further trouble from Dave O'Shea.

I suddenly jammed the hand brake lever forward, screeching to a full stop, narrowly avoiding a collision with the stationary car in front of me. I exhaled as my heartbeat slowly returned to normal, trying to pay attention to my driving as the traffic resumed its crawl toward downtown. But my thoughts soon returned to the upcoming meeting, beginning with its location. Susan Hecht had told me the meeting was not at the US attorney's offices in the federal courthouse, but in another building down the street. She'd repeated the location for emphasis, making it clear I was not to go to the courthouse. The mystery deepened.

I found a handicap space in a ramp adjacent to my destination. Then I unclamped my wheelchair, extended the ramp, and rolled out into the garage. With a few minutes to spare, I stopped on the first floor and checked out the directory to see who occupied this nondescript office tower. The tenants included several government agencies, some law firms, and a few marketing companies. I saw no listings at all for the fourteenth floor, where my meeting was to be held.

With clammy hands, I got onto the elevator, reached up, and pushed the button for fourteen. Suite 1418 was at the end of the hallway. I rolled down and saw a young man posted at the door. He wore an FBI class A uniform: dark suit, white shirt, muted tie. He opened the door for me, saying nothing. I paused, then went inside.

Three people sat at a rectangular table in a windowless conference room. Sitting nearest to me was a strikingly beautiful woman with Asian features. She sat across from US attorney Dave O'Shea, a stocky man with dark, unruly hair.

I was surprised to see the third person, a clean-cut, powerfully-built man in his early fifties. Lieutenant Dan Howard was the homicide commander for the Newport Beach Police Department. I'd had a run-in with him two years ago, when he had erroneously arrested my boyfriend, James Carter, for murder. To his credit, he had forthrightly assumed responsibility for the mistake, but I assumed he still had no love lost for me. And what was he doing here?

The woman stood up, and I was surprised to see she was about six feet tall. So am I, but people don't really see it. She extended her hand. "Ms. Wilkinson? I'm Special Agent Wendy Nomura. It's nice to meet you." We shook, and she gestured toward the table. "I believe you know these gentlemen." O'Shea and Howard nodded to me.

FBI, US attorney, and a cop who hated me. This was looking worse by the minute.

"Doris Penny Wilkinson," Nomura said. "Do you go by Doris?"

"I prefer Pen."

"Of course."

I had a feeling she knew full well what name I preferred, along with a lot of other things about me.

"Our first item of business," Nomura said, "concerns the confidentiality of this meeting." She handed me a sheet of paper with a space for my signature at the bottom. The sheet contained an agreement committing me not to disclose a word of anything I might learn at this meeting, with all kinds of dire consequences if I did. I hesitated, suspicious as hell. But I didn't want to get into further trouble before the meeting even started. Nomura handed me a pen, and I signed.

The FBI agent took the document from me. "Thank you for coming. There are a couple of things we'd like to show you." She switched off a bank of lights, darkening half the room, and gestured toward a screen on the wall. I rolled over for a better view while Nomura sat down at the table and tapped the touch screen on a laptop.

The picture of a man appeared on the screen. He was handsome and distinguished, with gray-flecked dark hair, wearing a gray pinstriped suit. "His name is Paul Landrum," Nomura said. "He runs a large hedge fund called Techinvest Partners, which is based here in LA."

Another slide appeared, showing a cluster of office buildings. A sign identified the complex as the corporate headquarters of DSI, Inc. "You may have heard of DSI," Nomura said. "It's a large defense contractor. It develops technology and weaponry that's essential to national security. The headquarters campus you see is in Huntington Beach. Techinvest Partners— Landrum's company—owns forty percent of the shares of DSI."

I nodded. What the hell did any of this have to do with me?

"Landrum doesn't run DSI," the FBI agent continued. "The CEO is a man named Pat Dalton. But obviously, as the largest single shareholder by far, Techinvest is very influential. They control four of the nine seats on the board of directors. Landrum is a vice-chairman of DSI and has an office at headquarters, but his fund has many other investments as well."

"Okay."

"DSI, with Techinvest's support, has agreed to buy a smaller defense company called Hulbert, whose technology is even more advanced than DSI's. The sale is set to close forty-five days from now."

Nomura paused. "Are you with me?"

"I guess so," I said.

Nomura glanced at Lieutenant Dan Howard, who nodded. O'Shea hadn't spoken.

Nomura said, "I'm going to play a recording of a phone call, which was received at the FBI two weeks ago."

She tapped on her laptop again, and I heard a woman's voice coming from the computer's speaker. She sounded young. And scared.

"You need to know," the voice said. "Paul Landrum is not who he appears to be. He has secrets, and he's dangerous. You need to know this before the Hulbert deal closes."

Nomura tapped her computer, then looked up at me. "That's the entire call. We didn't know the identity of the caller. The call came from a burner phone and went directly into our department, not to a tip line."

"And your department is?"

She hesitated. "Counterintelligence."

She slid the laptop across the table to Howard, who used the keyboard to bring up another screen. Another slide appeared. I gasped.

A woman's body lay sprawled on a hardwood floor, her head in a pool of blood. My stomach did a back handspring. "Who is she?" I whispered.

"This victim's name was Keri Wylie," Howard said. A new slide flashed up, showing a picture of an attractive young woman in her early thirties, with short, dark hair and a smile that looked genuine but with a touch of sadness.

"She was found a week ago," Howard continued. "She was shot in her home on Balboa Peninsula, a small house where she lived alone. No witnesses. Keri was thirty-three and worked as an attorney at DSI."

My mind raced. "Was she the one—"

"Yes," Howard said. "It was she who called the FBI about Paul Landrum. But we're getting ahead of ourselves."

"And this Landrum—"

"Has an alibi. A solid one. He was at a business meeting in Chicago, with plenty of people to vouch for him. Keri did have occasion to do some work with Landrum, and one co-worker at DSI acknowledged that their relationship had seemed strained recently, but they didn't know why."

"And," Nomura added, "no one has any idea what 'secrets' Keri was referring to."

Howard nodded. "We should add that there was no forced entry."

"Somebody she knew, then," I commented.

"The odds would support that, yes. It was a very solid door with a peephole. As a matter of routine, we contacted the FBI, which didn't have anything for us right away. But a couple of days later . . ." He looked at Nomura.

"Lieutenant Howard's inquiry about the murder came across my screen," she said. "When I saw that the victim worked for DSI, I remembered the call about Landrum. So, we checked out the voice with people who knew Keri, and sure enough, it was her."

Good Lord, I thought. Before I'd even realized it, I was already down the rabbit hole halfway to China.

"After the first call," Nomura said, "we took a close look at Landrum—really put him under the microscope. After the murder, we questioned him, along with a number of top management and legal personnel at DSI. We found nothing that would raise any alarms."

She glanced over at Dave O'Shea.

The US attorney leaned forward, hands clasped on the table. "Pen, would you be interested in coming back to work for us on a short-term basis? It wouldn't be legal work, strictly speaking. We'd be your official employer, but you'd be supervised by the FBI. We'd make it worth your while financially."

I was speechless.

"As you know," O'Shea said, "we've had mixed reports about your ability to function as a team player. We have a job in mind that would have no place for freelancing. Staying with the program would be critical. And if you can't, the consequences wouldn't be internal discipline; it would be prosecution and incarceration."

He let that sink in and then stood up, nodded, and left the room.

I was left with Howard and Nomura, and we were silent for a long moment. Finally, I said, "Excuse me, but what the hell was *that* all about?"

Nomura took a sheet of paper out of a file—my file, presumably. "You're proficient in HFA ClaimTrack software, version 4, is that right?"

I wasn't sure what I'd expected her to say, but it sure as hell wasn't that. "Yes," I said. "I used it when I worked at North Central Bank in Minneapolis."

"ClaimTrack 4 categorizes any claims made against a corporation, both in litigation and prior to that, am I right?"

"Yes."

She returned the sheet to the file. "We need to find out what Keri Wylie meant when she made that call about Paul Landrum. If he presents any national security risks, we've got major headaches, especially when DSI's takeover of Hulbert is completed."

"So?"

"DSI's law department has an opening for a paralegal, whose chief job it is to track and categorize claims using HFA ClaimTrack, version 4. The job has been vacant for some time, and we have it on good authority that they're feeling some urgency about filling it. Would you like to apply?"

"Why?"

"Because it would give us a set of eyes and ears in the department in which Keri worked. It's also adjacent to the company's executive row, where Landrum has his office. You'd work on finding out what secret of Landrum's Keri may have discovered."

I tried to process this. "You want me to work undercover?"

Nomura and Howard both nodded.

I was flabbergasted. "What on earth . . . how would it work?"

"We'd get you an identity and a legend—a background story—to go with it."

"You mean I'd have a phony name and identity?"

"Yes."

I nearly laughed out loud. "That's crazy. With the wheelchair, right here in my home city—I'd stick out like a sore thumb. Somebody would make me right away."

Nomura's response was measured and patient. "You've raised two issues, but they're really the same one. The wheelchair is a problem only if it causes somebody to think of Pen Wilkinson. In fact, it's my understanding that people in wheelchairs tend in some ways to be invisible."

She was right about that, I thought. And even when paraplegics are noticed, a lot of people tend to see them as slow, weak, and generally unthreatening.

Nomura continued: "If anything, a wheelchair would divert attention from your identity. People would wonder about your disability, not your background. So that raises the second question—would anybody recognize you? We don't think so. Your friend James lives in Newport Beach, and you spend some time down there. But your job was up here in LA, in an unrelated legal field. You live in Long Beach. You've never worked in the defense industry. You've only lived in California for about three years. There are more than eighteen million people in the LA combined metro area. Just for good measure, we ran your name through all our data banks and cross-referenced it with DSI and everybody we know who works there. We came up with no associations."

The FBI had obviously given the idea considerable thought. "What happens if somebody does recognize me?" I asked.

"You confess. You admit you were out of work and needed a job, so you gave a phony name and background to apply."

"What reason could I give for doing that?"

"That you were convinced the US attorney's office had blackballed you, and because you were afraid that if you'd told the truth about your background, DSI would have considered you overqualified and rejected you."

Both reasons were very plausible, I thought. I didn't know if O'Shea and his people had actually put out the word to steer clear of me, but they certainly could have. And I was definitely overqualified for the DSI job, just as I had been when I'd done the same work at North Central Bank, which had hired me for a totally unrelated—and sinister—reason. That helped answer the question of why I couldn't simply apply for the paralegal job as Pen Wilkinson. I was overqualified. And, of course, my background as a prosecutor might spook any wrongdoers I came across.

Howard spoke up. "Look, all they could do is fire you, Pen. And you're going to quit after six weeks, anyway."

I thought some more. It just might work. It also drove home the reality that I was essentially a nobody in this sprawling metropolis. No one would recognize me.

"Why me?" I asked. "Wouldn't you want a trained agent for a job like this?"

"Absolutely," Nomura said. "But unfortunately, we're pressed for time. Very pressed. The Hulbert deal closes in six weeks. That job in Legal is open now, and we have nobody skilled in that specific software. You're a trained prosecutor. You've worked for the Justice Department. Whatever political problems you had as an AUSA, no one has ever doubted your competence. You're available. We need you now."

Now. I had a million questions, a million concerns, a million preparations. "How much time do I get to think it over?" I asked.

"We'd like to do the job application tonight."

Chapter 2

That evening, I sat in my living room, looking down at the phone in my hand. I needed to make the call to James Carter. But I was still trying to get my head around the astonishing fact that I had been recruited for an undercover assignment. The recruitment was a fluke, arising from my knowledge of an aging software program. But the offer seemed genuine, and I was left to figure out what it meant for me.

I was, of course, relieved not to be in any immediate trouble with O'Shea, but that situation was easily reversible. It was also nice that he and his colleagues had expressed confidence in my abilities. But he'd been unrepentant about his past behavior and had offered me nothing beyond this assignment. Six weeks from now, I'd be unemployed again. And now, I was left to wonder if the choice offered me was a sham. Did I really have the option to say no to O'Shea? Or, if I refused the offer, would I risk cutting a hole for myself in the already thin ice on which I was situated?

During my half-year hiatus, I'd tried not to think too much about the future. It seemed increasingly unlikely that I'd be taking a conventional job, even though James thought that would be the safest course for me. He was right, of course, but the idea of "safe" didn't hold much appeal for me anymore. I wasn't an adrenaline addict, but I'd become used to challenge and novelty. More than that, I had discovered what it meant to do important work, something with a purpose beyond earning a paycheck, doing something for people who needed help.

There were lots of other things I could do to make that happen, I thought. I didn't have to take an undercover assignment that promised stress—maybe even danger. I told myself I just didn't need this.

But I did.

It was an investigative project, important work. But even with all the uncertainties—even the risk of bringing back the PTSD—this type of assignment seemed to be what I was built for. The abstractions of national security didn't stir me all that much, but the thought of a frightened young woman, an attorney trying to do the right thing, murdered in her home—that got my juices flowing.

Everything Nomura and Howard had told me about the assignment was plausible. But there had to be some significant things they weren't telling me. It was a national security case—everything compartmentalized and need-to-know. But the more powerful motives for withholding information tended to be bureaucratic in nature, and in working with the FBI, the US attorney, and the Newport Beach police, I was right at the intersection of three powerful bureaucracies. I would need to watch my back.

And then there was Howard. When I had rolled down to the elevator after our meeting downtown, he'd been waiting for me.

"I was against this," he'd said without preamble. "I still am. But Wendy is a friend. And I need the FBI's help to clear this case."

I knew I needed to stay on Howard's good side, even if I thought he was a rule-bound, tight-assed Dudley Do-Right. "Lieutenant, it doesn't have to be this way. I don't hold a grudge against you for arresting James."

"Who said anything about grudges? I'm just telling you this op is Nomura's thing."

"Fine."

"And everything O'Shea said about freelancing goes double for me. I can't take a chance on screwing up this case."

"So, your message is 'Don't screw up'? Gee, let me write that down."

"The message is 'Stay in your lane.' Don't get creative—just keep your eyes and ears open."

I'd shrugged. If that was really what they wanted, why didn't they just plant a janitor on Landrum's floor? Still, it was clear that the operation's sponsors were serious about keeping me under control. They had added me to the federal payroll, bringing me inside the tent and subject to their authority. But if you took the legalities out of it, I was more of a free agent, more like a cooperating individual (CI), a civilian working with law enforcement.

Which meant it wasn't exactly clear where I stood.

Now I looked down at the phone in my hand. Of course I wanted to do it. Needed to do it. Was intrigued, challenged, compelled. But I'd avoided the real issue. The project itself involved some risk. I could handle that, I thought. But what about the risk to my relationship, which both James and I had worked so hard to repair?

I sighed, took the phone, and called James.

Chapter 3

In a sense, my discussion with James Carter would be a continuation of the same argument we'd been having for three years. I felt compelled to do things that could be stressful or even dangerous, and he didn't want me to. But in another sense, we were breaking new ground. Since my last intense experience, a murder case in Minnesota, we'd each acknowledged a need to understand the other's position and to move outside our respective comfort zones. I was about to see just how far outside the zone he was willing to go.

"It's only six weeks," I said, fingering my wine glass. We sat on the deck of his boat, the *Alicia C*, at its dock at the marina on Bayside Drive in Newport Beach. The spring air was growing chilly as the sun sank hesitantly, then quickly, behind Balboa Peninsula. We waved to our friend Hal Dwyer on his boat at the next slip.

"Just six weeks—how sure are you of that?" James was a black man, trim, handsome, confident. But his features tightened as he struggled with my bare-bones explanation.

"Very sure," I said. After all, my work would become moot after DSI, Inc.'s acquisition of the Hulbert Co. closed. Of course, the closing might be delayed or extended, but I couldn't tell James that.

"And you basically can't tell me jackshit," James observed. Subtlety and indirection were buried pretty deep in James's playbook.

"Sorry about that."

James shifted on his deck chair. Nobody liked being kept in the dark, but James, a forceful man who owned his own business —who was used to being in control—liked it even less than most. "Who's recruiting you?"

I didn't answer.

"If it's that pompous gasbag Dave O'Shea, you should tell him to take a damn hike."

"I can't talk about that."

"I don't know, Pen. All this hush-hush stuff. You wouldn't even be able to call?"

"We're still negotiating that." That wasn't an outright lie; I hadn't actually asked yet. But I doubted they would let me call.

"And O'Shea . . ."

"You can be sure I'm not doing it because of him."

He flashed a knowing smile. "You're doing it because of a person, somebody who's in trouble or getting screwed somehow."

And her name was Keri Wylie, I didn't add.

"And you don't think there's any danger?" he said.

"I'm sure it will be fine."

He looked at me sharply. I hadn't answered quickly or convincingly enough.

He looked away, took a long drink from his glass, and returned his gaze to me. "You sure you're ready for this, honey?"

This was the critical question, we both knew. After nearly half a year of therapy, medication, and rest, had I recovered completely from my bout with post-traumatic stress disorder? I felt that I had. Early on, I had overcome the biggest hurdle, which was facing up to the problem. And after that, I'd made steady progress; the nightmares and anxiety attacks had all but disappeared. But now I was heading back into the type of high-pressure assignment that had created the problem in the first place. It would be a tough test of my recovery and newly acquired coping skills.

"I'm ready," I said. I really thought I was. But there was only one way to find out for sure.

He set his glass down, moved his chair directly in front of me, and took both of my hands in his. "I'm trusting you," he said.

"That's what I need to do, right? I'm not supposed to hold on too tight, to smother you. I'm supposed to let you go when you need to go."

I didn't answer.

He squeezed my hands more tightly. "It's just really hard." He let out a long sigh, which was interrupted mid-stream by a slight catch in his breath. "Just come back to me. I'll be waiting."

Chapter 4

Another day in LA for Viktor Kamensky. More sunshine. And more boredom. He pulled out into traffic and caught up with the plain-Jane sedan, then settled back to follow a man who had no idea he was being followed. A few blocks to the west, the sedan took its place in line, as expected, to get onto the I-10.

He had followed the target all the way up to LA to meet with . . . who? Kamensky didn't know, and that bugged him a little. He'd assumed it would be the Feds. But the man hadn't gone to the federal courthouse. So why was he here? Kamensky shook off his nagging doubts. There was no reason Lieutenant Dan Howard's trip downtown had to be related to the Keri Wylie murder; he handled plenty of other cases.

Kamensky had to admit he was going through the motions. The hit out on Balboa Peninsula had been too easy. The investigation had stalled immediately and was still going nowhere. Following the investigator seemed like pointless busywork; he was bored to death. But Kamensky wasn't about to complain to PACIFIC. It had taken him way too long to get to the States to begin with. He had the language, having been born to a Russian family in Brooklyn before returning to the old country at the age of nine. After years of assignments in cities ranging from gloomy to cold to downright crappy, he'd finally gotten his ticket, not just to the Promised Land, but to La-La Land. True, he was, and always would be, an illegal with phony ID. No diplomatic cover. No protection, no immunity. He was out there on his own. But there were worse situations to be in, he thought. On his own in La-La Land.

Kamensky dutifully followed the target all the way back to Newport Beach police headquarters and settled in at a parking lot down the street to watch. Idly, he took out his phone, swiped, and saw on his screen the smiling, toothless picture of a five-year-old boy, a boy with Kamensky's own face, his own hair. Vanya was seven now, but Kamensky hadn't seen him since the picture had been taken. Kamensky knew he could get custody of his son if he went back to Moscow — his friends in the security services could see to that. Sometimes he would look at the picture and think about it. But he was here, in LA. And he wasn't going anywhere.

He looked up, peering out his window in response to motion in his peripheral vision. A figure had come out of the white police building. He lifted the binoculars to his eyes: Howard. But he wasn't alone. He shifted the binoculars, focusing on the person with Howard, and . . . Oh, my, what have we here?

It was a woman, apparently leaving. Lieutenant Howard was seeing her to the parking lot. She was tall — the same height as the detective. She had exotic Asian features — Chinese or Japanese or something. And she was hot. He looked closer. She was probably older than he'd first thought — maybe forty. She wore a businesslike pantsuit. Her studied her demeanor — confident, no-nonsense. A cop?

Kamensky pulled out his camera and snapped a couple of long-range shots. Howard went back inside the building, and the woman headed for her car. It was a plain-Jane, definitely a cop or official vehicle of some type. He pulled out his phone, downloaded the picture from his camera, and sent it to PACIFIC. Then he started up his car. This one was worth following.

The woman headed east on Jamboree, then picked up the I-405 north. As they crawled through miserable traffic, Kamensky gave her plenty of room; she had looked competent. Sharp, in a way even Howard had not. By the time she finally exited, on Wilshire, he had long since guessed her destination: the Wilshire Federal Building, home to the Federal Bureau of Investigation. And PACIFIC had given him her name: Special Agent Wendy Nomura.

Chapter 5

Desiree Jane ("Dez") Walker sat in her van at a handicap space in the DSI employee parking lot. She hadn't slept much but figured nervousness on the first day of a new job was natural. She took deep breaths, doing the relaxation exercise her therapist had taught her. She unhooked her wheelchair, extended the ramp, and rolled out.

She was me.

This was insane.

As Special Agent Wendy Nomura had predicted, the hiring process had moved quickly—interview, drug test, and background check, all completed within a week. I'd spent most of the rest of the week memorizing the four-page, single-spaced background story, or legend, that Nomura had given me. This, too, must have been created in record time, although Nomura had confided that the Bureau maintained identities for adaptation and use in situations like this one. Nomura, it turned out, had once been the primary FBI liaison with DSI for counterintelligence matters.

At any rate, I'd had only a few days to become Desiree Jane Walker, a name that utilized my own initials. "Dez," I'd suggested. It was short and sounded something like Pen—a name that would be easier for me to answer to.

Nomura had shrugged. "Sure—whatever you're comfortable with." And so I was equipped with a new driver's license and credit cards. The van had been re-registered in Dez's name.

Dez had worked for an insurance company, using the all-important HFA ClaimTrack software. She'd recently relocated to California from Virginia, after breaking up with a long-time boyfriend and wanting to pack up, leave, and move as far away as possible. Dez looked a little different from me, sporting hair that was brown, shorter, and wavy—and fake. Much as I was committed to the project, I didn't want to cut my straight, blonde, shoulder-length hair. A wig would have to do. Dez also wore heavy, dark glasses, giving my contact lenses a break for a few weeks. Her wardrobe was a lot cheaper and more basic than mine, and I'd ditched my designer purse in favor of a knockoff. And Dez's personality? It was mostly my own, I suppose; I couldn't change that too much. But I'd have to restrain my tendency to express opinions that were, well, unrestrained.

I'd done a brief interview with the attorney I'd be working for, a youngish assistant general counsel named Bart Crosby. The interview had been weird, mostly because Crosby had been weird. He'd seemed distracted most of the time but would occasionally seem to notice my presence and give me a quizzical look through thick glasses. I noticed that other people in the office seemed to ignore him. After a few questions, he'd stood up and walked down the hall. After brief deliberation, I decided to follow him. He had stopped at the door of general counsel Nancy Griffin, then walked away.

I'd knocked at the door, gone in, and introduced myself to Griffin, a distinguished, no-nonsense woman of about sixty. After a noncommittal thirty-second meet-and-greet, I was back in the hallway by myself. By this time, I'd guessed that the interview was over, and I was worried that I wouldn't be hired, leaving the entire project stillborn. I'd left the building, sending a follow-up email to Crosby from the parking lot and copying Griffin. Late in the afternoon I'd gotten a call from HR telling me the job was mine, and they wanted me to start on Monday. "You really impressed them," the young woman from HR had said.

Now, as Dez, I headed into the main DSI office building, picked up a temporary badge at the front desk, and wheeled over to HR for an orientation session, joined by a dozen other new employees. For more than an hour, I struggled to stay awake as we learned about the company dental plan, 401(k), and the like. Then we watched a video explaining company policies and the employee code of conduct. They ran down a list of misdeeds that could get you fired, which included providing false information on your job application, and concluded with that all-purpose offense that hung over every at-will employee: No Reason at All. I noticed an emphasis on security and confidentiality, understandable for a defense contractor.

DSI, according to some research I'd done, produced a lot of sensitive products, including stealth technology for planes and ships. Less cutting-edge business lines included ammo, radio systems, and battlefield equipment. The company was also a subcontractor on various defense electronics projects headed up by other entities. "DSI" had originally stood for "Defense Systems International," but now, as with so many corporate names, it stood for nothing. Hulbert, the company being acquired by DSI, produced very advanced technology, including the latest electronic countermeasures to ballistic missile attacks.

After the orientation, an HR escort took me up to the seventh floor to Bart Crosby's office, which was situated in a row of offices along an exterior wall. My new boss wasn't there. The escort pointed out an empty cubicle across the aisle and left me there. The cube was next door to an assistant's desk. The assistant also wasn't there.

My cubicle was empty except for a desk, chair, and computer. I moved the chair aside, rolled up to the desk, and adjusted the height of the keyboard and screen. I managed to turn on the computer but was confronted by a login screen, which demanded a username and password. I was stymied.

"May I help you?"

I looked up. The offer had come from a black man in his early forties, squat and muscular, who'd emerged from the office next to Crosby's. His clothing—dark suit, white shirt, and striped tie—made him look like an FBI agent. But the Bureau might have frowned upon his hairstyle: dreadlocks.

He held out his hand. "McCartney Williamson." He spoke with a Caribbean lilt.

"Dez Walker," I said, shaking his hand. "Nice to meet you."

"I'm one of the attorneys. You're Bart's new paralegal?"

"Right. You have an interesting name. Were your parents Beatles fans?"

"Yes."

"They could have just named you Paul," I observed.

"Lots of Pauls around."

"Um—right." So much for my friendly icebreaker. I felt like a butthead.

He smiled. "Call me Mac."

"Sure."

"I don't work in Bart's area. I'm in the general corporate department."

"I see. Well, I guess I'll just wait until Bart gets back, since I'm not sure how to get started."

He took a yellow sticky note from my desk and wrote on it. "Here," he said. "This will enable you to log onto the system. You'll be able to start gathering the information that needs to be inputted into ClaimTrack, and I'm afraid there will be a large backlog of it."

"Thanks, Mac."

"My pleasure. I hope you'll join my friends and me for lunch at twelve thirty?"

"I guess so, sure."

I logged onto the computer and dug in. As Williamson had predicted, there was a ton of information from managers, lawyers, and loss prevention people at DSI facilities across the country and overseas. By looking at previous reports, I developed a pretty good idea how DSI processed the information. The procedures were only slightly different from those used by North Central Bank, the place I'd last used ClaimTrack. My legal expertise came into play in deciding how to categorize the claim. Was it an injury case? Defamation? Worker's comp? Discrimination?

Mac Williamson reappeared at twelve thirty and led me down to the company cafeteria on the first floor. The place was crowded, but there was an empty table in one corner. This, it turned out, was Williamson's regular dining spot, and he appeared to preside as much as to eat. Mac helped me bring a pre-packaged salad and a carton of milk back to the table. Half a dozen other people appeared, and Williamson made the introductions. It turned out that some of the people at the table didn't work in the law department, and I had trouble remembering all the names. Two of them stood out for their physical appearance. One was an intense-looking guy about my age, with unruly wavy hair and heavy glasses, wearing a sweater vest. His name was Clay something-or-other, and he worked in Finance. Another was a striking young woman named Marisa, who had blonde hair and large green eyes. I didn't catch where she worked.

"Why don't you tell us about yourself, Dez?" said Williamson.

I took the opportunity to relate my newly learned legend, including a basically authentic version of my car accident. I figured everybody would want an explanation for the wheelchair but would be too polite to ask.

The conversation continued, and I listened closely for any intelligence that might prove useful.

"You're working for Bart?" somebody asked.

"Yes, but I've only met him briefly." There were smiles around the table.

"He's a piece of work," said the guy named Clay.

"Yeah, Rain Man," somebody else said. "He can't say good morning, but you'd hate to play blackjack against the guy."

I just smiled.

"Bart doesn't relate to people in a normal way," Williamson said.

"What do you mean?"

"He's lacking in social skills. There's probably a diagnosis for it, but I don't get into that. He's useful to the company because he is a savant on the subject of government contract law. Really arcane stuff. There are untold volumes of regulations, laws, and procedures governing defense contracts. Bart can recall them in an appropriate and timely manner, and oftentimes can even explain them. That is an incredibly valuable skill set."

"That's true," Clay said. "But they've given him some other duties as well, and on those, he doesn't do so well."

"Tracking claims," I said.

"That's one of them," said Williamson. "That's why it's been difficult to hire someone, and that's why he—and Nancy Griffin—will be relying on you."

The young blonde spoke up. "If you have questions, I'm not sure Bart will be a lot of help. You'll have to figure it out for yourself."

I nodded. I wouldn't be able to bother Griffin with questions, either—my concerns would be far too insignificant to discuss with the general counsel of a Fortune 100 company.

"I wonder if I'll be doing anything besides claims," I said.

"Probably not much," Williamson answered. "There may be chores relating to the Hulbert acquisition—proofreading, collating, things like that."

"It's all hands on deck," Clay said. "We've worked late every night this week." With that, the conversation shifted to the Hulbert merger, with lots of speculation on who might be laid off or promoted or moved to another job.

When that topic wound down, somebody said, "You're going to hear about Keri."

I tried not to show undue interest. "Who's that?"

Williamson provided the answer. "Keri Wylie was an attorney—about your age, I'd guess—who was murdered a couple of weeks ago."

"*Murdered*?"

"Shot to death in her home. Nobody knows why, and the police don't appear to have made any progress."

"Wow," I said. "They don't think it was due to anything work-related, do they?"

"I don't see how it could be," Clay said. "Keri was well-liked and respected here. She was doing a lot of work on the merger. I think she was headed for bigger things down the line."

"They checked out the work angle, though," Williamson commented. "The police came in and interviewed several attorneys. Looked through her office, too, and took away some papers."

"Did they interview any of you?" I asked.

"They talked to me," Williamson said. But there were head shakes from the others around the table.

I decided to drop the subject, not wanting to appear too inquisitive. At the other end of the table, I saw the blonde woman named Marisa brush away a tear.

After lunch, Bart Crosby walked by my cube, noticed me, and came over. "You doing okay, uh . . ."

"Dez."

"Right."

"Yes, I've gotten started and things seem to be going fine."

"Good." He disappeared into his office. Later, I introduced myself to Bart's assistant, who also worked for two other attorneys. She seemed busy, distracted, and unsocial.

In mid-afternoon, I got a visit from the assistant to general counsel Nancy Griffin. She briefly welcomed me and gave me a little booklet with the names, positions, and family information of everybody in the department. An hour or so later, Griffin herself stopped by. "Hello, Dez. How is your first day going?"

"Fine."

"Bart has gotten you started?"

"Yes," I said, although it was actually Williamson who'd helped me.

"Great. Welcome aboard." She left.

I worked for about an hour, then decided to do some exploring. I set out for the bathroom, taking a circuitous route. I looked across the seventh floor, which was decorated in Classical Cube Farm—muted colors, efficient lighting, industrial carpet, and the inevitable neat rows of cubicles. Enclosed offices lined all four walls, with the cubes in the middle, split by a corridor, restrooms, conference rooms, and the elevator lobby. One side of the corridor was occupied by the offices of top executives, while the legal department took up our half. I'd learned, however, that additional law department offices were located on the next floor down. The corridors were well traveled, and there was a lot of back-and-forth between the legal and executive sides.

I wheeled past one of the executive rows and spotted the corner office suite belonging to the CEO, Pat Dalton. In the opposite corner I found the abode of the chief operating officer. Next door to him, I found the office I was looking for. The name plate said *Paul L. Landrum.* The office looked unoccupied, but I remembered that Landrum didn't spend all his time here. Even though he was a major investor in, and vice chairman of, DSI, his main business was running the Techinvest hedge fund.

"Hi, Dez," said a voice from behind me. I looked back toward the voice, but not as quickly as I should have. The greeting had come from the young woman named Marisa I'd met at lunch, who now sat at a desk in front of the entrance to the COO's offices.

"Hi," I said.

"Can I help you with something?"

"No, no. I'm just getting the lay of the land. Day one, you know?"

She smiled. "Right."

I nodded, waved, and continued on my circuitous route. Down the hallway from my cube and around a corner, I found an office with a closed door, which still bore the name of its former occupant: *Keri J. Wylie.*

Five-thirty eventually arrived. I logged out of the system, grabbed my purse, and joined the exodus. Glancing across the floor, I could see quite a few people still working, possibly on the Hulbert merger. Downstairs, I found my van in the lot and headed for home.

"Home" was, however, as novel an experience as work had been. My new abode was a rented condo in a complex overlooking Newport Peninsula, off Superior Street, up a hill from Pacific Coast Highway. It was a nice place, with balconies both front and back, and a spectacular view on the Pacific side. The rent was more than Dez Walker—or Pen Wilkinson—could afford, so I had, at Nomura's request, advertised for roommates. I would ignore the inquiries.

It wasn't until Nomura had told me about the apartment that I'd realized the seriousness of the whole endeavor. I'd assumed I would be going home at night as usual, giving DSI a phony address or mail drop. But Nomura was taking my cover seriously, building an identity that would hold up even in the unlikely event that somebody would follow me home, or really check me out in depth. Nomura had arranged for me to rent the place from its owners, her brother's in-laws. I was a bit surprised by that; I had imagined the FBI might maintain safe houses and other properties for undercover use. I glanced around as I approached the door, wondering if somebody, friend or foe, might be watching.

I rolled through the living room, which had been outfitted with rental furniture. The first thing I had done—the first thing I usually do when staying in a new place—was to check out the bathroom. It wasn't as accessible as I would have liked—there was just barely enough room to turn my wheelchair around—but it would do. Now, on the balcony, I sat with a glass of wine and looked out over the ocean, and in front of that, Balboa Peninsula. I was no more than a mile or two from Keri Wylie's house.

Day one had gone okay, I thought. I hadn't learned anything new about Keri or Landrum. But I'd found I could handle the work and wouldn't be closely supervised. I'd also avoided making any gaffes or, as far as I knew, arousing suspicions. I had gotten through the day without an anxiety attack, which gave me confidence about my recovery from the PTSD. But now that I was here at "home," what was I supposed to do? I couldn't see or call James. I'd had to cut off contact with my friends; the official story was that Pen Wilkinson had gone to Minnesota for a few weeks.

And now I was left here with my boredom. And my fear. It was hard to stop thinking about what would happen if I was caught. I wasn't so sure I would be able to just confess, quit, and roll out the door. My misrepresentations might be a crime. And I couldn't count on the FBI to come crashing in to extract me. Nomura had said there would be an intermittent, loose tail on me, which was actually safer than having an agent glued to my bumper twenty-four-seven. She had given me a special cell phone registered to Desiree Walker, but with a "panic button" on it, which would alert her immediately. The phone, which I'd come to think of as my Dez phone, also had the usual location tracking, so they'd know where I was at all times. Separately, I'd received a burner phone with which to report to Nomura every evening. She'd told me to call in any time after seven. I took a long drink from my glass and picked up the phone.

Chapter 6

Special Agent Wendy Nomura pulled out of the parking lot of Pen's new apartment after following Pen there from DSI headquarters. Wendy had visited DSI a number of times over the years, dating back to the period when she'd been the FBI counterintelligence liaison to the company. Tonight, no one had tailed Pen, not that she had expected anyone to. Wendy braced herself for the challenge of the next five weeks, supporting this undercover operation. She was already exhausted by the work of setting up the op in record time.

Wendy was relieved and a bit surprised that Pen had accepted the assignment. That seemed a good sign, an indication that Pen was ready to tackle another challenge. After hearing about Pen, Wendy had checked her out, and the reports on her skills and qualifications had been glowing. But then she had read about a series of undertakings Pen had been involved in: challenging corporate saboteurs; prosecuting a corrupt Congressman; taking down a Russian-backed hacker; and finally, solving the murder of a candidate for governor of Minnesota. All impressive feats, but they had taken their toll.

She'd seen the doctors' reports: PTSD. Not the worst case, but not the mildest, either. Pen had been shot at, and a madman had attempted to drown her in a swimming pool. She had killed a man and wounded another one. She had witnessed other murders. After the last incident, a shootout in Minnesota, Pen had gotten serious treatment, and by all accounts, it had gone well. All Wendy could do now was hope that the treatment would hold through the next five weeks. Because Wendy, and the FBI, were in a serious bind.

The entire op was fraught with risk, reeking of desperation. But when her superiors had asked what the alternative was, she'd been mute. Despite the clean bill of health Landrum had received in the Keri Wylie investigation, Nomura and a few select FBI personnel knew that the stakes were much higher than the death of a single woman. Leaving Landrum unchecked was not an option; the potential national security consequences were too serious. She hoped Pen was up to the job. And increasingly, Wendy hoped she herself was, too.

Chapter 7

DSI, Inc. got sued a lot. More than that, people *threatened* to sue the company all the time. Workers got injured in their plants. Suppliers got shorted in their payments. The military's regulations got flouted. Office employees got carpal tunnel syndrome. Job applicants got discriminated against. Faced with so much actual and potential litigation, the company needed Claim-Track and a full-time employee—me—to keep track of it. I collected and entered into the database the date and nature of the incidents, the names of the claimants, their demands, and who was handling things for DSI—usually an insurance company or law firm. Not the most exciting job, and in fact the work bored me to death, just as it had in Minnesota.

As I began my third day on the job, I started to seriously think about my real purpose here. Somehow, I had to find clues as to what Keri Wylie's warnings about Paul Landrum were all about, and as to why Keri might have been killed. So far, I had discovered . . . nothing.

The most promising lead seemed to be Marisa Costas, the young woman who worked for the chief operating officer. From my conversations at lunch, I'd heard that Marisa had been a friend of Keri's. Although Keri had been older, they had gone to the same high school. Marisa, however, seemed disinclined to talk about her friend.

Around nine o'clock, Bart Crosby emerged from his office to give me an envelope of documents to be delivered to CEO Pat Dalton. I rolled across the floor to Dalton's corner office suite but found his assistant's desk unoccupied. I sat there for a moment, wondering whether it would be okay to just leave the documents on her desk. Then the man himself walked out of the inner office.

Pat Dalton was a beefy, genial man in his mid-fifties with graying, sandy hair. "Well, hello," he said.

"Hi. I, um, have some papers for you."

He walked out and shook my hand. "Pat Dalton."

"I'm Dez Walker. I work for Bart Crosby in Legal."

"Nice to meet you, Dez. You're new?"

"Right. Just started this week."

"Welcome." He took the envelope from me, gave me a little wave, and returned to his office. It looked as though that little encounter might be the highlight of my week.

When I returned to my cubicle, however, I found a note on my desk. The yellow sticky Post-it was from Nancy Griffin's assistant, telling me I had an appointment at ten with a guy named Royce Pearson in Security. My breathing grew shallow. I calmed myself down enough to pick up the phone and call Griffin's assistant to ask if she knew what the meeting was about.

"Probably just routine," she said. "I'm sure it's nothing to worry about."

Easy for her to say, I thought.

I looked at my phone: 9:12. Less than an hour to go. I tried to look busy while I wondered what was going on. Had they spotted a red flag on my job application? Had one of my FBI-supplied references been unconvincing? Or was it just some paperwork glitch?

I closed my eyes and did breathing and relaxation exercises, gradually returning my breathing and pulse to near normal. Then, after rehearsing my legend yet again, I forced myself to return to working, which helped to pass the time. At 9:50, I repeated the relaxation routine, mentally transporting myself to a sunny beach and paying close attention to my breathing. Then I left for the security office on the first floor.

Royce Pearson was a young guy, clean-cut and friendly, dressed in dark slacks and an open-necked blue dress shirt. He showed me into a windowless interview room, moving a chair away from a table so I could sit across from him.

He placed a file on the table along with a laptop and notebook.

Pearson smiled. "When we processed your conditional security approval, we ran into a couple of minor snags. We just have a few routine follow-up questions."

"Okay."

"Now, your last employer was the Tidewater Delmarva Insurance Company, is that right?"

"Correct."

"And how long were you there?"

"Six years."

He frowned. "They do confirm that you were employed there for that length of time but have declined to provide any further information. Do you know why that might be the case?"

"No. Probably a liability thing."

He nodded slowly and looked at the file again. "And before that you were employed at Richmond Fidelity."

"That's right."

"They were apparently bought by Travelers Insurance three years ago."

"I think I heard that, yes."

"And your paralegal school merged with another institution more than ten years ago."

"That's true."

"That has made it harder to confirm your employment and school attendance."

I shrugged. "Sorry."

The door to the little room opened, and a large man entered. "I'll take it from here, Royce," the man said in a sharp baritone. Without a word, Pearson disappeared, and the new man crisply moved in and took his place. His face, flat and merging into a wide, jutting chin, looked like a mask or face shield. He was dressed in a long-sleeved white shirt and frayed tie, his short, salt-and-pepper hair brushed straight back.

He sat in the chair and simply studied me for a long moment, and I suspected this guy might have been watching me via a camera or one-way mirror. Finally, he said, "My name is Les Hornsby. I'm DSI's head of security. I have a few questions of my own."

I waited.

"What was your boyfriend's name?"

What the hell? "Mr. Hornsby, I don't believe that's a legal or appropriate question." I regretted the words as they left my mouth, realizing they had come from Pen, not Dez.

The response didn't appear to faze Hornsby. "I don't debate legal or appropriate. You answer my questions, truthfully and to my satisfaction, or we revoke your security status, which means you don't work at DSI. What was your boyfriend's name?" He spoke with the formal, condescending monotone common to military and police types. He appeared to be annoyed not by my challenging his authority, but by my wasting his time.

I quickly shifted to Dez mode. "Trevor McNeil."

"What's his middle name?"

"Edward."

"Where did he go to high school?"

"Langley High School in McLean, Virginia."

"What is his father's name?"

"Ed."

"Did you go to your senior prom?"

"Yes."

"Who was your date?"

I allowed myself to show just a bit of exasperation. "His name was Tommy Ashe."

"Who was your favorite teacher in middle school?"

"It was called junior high school in our district."

"What was the teacher's name?"

I showed slightly more exasperation this time. I kept my hands clasped so he wouldn't see them shaking. "I liked my eighth-grade social studies teacher. Her name was Alice Fitzgerald."

"Is she still teaching there?"

"I have no idea."

"But if we went back and checked, the records of your junior high school would show a social studies teacher named Alice Fitzgerald at the time you were there?"

"Presumably, yes."

He studied me for another long moment, then gave me an unpleasant smile, showing yellowed teeth. "Have a nice day." He got up and left.

I made it back to my cube, where I stared at the wall, fighting off the panic attack I felt coming on. I took deep breaths, using every relaxation exercise I knew. Within a few minutes the attack subsided, but I was still badly shaken. I had successfully answered all the questions; having used all the idle hours at my new home, I had memorized the answers to everything Hornsby had asked, and a lot more. But everything else about the interview had been profoundly disturbing.

First, there was the fact that it had taken place at all—what had triggered Security's suspicions? It was a pretty common practice for employers to provide only minimal information about former employees, and to merge with other companies. Then there was the appearance of Hornsby, the top security official at a massive company where security was necessarily a huge issue. But most disturbing of all was the nature of Hornsby's questions. The young guy, Pearson, had addressed possible gaps in my resume, but Hornsby had questioned my identity, whether I was actually the person I claimed to be. That was terrible news. I hoped I had put their concerns to bed.

But I doubted it.

*   *   *

I sat at lunch at McCartney Williamson's table, where I seemed to be fitting in as a regular. The other diners were a rotating cast. It was an eclectic, egalitarian group, including attorneys, analysts, assistants, and executives. Marisa Costas had appeared twice. The other person I remembered from the first day, Clay Ritchie from Finance, had also made two appearances, the second of which was today. He sat across the table, giving me the chance to check him out more closely. Despite the glasses and nerdy clothes, he wasn't bad looking. Several times, I caught him eyeing me suspiciously.

During a break in the conversation Ritchie said, "I heard you met with Iron Man."

"Iron . . ."

"Les Hornsby."

"Oh, the security director. Right." In fact, Hornsby's face did look a bit like the superhero's helmet shield.

"You don't want to cross him. He's paid to be paranoid."

"But he'd do it for nothing," somebody commented.

"He's ex-CIA," another person said. "I heard he was involved in rendition—you know, enhanced interrogation in those secret prisons."

I could easily imagine Hornsby waterboarding somebody.

"Why did you have to go in for a follow-up interview?" Williamson asked.

"Didn't you?"

"No, I didn't."

"I didn't, either," somebody else said. There were other head shakes around the table. I found this unsettling. These people handled matters a lot more sensitive than the ones I did.

Ritchie shook his head gravely. "Rogue paralegals. Big security threat."

A couple of minutes later, during a lull, I said, "I met Pat Dalton."

"What did you think?" Williamson asked.

"Nice man. Could be a politician."

"A good description," Williamson said. "He's not confrontational. He's a consensus-builder. A bit old-fashioned."

"A bit?" somebody said.

"He came up through the ranks," said a young guy with thinning hair. "He was an IT guy, got his degrees from Ohio State and Berkeley. Nice to see a geek make it all the way to CEO. Some people don't think he's aggressive enough for this era. He enjoys living well—gives that corporate jet a lot of use. He's got a helicopter, too."

"Air Dalton," Ritchie cracked.

"He deserves a break," Williamson said.

Ritchie's look turned somber. "His daughter."

Williamson turned to me. "Pat's daughter—I forget her name—she must have been in her mid-twenties—was killed in a surfing accident a couple of years ago in Thailand. He took it very hard."

"There was some talk that he might quit," an older woman said.

"He hasn't, though," Ritchie pointed out. "He's still in the game, pushing the merger and now seeing it through. He wants to stay on afterward, too."

"I thought I heard somebody was trying to take over the company," I ventured.

Williamson answered. "Our vice chairman, Paul Landrum, is a hedge fund investor, and he owns forty percent of the company. He attempted a takeover a couple of years ago."

"And he's a vice chairman of the company? How does that work?"

"When Landrum tried to take control, Dalton fought him off. Eventually they reached a standstill agreement. Techinvest

—that's Landrum's company—agreed to take four board seats and not seek to acquire ownership beyond the forty percent it owns without advance notice. At this point, Pat and Landrum stay out of each other's way."

"But Landrum supports the Hulbert deal?"

"Reluctantly, I've heard. Dalton has been the driving force behind it."

"Why would Landrum be reluctant?"

Williamson shrugged. "A lot of shareholders believe we're paying way too much."

After lunch, Ritchie walked with me back to the Legal side of the floor. "Hope we didn't scare you too much about Hornsby," he said.

"I don't know what I'd have to be scared about."

"No skeletons in your closet?"

"My life has been pretty boring."

"Really?" We paused at the entrance to my cube, and Ritchie gave me a shrewd appraisal. "This is just a hunch, but I'd bet that underneath those thick glasses and your unassuming personality, you're a pretty interesting person, Dez Walker." He smiled and walked off.

What was *that* all about? I wondered. Was he hitting on me? Very unlikely. I wasn't a frequent target for romantic attention to begin with, and with the geeky appearance I'd adopted for the Dez role, it would have made even less sense. His inference that I was hiding something was troubling, even though I saw no way this guy from Finance could know anything about me. But he seemed to want to know more; he'd made it a point to chat me up. I'd have to keep my eye on him. But I'd had harder tasks. Underneath the Clark Kent glasses, Clay Ritchie was a good-looking guy.

Chapter 8

Wendy Nomura walked at a measured pace down the hallway toward her boss's office, mentally reviewing all the things that could have gone wrong. The man was no dummy and had been on edge ever since the call from Keri Wylie. She reached his door, let out a breath, and knocked.

Ward Gilbertson looked up as she entered. "Come in, come in, Wendy. Have a seat."

Wendy shut the door behind her and sat down without comment.

Gilbertson, a nondescript man in his mid-forties, leaned forward, concern on his face. "How's everything going, Wendy?"

"Fine."

"I haven't seen a lot of you around the office lately. You've been pushing hard, looking a little tired. Are you sure everything is okay?" He flashed a knowing smile that stopped just short of predatory. Wendy didn't care; when it came to predatory, they always got there eventually.

"I'm fine."

"And how is everything at your companies?"

"Okay, I guess."

"They're giving you everything you've asked for?"

"For the most part, yes."

"There's still that strange situation at DSI."

"You took me off DSI."

"Right. But I'm sure you hear things. You haven't picked up any bad vibes about the Hulbert acquisition?"

"Not really, no."

Gilbertson sat back and crossed his legs. "Well, there is that attorney who was murdered. You were involved with that, right?"

Wendy kept her voice steady. She always had to resist the temptation to dismiss her boss as an empty suit; he was a survivor, and he was cunning. "I did help in checking that out. Newport Beach found no indication that the murder was work-related."

"Even after the strange phone call."

"That's my understanding. I helped check out this Landrum again, thoroughly. I interviewed him, and others at the company. Others in the industry, too. Bottom line, we don't know what Keri Wylie was talking about." Wendy hoped Gilbertson would buy the explanation. Above all, she hoped she had avoided showing her hand, of revealing the secret she knew about her boss. If she hadn't avoided tipping him, there was a good chance of her ending up like Keri Wylie.

"So, all this has been put to bed, and you've completed handing over the DSI relationship to Connie."

"Yes." She studied him, unable to tell if he believed her.

Gilbertson finally nodded. "And your recent meeting with Lieutenant Howard had nothing to do with that?"

Wendy tried to think through the deafening sound of the mental alarm bells. "Not that, specifically."

"Then what led you down there?"

He was making no pretext now, she thought. Somebody had spotted her with Howard and passed it on to Gilbertson. Or Gilbertson was having her watched. More ominously, he seemed to understand that her meeting with Howard was significant.

"Mostly I went down there to have lunch, Ward. Dan and I are old friends. We worked together years ago on that big case at Horrey Technologies."

"The one where Horrey's CEO was killed?"

"Among other victims, yes. That was before your time." In fact, Gilbertson had been promoted over her in the years that followed.

"So, you went down there to have lunch?"

"In part. I also followed up with the department on some background check information I've been coordinating with them on."

Gilbertson paused. "I see. Well, I'm glad the DSI situation is under control. That's why I put you there, after all—to oversee things and make sure they've resolved all their past problems. And that's why I felt comfortable taking you off the relationship."

Wendy said nothing.

"So," Gilbertson said, "how are things at home, Wendy?"

Wendy had wondered how long it would take him to get down to it. He'd been waiting to make his move. She was divorced and Gilbertson knew it. He hadn't called her in here solely for information. He wanted . . . She sighed. He wanted what all too many of them seemed to want. "I don't think that's really an appropriate topic for discussion."

Her boss looked hurt. "We don't have to have that kind of relationship. I'm just trying to be supportive."

Wendy remained stone-faced.

"I'm thinking if I knew you better, on a personal basis, my concerns about your cooperation and being a team player might be put to rest."

More stone face.

"You know you can come to me any time if you need support."

"Are we done here?"

His features hardened. "I guess we are. For now."

*　　*　　*

After Wendy left, Gilbertson sat at his desk, trying to make sense of what she had told him. She hadn't been defensive—hadn't pressed him on how he'd known about her meeting with Dan Howard. But now she knew she was being watched, if not exactly by whom. Her reason for visiting Howard two days ago was plausible. Was she lying? He shook his head; she was so damned unreadable. And so damned hot. Why did she have to act like a cold bitch? She'd come around, damnit.

Gilbertson stood up. He was forty-four, not bad looking. He was tall, with his hair thinning a little as his waist thickened just a bit. He looked out his window at the gridlocked traffic on the I-405. Life should be pretty good, the problem with Nomura notwithstanding. Gilbertson had four kids and an adoring wife, who liked the big city after their upbringing in Idaho. He enjoyed his job as a field supervisor in the FBI's counterintelligence division, even though it was tough staying ahead of the Chinese and the Russians. Cyber-hacking remained the preferred method of penetration, but both the government and private sectors were hardening their systems, forcing foreign foes to shift some of their resources back to old-fashioned spying. Wendy Nomura was good at thwarting that. And now, to find out what she was up to, he'd have to be better.

Chapter 9

At "home" that night, I made my daily call to Nomura and reported the bad news about my interview with Security. She sounded a little unsettled but gave me some hope. "I've met Hornsby," she said. "Even worked with him a little. He really is paranoid. He wouldn't have to have any factual basis to grill you like that. It's just the way he is."

"I hope he's satisfied. I really don't want to see him again."

"He's a little creepy," Nomura acknowledged. "Now, how's the information collection going?"

I told her what little I knew, and for the first time, I sensed impatience on her part. I was fitting in at DSI and apparently hadn't aroused suspicion, but that wasn't enough. I wasn't getting any hard information that would move the investigation forward. I had thought about pushing harder, asking Marisa some pointed questions about Keri and Landrum. But that seemed premature and risked backfiring.

After ending the call with Nomura, I spent an hour online, using an anonymous browser to research Paul Landrum, looking for some clue as to what about him could be "not what it seemed." The pictures I saw showed a formidable man, more confident and powerful than distinguished and genteel. I found lots of articles about Landrum's attempted takeover of DSI two years earlier. He had attacked Pat Dalton and his allies on all fronts—financial, legal, and public relations. But in the end, he hadn't been able to convince enough institutional shareholders —pension funds, insurance companies, and brokerage houses— that he'd produce better results than Dalton would. The federal government was also known to be uneasy about having a hard-charging hedge fund manager in control of a critically important defense contractor. Most commentators expected Landrum to make another move on DSI eventually.

Landrum, a New York native, had built his hedge fund empire in Minneapolis after a stint on Wall Street. He had made shrewd investments in growth companies and had made a killing in the high-risk field of commodity and currency trading. He had done especially well in the trading of oil futures and was regarded as an expert in world oil markets. Four years ago, he had begun Act Two of his business career. He had moved from Minnesota to Beverly Hills and changed the name of his fund to Techinvest Partners. The new venture had quickly become a player in financing tech acquisitions and startups and had done well for its investors as well as its founder. Its ownership stake in DSI was its biggest by far.

Shortly after leaving the Midwest, Landrum had divorced his longtime wife, Diane, and married Irina Petrenko, a Ukrainian model and actress twenty years his junior. I Googled Irina, who, it seemed, was better known as Landrum's wife than for her career. She'd modeled in a few magazine spreads and had appeared in several minor television roles.

I glanced through the image results. Irina was very attractive in a vacant sort of way, a blonde with sultry Slavic features, wearing too much makeup. In a lot of the images, Irina was scantily clad and/or provocatively posed. If Landrum was the architect of a secret, evil scheme, I'd have a hard time believing this woman was in on it. In some of the images, she was featured as arm candy for Landrum, who'd become a regular at Hollywood openings and charity events in the LA area. Social doors always swung open for billionaires, even recent transplants.

I went back to the web page search results, where various profiles left a clear and consistent public image of Paul Landrum. He was regarded with fear and respect, a man of frightening intelligence, magnified by a healthy dose of ruthlessness. This was the guy I, a lowly paralegal with three days on the job, was supposed to get the goods on, where the FBI had failed.

I closed my browser, wondering what was really going on with Nomura. She had been my only FBI contact for the project —she'd never mentioned a boss or any other person who was helping her. I understood the need to compartmentalize, but she couldn't keep the whole rest of the FBI out of the loop.

Or could she?

I tried to put it out of my mind. I couldn't worry about the FBI, the US attorney's office, or their political maneuverings. I had a job to do, a job that consisted of alternate periods of boredom and terror.

Why the fear? There would be a lot of embarrassment if I was caught, of course. Just the thought of coming face to face with Les Hornsby again made my skin crawl. I might even be prosecuted, if it was a crime to lie on your job application. Worse than any of that was the prospect of having to tell Wendy Nomura and Dave O'Shea not only that I'd failed, but that Paul Landrum would now be on full alert. Any chance of rehabilitating my career prospects would be trashed.

Bad as all that was, it wasn't truly the stuff of nightmares. But the thought of Keri Wylie was. I couldn't shake the image of Keri alone in her little house, terrified, probably betrayed by someone she trusted, and then shot in the head. This was the reason I'd taken the assignment—and the reason I couldn't sleep. If I found damaging information about Landrum—if I "succeeded" —I could end up like Keri.

I turned on the TV, hoping to relieve the boredom before the next round of fear kicked in.

Chapter 10

Thursday

Nancy Griffin took the elevator up to the seventh floor at DSI headquarters, exhausted after a full day downtown. The meetings relating to the Hulbert merger had been attended by representatives from no fewer than five law firms, plus a team of three in-house attorneys from DSI, led by Nancy herself. As usual, there had been a lot of lawyers trying to justify their exorbitant fees, which they did, as usual, by finding problems. But Nancy had done plenty of deals during her career and wasn't seriously concerned about the prospects for this one.

Wall Street liked the merger. Hulbert shareholders would be collecting a nice premium, thanks to an overall purchase price of $20.7 billion in cash and stock. Federal antitrust regulators had, following intense lobbying, gotten on board, having requested only a few minor divestments for competitive reasons. The deal was on track to close in about three weeks. But the attorneys still needed to create a little drama, and of course everybody had to complete the paperwork. Oh God, the paperwork.

She walked past her assistant's desk into her spacious office, closed her door, and plopped down, swallowing a couple of Advils to preempt the headache she felt coming on. Among the beneficiaries of the Hulbert deal would be Griffin herself. She would become general counsel of the new, combined company, with additional prestige, responsibility, and income. Why, then, did she need the Advils?

One source of unease was the unclear agenda of Paul Landrum. He had given the merger his reluctant blessing and, for a change, he and Pat Dalton were rowing in the same direction.

Nancy owed her job to Landrum, who, although he was a minority shareholder, still exercised considerable influence. In an unwritten part of the standstill agreement with DSI, Landrum had received the right to fill a few important jobs. One was general counsel, for which he had plucked Nancy from her previous post from Techinvest's law firm. Despite recruiting her, Landrum had never asked her to do anything specific, other than to have lunch occasionally and keep him informed.

Nancy had no doubt that if it suited his purpose, Landrum would jettison her in a heartbeat. In that respect, he was different from Pat Dalton, for whom personal loyalty still mattered. But what did Landrum want from her? She sensed that she would soon find out.

Her phone rang. She glanced at the ID and took the call without hesitation. "What can I do for you, Les?"

Les Hornsby, whose official title was Senior Vice President —Product and Process Integrity, was another of Landrum's protégés. For that reason alone, Nancy made it a point to take his calls.

"Hi, Nancy. I want to ask you about that new paralegal you hired for Bart Crosby. Dez?"

Nancy was puzzled. Why would Hornsby be concerned about such a low-level employee? Especially an inoffensive-looking woman in a wheelchair? "What's the problem?"

"How is she working out?"

"Fine, as far as I know. She just started this week. I asked Mac Williamson, who said she's friendly enough and seems to get along with everybody. And she's working through the backlog of claims."

"I had Royce talk to her yesterday," Hornsby said. "And I interviewed her after that."

"And?"

"There are no red flags per se. It's just that her background is a little obscure. She's from the opposite end of the country. She has no family. Her previous employer confirmed that she worked there, but nothing more. And the company she worked for before that has been acquired, so her records are unavailable. Ditto for the paralegal school she went to."

"And you think that's suspicious?"

"A little bit, yes."

"Les, she has no access to anything remotely classified or confidential." Griffin massaged her temples, waiting for the Advils to kick in. With all the critical national security issues the Pentagon was concerned about, with all the informational requests from the new FBI liaison—Hornsby was worried about this lady in a wheelchair?

"She has proximity," Hornsby said. "My sources say she's blended in quickly. Made friends, ingratiated herself. She's very confident and comfortable in dealing with the attorneys."

"And here I was, congratulating myself on hiring her, for those very reasons. What's going on here, Les?"

"She just doesn't feel right."

Griffin forced herself to calm down. "All right. They pay you to be suspicious. What do you want me to do?"

"I'm not sure. Just keep an eye on her."

Right, Griffin thought. *With a large department to run and a huge merger coming up, I'm going to babysit a paralegal?*

"I'll do what I can," Nancy said. She hung up and returned to work, with no time to reflect on Hornsby's most annoying attribute: He was usually right.

Chapter 11

Wendy Nomura walked into the Newport Beach police station, involuntarily glancing around, assuming she was still being watched. A second visit to Howard within a week would certainly catch the attention of Ward Gilbertson. Dan Howard had asked her to come down; he could help her think up an excuse for the visit. She wondered why the detective had summoned her, but it would be even more interesting to learn who was watching her and why.

Howard came out to reception, sporting his standard detective look and demeanor, but Wendy thought she could detect a slight spring in his step, maybe even a bit of excitement on his face. "Come on back," he said. "Something to show you."

Howard escorted her to a conference room, where she took a seat. "First things first," she said and told him that word of their last meeting had gotten back to FBI headquarters.

The detective lifted an eyebrow. "Did you cover it okay?"

"I think so. We'll have to think of something to explain today."

He nodded. "But who's the snitch?"

"Somebody from my end."

He didn't dispute this. "But why is somebody interested?"

Wendy looked away, then back. "Something to do with . . . the security situation."

"That could be a lot of things."

"I know. I think it will come to a head after the DSI-Hulbert deal closes."

"I hope so. We shouldn't have to sneak around to do ordinary business. Or, in this case, extraordinary business."

"Extraordinary? Well, out with it."

"We have a person of interest in the Keri Wylie case."

"Do tell," she said.

"We—uh, don't have a name. But we have a face."

"Surveillance footage?"

"Yes." He placed a picture before her.

Wendy squinted at the photograph, which showed a clean-shaven man, about forty, with light hair and eyes that seemed to bulge a bit. "Taken through a car windshield?"

"Yes. There are cameras at both entrances to the Peninsula. Mostly they're used to capture vehicle tags. Every once in a while, if the lighting is right, and the positioning of the car in the lane and the person in the car are right, we can get an actual face inside the car. In this case, we got lucky."

"He seems to be looking up."

"I think he spotted the camera. Too late."

"What about the vehicle?"

"Dead end," Howard said. "We've spent nearly two weeks tracking down vehicles that came off the Peninsula that night after the murder and checking out the owners. There were a handful of suspicious owners, but we cleared them all. Except this guy." He tapped the picture with a finger. "He came by at the right time, but the vehicle didn't check out."

"Stolen?"

"Nope. Registered to a dead-end corporation. A defunct shell with closed offices and foreign owners."

"Suspicious," Wendy said.

"Definitely. But that means all we have is a face. I've had it run through the state databases but came up empty."

"And you're wondering if I can run it through federal?"

"Yes."

Wendy thought for a full minute. "There's a chance I could slip it through," she said at last. "But I can't take the chance of catching somebody's attention. And I don't want to put anybody else at risk."

Howard nodded. He seemed to have expected this response.

She let out a long breath. "How sure are you, Dan?"

"This is the guy," he said without hesitation.

"Let me think about it. There has to be a way."

"Take the picture with you." They stood up. "Damnit, let's get this asshole."

*   *   *

From the parking lot of the office building down the street, Viktor Kamensky called PACIFIC.

"He's met with the FBI agent again."

"At the station?"

"Yes, for about half an hour."

A long pause. "I think," PACIFIC said, "that it's time to switch targets. Go with Nomura."

Chapter 12

After a full week on the job, I wasn't panicking. Not yet. But I appeared to have reached a dead end. Nobody seemed to want to talk about either Keri or Landrum. I continued to do my work, keeping my eyes and ears open. I spent my time processing claim reports, although I'd had a proofreading assignment on Wednesday. I'd had to review and check, line by line, more than a hundred pages of inventory and equipment belonging to Hulbert that was to be included in the DSI acquisition. I'd needed an extra cup of coffee to stay awake through the tedious project, which had stretched into the evening hours.

I'd had little opportunity to interact with people outside my immediate area. I had attended a couple of meetings with attorneys who managed litigation for the company, and I often called DSI's risk managers at its various locations to ask questions about the reports they submitted on claims against the company. But that was about it.

I attended lunch faithfully at Mac Williamson's table. I'd taken to fixing my fake hair and minimal makeup in the ladies' room, reasoning that I might pick up some scuttlebutt. I hadn't so far. Paul Landrum was a remote, near-legendary figure. None of the attorneys seemed to have been intimate friends with Keri. Marisa Costas had been a friend of Keri's, but it was hard to tell how close they had been, and Marisa didn't want to talk about it. Interestingly, the attorney who had seemed to work mostly closely with Landrum had been Keri herself, but that shouldn't have been surprising, since she'd learned enough to phone in an anonymous warning about him. In all, DSI's legal department seemed an unremarkable workplace—except for that pesky murder.

I looked around the table at lunch. "Where's Ritchie?" I asked. Clay hadn't made an appearance since Wednesday.

"We actually don't see him all that often," Mac Williamson answered. "This week has been an exception. I think he just wanted to meet you, Dez."

I blushed. "Well, he's not here now. So, whether he liked what he saw—you be the judge."

When we'd finished eating, I started to pick up my tray but felt a hand on my arm. "Stay a minute," Williamson said.

When everybody had left, he said, "I'm a bit hesitant, but I'm convinced that telling you is the right thing to do."

I waited.

"I got a visit from Les Hornsby yesterday. He asked about you."

My guts churned.

"He asked if you had talked about yourself at all," he continued. "I had to say, truthfully, that you hadn't, but that I didn't consider that suspicious. Hornsby said your background was somewhat fuzzy."

"I answered all his questions," I said. "I can't imagine what they think is so suspicious about me. I'm just a paralegal."

Williamson let out a thoughtful sigh. "I'm not sure what he thinks. I'll say this much, Dez. I've known many fine, capable paralegals. You're sharper and more sophisticated than any of them. Have you ever thought about going to law school?"

"I'm kind of old for that now."

"No, you're not. You should think about it."

I smiled and nodded. As we got up to leave, I reflected that as scary as Les Hornsby had been, the prospect of repeating law school was worse.

*   *   *

Late in the afternoon, restless, I found myself headed toward the bathroom. My route took me only a couple of doors away from Keri Wylie's office. I glanced around, saw no one, and took the detour. I lingered in front of Keri's door, checked my surroundings again, and tried the doorknob. Locked.

"Dez?"

I jerked around. Clay Ritchie stood behind me. He'd appeared from nowhere.

"Oh, hi," I said.

"The bathroom is back there," Ritchie said.

"Um, right."

"But I guess you probably know that by now."

"Sure."

He gave me a knowing smile. "Have a good one."

Chapter 13

Wendy Nomura trudged toward her boss's office for her second appearance in less than a week. Gilbertson had stepped up the pressure on her; he'd sent her an email accusing her of deficiencies in her job performance. Was that what he wanted to see her about today? Or would it be about the meetings with Howard? And in either case, what was his real motive? Straightforward sexual harassment? Or something even more sinister?

At least she now knew she was being watched. But how was Gilbertson doing it? Who was watching on his behalf? She rehearsed the cover story she had agreed on with Howard about their meetings—further coordination on background checks. It sounded lame. But there was no way to know what today's agenda would be—she'd have to rely on her wits. She knocked, walked in, and sat down without a word.

This time the smiles had disappeared; Gilbertson's expression conveyed grim disapproval. "Did you get my email?" he asked.

"Yes."

"So?"

"What do you want me to say? I get a message telling me my job performance is subpar and to come up with an improvement plan. May I ask a question?"

He nodded.

"Are you for real? You expect me to take this seriously?"

He sat up and cleared his throat. "Item one on the improvement plan might be to take your boss seriously, yes."

"I've never gotten anything but glowing job reviews. Your criticism is bogus, and you know it."

"You're not helping yourself, Wendy. You need to respond."

"My response will be that the email is part of a campaign of harassment and intimidation against me. The proper authorities will be copied."

His face darkened. "You really don't want to do that."

"I'm sorry; harassment, intimidation, *and threats*."

A flash of doubt crossed Gilbertson's face, but he seemed determined to stay on the offensive. He calmed himself, then sat back in his chair, studying her with a practiced look of disappointment. "Think about it. You don't want this to go on your permanent record."

Wendy stared straight ahead.

He stood up, came out from behind his desk, and walked slowly toward her.

Here it comes, she thought.

He stood beside her. "I had high hopes for you, Wendy. That we could work together, as a team." When Wendy didn't react, Gilbertson moved around behind her. "I've been disappointed in your attitude. Very disappointed. How do we get out of this situation? I don't want to report you."

She remained silent.

"The key is cooperation," he said, one hand coming to rest on her shoulder. "Cooperation with me. Responding to what I need, and to what I'm trying to do for you. Going along. Think about it. If I see a change in attitude, then maybe we can take another look at your behavior." His other hand came to rest on her other shoulder. He began massaging her.

Wendy got up and headed for the door.

"Wait a minute. This meeting is not over yet."

She turned and gave him a rare smile. "Oh, yes. I'm afraid it's definitely over."

She headed straight for the ladies' room. Inside a stall, she composed herself. Shaking off her disgust, she reflected on Gilbertson's approach. Appalling though it was, at least it was straightforward. There was no mention of the meetings with Howard.

It wasn't the first time she had encountered harassment, and it probably wouldn't be the last. But was there something else, another agenda, behind it all? And what, if anything, did it have to do with Keri Wylie?

Chapter 14

It was past six in the evening when Viktor Kamensky picked up Wendy Nomura's sedan, down the road from the FBI's headquarters in Westwood. For the past couple of days, he had followed her off and on during the workday and seen nothing remarkable. Since he didn't know what he was looking for, that wasn't surprising. Still, PACIFIC had told him that Nomura, rather than Howard, now posed the biggest threat among law enforcement assets. So, he had dutifully tailed her to meetings at two large defense contractors and then back to the office for the rest of the day. He tried to concentrate on the surveillance, but his mind kept going back to the phone call last night from PACIFIC.

"You've got to be careful, Viktor," PACIFIC had said.

"I know that, for God's sake."

"I'm afraid you might be losing the edge. You're blending right into cushy, laid-back LA. Maybe you need to go back to Moscow to sharpen your skills."

Kamensky's mouth went dry. "Look, my vehicles are clean. My identity is clean. My apartment—"

"Yes, yes. But now you've got to keep your *nose* clean, especially in places where they might use facial recognition routinely."

A pause. "They're running my face?"

"Not deliberately or consciously, as far as we know. But they could get a hit, if they picked you up at places like the FBI building, the courthouse, the airports."

Kamensky found the warning unsettling. PACIFIC was supposed to have things like facial recognition under control; how else could he have gotten into the United States? But as much as he was concerned about the authorities, he was more concerned about PACIFIC.

"Have you picked up anything else on . . . your last project?" PACIFIC wouldn't say *Keri Wylie's murder* over the phone.

"Nothing at all," Kamensky replied.

"Let's keep it that way."

He hung up, relieved, and returned his attention to tailing Nomura.

Kamensky reflected that he and Nomura were basically in the same business. But he wouldn't be able to tolerate all the hassles involved in working for the FBI. Warrants, rights, rules, guidelines, evidence. It was a miracle they got anything done. The Bureau, with its limitations, was a reflection of a weak government, a weak system, a weak mentality. Weak men who let terrorists mess with them, who let foreign governments mess with their elections. Kamensky felt nothing but contempt for these people, and for the people he had killed. Whiners and weaklings who deserved their fate.

Peering ahead at Nomura's car, he reflected again on how lucky he was to be surveilling not only a woman, but an attractive one. He'd found that she lived in a small house in Fountain Valley but hadn't learned anything about a husband or boyfriend. He maintained a loose tail as she got onto the 405.

He told himself there was no reason to worry. The authorities didn't know he was in the country. The FBI was supposed to be under control. But now PACIFIC was worried about facial recognition and seemed at least mildly concerned about Wendy Nomura. So far, Nomura hadn't done anything suspicious. Maybe that in itself was suspicious.

He jerked back to present awareness as Nomura abruptly exited the freeway. She took a right, and Kamensky had to wait at a light before following. When he was finally able to make the turn, he couldn't find her. He sped up, threading his way through traffic, until finally, he saw her . . . coming back in the opposite direction. He couldn't make a U-turn and follow her now, not without showing himself. She suspected a tail or was at least concerned about one. He slammed his palm on the wheel. Damnit, what the *hell* was going on? Nomura was messing with him.

One thing was certain: He was pissed off now, to go along with being bored and restless. And when Viktor Kamensky got pissed off, somebody had to pay.

Chapter 15

Wendy Nomura stopped by at nine on Friday night. I had spotted her car in the back of my parking lot about fifteen minutes earlier, and now she slipped in quickly.

"All clear?" I asked.

She hesitated. "Nobody saw me come here, if that's what you mean. But it's possible somebody has been trying to follow me."

"To follow *you*?"

"Yes." She followed me through the condo to the living room, where she took an easy chair. I'd already pulled the curtains, blocking our view of the ocean. I studied Nomura and was, as always, struck by how beautiful she was. Her demeanor was very direct and no-nonsense—maybe even a little severe at times, and I wondered if acting that way was part of an effort to be taken seriously. Men probably found it sexy.

"What's the latest?" she asked.

"I don't know if they're on to me, but they're suspicious." I told her about my conversation with Mac Williamson, and Les Hornsby's extra scrutiny.

"That's not good," she said. "But there's nothing in your legend that won't check out. In the meantime, I've seen no signs of interest in you outside of the office. I've checked your van for trackers and haven't found any. We had this place swept for bugs yesterday, and it was clean. I'm having your phone monitored, and nobody has tried to slip tracking malware onto it. I've watched this complex at night—nothing."

"You've watched it every night?" I asked. "All night?"

"No and no."

Not for the first time, I wondered how closely the FBI was watching me. The project had the sanction of Dave O'Shea, and presumably of higher-ups at the FBI, people who could, with a phone call, summon up the resources for more surveillance. But Nomura didn't seem inclined to explain. She had also never discussed how the FBI had learned of my expertise in ClaimTrack, or my availability for a six-week assignment.

"What's the latest at DSI?" she asked.

I reported that I'd made no real progress on either Keri or Landrum. I was still trying to get closer to Marisa Costas, the only person I'd met who claimed to be a friend of Keri's. "I've got proximity," I said, "but I don't regularly interact with other people on the floor. I deal mostly with risk managers out in the field, and that's over the phone. I'm left mostly with conversations at lunch, or in the restroom or hallways."

She frowned. "Any social interaction outside of work?"

"I'm hoping there might be a happy hour or weekend party. But I'm just a paralegal. I wouldn't necessarily be invited. I'm lucky some of the attorneys include me at their table at lunch."

"Have you actually met Landrum?"

"No. He doesn't spend a lot of time at DSI. I saw him walk by in the hallway on Thursday. That's about it. People seem afraid of him."

"You need to get closer to him."

"Damnit, Wendy, I'm about eight levels below Landrum. He's not even there most of the time. I happen to have a cube on the same floor. And I've been there all of a week."

She held up her hands. "All right, I get it. Aren't there some attorneys who were close to Keri?"

"I haven't found any I'd describe as close, no."

"How about attorneys who are close to Landrum, other than Keri?"

"I haven't found any yet, but there could be. We have a lot of attorneys, and not all of them are on the executive floor."

She shook her head in frustration. "We're running out of time."

Nomura stood up to leave, and I felt like telling her to sit down, that there were some serious questions I wanted her to answer, right now, about the FBI's monitoring and level of support for the project. But I let her go. What had happened to my usual assertiveness? I wondered. Was I becoming a shy paralegal?

*   *   *

The phone call to PACIFIC was a tense one. "I told you," Kamensky said, "I don't *know* what's going on. Maybe nothing."

"But it was definitely deliberate counter-surveillance."

"No question."

"And you lost her."

"I lost her."

Silence. "This is really not good, Viktor."

Kamensky couldn't hold back any longer. "You're trying to put this all on me. You're supposed to have these people *under control.* The fact is, you're fucking clueless."

This time the silence was longer. Kamensky was left to wait. To wait, and to regret running his mouth. His relationship with PACIFIC was uneasy at best. He was under PACIFIC's nominal control, but if push came to shove—if their respective sponsors in Moscow came into serious conflict—it was far from clear who would prevail.

Finally, PACIFIC said, "If nothing else, I guess it's rather obvious what you need to do now. So do it. I will forget about your last comment."

*   *   *

Wendy drove home, exhausted after a long day of juggling two lives. Even Pen only had to manage one life at a time; stressful though her undercover assignment was, she could at least sit in the apartment at night and relax. But Wendy had to contend with a day job along with an undercover op at night. And the day gig included fending off Ward Gilbertson.

She knew that solving Keri Wylie's murder was critical. But her superiors had made it clear, for reasons she well understood, that no further resources would be forthcoming. Which meant that for the most part, the job would be up to Pen.

Chapter 16

Saturday

Wendy Nomura sat her desk, hoping to catch up on work without the distractions of Ward Gilbertson and Pen Wilkinson. She frequently worked on Saturdays, her anemic social life leaving her with little else to do. On Sundays she'd dutifully visit her parents, absorbing their unspoken disapproval, their disdain for her status as a childless divorcée. And her brother, a hot-shot corporate lawyer, would be there with his perfect wife and three kids, just in case Wendy's marital failure, childlessness, and languishing career weren't obvious enough.

She picked up the picture of Howard's mystery suspect and studied it. She'd discreetly passed the picture around the office on the off chance somebody might recognize the suspect's face. It seemed incredible that she wasn't free to identify and track the guy down, but bigger forces were in play. This hard-looking man might have fled the area, or even the country. But he could still be on the loose, somewhere here in LA.

"Wendy?"

She looked up. A fellow agent, Sophie Thomas, was standing at the door, holding a copy of the picture. Sophie was a fellow counterintelligence agent, a large woman with washed-out features.

"Hi, Sophie."

Thomas approached and laid the picture on Wendy's desk. "I recognize this guy," she said. "You have a problem."

*   *   *

Sixty-four minutes later, Wendy waited in the windowless, nondescript conference room, in a section of the building well away from her own office and that of the man she would be meeting with. She couldn't stop looking at the picture of Howard's suspect, feeling in her bones that the man's presence here in LA signaled a potential disaster.

She stood up when a man, lanky and blond, entered. Assistant Director in Charge Kirk Hendricks motioned for her to sit. The large and critically important Los Angeles field office was one of only a handful that rated an assistant director, rather than a special agent in charge, as its leader, and Hendricks, the ADC, far outranked Nomura. When he had personally approved the DSI operation, he had given Wendy his personal cell phone number. She hadn't had any cause to use it until now.

The ADC was a formidable man, confident, with keen intelligence, tempered by a bit of shyness. He sat alone at the conference table, which was unusual; he was nearly always accompanied by assistants to record the conversation and take care of follow-up matters. At least Hendricks's friend, US attorney Dave O'Shea, wouldn't be here. Wendy handed Hendricks the picture, which he stared at with a thin smile.

"Viktor Kamensky," he said, shaking his head. "Where do we even start?"

"I'll have to study up on him, sir. I just haven't had time."

"No problem. You did the right thing by calling me immediately. This is a situation." He looked back at the picture. "You're probably familiar with his crimes, if not with his name or face."

She nodded. "The London operations."

"More than that. He's a full-blown thug in the employ of Russian military intelligence—GRU—and people keep ending up dead wherever he's stationed. The London killings are the most notorious, of course—you use poison umbrellas and nerve gas, you tend to get people's attention."

"I assume that was the idea."

"Of course. The Russians were sending a message to would-be dissidents and journalists and assorted troublemakers. But when it has served their interests to kill people quietly—well, Kamensky's done that, too. In London, Kiev, Bucharest. And now here. The big questions relate to the why. Why would they risk bringing him in illegally? And why is he here, if he's still around?"

"I think it's safe to say he's here for a bigger purpose than just shooting a young attorney."

"Absolutely. They could have used street muscle for that." A small chime sounded, and Hendricks pulled the cell phone from the inside pocket of his weekend blazer. He glanced at the screen, then looked up. "It's a big negative. He's not in our face databases."

She nodded. "I *knew* it." Among the perks of being an ADC was the ability to run a face discreetly and instantly, using Washington channels Wendy hadn't been aware of. Wendy hadn't asked him to do it; she'd gotten lucky when Sophie Thomas had recognized the face from a stint at the FBI's London office. Since they now had a name, the search hadn't taken long, and it had confirmed their fears: Viktor Kamensky's face had not been in federal databases.

Hendricks said, "Any idea, Wendy? Any thoughts at all about what the Russians might be up to?"

"So far all we have for sure is the Keri Wylie murder. That may tie into Paul Landrum, DSI, and the Hulbert merger. All indications are that they're protecting a big secret, and bringing Kamensky in almost certainly means they have killed, or intend to kill, other people to keep the lid on."

"It's got to be something major. And here we are, with our hands tied." The ADC slapped the picture onto the table. "We've got a Russian killer running loose, planning who knows what, and we can't even BOLO the guy. Incredible."

Incredible might be too weak a word, Wendy thought. With all the resources of the Bureau—of the entire federal government, theoretically—with all the power and authority of an official like Hendricks, they were pathetically helpless, hampered by the need for secrecy. "If Kamensky's still here," she said, "that would mean they still need him for something."

"Yes. If we get the clear sense something is imminent, then all bets are off. That's especially true if it looks like any of the Hulbert products are at risk. If their missile countermeasures system should fall into the wrong hands, God help us. We'd be open to blackmail at best, attack at worst."

And our careers would be over—they might even prosecute us, Wendy thought.

"If there's anything imminent," Hendricks continued, "we'll have to abandon the project, forget about secrecy, and make our move. In the meantime, I'll have to consider talking to CIA and Homeland."

Wendy suspected he would do no such thing. Sharing this kind of knowledge was nearly unthinkable from a bureaucratic standpoint, and bringing more people into the loop would only increase the odds of a security leak.

Hendricks thought for a while. "Is Howard okay?" he asked.

"He's solid. I'm not worried about him."

"I'm going to have a personal chat with Sophie Thomas and send her out of town on a temporary assignment for the next month, just as a precaution. In the meantime, I'll be ready to put out an interagency net for Kamensky, using antiterrorism protocols, if we sense something is going down soon."

"Keri Wylie seemed to think there was something tied to the DSI-Hulbert merger. That would give us less than a month."

"I want this thing solved a lot sooner than that," Hendricks said.

"We need assets, resources."

"We can't chance that now. That could blow our entire operation."

Wendy, though frustrated, couldn't dispute his logic. "And so, for now, that pretty much leaves me."

"You and Pen." He smiled. "No pressure." The smile vanished. They couldn't avoid talking about Pen any longer.

"Do we tell her?" Wendy asked.

"We'll have to. It goes against every principle of compartmentalization, but she has to know. If we put a civilian out there, facing this kind of potential risk, without telling her, we're no better than the Russians."

Wendy was relieved at not having to make the decision herself. She had no idea what she would have done.

"The best way to protect Pen is to stay away from her as much as possible," Hendricks said. "They spot us protecting her and she's blown."

"Agreed. I never visit her unless I'm a hundred percent sure the place is clear."

"Let's review what we're doing to keep tabs on her."

"We've proceeded on the assumption that she's okay at the office," Wendy said.

"Reasonable enough. What about to and from?"

"I've been out of visual for the commute, but nearby. And we've got the tracker on her phone."

Hendricks considered it. "I don't see how we can do more. What about at home, and trips after hours and on weekends?"

"She tells me ahead of time, and I make sure she's clean."

Hendricks thought some more. "Are we spinning our wheels here, Wendy? Do we really expect her to find anything?"

"Expect? I'm afraid not. Hope? You'd better believe it, sir. Because we don't have much else."

*   *   *

I sat in my living room late at night, sipping wine, not watching the picture on TV, bored to death. My legend sat next to me on my end table, along with a dozen pages of notes. I'd spent hours memorizing all the facts of my phony background, trying to anticipate all possible questions and preparing improvised answers to queries that might not be covered in the legend. That preparation had served me well during my encounter with Les Hornsby, and I hoped I wouldn't need to draw upon it again. Now, my brain hurt, and I just wanted to get out and go somewhere. But I couldn't do that without notifying Nomura, which I hated to do on a weekend.

I'd studied my legend for more than three hours before tossing the document onto the coffee table. After a week at DSI, I hadn't found any natural channels, any "ins," that might give me access to the truth about Paul Landrum and Keri Wylie. It had to happen soon.

Chapter 17

Sunday

Even deep-cover spies need to do some shopping occasionally, so I reluctantly called Nomura in late morning.

"Fine," she said. "And when you're done, I want to see you."

I drove to a Target store, where I picked up some groceries and other items, then returned around three. I hadn't seen Nomura or anybody else trailing me, and I guessed that was a good thing.

Nomura appeared at my door about half an hour after my return, looking grim.

I led her to the living room. "Something to drink?" I asked.

"No, thanks," she said.

She sat down and pulled a sheet of paper out of her purse. It was a picture of a serious-looking, middle-aged man.

"Who's he?" I asked.

"His name is Viktor Kamensky. He's a Russian assassin. And we think he killed Keri."

I clutched the wheels of my chair. "Tell me you're joking."

She wasn't.

"What does this mean?" I asked.

"It could mean a lot of things. We're still evaluating it. But for you, it has a couple of specific applications."

I waited.

"First of all, as you investigate Landrum, you need to look for any Russian connections."

That made sense, I thought.

"The second consideration is your safety," she said. I found myself gripping the wheels again.

"Now, don't be alarmed," she said hurriedly. "This is theoretical. There is no current threat to you, as far as we know. We just believe you deserve to know what we're contending with."

"Do we need to change our security procedures?"

"We don't think so. If we start openly guarding you, that's going to give you away."

"I guess. What do we know about this . . ."

"Kamensky."

"Kamensky, right."

"I don't want to get into details. In fact, the less you know about him, the better. I'll just state the obvious: he's incredibly dangerous. Look, we already knew Keri's killer was still out there. Now we just know who he is."

"The search just got a lot easier," I said.

"Um, right. Absolutely."

There was a long moment of awkward silence. I'd caught her hesitation, and she knew I'd caught it. But she wasn't going to say anything about it.

She stood up, returning the picture of Kamensky to her purse. "I need to get going."

I went with her to the door.

"Let me know if you need anything," she said. "I'll talk to you tomorrow night."

"Sure. And Wendy?"

"Yes?"

"Thanks for telling me."

I'm not sure how long I sat there, looking at the blank TV screen. Maybe two hours, maybe three. I had to muster as much lawyerly mental discipline as I could to sort out what Nomura had told me and, just as significantly, what she hadn't. I started by taking at face value her explanation for why she had told me about the Russian. I felt she was sincere in saying I deserved to know, and that I needed to watch Landrum for a Russian connection.

76

So far, so good. But what had she left out? Basically, every-thing else. I pulled out my iPad and Googled "Russian assassin." After filtering out the fictional references, I spent the next hour reading one horrifying article after another, detailing how the Russian regime had killed its opponents, both in Russia and in the West. The two most notorious incidents had been a radiation poisoning in England in 2006 and a nerve gas killing, also in the UK, in 2017.

So far, so bad. But further research left me profoundly dis-turbed. One article listed more than thirty-eight suspicious deaths of political activists, journalists, and the like who had op-posed the Kremlin. Some were shot. Some were killed in acci-dents. And a few had died of mysterious heart attacks or causes that were unknown. In each case, even though no assassin had been identified, or even a crime proven, Western intelligence agencies believed the victims had been murdered. None of the articles mentioned Viktor Kamensky by name, but as a known killer, sent abroad to commit a murder, he fit the profile. How many of these crimes had he been responsible for?

And what did all this mean for me? First of all, Nomura, and presumably Howard, had already made the leap and believed that Landrum might somehow be connected to the Russians. Whatever Keri had learned about Landrum—that he was not who he appeared to be and needed to be unmasked before the Hulbert merger closed—was apparently a secret worth killing to protect.

Really? I thought. Keri's statements were just vague accusa-tions, with no facts—no allegations of actual criminality or other wrongdoing. Which meant Keri seemed likely to have found something more—something specific—such as an actual Landrum connection to Russia. Finding those additional facts seemed the key to understanding her death. There had to be more; why else would the Russians risk bringing in a professional killer to do the job? There had been nothing exotic about Keri Wylie's

murder—just a shot to the head. An American contract killer—
even a street criminal—could have done the job. Had Kamensky
already been in the United States for another reason? And, somehow, a known Russian operative had eluded US border controls
—how?

Nomura's information also reframed Keri's murder as
something both professional and personal. There now seemed
little chance that the motivation for the killing had been personal
somehow, as with a crime of passion. The motive looked professional. But the odds were now much higher that a second person,
someone Keri knew, had talked his or her way into Keri's house
to make way for Kamensky. There had been no forced entry, and
it was hard to imagine a Russian thug using charm or trickery to
induce Keri to open her door in the middle of the night. If the
motive appeared professional, the means looked personal.

Of course it made sense that the FBI had an urgent interest
in finding a Russian intelligence operative who had somehow
gotten past American security. And any secret Russian connection to a major defense contractor was a matter for official concern
—even alarm. Then why Nomura's hesitation when I'd mentioned the subject of a manhunt? There was something about the
FBI's approach that didn't seem right, something I couldn't put
my finger on, a fact that seemed to be playing hide-and-seek in
my subconscious.

I leaned back in my chair, exhausted. Was I overthinking it?
Was I better off just doing my job every day at DSI, not worrying
about anything deeper? I knew I didn't have that option.

Chapter 18

Week 3

Monday

I was both apprehensive and relieved to be back at work after a weekend that had alternated between learning alarming facts and fighting off sheer boredom. With less than four weeks left before the Hulbert merger closed, I'd have to make a move soon, to be more direct in my approach.

Bart came out of his office a little before 4:00, carrying a file. "Proofreading," he said. "Finish it before you go home. You can put in for overtime." He handed me the file and disappeared back into his office. I knew I wouldn't receive any more direction.

I looked over the document. It was a revised shareholder agreement between DSI and Techinvest Partners, Landrum's company. The document had been prepared by Techinvest's law firm and sent to DSI's law firm. From there it had gone to Nancy Griffin. There was a handwritten yellow sticky note on the file: "Bart: One final proofreading before execution. Your new para can do it. Thx, Nancy." It might be interesting, I thought.

Judging from the length of the document, nearly two hundred pages, I'd be working late. Another note on the document contained an online address, where I found the email transmitting the electronic version of the document to DSI. I needed to make sure that changes highlighted in the online version had made it correctly into the printed copies Bart had given me. I knew from my previous proofreading assignment that I'd need to send a return email to DSI's law firm either confirming that the changes had been made correctly or specifying any problems. I settled in and started reading.

After an hour or so I went and got myself a cup of coffee. The going was slow, partly because I was interested in the substance of the document. It was a revision of the legal truce reached by DSI and Techinvest Partners after the latter had tried to take over the former nearly two years ago. Techinvest had agreed to cease its efforts to take control without giving advance notice, and in return, DSI had granted it certain rights and privileges as a major shareholder, including the right to name four of the nine members of the board of directors. Lawsuits between the two parties had been settled and dismissed.

At seven, I bought a sandwich from a vending machine downstairs, returned to the seventh floor, and resumed the drudgery. By nine I was nearly done, but my eyes were starting to glaze over. I'd needed more coffee to keep going. So far, all the changes I'd seen on my screen had been faithfully reflected in the final written version. Then I did a double take.

I'd nearly missed it. There was a difference in the two versions, but it had not been marked. A single word had been added to the paper version, the final document to be executed by the parties. But the word wasn't on the marked-up version on the screen.

I double-checked. And checked again. But the word was definitely missing. The word was "not."

What was going on?

I read the text again in detail. To understand it, I first had to refer back to a Section 5.1.1, which limited Techinvest to naming only four of the nine members of DSI's board of directors. Next, several paragraphs later, there was a provision that allowed Techinvest to increase its forty percent stock ownership stake in DSI under certain conditions, but if it did, it had to give DSI a six-month written notice of its intent to do so, and to meet other requirements. Furthermore—and this was the kicker—the "provisions of Section 5.1.1 shall apply." In the paper version, "not" had been added, so that it read: ". . . the provisions of Section 5.1.1 shall *not* apply."

Whoa, I thought. The effect of this one-word insertion was a complete game-changer. I read it over again. And then again. But there was no doubt: Techinvest would now be allowed to increase its ownership stake in DSI and would no longer be limited to four board seats. It might be able to take control of the board of directors, and thus of DSI, at any time, before or after the merger. This year, or next, or tomorrow. This change would undo the uneasy truce. And somebody was trying to slip it in.

They had nearly succeeded. It was a single word, in a document of two hundred pages, inserted as the last word of a page, so inconspicuous that I had found it almost by accident. Paul Landrum and Techinvest, or someone working on their behalf, had tried, in crude fashion, to pull a fast one.

I stopped and sat up. The seventh floor was dark, illuminated only by my cubicle light and faint after-hours lights. The building was quiet, with only the hiss of the ventilation system.

As I turned the problem over in my mind, my right foot, which I couldn't actually feel, did a furious phantom fidget. Would Landrum really be so brazen? So underhanded? Did he really think he would get away with it?

Of course he did. He nearly had.

If Landrum tried to invoke the changed language and take over, DSI would undoubtedly sue to block the move, claiming that it had been defrauded. DSI might prevail in making that argument. But maybe not. The fight would be uphill for DSI, trying to overturn a document it had signed. Techinvest would, of course, claim that DSI had agreed to the change, probably in exchange for Techinvest's support for the Hulbert deal. In any event, the wording would give Techinvest leverage, including the ability to tie DSI up in litigation. Someone obviously thought it was worth a try to slip in the change.

I thought about it some more. The change had been inserted at the last minute to minimize the risk of discovery. The next stop was execution by the parties. The culprit had probably figured the document would be proofread by a low-level employee—an assistant or paralegal. They had no way of knowing the proofreader would be an experienced—and suspicious—attorney. Even less would they expect the proofreader to read the entire document word-for-word; almost anyone would simply skip from one highlighted change to the next.

But the most inexplicable, and possibly sinister, thing about the change was that it had gone through DSI's law firm. Did Landrum really think the change would be missed by the corporation's high-powered attorneys? And yet it apparently had been missed. Or someone at DSI's law firm was in on the scheme, risking disbarment or worse. Or—and I hated to consider this possibility—the change had been slipped in by Nancy Griffin, a Landrum protégée, whose desk had been the last stop before Bart had given the document to me. In all, there was no question whose interests the insertion of the language served: Paul Landrum's. But the question of who had actually inserted the language was a genuine mystery. I suspected the offender had covered his or her tracks thoroughly.

I sat for several minutes, trying to let the magnitude of this discovery sink in, and gradually turning my attention to the hazardous question of what to do about it. It was now after nine. Bart Crosby had left for the day. So had his boss, Nancy Griffin. So had nearly everybody in the building. I could ask Nomura what to do, but I couldn't safely make the call from here; my burner phone was at home. The assignment needed to be turned in before I left for the day. If I was going to blow the whistle, I'd have to do it by email. But should I blow the whistle?

The risks were potentially huge. I'd be calling attention to myself, which would invite scrutiny and risk blowing my cover. Worse, I'd be making an enemy of Landrum, the guy I was supposed to be investigating. DSI's law firm would be embarrassed at best, vindictive at worst. Nancy Griffin wouldn't be happy. And what was the upside?

Truthfully, I really couldn't say what the potential benefit of blowing the whistle might be. But I sensed that I needed to make something happen, even if it might raise my profile. I was spinning my wheels and running out of time. I couldn't predict the reaction of all the players, but the stench wafting out of DSI was getting pungent, and this might be my only chance to force the complicit parties to show themselves. And so, I decided to go for broke.

I was supposed to communicate the results of my proofreading to DSI's law firm by responding to the email they had sent to convey the documents to the online site. I had to either tell them that everything was okay or that there had been discrepancies. Technically, the inserted "not" didn't even qualify as a discrepancy. It was outside the scope of my assignment, which was to check out highlighted changes. The "not" obviously hadn't been highlighted.

I composed an innocuous reply, which stated that all changes had been accurately reflected in the written version, but that there was an additional discrepancy. I referenced the inserted "not," but I didn't explain what it did. It was more a pink flag than a red one.

Now it was time to send the message. I had the option of clicking "Reply," which would send the response back to DSI's law firm. That was all I needed to do—all I was supposed to do, really. But there was another alternative.

I also had the option of clicking "Reply All," which would send the response to everybody who had been routinely copied, including Paul Landrum, Pat Dalton, and Nancy Griffin.

I took a deep breath and hit Reply All.

Chapter 19

Tuesday

My drive to the office the next morning seemed three times longer than its usual fifteen minutes. I didn't know if I'd still be employed by the end of the day, but I held out a slim hope that company officials would smooth everything over, sweeping the incident under the rug. I had barely slept.

When I'd reported in to Nomura last night, I'd decided to come clean, telling her in detail what had happened. Predictably, she had been mortified.

"Good God, Pen. What were you thinking? This will really shake the tree."

"Yes."

"And not in a good way. Landrum might be tipped off."

"I hope not. But if so, we can see how he reacts." *And hopefully, he won't send Viktor Kamensky after me,* I thought.

"Damnit, Pen, that was not your call."

"I couldn't reach you. I had to make a decision."

"No, you didn't. You promised no freelancing."

"A decision to do nothing is still a decision."

"Let's hope it wasn't the wrong one."

We talked for a while about possible reactions by the players at DSI. We also discussed possible responses by me, but when push came to shove, I'd probably have to wing it. She hadn't been mollified by the time our call had ended.

Now I could feel my heart pounding as I pulled into the DSI parking lot. I tried to collect myself as I waited for my van's door to open and the ramp to extend. *You're Dez,* I reminded myself. An innocent, bewildered paralegal.

"Dez?"

I looked up, startled. Mac Williamson had pulled in next to me. He was driving an ancient, battered Toyota Land Cruiser.

"Good morning," I said.

"My wife's car," he said, gesturing toward the Toyota. "She's attached to this old heap."

We chatted as we moved across the lot toward the building. I paid little attention to the conversation. As we got off the elevator on the seventh floor, I was bracing myself for the blowback.

Nothing happened. I rolled into my cube as usual, did my job as usual. I supposed it might have been a little early for the fallout to begin. The day went on, and I tried not to look over my shoulder too much. At lunch, nobody mentioned hearing anything about The Typo.

At quitting time, I wanted to get out of the building as quickly as possible. But I felt glued to my cube. I realized that as much as I didn't want to be here, I didn't want to go home, either.

The seventh floor had grown quiet and increasingly dark when a figure appeared in my doorway: Mac Williamson. He was dressed, as always, in a dark suit and a tie, which was never loosened or askew.

"Hey," I said.

"Good evening, Dez."

"Headed home?"

"In a bit," he said. "May I sit down?"

"Sure."

He slowly lowered himself into my visitor's chair. "You're working late."

"Yes."

"Last night, too."

I nodded.

"A proofreading project, I hear."

Uh-oh, I thought. "That's right."

"You're new," he said. "No one should expect you to be familiar with all the company's politics."

"What did I do wrong, Mac?"

"Maybe nothing. I just heard some rumbles today. Received some vibes."

I waited. There was little sound on the seventh floor, apart from the usual hiss of the ventilation system.

"You don't want to make an enemy of Paul Landrum, Dez. He's a very formidable man. But I have a feeling you may know that. In fact, I'm guessing, without any real proof, that you may have a rather sophisticated grasp of the power relationships on the seventh floor."

"Me?"

"Forgive me if I'm wrong," he said. "But you seem very discerning, and very curious, beyond what would be expected from a new employee in your position. It has led me to wonder if you have a purpose here that goes beyond earning a living and pursuing a career."

"Mac, I—"

He held up a hand, silencing me. "As I said, I could be completely wrong, and if I am, please forgive me. It's none of my business. But based on what I heard today, others may begin to have similar suspicions. You don't want to get on the wrong side politically."

"All this is way above my pay grade, Mac. I just try to stay out of the politics." I decided I'd better change the subject. "What about you? Do you shift with the political winds?"

He laughed, long and loudly. "I'm sorry, Dez. But that's a pretty surreal suggestion. No, I don't play politics. In fact, I've sort of made a career out of not doing so."

"And you've gotten away with it?"

"So far. But none of us are guaranteed anything. I could be out of here on my ear tomorrow, hitting the streets and looking for a way to support my wife and five kids."

"How have you made a career out of avoiding politics?" I asked.

"I didn't ask for it. I guess I did have somewhat of a reputation for integrity after my first couple of years here. And then it became institutionalized. Pat Dalton was named CEO. He walked into my office one day and handed me a little metal container. It contained the corporate seal. As you know, the seal needs to be applied to all major company contracts and transactions. Normally it's a formality. But Pat said, 'Congratulations. You're the new corporate secretary. Every deal goes through you. You're our last line of defense. And you have one job: Keep our ass out of trouble. Anybody objects, I've got your back.' Then he walked out."

"How has that worked out?"

"I took Pat's instructions seriously, which quickly made me unpopular. I'm picky. Every deal needs to be done right, or it gets sent back. I still reject probably a quarter of all the transactions that come across my desk. I's dotted, T's crossed, rules followed, legalities observed. I'm a pain in the ass. It's my job. And, as much as it infuriates people from time to time, I think most would grudgingly acknowledge that every company should have somebody like me. A last line of defense."

"You don't mind being unpopular?"

He shrugged. "The role fits well with who I am, and the reputation I already had."

"How did you become such a Boy Scout?"

"Because I *was* a Boy Scout. Literally. I joined up shortly after we moved to New York from Kingston, and I loved it. Most guys my age thought it was ridiculous—wearing a hokey uniform, lining up to salute the flag, earning merit badges. But I ate it up. I loved the purpose and the structure and the advancement. Plus, it was a chance to go camping and hiking and canoeing. I was the best damned Eagle Scout you ever saw. I wasn't popular or cool, of course. But then, as now, I believe I was respected." He smiled. "You're good, Dez. How did this conversation become about me?"

"All I can say is, I can do without the unpopularity."

"When it comes to Landrum, you certainly can."

"I'm just trying to do my job, too, Mac." Having broken the ice with Williamson, I decided to risk asking about Keri. "You know, I like this job. I like it here. But I'm really bothered by the fact that one of our people was murdered just a few weeks ago."

Williamson nodded.

"Are the police sure it had nothing to do with her job?"

"They seem to be satisfied." I knew, of course, that Howard was anything but.

"What do *you* think?" I asked.

"I can't really say. Keri was a very private person."

"Did she have any family nearby?"

"Not really. She was an only child, grew up in Arizona. Her mother is still alive and lives in Phoenix, but they weren't close. I probably knew Keri as well as anyone did, and she didn't confide any problems to me. She really had no other close friends here, except Marisa and possibly Bart."

"Bart? Really?"

"Yes, they seemed to be friendly, for whatever reason. But at the end of the day, I think she found it hard to trust anybody she worked with."

His features softened. "I learned this much about her: Ten years ago, just out of law school, Keri married the love of her life. He was everything she wanted, except faithful. About five years into her marriage, she found out he had been cheating on her from the very beginning. He had seemed totally devoted to her —even doting. It was all a lie."

"So she divorced him?" I felt as though Nomura or Howard should have told me these things, though I couldn't exactly say why.

"Yes. The ex had an alibi for the murder, by the way—he lives in Seattle. Anyway, Keri continued to show up here for work every day, putting a brave face on the whole situation. But make no mistake about it: She was shattered. She used an inheritance from her grandparents to buy that little house out on Balboa Peninsula. She went out surfing and biking and swimming by herself. It was sad."

"Right," I said. "Sad."

Chapter 20

Nomura was still upset with me. She stopped by at nine thirty that night, looking haggard and stressed out. It was a nice evening, and I wished we could go out on the balcony, but Nomura had deemed that insecure, vulnerable to long-range observation. We sat in the living room. "How about a glass of wine?" I asked.

She started to decline, then reversed course. "Why not?" She got up, and I directed her to the glasses and the bottle in the refrigerator. She brought everything out and poured the Chardonnay, and we drank it without ceremony.

"I'm afraid to ask," she said. "What happened today?"

"Nothing, but I think there is blowback yet to come." I described the ominous-sounding warnings from Mac Williamson.

"Pen, is there any chance this was a genuine typo? A mistake?"

"Almost none, I'm afraid. It seems crude, but apparently Landrum thought it was worth a try. And it almost worked."

"So now we prepare for the blowback."

"I guess so," I said. "At least we'll know we've hit a nerve."

"But maybe the wrong nerve. We know Landrum was trying to screw Dalton. So what? What does that tell us about Landrum not being who he appears to be? He tried to cheat a fellow shareholder; based on what we know, that sounds like exactly who he is."

"It might be too early to form a conclusion about what happened," I said. "Let's give it a little more time—maybe there will be some other reactions that will be revealing."

She sipped from her glass. "I really hope you're right, Pen. But from where I sit, it looks as though you've put the entire operation in jeopardy, calling attention to yourself and putting Landrum and his people on their guard."

I didn't respond. She could be right.

Nomura looked into her wineglass for a long time, then said, "Why are you doing this, Pen? Working for us, I mean. We never really asked you the reason. We had some ideas, I suppose. But now you've got me wondering why."

I started to give the first answer that came to mind, that I wanted to do something interesting, something useful and worthwhile. That was true, but I sensed she wanted something more.

"You mean what am I trying to prove?"

"Exactly. And whom are you trying to prove it to?"

I reached for the Chardonnay bottle and topped off my glass. "I'm not trying to prove anything to anybody else."

"To yourself, then?"

"I guess I'm trying to be independent. Capable of functioning on my own."

"To prove that you don't need anybody else?"

"No, I've moved beyond that."

"Completely?"

"Mostly, I think. I've been working hard on it during the past half-year. But I've had help."

"From James?"

"And from his daughter, Alicia, and from my sister, and from my friends, Cassandra and Pam. I learned my lesson after my last . . . episode, up in Minnesota."

"The murder case?"

"Right. Ever since the accident, I've fought the feelings of helplessness from being handicapped. But after the murder investigation, I started to realize that we're all helpless, to some extent. We're all dependent, on somebody or something."

She nodded slowly, still studying her glass. She probably wasn't buying it.

"How about you?" I said. "You seem pretty intense about your job. What's your agenda?"

I could tell she didn't want to answer, but she could hardly refuse, since I had opened myself up to her. "I made a decision early on," she said, "that I wanted to be taken seriously. It was either that or go into modeling."

"I suppose law enforcement is about as serious as it gets."

"And in law enforcement, the FBI is about as serious as it gets."

"You didn't want to be just another pretty face."

"Of course I didn't. You should understand that. You're easy on the eyes yourself. Don't you ever want to silence all the catcalls and sexist remarks?"

"I never thought much about it before the accident. It was annoying, and I didn't like it, but I guess I have a knack for putting piggy guys in their place."

She nodded and smiled, taking a sip from her glass.

"And since the accident," I continued, "I don't get a lot of that. I get plenty of other thoughtless, insensitive comments, but I'm usually pretty thick-skinned. I have other insecurities to worry about. Let me ask you something."

"All right."

"Has working in law enforcement actually silenced the catcalls and sexist remarks?"

She paused, appearing to really ponder the question, as if for the first time. "No."

We were silent for a minute. Then she said, "O'Shea warned us about you, that you were a loose cannon."

"O'Shea doesn't like me because I showed him up. But all I did was show a little initiative in doing my job."

She finished her wine and stood up. "Initiative is great, Pen, when it works. When it doesn't . . ."

She didn't finish the thought. She didn't have to. It was obvious what had happened when a young attorney named Keri Wylie had tried to show initiative.

Chapter 21

Wednesday

I didn't have to wait long for the blowback. When I reached my cube the next morning, a message to see Nancy Griffin already sat on my desk. I closed my eyes and practiced one of the relaxation routines my therapist had taught me. Then I exhaled and set out to learn my fate.

You're Dez, I reminded myself.

Griffin wasn't smiling when I knocked and pushed open the door. She was talking to someone; I looked over and saw Bart Crosby sitting off to one side.

"Come in," Griffin said. As I rolled to a spot in front of her desk, she said, "We need to talk about the proofreading assignment."

"You mean the typo." I was basically going to play dumb, but I figured it wouldn't pay to be too dumb.

"I mean this," she said, handing me an electronic tablet. I recognized the Techinvest shareholder agreement on it, displaying the page with the added "not."

I looked up from the tablet. "Yes?"

Griffin took the iPad back and removed her reading glasses in a practiced gesture. "Do you have any idea how much trouble you've caused?"

I feigned a puzzled look. "You mean by pointing out this typo?"

"All you were asked to do is confirm highlighted changes to this document. Do you see any highlighted changes here?"

"No."

"And then, to compound the blunder, you apparently clicked Reply All."

"I did?"

"Yes, you did. Which means that Paul Landrum and Pat Dalton saw it."

I assumed a troubled, contrite expression. "Oh, wow. I'm really sorry, Ms. Griffin. I didn't mean to do that. I mean, bothering the top executives of the company with a one-word typo. That's really embarrassing. I really feel bad."

She studied me with an intensity that was almost frightening, trying to decide if I was really that obtuse. Finally, she said, "You embarrassed the department, embarrassed me, and sowed suspicion. This is not the way we do business here. If it happens again, you're out."

I hung my head in shame, repeated my apologies, and left. Bart Crosby hadn't said a word. Back in my cube, I replayed the scene in my mind. There might have been a chance she had bought my innocent act. In any event, I thought it had been my best play. She had hinted at high-level discord by saying that the email had "sown suspicion." I'd just have to wait to find out what that meant.

And then, reliving the meeting again, I realized Griffin hadn't been buying the innocent routine one bit. I remembered taking the iPad from her and then handing it back. The move had seemed a bit pointless at the time. But it wasn't.

She now had a complete set of my fingerprints.

*   *   *

A couple of hours later I rolled toward the bathroom and saw Marisa Costas going in. I slowed down, pondering the wisdom of engaging her directly. She appeared to be my best prospect for learning more about Keri but had shown no inclination to talk about her. How much longer could I go on as I had, smiling at her in the hallway and hoping? Griffin apparently wasn't going to fire me right away, but I was on thin ice and short on time. I pushed my way into the bathroom.

Marisa had finished and was washing up. "Hi," I said.

She spotted me in the mirror and forced a quick smile. "Hi."

"Marisa . . ."

She turned her beautiful face toward me.

"I know you were a friend of Keri's," I said.

Her already guarded expression closed up completely.

"Maybe you'd like to talk about Keri sometime," I persisted. "What she was like, and—" I hesitated. "Why she died."

Her features relaxed briefly, and I couldn't quite identify the split-second expression I saw. Was she doubtful? Tempted? It didn't matter; the expression disappeared. She turned and stared directly at me. "Who are you?"

"A friend."

Again, a momentary hesitation. But then, "I can't." She threw her purse strap over her shoulder and left.

That went well, I thought. If I really tried, maybe I could now dream up yet another impulsive, counterproductive idea. With my head down, and cursing myself under my breath, I left the restroom. Outside the door, I nearly ran into Clay Ritchie.

"Hey," he said.

"Oh, hi."

"I saw Marisa come out just now. She wasn't looking good."

"I noticed that, too. She must be upset about something."

He studied me briefly, then nodded and walked off.

*   *   *

I was staring at my screen in late afternoon, rehashing all the events of the previous forty-eight hours and imagining all the ways I could have handled things differently. I'd tried to force things, and it had backfired, badly. From the corner of my eye I saw a figure appear in the doorway of my cubicle. I turned to look and nearly recoiled in fear. It was Paul Landrum. He looked like Darth Vader in a dark three-piece suit.

"Hello, Dez," he said pleasantly.

"Hi."

"Do you know who I am?"

"Yes."

He sauntered in, looked around, and took the visitor's chair next to my desk. My cube wasn't big, and his knee nearly touched my wheelchair. He was expensively dressed, tanned, and immaculately coiffed.

He gave me the creeps.

"So," he said, "you're new to the company."

I nodded.

"Would you mind a personal question?"

"Sure, why not?"

"How did you end up in a wheelchair?"

"A car accident."

"And when did that accident occur?"

"About four years ago."

"I see. And after the accident you returned to work as a paralegal?"

"That's right."

He nodded to himself, apparently considering what I'd said. I studied him and wondered if he could really be working secretly for the Russians. Then I thought about all the lobbyists and politicians and scandals in the news in recent years, all the players who'd gotten mixed up with the Kremlin. If the money was right, plenty of people seemed willing to do it.

"Do you enjoy being a legal assistant?" Landrum asked.

"Mostly. It's partly drudgery, but I guess most jobs have some of that."

He nodded thoughtfully. "What brought you to DSI?"

I briefly recounted my cover story of breaking up with a boyfriend and moving to the opposite coast.

"The Rand-McNally solution to life's problems?"

I shrugged. "It's worth a try."

"Do you enjoy your job here?"

"It's okay. Unfortunately, I made a mistake yesterday, and Ms. Griffin isn't too happy with me."

He flashed me a smile that contained not a bit of humor. "Ah, yes. The now-famous typo."

I didn't comment.

"Well," he said, "you certainly showed pluck and initiative, didn't you?"

I waited for the inevitable follow-up line: *And I* hate *pluck and initiative.* But it didn't come. He was the very embodiment of control, his expression unreadable.

Landrum slapped his knees and stood up. "Well, it's been nice chatting with you, Dez."

He left.

*   *   *

Back in his office, Landrum sat down at his desk, grabbed his phone, and hit a speed dial number. "You have them?" he asked.

"Yes. Nancy got her prints."

"Why wasn't she printed when she was hired?"

"She's low-level and has no security clearance. She doesn't have access to sensitive or classified material."

"Well, we've got them now," Landrum said. "Run them."

"Will do."

"What about that wheelchair? Do you think she really needs it, or is it just a prop?"

"She needs it. Did you notice how skinny her legs are?"

"All right. Put her under the microscope and find out who the hell she is."

"Got it," said security director Les Hornsby.

*   *   *

About twenty minutes after Landrum left, I packed up to go home. The backlash had arrived. I wasn't looking forward to telling Nomura about it. I wasn't even looking forward to coming back to work tomorrow. Who knew when the other shoe might drop? I rolled down to the elevator and nodded to two other people who got on with me. And then Clay Ritchie got on.

"Hey, Dez."

I forced a smile and nodded. A couple more people entered the elevator on the fourth floor. Then we stopped on two. One woman got on.

"Pen? Pen Wilkinson?"

I looked up, far too quickly. A woman stood outside in the hallway, apparently having decided to wait for the next elevator instead of getting on. But she saw me clearly, and half a dozen people saw me respond to my real name.

I recognized the woman, but more importantly, she recognized me.

The elevator door closed, and we resumed our descent.

We got off on the ground floor, and Ritchie walked with me to the parking lot. I wished this attractive-but-suspicious guy would just go away. "Somebody you knew back there, Dez?"

"I don't think so."

"Well, have a good one." He walked off toward his car.

Chapter 22

At home, shaking and near tears, I called Nomura. I described everything about my disastrous day.

The FBI agent kept her cool. "Tell me about the woman who recognized you."

"Her name is Laura Dixon. She's about thirty, I suppose. She worked at the US attorney's office when I was there. She was an assistant for three attorneys who worked on employment law cases. I encountered her on the second floor at DSI, not my floor. I don't know whether she was visiting DSI, or had business there, or now works there."

"And she clearly said your real name?"

"Yes. Once. And I'm afraid I did look up."

"But you didn't say anything?"

"No."

"Is there any doubt she recognized you?"

"She might have had a bit of doubt that it was me. I haven't seen her for several months, and I do look a little different, and I didn't confirm for her that I was Pen. But, you know . . ."

"I know. The damn wheelchair. How about the people in the elevator, or out in the hallway? Do you know any of them?"

"Yes. There was a guy named Clay Ritchie. I run into him at lunch occasionally."

"Is he going to be a problem?"

"I don't know." I didn't tell her that from my first day of work, Ritchie had been keeping a wary eye on me. Still, I found it hard to believe he was working for Landrum.

"Probably best to try to steer clear of him for now. How well do you know Laura?"

"Not very well. I came into contact with her three or four times, all in connection with a case I was working on with one of her attorneys. That's all."

"Of all the crappy luck. What are the odds?" A pause. "Don't talk to anyone. Stay where you are. I'll call you back."

She called back an hour later. "Here's what we know," she said. "Laura Dixon was hired at DSI two weeks before you were. She wanted a job in OC to be closer to her boyfriend. She doesn't work in Legal—she was hired by the HR department to work on employment compliance issues."

"Then she might have access to DSI's employment records," I said.

"She might. She won't find any Pen Wilkinson, and she wouldn't be looking for a paralegal. She'd have to put in some serious effort to link Pen with Dez."

"But she'll probably assume that I'd be working for Legal, on either the sixth or seventh floors."

"Would she have occasion to come up to seven and look for you?"

"Possibly. But any interaction would likely be with the attorneys who do employment law. I believe they're on six."

"Let's confirm that. We know her normal work day runs from nine to five forty-five. Her lunchtime is at noon, but she usually eats at her desk."

"How do you know all this?"

"That's confidential. You can pretty much set your own working hours, right?"

"Yes. Bart has no idea when I come and go."

"Then make sure you avoid Laura."

"You mean I'm going to just go back to work?"

"Yes. We believe it's worth the risk."

Easy for you to say, I thought. "What if I run into her again?"

"That seems very unlikely."

"But what if I do?"

"Do what you have to do to shut her up. Give her your confession cover story if you have to."

I thought about the next three weeks, looking over my shoulder, knowing I could be identified at any moment. "Okay."

"The rest of your day certainly sucked, too," Nomura said. "I'm not concerned about the fingerprint thing, per se—we've got that covered. But the fact that they *wanted* your prints is not good at all. That confirms that they doubt your identity as well as your motivation. And Landrum showing up personally, apparently to size you up . . ."

I had no idea what to say.

"We're not giving up," she said. "We're still counting on you."

I hung up and started rolling toward the kitchen and the wine bottle. Then I stopped myself.

Everything was coming apart. I'd failed, in multiple ways. I was trapped. But, thanks to reflection, therapy, and some good luck, I knew enough not to try to carry the burden myself. I dug my personal phone out of my purse and hit speed dial number one.

James.

*   *   *

Viktor Kamensky was enjoying a rare night off at a club just off Sunset when he felt his phone buzz. He thought he was making progress with one of the two young women he was chatting up. The blonde seemed impervious to his charms. But the redhead . . . He sighed. "Excuse me, ladies. I'll be right back."

He walked outside to take the call, putting a finger in one ear to block out the street noise. "Yes?"

"Anything?" PACIFIC asked.

"More of the same," he reported. "Counter-surveillance whenever I try to pick her up."

"Any chance she's made you?"

"No way. I break it off. I'm not taking any chances. That's what you told me to do."

"Yes, that's what I told you. All right, we know something is going on with Nomura. You don't do counter-surveillance on your off hours when you're going to Publix or Walgreens."

Well, duh, Kamensky managed to avoid saying.

But then PACIFIC surprised him. "We have some additional surveillance we need to do."

He waited.

"We'll stick with phone tracking for now, but stand by in case we need to do more."

"Who is it?"

"A DSI employee. Her name is Desiree Walker. She works in Legal."

Kamensky clicked off and went back inside. As usual, PACIFIC had told him no more than he'd needed to know—probably less. He had plenty of work to do, keeping an eye on Wendy Nomura when he could, maintaining the safe house, and, most importantly, planning the end game, in which he'd be instrumental. PACIFIC would coordinate with Mother to set up the phone tracking on this new woman. Although their own phones were virtually impenetrable by the NSA, they avoided using words like "Russia" and "Moscow," which might trigger scrutiny. Thus "Mother," shorthand for "Mother Russia."

He returned to the bar. The women were gone. Shit.

But there would be more. This was LA.

Chapter 23

I tried not to be a total wreck when I went to work the next day. I tried to be logical about Laura Dixon. Not only was a chance encounter improbable, but it was unlikelier still that Laura would come looking for me. Why, exactly, would this woman, whom I barely knew, care whether I worked at DSI or not? But it could still happen, and I'd have to keep my guard up. And there was a definite possibility of more pressure or investigation by Paul Landrum and his allies, including Nancy Griffin.

It had helped to talk to James. I wasn't supposed to communicate with him, or with anybody else from my real life. I felt weak making the call and hated myself for feeling weak. It probably hadn't been wise to respond to Nomura's displeasure about my freelancing with more freelancing. But sometimes, as with last night, you do what you have to do. I hadn't gone into specifics with James, but I'd let him know I was in trouble. I just needed to talk, to hear his voice, to get some reassurance that he was still out there. I told him I'd ask Nomura if we could sneak away together next weekend.

The morning passed uneventfully as I tried to stay engaged with my work while keeping one eye out for trouble. At lunchtime, I went down with Mac, who said nothing further about our conversation night before last. Marisa was not at Mac's table today, but Clay Ritchie made a rare appearance, and I had a feeling he was there out of curiosity about me.

"Pretty active over in Landrum's office," Ritchie commented. "Is there a crisis of some kind?"

"Busy everywhere," McCartney Williamson said. "We're less than three weeks out."

"This sounds a little different," Ritchie said. "I heard an interesting rumor that Dez may have done something to get Landrum's attention."

Everybody looked at me. I responded with a *Who, me?* expression.

"Dez?" somebody asked. "What did you do?"

I forced a smile. "I'll plead the Fifth."

Ritchie said, "There was a Landrum sighting in the vicinity of your cube yesterday."

I tried to think of another lighthearted response, but the guy on the other side of the table saved me. "Landrum was reportedly mad at his own law firm," he said.

"I wouldn't want to be his law firm," somebody else said.

"I heard him hollering on the phone at somebody," Ritchie said. "I hope nobody's job is threatened."

"A lot of us may have different jobs after the merger," Williamson said. "Some of us will be gone."

"You have nothing to worry about, Mac," somebody said. "Nobody else wants the job of official pain in the ass." Everybody laughed.

People started to get up to leave. I jumped when I felt a hand on my arm. It was Mac.

"Are you meeting someone, Dez?"

"Um—no."

"All through lunch, you were glancing around the dining room."

I forced a smile. "Just a short attention span today, I guess."

Chapter 24

I wheeled back to my cubicle, past Bart's door, and sat in front of my screen. I looked at the screen for a moment, then glanced out to the hallway. Bart was, as always, closeted in his office. Before I could stop myself, or consider why I felt compelled to do it, I had rolled across the hall and knocked on his door.

"Yes?" came the soft voice from within.

I pushed the door open. "Do you have a minute, Bart?"

He hesitated, apparently unable to come up with a quick excuse for putting me off. "Okay."

I entered his office for the first time. The floor was mostly covered with neatly stacked piles of files and papers, arranged in rows, with a path leading around the desk to his chair, and another to the visitor's chair in front of the desk. I made my way carefully along the path to a small space beside the visitor's chair. The office walls were totally bare—no photos, artwork, or diplomas. The blinds were shut.

Bart was fortyish—not much older than I was. He sported longish brown hair and wore older-style gold-rimmed glasses. He looked me steadily in the eye, and I sensed that he'd been trained to do this. He seemed fidgety, but after a few seconds he made it a point to clasp his hands together and remain still. More training, I assumed.

"What do you want?" he asked. Coming from him, the question didn't seem abrupt or rude.

"I just wanted to say I'm sorry about the typo. I hope I didn't get you into any trouble."

He seemed surprised but nodded briefly. We were silent for a few moments. Then he said. "I think it will be okay. You shouldn't have pointed out the typo, though."

"I guess not. I was just trying to show a little initiative and be helpful."

"Nancy doesn't think so."

"I know."

There was more silence, but it wasn't uncomfortable. "I've noticed," I said, "that what I do doesn't really have anything to do with what you do."

"That's true." A pause. "Last year they wanted to promote me to this job, to assistant general counsel."

I waited. So did Bart. Finally, he seemed to realize that additional explanation was necessary. "For this level, you have to have supervisory duties," he said.

"So they gave you my position to supervise."

"Yes." Probably because the job didn't need a lot of supervision, I thought.

After more companionable silence, he said, "Nancy is a good person. She's under a lot of pressure."

"Right."

"She owes her job to Landrum."

I nodded. Bart's social limitations may have placed him somewhere on the spectrum, but he was no fool. I said, "I heard you were friendly with Keri."

His expression changed in some slight but discernible way. "I liked her. A lot, actually. She was always nice to me. I'm, well, not always easy to get along with."

"Why do you think she was killed?"

"I don't know."

"Do you think it had anything to do with her job?"

"I hope not."

I nodded briefly and turned to go. Then I heard his voice behind me.

"But I'm afraid maybe it did."

I turned back. He was fidgeting again.

*　　*　　*

At home, I rolled out to the balcony overlooking the Balboa Peninsula and the ocean, trying to fight through the exhaustion enough to fix some dinner. I'd gotten through the day, but it had been a struggle. My brief, impulsive encounter with Bart Crosby had given me yet another angle to consider: Did Bart himself have to be considered a suspect? Had he gotten into a relationship with Keri and then been jilted? And why had he been concerned that Keri's death might have been job-related? I looked around at the impersonal rental furniture and wanted badly to go home. Just a couple more weeks, I told myself. Then I could admit my failure and go back to my life.

But would it really be that easy? Could I just move on to the next thing, knowing that Keri Wylie's killer, probably a Russian thug, was still out there? That the largest shareholder of a major defense contractor might be a fraud, or even a Russian agent? That I would be remembered in the law enforcement community as part of a rushed, half-assed, unsuccessful undercover operation?

The phone rang—my Dez phone. I didn't recognize the number.

I quickly rolled inside and answered. "Yes?"

"Hello, is this Dez?" asked a male voice.

"Yes."

"This is Pat Dalton. How are you doing today?"

I looked at the phone in disbelief. "Fine, Mr. Dalton. What can I do for you?"

"I wonder if you'd be free to join my family and me for dinner tonight?"

"I—sure, I guess so."

"Great. My driver is outside. Whenever you're ready, just go out and he'll bring you over. See you soon." He hung up.

I tried to calm down and think. I was reasonably sure the caller had been Dalton; I recognized his strong baritone voice from the brief introduction I'd had last week. I had given the cell phone number he had used only to DSI. But dinner? With his family? I called Nomura, got a rare voicemail instead of an instant pickup, and left a message.

My next concern was what to wear to meet the CEO. *You're Dez,* I told myself. Pen would change to a stylish outfit from her extensive wardrobe. But Dez . . .

I looked down at my work clothes and decided that's what Dez would wear. I primped a little in the bathroom, then grabbed my purse and went outside.

Chapter 25

Pat Dalton's driver was a powerfully-built youngish man with closely-cropped hair. He was polite, formal, and observant —maybe a security guy or bodyguard as well as a driver. He helped me transfer into the back seat of the inevitable black SUV, then stowed my chair. As we pulled out of my parking lot, I realized I had no idea where we were going. I thought about asking the driver, but he didn't seem in the mood for conversation.

From the Coast Highway we swung east on Highway 55, then south on Toll Road 73, and eventually onto the I-5. We got off at one of the San Clemente exits, then made our way southwest toward the ocean. Our destination proved to be a sprawling gated oceanfront estate, built in a sixties modern style. A heavy automatic gate opened to a cobbled driveway, and we entered past a staffed guard hut. The car then wound through a thickly-landscaped approach to what appeared to be the main house. I looked toward the house and saw another security guy standing in a little alcove off to one side of the main entrance. Off on the far side of the property, shielded by a line of short trees, I saw a helicopter parked on a landing pad.

The driver/bodyguard brought my chair out of the back, helped me into it, and offered to push me inside. I accepted, and we entered, not through the main front door, but along a stone colonnade that followed the edge of the bluff overlooking the ocean.

We emerged on a huge stone patio. A handsome woman in her late forties with olive skin and flowing black hair walked over. "Hello," she said. "Thank you for coming, Dez. I'm Jackie." She spoke with a light accent I couldn't quite identify.

We shook. Dalton, I recalled, was divorced. Presumably Jackie was his girlfriend or fiancée. "I'm sorry about the short notice," she said.

"No trouble," I said, "although it was disappointing to have to put my Lean Cuisine meal back into the freezer."

She laughed. "Maybe we can do a bit better than that. Go on over and say hello." She gestured toward the edge of the patio. Pat Dalton was seated on a palm tree-shaded couch with a drink by his side, studying papers from a briefcase.

The CEO looked up and removed his reading glasses when I approached. "Hello, Dez. Glad you could join us." He put his papers aside, stood up, and shook my hand.

"Thank you," I said, wondering if I looked as bewildered as I felt.

The answer came an instant later, when Dalton studied me and broke into a laugh. "Relax," he said. "You're among friends. Drink?"

"I—um, sure. White wine, please."

A woman, apparently a maid, had been standing behind me, I now saw. She disappeared into the house.

"Make yourself comfortable," Dalton said, gesturing to a spot beside the couch. I rolled over next to him, taking in the breathtaking ocean view, down across Dana Point and, out over the water, Catalina. I'd known some wealthy people and been to some expensive homes, but I had never seen anything like this.

The maid, a thin, older Filipina, brought my wine. I took a sip; it was dry and delicious, and although my wine taste is fairly well developed, I couldn't identify it.

"It's from Douro."

I looked up. Jackie had appeared beside me.

"That's in Portugal," she said. "We brought some back on my last trip home." That solved the mystery of her accent.

"It's wonderful," I said.

"I'm glad you like it." She left.

"I invited you here to thank you," Dalton said. "You did a very courageous thing, and I appreciate it."

"I corrected a typo. I didn't know it would be a big deal."

He gave me a knowing smile. "Even if you didn't fully appreciate all the implications, I have a feeling you knew exactly what you were doing. Not everyone would have chanced that—not in their first month at a new job."

"Thank you," I said.

"How do you like the job so far?"

"It's fine."

"Have you ever considered going to law school?"

"I've thought about it, off and on. I'm getting a little old to do it now."

"You should make a conscious decision. Don't just let it slide until your options are closed."

Good advice, I thought.

Jackie called us to dinner, which was also served on the patio at a table closer to the house, next to a swimming pool. Heating towers blunted the spring chill. Dalton got up and led me over to the table, at which a place without a chair had been set for me. Dalton had said I'd be having dinner with his family, but only Jackie had yet appeared.

After we were seated, a lanky young man appeared and took a seat across from me. He appeared to be in his mid-twenties, wearing shorts, flip-flops, and a Hawaiian shirt, with a stubbly beard. His head was buzz-cut on the sides, with a shock of brown hair flipped over the top. Even a scruffy appearance, however, couldn't hide a baby face. "My son, Tim," Dalton said. "Meet Dez Walker."

Tim gave me a grudging nod but didn't say anything.

The maid arrived with delicious pineapple salads, and we commenced eating. The conversation was innocuous. Tim said his day had been fine but volunteered nothing more. Jackie kept the conversation going, inviting me to talk about myself. I gave an abbreviated version of my legend, reciting the details of my upbringing, career, and move to California. The main course, stuffed halibut, was delicious. Tim pushed his food around his plate and said very little. Jackie, Pat Dalton, and I talked a little about the weather and items in the news. A couple of times, I thought I caught Tim looking at me. Just curious, I supposed.

"Mr. Dalton?"

My host looked up. "Yes, Gloria?"

"Mr. Li is here," the maid said.

I glanced to my right; a youngish, smiling, Asian-looking man stood at the doorway. "My apologies," Dalton said, placing his napkin on the table. "You'll have to excuse me for a few minutes."

He disappeared into the house, followed by the Asian guy. Gloria shot them a disapproving glance. Jackie said nothing but got up and helped Gloria clear the table.

"Do you want to . . . sit over there?" Tim asked me, gesturing toward where his father and I had sat before dinner.

"Sure."

We sat and watched the sun descend over the Pacific. Tim, sullen and fidgety, said nothing. "What do you do, Tim?" I asked.

"I'm a barista," he said with a touch of defiance. "Up in Westwood."

"A long way."

"No kidding. He has me come all the way down here, then he blows off dinner to talk to his lawyer."

"That guy is his attorney?"

Tim nodded. "Steve Li has represented him for a couple of years. He seems to just cruise in here whenever he feels like it."

"Do you have any brothers or sisters, Tim?"

"Not anymore. I had a sister, Mikayla. She died in a surfing accident when we were on vacation in Thailand."

"Oh, Tim, I'm so sorry. I had no idea." In fact, Mac Williamson had told me about the accident, but I'd spaced on it, and covering myself with a lie seemed to come automatically these days.

"She was three years older than me." He looked out at the ocean but wasn't really seeing it. "We were close. I miss her a lot."

I didn't know how to respond to that, and neither of us said anything for a couple of minutes.

"I'm the family screwup," Tim announced finally, in a tone that combined nonchalance with defiance. "The black sheep."

"Oh, I'm sure—"

"It's no big deal. It's just what I am. I dropped out of college. I work at a coffee shop. I share an apartment with a couple of other guys."

"Not everybody has a straight path to where they're going."

"I just keep going along in no particular direction, and I'm not sure Dad cares anymore."

"He did ask you to dinner."

"Sure, to drive an hour and a half down here just to—" He stopped himself.

"To have dinner with some paralegal from his company, whom you'll never see again—whom *he'll* probably never see again. Don't you get it, Tim? It has nothing to do with me. He wanted to see you."

His calculated nonchalance gave way, as though he'd been confronted with something he couldn't avoid caring about. "That's something, I guess. I wish he would just quit. He spends all his time dealing with the merger and fighting with that shark, Landrum."

Pat Dalton emerged from the house, sans his attorney, looking sheepish. Tim stood up. "I need to get going."

"Thanks for coming down," Pat told him.

"It was nice meeting you, Tim," I added. "Best of luck."

He grunted and left, giving me one last look.

I gathered up my purse and prepared to leave. Jackie appeared and thanked me for coming. In a lower voice she added, "Thanks for talking to Tim."

Dalton came over. "I'll walk you to the car."

As we proceeded back along the colonnade, he said, "I hope it went okay for you—talking to Tim, I mean."

"It was fine," I assured him.

"It hasn't been easy for him. First his mother and I divorced. And then his sister . . . I've worked hard on my relationship with him."

Dalton's bodyguard was waiting by the SUV. He helped me get in, and Dalton shook my hand through the car window. "DSI has technology that you literally wouldn't believe—sci-fi stuff. But it always comes back to people, to loyalty. That's our currency. If we can't count on each other, if we can't develop the human connections we all need—not only will the business fail, but life won't be worth living."

I found this pontificating hard to take seriously. No American corporation actually behaved as though employees were their most important asset—Wall Street and shareholders would never allow that. It was a lesson I'd learned from the hard-headed James Carter.

Dalton looked out at the darkened ocean, then back at me. "Thank you again," he said. "You helped to save the company and me from a hell of a fight. I think we would have won, but who knows? It was something we really didn't need. Anyway, it took guts."

I nodded briefly and thanked him for dinner, and the car pulled away.

I spent the ride home racking my brain, trying to think of some ulterior motive Dalton might have had for inviting me, but I came up empty. He didn't need anything more from me; the dinner was just a kind gesture. Both Dalton and Jackie had seemed grateful to me for talking to Tim, a troubled guy who alternated between surly defiance and sneaking glances at me. Maybe Tim even appreciated having me there, on some level he couldn't really understand.

The SUV pulled up in my parking lot, and I thanked the driver and headed inside to call Nomura.

Chapter 26

Friday

I showed up at work the next day burdened by a secret. Any other lowly employee who'd been invited to dinner by the CEO would be dying to tell people about it. In contrast, I was afraid of anybody finding out. Pat Dalton hadn't told me to keep my evening with him a secret; he had trusted my discretion. I appreciated that.

At lunch, no one mentioned my run-in with Landrum, which was apparently yesterday's news. While we ate, I continued to keep an eye out for Laura Dixon but tried to be less conspicuous about it. As everyone got up to leave, Clay Ritchie, who'd appeared at our table for the first time in about a week, hung back until only the two of us remained.

"So, Dez," he said. "Just one question: *What the hell were you thinking?*"

I tried to laugh off his remark, but he was serious.

He leaned forward. "I'm trying to decide whether you were clueless, gutsy, or have an agenda."

"I hate to admit it, but clueless is probably the leading contender."

"I don't believe that for a minute. But at the moment, I don't see a plan behind what you're doing, so I'm going with gutsy."

"So, what do you hear? Am I going to get fired?"

He shrugged. "I doubt it. Of course, if Landrum eventually gets control of the company, you'd want to start updating your LinkedIn page, since Griffin is in his pocket."

"What was *Landrum* thinking?"

"Hard to say. Most people thought he and Dalton had declared a truce until the Hulbert deal is complete. But I guess that little typo you found proves otherwise. Maybe Landrum was cooperating just to lull Dalton to sleep."

"Could be."

He stood up and began to walk away. I exhaled, relieved to have weathered the cross-examination. But then he turned back. "Who is . . . Pen Wilkinson, Dez?"

"Who?"

"That woman by the elevator—that's what she called you."

"Is it? I don't think I've heard the name."

"She seemed to know you."

I shrugged. "She must have thought I was somebody else."

He smiled. He didn't believe it for a moment. "I guess so. See you later."

*   *   *

Somebody followed me as I drove home. Or at least, I thought somebody did. A battered blue pickup truck emerged from a side street as I left the DSI parking lot and headed for the freeway. And then it disappeared. I put it out of my mind and got onto the 405.

Where I saw the blue pickup again. I wasn't sure if it was the same one; there were other blue trucks on the road, though not a multitude of them in fashionable Orange County. I fingered my Dez phone, poised to hit the panic button. I checked to see that the knife I kept in the van was in its spot beside the seat. Then the truck disappeared again.

I had never noticed anybody following me before. But I hadn't been paying much attention. I'd assumed Nomura was watching my back. But increasingly, I'd wondered about that. And, thanks to The Typo and the reaction of Landrum and his allies, I had good reason to care about it. I pulled into my parking lot and looked around. No one had followed me up the hill from PCH.

Inside, I pulled out my burner phone and called Nomura.

"You're early," she said. "Is something wrong?"

"This guy Ritchie, who saw the incident in the elevator, might be a problem. He asked me who Pen Wilkinson was—he remembered that's what Laura called me."

"What happened next?"

"I told him I had no idea who Pen was. Whether he believed it or not, I don't know. I'm afraid he might Google her—me."

"We've managed to remove all images of you from the Internet, or at least un-link them from your name."

"How did you do that?"

"Child's play for the geeks in Washington, I'm told. There actually weren't many images. But there were a lot of stories about you. He'd find them if he looked. Do you think he's tied to Landrum somehow?"

"He talked disparagingly about Landrum, but of course it could be an act."

"Well, steer clear of him, I guess. Is there anything else?"

"As a matter of fact, yes. Did you follow me home from work tonight?"

A slight hesitation. "No."

"Did anyone from your team follow me?"

Silence.

"We need to talk," I said.

"All right. Tomorrow."

Chapter 27

Saturday

It was nearly ten o'clock when I woke up; I'd slept off some serious exhaustion. The last week had been a whirlwind, dealing with a Russian killer, The Typo, and my unanswered questions about the FBI's operation. And at the end of it all, I had zilch to show for it.

By the time Nomura arrived, I'd completed a leisurely shower and breakfast. She came in and took a seat in the living room without pleasantries. I rolled over in front of the picture window, looking out over the Balboa Peninsula, where Keri Wylie had lived and died. Nomura knew I had some things I wanted to discuss. But she took the offensive.

"Pen, I'm still not happy with you. You alienated and alerted Landrum. More than that, you're appearing to take sides with Dalton—somebody may find out about that visit to his house. It's hard to see how you're going to quietly insinuate yourself into the situation and find out what's going on."

"Wendy, is anybody watching this apartment right now?"

This checked her momentum. "No. I made sure it was clean."

"Did anyone follow me home from work last night?"

She hesitated. "I don't know."

"Thanks for being honest. I'm sorry about the typo thing. Maybe I made a mistake, maybe not. But I don't go to DSI every day with a receiver in my ear. I have to be able to use some judgment. Now, I've worked with law enforcement before, and I've always felt a little sheepish when I've expressed concern for my personal safety. But you know what? I'm way past that now. I'm going to ask you some questions, and if I don't get what I believe to be straight answers, my involvement in this project is over, effective tonight."

Her expression hardened, but she didn't say anything.

I plunged on. "Do you have a team supporting you on this operation?"

She didn't answer.

"Because I've never seen or heard of anybody helping you. You appear to be running this not only by yourself, but on your own time."

She sat up straighter, giving me a defensive look. "You don't know everything we have."

"Let's remedy that. Who else is on your team?"

Nomura didn't answer.

"I'm taking that as an admission that you don't have a team. Now tell me this: Somebody, somewhere, recognized and identified the Russian assassin. You have facial recognition databases. Why didn't they spot this guy coming into the country?"

"We don't know."

"I think you do know. Who's your boss, Wendy?"

"Pen, you need a little refresher on what our respective roles are here. I have a lot of functions, but sitting here and answering your questions isn't one of them. It is not your place to question or second-guess how we run FBI ops."

"My only role tonight is as a person who's trying to decide whether to quit. Who's your boss, Wendy?"

"I'm afraid that is not a topic that's open for discussion."

"Why didn't the facial recognition databases catch the Russian?"

"I can't discuss that."

"And you're running this op on your own."

"We're understaffed."

"I need answers. I can't go on working like this."

"Yes, you can. You don't need answers. You want answers. There is a big difference."

I didn't respond.

Her features softened. "Pen, I know I sound like a bureau-crat. Believe me, I'm not withholding information just for the fun of it, or because I can. We have sensitive security issues involved here, which I am absolutely forbidden to discuss."

"What if I decide I can't accept that?"

"Then you do what you have to do."

I sighed. She had called my bluff. Did I trust her?

"If I'm on a need-to-know basis," I said, "I do need to know this: I think somebody followed me home from work. What are we going to do about that?"

"If it happens again, let me know. We'll figure something out."

I listened to the silence in the room. I had created this con-frontation; who was going to blink?

"All right. I'll go back to work on Monday morning. I'm trusting you, Wendy."

Nomura's expression was, as always, unreadable.

"I have another question. You don't have to answer it if you don't want to. I'm curious as to how you got my name for this op. I strongly suspect Hal Dwyer."

She looked away with an exasperated sigh, then returned her gaze to me. "Yes, I can tell you that. It was Hal."

Hal Dwyer, a good friend of James's, and increasingly of mine as well, owned the boat next to the *Alicia C* at the marina on Bay-side Drive. Dwyer's teenage daughter had been murdered more than a decade ago. I'd heard, from either him or James, that Hal had worked with a female FBI agent to solve the case, which had also involved crookedness at his company, Horrey Technolo-gies. Hal knew I had used claim tracking software when I'd worked at North Central Bank and that I was currently unem-ployed. He probably also knew that James would wring his neck for getting me involved in this operation.

"I have two other requests," I said.

Her nearly superhuman self-possession nearly gave way. "Yes, Pen," she said with exaggerated patience. "What else can I do for you?"

"First of all, could you please check out a local attorney named Steve Lee or Li? He works for Pat Dalton, and something seemed a little off about him."

She nodded and wrote the name down. "Is the next request easier or harder?"

"You be the judge: I want to go away for a weekend with James."

*   *   *

I had trouble sleeping that night. In addition to pondering ways of moving the investigation off dead center, I now found myself worrying about the FBI. Nomura hadn't denied running the operation virtually alone. She had also refused to explain why federal facial recognition systems hadn't picked up Viktor Kamensky entering the country. She had been willing to let me walk rather than discuss any of it. All this added up, I suspected, to a serious internal problem at the Bureau. The problem could have been anything from a security leak to covering a mistake to—and I shuddered to consider it—Nomura running an unauthorized op. The bottom line was that I was putting myself in Nomura's hands.

But it also looked as though she was putting herself in mine.

Chapter 28

Week 4

Monday

Wendy Nomura sat in her car, watching Pen's van arrive in the parking lot of her apartment building. Wendy took deep breaths, fighting off exhaustion, frustration, and despair. The unraveling was continuing. She'd been a fool to think she could run this op on her own. And she'd been an even bigger fool to think she could keep Pen in the dark. Hal Dwyer had warned her that Pen was not the type to blindly follow orders and meekly accept what she had been told. Wendy had accordingly given Pen an extraordinary amount of information at the beginning of the project, far beyond her need to know. But it hadn't been enough.

Wendy had already been thinking about putting someone into DSI to investigate the Landrum situation. She had talked in general, hypothetical terms about the idea to Lieutenant Dan Howard, a man she had worked with before and trusted. Howard, who had been stymied in his attempts to solve the Keri Wylie murder, had been supportive. Wendy had then printed out from the DSI website a list of open jobs located on the seventh floor of its headquarters. And then she had, after a couple of drinks, confided way too much to a civilian, her longtime friend Dwyer. He had grabbed the list of job openings from her, and she hadn't objected too much. The openings were, after all, publicly posted information.

After scanning the openings for a minute, Dwyer had given her a little smile. "I just might have somebody for you." After Hal had spoken in glowing terms about Pen Wilkinson, Wendy had done her own research on the paraplegic former prosecutor. It had taken some persuasion to get Howard on board, given a previous run-in he'd had with Pen, but she'd succeeded. She had then requested and received an appointment with Assistant Director in Charge Kirk Hendricks. The ADC had, with US Attorney Dave O'Shea's blessing, approved the op, but its success or failure was all on her.

Wendy maintained her surveillance on the parking lot. Nobody else watched as Pen completed the process of exiting and closing up her van, rolling up to the apartment's door, and letting herself in. If the operation failed, or even if it succeeded, it was doubtful that anyone would ever appreciate the incredible speed with which Wendy had set up the op. With Hendricks's assistance, she had enlisted the help of agents in Washington to put together Pen's legend. Then she'd done the high-speed recruiting and briefing of Pen herself. Since then, she had run herself ragged, trying to put in normal days at work while running Pen during off hours and spare moments. She had followed Pen sporadically and watched her apartment off and on at unpredictable intervals, after making sure she herself wasn't being followed. This spot-checking was the best she could do, and so far, she hadn't spotted any surveillance on Pen. But Landrum and his allies at DSI, who knew where Desiree Walker lived, could begin watching her at any time.

And Ward Gilbertson might be having Wendy watched already.

Through it all, Wendy had tried to keep her eye on the central objective of the operation: to learn what Keri had known about Paul Landrum that had concerned her so much. Somehow, the secret seemed related to the Hulbert acquisition, which would be finalized in less than three weeks. It seemed no stretch to conclude that whatever had troubled Keri had gotten her killed. But who or what could have gotten her to open her door to the person—probably Viktor Kamensky—who had killed her? Howard hoped that Pen's operation might be able to answer that question, which seemed even more critical now that they'd identified the trigger man.

Dwyer had warned her of Pen's independence and unpredictability. "But that's something you should use," he'd said. "Let her run with it." Allowing CI's, or cooperating individuals, to run with undercover ops was, to put it mildly, not the FBI way, nor was it Wendy's. But Pen hadn't left her with much choice. And now, Pen had asked permission to drop her cover next weekend to go to Minnesota with James Carter, who would be visiting his daughter. Wendy had agreed; there was little Pen would be able to learn about DSI over the weekend. And it would give Wendy two days to rest and figure out how to protect Pen without blowing the op—if it wasn't already blown.

Chapter 29

Viktor Kamensky cruised by the small tract house in Fountain Valley. Lights were on inside, and he could see movement through the blinds on the bedroom window. He fantasized about catching a glimpse of Wendy Nomura, but of course it wouldn't happen. She was as buttoned-up as they came. Still, he liked the idea of hanging around, being close to her. Now driving a battered Toyota pickup, one of his four surveillance vehicles, he made one more pass, then turned and headed for home.

PACIFIC had told him to use his discretion in conducting the surveillance. It didn't have to be twenty-four-seven—just some lengthy spot checks at times she might be going somewhere other than work. She'd been avoiding him, but she couldn't do it forever. He really enjoyed looking at her. He was a professional, but if he ever got the chance, he'd do a lot more than just look.

Oh, the things he'd do.

It had taken him a while to acknowledge that he enjoyed killing. It gave him an inner buzz, a high that continued for some days after the event. It wasn't something he wanted to analyze— who knew where that might lead? And sometimes he'd relive the buzz, as with the one he'd gotten with Keri Wylie. That had been a good one.

He hadn't been the only one to enjoy it. He could remember almost word for word what his boss had said over the Facetime phone connection. After he'd been admitted to Keri Wylie's house and had secured his victim, he had carefully positioned the phone in front of her. She had watched with terrified eyes above her taped mouth as the boss spoke:

"Keri, you know why this is happening. And this is not just business—it's very, very personal. You didn't have to make that call. It didn't benefit you in any way. It was gratuitous."

The boss was getting red-faced. "Who the hell do you think I am? Who do you think we are? And who the hell are you?" The boss disconnected, and for Kamensky, the time for the buzz had arrived.

Now his phone trilled as he reached the 405. He pressed the button to answer.

"We have a problem," PACIFIC said. "Mother can't get the tracking spyware onto Dez Walker's phone."

"What's going on?"

"They're not sure, but the line and the phone seem protected."

"Suspicious, right?"

"Yes, a little. It's one thing to be blocked from getting onto an FBI or police phone. But this one would be surprising. Her fingerprints have been checked out, and it appears she really is Desiree Walker, but the situation still doesn't smell right."

"If you say so," Kamensky said. Just for a change of pace, he had followed Desiree Walker home, using his pickup truck, on Friday. She'd certainly looked harmless enough; no one had told him she was a cripple. "So, what's next?" he asked.

"We'll put a vehicle tracker on."

"When and where?"

"In the next day or two, while she's at work—we'll let you know. The tracking link will be sent to your iPad. Keep track and report anything unusual."

"All right. What's her job?"

"She's a paralegal."

"I'll be looking for the information."

Kamensky hung up. A paralegal? It was a fairly low-level job; he'd expected a senior person, an executive vice president of something-or-other. He couldn't imagine what the threat from this woman might be, especially given her handicap. But he always went along with PACIFIC.

You never wanted to cross the wrong people.

Chapter 30

Thursday

It was metaphorically, if not physically, accurate to say that my step was a little lighter as I left work and headed home. No, I hadn't learned anything more about Paul Landrum, or about Keri Wylie's murder. And my work with ClaimTrack certainly hadn't gotten any more interesting. But I was excited because I'd gotten the go-ahead to spend the weekend with James. I had told Nomura I'd been unable to think of anything I could do to move my work forward over the weekend—in California. And she had agreed.

James and I were going to Minnesota, where he and I had met, and where his teenage daughter, Alicia, lived. He went to Minneapolis frequently, and the city had become a second home for me, too, the place where I had completed two major investigations during the past year. Increasingly, our visits to Alicia had also become important to me; she and I had become close during the past few years. Wendy Nomura, sensing my mounting frustration with my undercover assignment, as well as the stress from the relentless scrutiny, had approved the trip as a mental health break.

As if, I thought. As if, with only a couple of weeks left on my assignment, and the clock ticking toward a potentially catastrophic climax, I would bail and take a vacation. I was merely working another angle, which I had set up with some calls last night—not that I wouldn't welcome the change of scenery and a break from the pressure.

I pulled into my building's parking lot, glancing around as I always did and not spotting anybody who might be watching.

I had hoped Nomura might be out there somewhere. I exhaled as I parked and got out. No, I wouldn't mind a break.

Chapter 31

Friday

I felt a tremendous sense of relief as I drove to LAX Airport from work. I had permission to be myself for a couple of days. I could ditch the wig and glasses. I could lose the constant fear of being recognized and unmasked. Best of all, I'd be with James, a fact that nearly always made me feel more relaxed and secure. I was, however, afraid that at some point he'd bring up the danger that the FBI operation might pose to me.

We drove separately to the airport. I didn't even risk a stop at Pen's apartment in Long Beach; I'd called James and had him bring some clothes for me that I'd kept at his place. I found a handicap space in an airport ramp, plopped my bag onto my lap, and propelled myself inside.

After the usual hassle at security, I made my way to the gate. During pre-boarding, I gate-checked my wheelchair, then switched to an aisle chair for the short ride to the first-class cabin. I transferred to my seat, grateful to be travelling with James, who did everything first class. And after a minute, there he was, sitting down beside me.

He held my hand as we took off. "God, it's good to see you," he said quietly.

"Likewise."

"How many rules did you break by telling me about Landrum?"

I thought about all the strict secrecy agreements I'd signed. "Enough to get me prosecuted and put away for a pretty long time."

"I can keep my mouth shut."

"I know."

"And I don't mind helping."

"I know that, too. But mainly I just . . . need you."

He smiled. "You? Need somebody?"

I punched his arm.

He leaned over and kissed me. Then kissed some more. Finally, breathing hard, we broke it off.

"Somebody will be yelling at us to get a room," I said.

"It's been a while."

We both smiled and settled back into our seats.

The three-hour flight gave me time to think about the gravity of what I was doing. In telling James about the operation, and then enlisting him to contact Landrum, I had committed grave breaches of security. Yesterday James had, at my request, called Landrum, purportedly to pitch a venture capital deal James was in the process of lining up investors for. The two had chatted briefly and agreed to meet soon. That breach was serious enough.

But what I was doing now, breaking cover and flying off for an unauthorized undertaking, was even worse. I was betraying Nomura's trust. I was—there was no denying it—going rogue. But I had a better description for this risky maneuver, something I had never set out to do, but which in hindsight seemed inevitable: Going all in.

*   *   *

"The airport?" PACIFIC exclaimed. "What is *that* all about?"

"I have no idea," Kamensky replied. He had made a routine check on the locations transmitted by the tracker on Dez Walker's van. "The last couple of days, since the tracker was placed on Wednesday, have been nothing out of the ordinary. Just to work and back. I wasn't even going to check tonight, but . . ."

"How long has she been there?"

"A couple of hours."

"Probably too long to be meeting somebody. I'll get Mother to check flights. In the meantime, find the car. Stay on it for the rest of tonight. But let's assume she's gone someplace for the weekend. Be prepared to pick her up Sunday afternoon." After a moment of silence PACIFIC said, "I'll be damned. And I'd thought we might be overreacting."

PART TWO

The Fall

Minneapolis-St. Paul

Chapter 32

Saturday

A t 11:10 AM, we sat in our rental car outside the gate of a massive stone mansion on Lake Minnetonka, west of Minneapolis. Buds were appearing on the huge trees that lined the wrought-iron fence.

"Nice digs," said James, who hadn't been here before. "Shouldn't there be peasants at the gate with pitchforks and torches?"

"Five more minutes," I said. "We need to be good and late."

We chatted for a few more minutes. Finally, James looked at his Rolex. "Now?"

"Now."

We pulled forward and up to the gate. James rolled down his window to access the intercom.

"Yes?" a female voice asked.

"It's James," he answered.

"Come on around to the kitchen."

The gate slid slowly to one side, and we drove up a long, winding driveway, which was flanked by vast lawns broken up by patches of trees. The estate belonged to Simone Woodruff Lofton. James's ex-wife was married to Simone's brother, Andre. That made Simone a step-aunt of Alicia. Simone and Alicia had become closer over the past half-year, since Alicia's mother had ceased to be involved in her life.

I directed James up to the cobbled circular approach, then down a short driveway off to one side of the mansion. James parked the car, retrieved my wheelchair from the trunk, and brought it around to the passenger side. After helping me transfer, he pushed me over to a side door, then held it open for me. I did a little wheelie up a short step and into a small entry-way.

"Come on in," a female voice called from the next room. We went around the corner into a spacious dining alcove, which was adjacent to an industrial-sized kitchen. Three women sat at the table, two with cups of coffee and one with a can of Pepsi. The wonderful aroma of fresh cookies or muffins filled the room.

Simone stood up to greet us. She was a striking, vibrant black woman in her late forties who looked content and healthy despite the murder of her husband last year. She came around to embrace both of us but was beaten to the punch by Alicia.

"Dad!" She was nearly fifteen now, taller than Simone, los-ing the awkwardness on her way to becoming a lovely young woman.

After the exchange of hugs, the third woman stood up. She looked to be in her mid-forties, short, expensively dressed, with honey blonde hair, good-looking in a wholesome, Midwestern sort of way. She stepped forward, extending her hand. "Hi," she said. "Nice to meet both of you. I'm Diane Landrum."

James and I shook her hand. "Diane and I were just talking about an upcoming item for the next planning commission meet-ing," Simone said.

"And here we are, late to pick up Alicia," James said. "Sorry about that. We'll get out of your hair."

"Nonsense," Diane said. "It was great talking to Alicia. Can you stay a bit?"

"Yes, stay and have some coffee," Simone said.

After suitable hesitation and protestations of not wanting to intrude, we stayed, and a few minutes later we were seated around the table and supplied with coffee.

It was all a put-up job, of course. Thanks to James's connec-tions as a former corporate CEO, I had some access to the rela-tively small world of wealthy movers and shakers in Minnesota.

I had come across a connection after only three phone calls, when I had called Simone and asked if she knew Diane, whom my research showed was a neighbor of hers. As an attorney in private practice, and as a prosecutor, I'd learned that if you needed the skinny on somebody, ex-spouses were often a willing source.

Simone not only knew Paul Landrum's ex-wife, which wasn't surprising, but she was a fellow member of the local planning commission, which was. She'd agreed to ask Diane over today. More than that, she had agreed to host Alicia just prior to Diane's scheduled arrival. We had created an overlap by being late to pick up Alicia. Simone had been inclined to do almost anything for me since I had solved the murder of her husband, CEO and gubernatorial candidate Blake Lofton, last year. But she was the kind of person who would be that helpful anyway.

"Diane and I were just talking about the plans for this new luxury condo project," Simone said.

Diane smiled. "We might be violating the spirit of the state open meeting law, but when friends get together and the subject comes up, what can you do?" She gestured toward Alicia. "It's been such a pleasure to meet Alicia. She reminds me a lot of my own daughter."

"I hope to see more of her," Simone added. "It gets pretty quiet here, without Blake and with my boys launched and moved to the coasts."

Alicia looked embarrassed. James beamed.

After a couple more minutes of small talk, James said to Diane, "I talked to your former husband a few days ago." This was a crucial opening; Simone wasn't sure how Diane would feel about discussing her ex.

"Really?" Diane said, sounding at least neutral if not enthused. "How was Paul?"

"We just talked briefly. We agreed to meet and discuss doing a deal."

She gave James a knowing smile. "And you're wondering whether you can trust him?"

James shrugged. "I don't know him, that's all."

"I assume you're aware of his business track record."

"Sure. Who isn't?"

"Even a non-business type like me has heard of him," I said. "A self-made billionaire. A wizard at predicting changes in commodity prices, and now investing in tech companies."

Diane nodded. "He's all that and more—when it comes to business."

He was, I reflected, also a cheat, nearly succeeding in his attempt to defraud DSI by slipping a word into his contract with the company. How much of his success, I wondered, was due to similar shady dealings?

"I need to acknowledge Paul's success," Diane continued, "and separate it from my personal experience with him. There's nothing remarkable about our marital story—a man becomes successful, dumps his dowdy first wife, takes up with a . . ." She stopped and sighed. "I need to be charitable here. I won't characterize Irina."

"Paul also moved to the West Coast," I said.

She nodded. "He was a big fish who needed a bigger pond, and he's done very well out there. Of course, Paul is a New Yorker. I'm from the Midwest—Kansas, actually. I like living here. Unfortunately, our daughter, Meghan, opted for the West Coast, too. She's in college out there. UCLA."

"Does she get home often?" I asked.

"Not very. But I get out there to see her regularly. I was pretty lonely during fall semester, when she was studying in Australia."

"You said Paul was originally a New Yorker," James noted. "How did he end up in Minneapolis?"

"After he graduated from Wharton, he took a job with a big mutual fund company here. That's when we met; I'd finished college at the University of Minnesota and was working in HR at Honeywell. Within a couple of years, Paul had lined up investors and started his own hedge fund. And the rest is history."

Our conversation continued for a while longer, expanding to include Simone and even Alicia. Finally, we said our good-byes, apologizing again for being late. We had barely cleared the property when Alicia said, "That was a setup, wasn't it? You wanted to meet Diane."

James and I looked at each other. If Alicia had been able to figure it out, Diane might have, too. I consoled myself with the thought that Alicia knew us, and Diane didn't. And if Diane did see the situation as a setup, she'd think it was because of a possible business deal between James and Landrum. But at this point, I wasn't concerned about a little embarrassment. I had, however, every reason to remain concerned about Paul Landrum.

Chapter 33

After dropping Alicia off at home, we drove toward Minneapolis on Highway 7. "I'm glad to see Simone and Alicia hitting it off," I said.

"So am I," James said. "With her mother out of the picture, Alicia needs someone, and I can't think of anybody better than Simone."

"At least we were able to meet Diane."

"What did you think of her?" James asked.

"On the surface, she seems pretty unremarkable," I said. "A nice person. A mother. Dealing with being discarded by her husband."

"We didn't learn much of anything about Landrum. She didn't have any dirt."

"That could be because there isn't any, because she's too classy to talk about it, or because she's protecting him."

"I think we can discard number one. That leaves two or three."

"Could be either," I said. "I got the feeling there's more to her than what we saw."

"So did I. It was almost as though she wanted to tell us something but couldn't."

I had to agree. We appeared to have struck out, although over the years I'd learned not to judge too quickly what might or might not be relevant. I could still hope we'd learned something, even if we didn't realize it now.

"What about Landrum's current wife?" James asked.

"Irina?"

"Right. Isn't she Russian or something?"

"Ukrainian."

"Isn't that suspicious? Could she be involved in—whatever you're looking for?" I had told James nothing about what Landrum was suspected of, or of any Russian connection. He didn't know my assignment was at DSI, or that I was working for the FBI, or posing as a paralegal. He had never heard of Keri Wylie. He knew only that I was interested in Landrum, who was suspected of wrongdoing of some type.

"I'm leaving her to the people I'm working for," I said. "As far as I know, she's been checked out thoroughly. At any rate, I don't have time to start investigating her."

We turned east onto I-94 and drove through a long tunnel on the western edge of downtown. A few minutes later, we crossed the Mississippi and entered St. Paul. I had rarely ventured to this side of the river over the years, but the city had its charms. We approached downtown and took an exit that was flanked by two impressive competing domes, belonging to the state capitol off to the left and the St. Paul Cathedral up the hill to our right.

The downtown skyline was undistinguished; St. Paul was more of a government and cultural center than a business hub. We reached our destination, a fairly new but plain-looking brick building, almost as soon as we exited the freeway. As we drove past, we saw scruffy-looking people standing around or sitting on benches outside the building. We circled the block and finally found a spot down the street. James retrieved my wheelchair from the trunk, unfolded it, and helped me transfer. Then, after a glance at some of the dubious characters who populated the street, he locked the doors of the rental.

The front entrance to the St. Francis Center smelled of cigarette smoke. We went past it and around to the side of the building, where we found another entrance. James pressed a button, and a few seconds later we were buzzed in. A woman appeared at the end of a short hallway. She saw James and beamed. "Well, if it isn't Dandy Jim."

James walked forward and embraced the woman, who looked to be in her early forties, with sharp features and short, dark hair fringed with gray, wearing oversized glasses. James turned back to me. "Pen Wilkinson, meet Courtney Stapleton." Her smile was warm, her handshake firm and businesslike.

"Come on in," she said. We followed her past an open door, which revealed a cramped, windowless office. Courtney gestured toward the room. "Just like my old digs on the twenty-third floor, right, James?"

We kept following as she led us to a larger room, equipped with a refrigerator, coffeemaker, sink, and microwave, and a table surrounded by chipped plastic chairs. On the other side of the room sat a battered couch and two upholstered armchairs, their surfaces shiny with wear. "Have a seat," she told James. For me, of course, the request would have been redundant. "Coffee?" she asked. We declined, and she plopped down on the couch, next to the chair occupied by James. I rolled up to the side.

"I suppose James told you a bit about me, Pen," Courtney said.

"Just that you two worked together, and—"

"We survived each other." She laughed.

"More than that," James said. "I put her in charge of an entire business line."

"What line?" I asked.

"Treasury management," Courtney answered. "High-tech bank accounts and money management tools. But promoting me wasn't the best thing James did."

"I also needed somebody to run a key area in Trust," James explained, "so I brought Tanya over from my old bank in Charlotte."

"Tanya and I sort of hit it off," Courtney said. She held up her left hand, displaying a wedding ring. She and James laughed.

"Congratulations," I said.

"Thanks. But that's not why you're here now. You're here because of who I worked for before I was hired at North Central. I was at MinnFund Partners."

"Paul Landrum's hedge fund," James said. "That's what Techinvest Partners was called when it was located here."

"Quite a journey for me," Courtney said. "High-flying hedge fund to corporate banking executive to lowly social services provider."

"Don't say lowly," James said. "I checked this place out. The St. Francis Center is a leader. You're ahead of the pack in services for the homeless."

"No place I'd rather be," she said. "One night, a year and a half ago, when Tanya and I were still at the bank, we found ourselves eating takeout at the office at 8:30 PM. We sort of looked at each other and asked, 'Why are we doing this?' We started volunteering here, and eventually I took the center's CFO job. Everybody pitches in, though; I often go out and help serve lunch."

"That's wonderful," I said.

She shrugged. "I've still got a way to go before I've atoned for all my corporate sins."

"Careful, now," James said.

"Don't worry, I haven't gone all mushy and liberal on you, James. Tanya still works over at the bank. We need health insurance and a 401(k), after all."

"So," I said, "did you commit some of your sins in the service of Paul Landrum?"

"Depends on how you look at it. He never asked me to do anything flat-out crooked. I guess the only real sin I was guilty of was blind greed. But as sins go, that one rocks, let me tell you."

"What did you do for Landrum?"

"Trading and banking, mostly. It was an exciting environment, I'll admit. High stress, but a lot of action."

"What businesses was MinnFund Partners in?"

"It was an unusual mix. We did commodity and currency trading, but also made equity investments in individual companies. It required two different skill sets."

"Commodities are supposed to be Landrum's superpower," James said.

"Absolutely."

"What was his decision-making process for his trades?"

"He did the things other commodities guys do," Courtney said. "He'd look at fundamental reports by analysts—you know, what are the inventory levels on the world oil and soybean markets? And he'd also look at reports from the quantitative analysts. Models and algorithms—that sort of thing. But in the end, he went with his gut. He made big bets, and he was right more often than not, especially on oil. Oil is just his thing, that's all. And the money rolled in. He became a billionaire who flies around in his own jet."

"How did he raise the capital for his hedge fund?" James asked. It was, I realized, a really good, and really obvious, question. I was glad to have James's expertise.

A brief, troubled expression crossed Courtney's face. I knew James had seen it, too. "That goes back a long time," she said. "More than twenty years. Before I worked for him."

"So you have no idea?"

"Nobody is really sure."

James leaned forward. "Courtney, if I did a deal with the guy, I'd want to know."

Clever, I thought, *phrasing it as hypothetical.*

She looked toward the door, then lowered her voice. "There was speculation about it. He was vague; he said he'd developed connections in New York."

"What was your take?" James asked. His presence was powerful; dodging the question would be difficult.

She glanced at the door again, hesitated again, looked up tentatively at us. "This has to stay confidential, James. There's no way—and I mean *no* way—this comes from me."

"Of course," he said.

"It was all hidden well. But I'm familiar with international money transfers. I know the types of entities and techniques that are used. I could never prove it, but I'm telling you it's true: The source of his capital was Russia."

We were silent for a long moment as I struggled to take this in. I knew Landrum might have employed a Russian hit man to take out Keri. But what did it mean that he had a financial relationship with Russians, going back twenty years?

"Was there any evidence that he was working with the Russians over the years?" I asked.

"Not really."

"That's not quite the same thing as 'no,'" James observed.

"No, but . . ."

We waited.

"I overheard him speaking Russian once. It was late at night, in his office. He didn't know anybody was there."

"Why was that suspicious?" I asked.

"I worked with him for four years, and there was never a hint that he knew Russian. He's got Spanish and French listed on his resume."

Suspicious, but not conclusive, I thought. I decided to switch subjects. "How did he treat people?"

"His expectations were clear. If you didn't produce, you were out." She glanced over at James. "Sound familiar, big guy?"

James, a notoriously demanding boss, managed a sheepish smile.

"I knew that sooner or later, someday, I wouldn't make the numbers, and I'd be cut. I decided to get out ahead of the curve. I moved over to North Central."

"Did he have conflicts with people?" I asked.

"Not many—it was his company, after all. He had only one real fight that I remember. He had just a ferocious disagreement about something or other—I don't know what—with a guy named

Stew Kyler, who was an early associate. Paul ended up forcing him out."

"Where did Kyler go after MinnFund?" I asked, hoping we might track him down.

"He was killed in a car accident—just a few weeks after he left, as I recall."

James and I exchanged discreet glances. James asked, "Were you surprised when Landrum moved to California?"

"I wasn't shocked. Professionally, he was ready for something bigger, so he moved. He left Diane here—that did surprise me. I thought he'd been pretty close to his family."

"Did you know Diane?"

"I got to know her a bit. We still have lunch a couple of times a year. She seemed more resigned than shocked when Paul left her. But she's doing okay, I think. Gets out to see Meghan regularly. She has friends in New York, too, and gets out there frequently. Of course, she's well situated—Paul paid handsomely to get rid of her."

I felt frustrated. I thought we were getting a surface view of Landrum. "What was he *like*?" I asked.

Courtney thought for a moment. "He was a little distant. He was correct. He could be civilized, elegant. Always under control."

"Always?" James said.

Her smile was wary. "There were a couple of lapses during the time I worked for him."

"How many?"

"Two."

"That you know of?" I asked.

"No, two, period. If there were any more, I definitely would have heard about it."

"What happened?"

"Let's just say that when the ultimate control freak loses control, it ain't pretty. The explosions were violent; the man basically went berserk, red-faced and screaming. In one case, he hit the person."

"*Hit* them?" I exclaimed.

James said, "Any chance the outbursts were contrived? Just to send a message, keep people in line?"

"Not a chance, James. You could never fake something like that, although it certainly did keep everybody on their toes."

We couldn't think of any more questions, so we thanked Courtney, and she walked with us to the exit. "Are you really thinking of doing a deal with Paul?" she asked James when we reached the door.

"Just thinking."

"If you ever get a deal on the table, don't walk away from it," she said.

"Run?" he guessed.

"Like the wind."

Chapter 34

In the car, James was on my case immediately. "What the *hell* are you into?" he demanded.

"I can't talk about it."

"This guy is trouble."

"I know. That's why I'm investigating him."

He shook his head in frustration but didn't say anything more. I was thinking about what to tell Nomura.

We drove back toward Lake Minnetonka. With a couple of hours to kill before picking up Alicia for dinner, we stopped at a large shopping mall called Ridgedale, where we wandered around and did some half-hearted shopping. Mostly, we were just quiet, which was just as well, since I couldn't talk about what I was doing, and all we really seemed to want was to enjoy each other's presence.

James was a clothes horse (as Courtney had noted, people at his old company had called him Dandy Jim), so he couldn't resist shopping for a new pair of jeans, even at a middlebrow store like Nordstrom. I was no slouch at shopping myself but generally didn't buy stuff at malls, even though, given my budget, that's where I should have shopped. James began trying on jeans, and when he came out of the dressing room after the fourth attempt, he asked my opinion.

"A little snug," I said.

He nodded glumly. "Guess I'd better try the relaxed fit."

"The big-butt sizes."

He gave me a mock glare.

On his seventh attempt, he finally found a pair he deemed acceptable. "I like this brand," he said. "What is it called?"

I took a pair of the same brand off the shelf and pretended to study the label. "It's called Old Fart."

He rolled his eyes and started to return to the dressing room, then looked back at me, stunned. "What's wrong, honey?"

I was sniffling, stifling a full-blown jag. He came over, leaned down, and embraced me. "What's wrong?" he said, more softly.

"I just—I'm just . . . oh, God, I just don't know."

"Don't know what?"

I got myself under control, wiping my tears with the handkerchief he handed me. "I'm sorry, James. I'm so sorry."

"No, no, no. What's the matter?"

I took a deep, ragged breath and let it out. "This—you and me. Just hanging out, being together. Relaxed. Fun. It's just so right. But . . ."

"I know, I know," he said, suppressing his exasperation. "There's always a *but*."

"I just need to do . . . other stuff, too."

"I know. It's all right."

I nodded and gripped him tighter, knowing it wasn't really all right.

*   *   *

After dinner with Alicia, we drove her back home to her stepfather, Andre. James had gone through considerable soul-searching before deciding to leave Alicia with Andre, with familiar surroundings, friends, schools, and activities, rather than uprooting her and bringing her to California to live with him. After dropping Alicia off, we made the fifteen-mile drive to the condo James maintained in downtown Minneapolis. Since I had first been to this place, located in a high-rise building on Nicollet Mall, James had gradually added some personal touches—pictures of Alicia and of James and myself, and a few books and souvenirs from trips.

We sat in the living room, watching the news on TV and sipping wine. He had helped me out of my chair and onto the couch next to him. Neither of us had spoken for a while.

"Go ahead and say it," I said.

He started at the television set and lifted the glass to his lips. He stopped short of drinking, putting the glass down again. "You can't expect me to just shrug this off," he said. "I know I'm supposed to let you do your thing. The counselor we saw convinced me of that. But you're into something dangerous—I can sense that."

"I don't expect you to shrug it off. I'm sort of . . . concerned myself." I figured "concerned" sounded better than "scared shitless."

"I'm glad you're concerned. You need to be careful."

"I am."

He turned toward me, his frustration bubbling over. "You say that automatically. But why do we have to keep having this conversation? Why does it always have to be dangerous?"

I took my time, formulating my response. "James, what if somebody told you that you couldn't run your business?"

He gave me a sharp look.

"That you just couldn't handle it?" I persisted. "That you weren't emotionally up to the job? That it was just too much, too stressful for you? That you were too fragile, too wounded, too handicapped?"

This time the wineglass made it all the way to his mouth for a long drink, followed by a long silence. "I don't have an answer for that," he said at last. "I guess I'll just have to live with it." He put his arm around me. "God, just be careful."

The TV news was gone, replaced by some inane talk show. "What do you feel like doing?" he asked.

"Well, we could do what we talked about on the plane."

"What was that?"

I smiled. "Get a room."

Chapter 35

Sunday

Los Angeles

Wendy Nomura tried to look nonchalant as she walked toward the conference room, located in a quiet corner of the Wilshire Federal Building. She was meeting again with an immensely powerful man who wouldn't want to hear what she had to say. She would not tell him that she had allowed Pen to break cover and go away for a weekend, even though she was still convinced it was the right call. There were plenty of other things to talk about. She nodded to the two agents from Assistant Director in Charge Kirk Hendricks's security detail. Then she slipped inside.

Hendricks already sat at the conference table, holding a cup of coffee.

Wendy nodded and sat down.

"We have a number of things to discuss," Hendricks said. "But let's start with the big one. Has she learned anything?"

"No."

He nodded, not pleased but clearly not surprised.

"It gets worse. Pen has also come close to figuring out . . . our problem."

"Our Gilbertson problem?"

She nodded.

Hendricks drummed his fingers on the table, looking off into space. "Ward, Ward, Ward. What the hell do we do with him? It's bad enough that he sold out his country, but hell, that's nothing compared to the havoc he's created with our investigating capability. Here we are, utterly hamstrung in trying to get a handle on this Landrum business. If we'd had Kamensky's face on file, we could have prevented most of this from happening."

"Will we be able to prove Gilbertson pulled Kamensky's face out of the database?" Wendy asked.

The ADC shrugged. "I suspect it will be tough. That's for the OIG's cyber-geeks to figure out. But unfortunately, it could have bigger ramifications."

It could, indeed, Wendy thought. Gilbertson might have accomplices in the federal security bureaucracy. Or the Russians could have other well-placed operatives, unknown to Gilbertson.

The inspector general's office was already very familiar with Wendy's boss, who'd been under suspicion even before everything had hit the fan with Landrum. Ever since Gilbertson had served a stint in Moscow, the intelligence failures had been accumulating. A discreet investigation had turned up indications that female Russian agents might have compromised Gilbertson, a married father of four. And so internal investigators had begun monitoring him. And the small discrepancies, the little actions that seemed a bit off, had begun to pile up. Removing a Russian assassin's face from the database to facilitate his entry into the United States fit the pattern squarely.

The Bureau's suspicions about Gilbertson were tightly held. But Wendy had been admitted to the circle of knowledge a month ago, in this very conference room. Answering a summons from Hendricks, whom she had never met beyond a brief handshake at an official function, she had entered the room to find Hendricks and the head of OIG seated at the table. After she'd taken a seat, Hendricks had said, "Something is wrong with your boss, Wendy. But I suspect you already know that."

After a long hesitation, she had nodded.

"We have a problem," the ADC had continued. "And we need you to help us solve it."

Now Wendy said, "Is it time to bring Gilbertson in, sir? Sweat him? Find out what they're up to?"

"If I thought it would work, I'd do it in a heartbeat. But I've talked to OIG. They feel, and I agree, that we can't risk it. What if he lawyers up and keeps his mouth shut?"

Wendy was skeptical of that concern. Hendricks could, with minimal accountability, have Gilbertson thrown into a deep, dark hole and subjected to enhanced interrogation techniques. He would talk. But . . .

Hendricks completed the thought. "What if he doesn't know? If you were the Russians, would you give Ward Gilbertson the big picture?"

Wendy shook her head. The question answered itself. And if they pulled her boss in, the Russians would lose no time folding up whatever operation they were running, its perpetrators disappearing or fleeing the country. The Bureau would be left empty-handed, not only with the guilty unpunished, but with no one to debrief, no way to assess the damage that had been wrought. And neither wanted to think about an even bigger nightmare: other Russian operatives planted in the FBI, maybe even higher-ranking than Gilbertson. Which was why Hendricks couldn't risk further involvement by his office, beyond a secret op run by lowly Special Agent Wendy Nomura.

"Hell," Hendricks said, "I would love to just swoop in on the whole crew and round them up. But beyond Gilbertson, we don't know who the 'crew' consists of. If there are others, we might miss them, maybe including the ringleaders. The ones we missed would flee the country. And the attorneys would go nuts. How would we get warrants? There's no probable cause for, well, anything. If it was terrorism-related, we've got all kinds of extraordinary authority there. But if it's 'just' national security . . ." He sat up, hands steepled on the table top. "Any indications, Wendy—any hint—of something imminent? Something irreparable?"

"The only time-sensitive event we're aware of comes from the Landrum investigation."

"The closing of the Hulbert merger. That's what Keri was concerned about."

"Should we have told Pen of our suspicions relating to Landrum and Russia?"

Hendricks shrugged. "Maybe. But when we put her into DSI, all we had was a few of Landrum's transmissions that NSA had flagged as suspicious. Now, of course, we have Kamensky."

She nodded.

"It's based on a chain of causation," he continued, "but it's a strong chain. We think Kamensky—meaning Moscow—killed Keri Wylie, and we know Keri was trying to blow the whistle on Landrum. Just for good measure, we have Gilbertson, whom we know is dirty, trying to monitor your involvement in the Wylie investigation. We've nearly completed the circle, Wendy. It all ties together, but we don't know how. We didn't tell Pen about Russia, but she had no need to know."

"Knowing Pen, she may figure it out anyway."

"So Keri was concerned about Landrum and the Hulbert merger," Hendricks said. "But Landrum will not have control of Hulbert, thank God. He doesn't even have control of DSI."

"I know, and I can't explain it."

"Damnit, we *have* to find out what she meant," he said. "Is Pen our only hope of doing that?"

"I'm afraid so. But there are some problems."

He shook his head. "There always are."

"She's under serious scrutiny." Wendy described the extra interviewing and possible fingerprinting by DSI security personnel.

"And these people are working with Landrum?"

"Pen believes so, yes. The head of security is reputed to be Landrum's man. And today, I discovered that they've put a tracker on her vehicle." Wendy had checked out the van in its parking spot at LAX. She had also had the apartment swept but found nothing.

"Good Lord," Hendricks exclaimed. "Do you think she's flat-out blown?"

"Too early to say."

"You left the tracker in place?"

"Yes. We may have to be prepared for physical surveillance, too. And there's another thing. She—well, got involved in a controversy between DSI and Landrum."

"A paralegal? How did she do that?"

"She's got the knack, sir." Wendy described the uproar over The Typo.

"So that's probably what made them suspicious," he observed.

"She was already under suspicion, but it obviously didn't help."

"Poor judgment."

"Yes, although it earned her a personal dinner invitation at Pat Dalton's house."

Hendricks let out an astonished chuckle. "Who the hell *is* this woman?"

Wendy shrugged.

"So," he said, "it's unlikely she's going to find out anything about Landrum. He's on full alert."

"I'm afraid so. But their suspicion might provide us with an opportunity."

Hendricks leaned further forward. "You want to use her as bait."

"Yes. Let's find out who's interested in her. Let's see who else is in 'the crew.'"

"There's an obvious problem with that."

"Resources."

He nodded. The use of more resources risked exposing their operation. "We're already playing a dicey game. How is security holding up at our end?"

"So far, so good. I see no indication that Ward is suspicious about Pen, but of course Landrum or his people at DSI could have passed it on to him, assuming they're all in cahoots."

"They are," Hendricks said flatly. "This is all part of the Russian game on the West Coast, part of PACIFIC. I just know it. But we still have no feel for the extent of the operation, or who all is involved, or least of all, what their current project is, the one they brought Kamensky in for. I don't see any alternative, Wendy. We'll have to keep running Pen out there, see who reacts."

"Fine. But my one-person show is creating a different problem. Pen has figured out that I'm soloing."

"She's concerned that nobody's watching her back."

"Correct," Wendy said.

"How serious is her discontent?"

"She's still with the program, but just barely. She feels insecure, especially since we told her about Kamensky."

"I get it. We need to deploy additional assets, both to find out who's interested in Pen, and to keep Pen safe and with the program. But if we do anything more, Ward might find out about it. A supervisory agent like Gilbertson has a lot of access; it's difficult to wall him off."

"Right. And there's another complication."

Hendricks looked exasperated. "What?"

"There's always a possibility that the other side could be using Kamensky for surveillance on Pen."

"That would be the type of connection we're looking for, to link Landrum to the Russians."

"True. But it also means we can't really enlist Newport Beach to help with our surveillance, even if all the work would be on their turf, which it wouldn't be."

The ADC nodded slowly. "Newport Beach has probable cause to bust Kamensky for the Keri Wylie murder."

"Yes. They've held off issuing a warrant or conducting a manhunt."

"Hell, we'd like to bust him, too, for a number of things. And we will. He will *not* escape the country. But we can't do it now, not without showing our hand and folding the operation. *Damn* it." He leaned back, staring at the wall. Wendy said nothing.

Finally, Hendricks stood up abruptly. "We'll keep Pen in place for now. Let me call in some markers—I'll get back to you. But if they get any closer to her, we'll have to pull the plug."

Chapter 36

Viktor Kamensky finished replacing the draperies in the second bedroom of the cabin in the Santa Ana Mountains, not far from Silverado. He admired his handiwork: the room now sported heavy blackout-type curtains on the window. It wasn't as though the neighbors took much notice of what he did or could really see much at all; the place was fairly isolated. He hadn't made much use of the cabin, but it would serve his purpose. It featured an enclosed garage and a guest bedroom he could use as a workshop, a place to gather information. Somehow, someone was doing something under his nose, and that made him angry. He put away the tools he had used to install the blinds, then checked his equipment: an electric cord, some wires and electrodes, smelling salts, a water bucket, and duct tape.

Kamensky didn't exactly enjoy this kind of work, but he didn't shy away from it, either. He never had a problem giving fools what they deserved. Soft-headed people who didn't understand the world, who acted out of principle, idealism, or often, just foolishness. They all had one thing in common: they ended up crossing the wrong people. In this case, after his conversations were complete and he knew what he needed to know, he wouldn't have to wrap it up with anything exotic. A simple bullet would do the job, as it had with Keri Wylie.

But before the bullet, they would need to find out what Desiree Walker knew. It wouldn't be like London, where he'd used a prick with an umbrella, which had administered a fatal dose of radiation to a fool who'd continued to organize opposition to the Kremlin. The process of dying hadn't been short or easy for that guy. And it wasn't as though the target hadn't been warned; he had been forced out of the country and had his assets confiscated. All he'd had to do was keep his mouth shut, but the idiot couldn't even manage that. He'd crossed the wrong people.

The second British target had been even worse. The guy was a former journalist who'd continued to put out tweets and articles critical of the Russian regime. He'd even gone to Washington and Brussels to round up support for sanctions against the oligarchs. Utterly clueless. The nerve gas had spooked Viktor, though. He was really glad he didn't have to use that stuff again. It had killed the target and nearly killed the target's girlfriend, who was still recovering. The murder had created an international brouhaha, of course, but that wasn't Viktor's problem. He'd done his job.

And, boring or no, he'd do it again here in LA.

Chapter 37

It was midafternoon on Sunday when we returned to LA. As we landed, the warm glow of a weekend with James began to wear off. Unpleasant realities—the dwindling time left to finish my assignment, along with the acknowledgement that the Minnesota trip had been only marginally productive—seeped into my consciousness. Now I had to shift back into Dez Mode.

I told James we shouldn't be seen together going through the airport, or outside, so we said goodbye at the gate. We moved into a corner, away from the crowd.

"Just a couple of weeks," I said.

"Right." In a couple of weeks, I'd be back to my regular apartment, and life would return to normal. Or would it? Would I last the two weeks? Or would I be exposed by Paul Landrum and Les Hornsby? I tried to ignore the nagging fear that they were closing in on me, which led to an even bigger fear.

I didn't want to end up like Keri Wylie.

James looked straight ahead, but I knew he had something to say.

"What?" I asked.

"Just so you know, if anything happens to you—*anything*—I will personally see to it that all responsible parties are held accountable. Fully accountable. I don't care if it takes me the rest of my life and every penny I own, but it will happen. Guaranteed."

And the process might well include James beating the crap out of the offenders, I thought as he walked away.

*   *   *

Carter waited in his car at a spot along Century Boulevard, near the airport, sipping from a Starbucks cup. He didn't know where Pen was living her alternate life. And so he waited. He'd spent the last few weeks worrying about her, and then worrying about worrying. Pen's PTSD symptoms had only recently subsided. They could easily return. And yet, as Pen had pointed out, these stressful undertakings defined her as much as Carter's business defined him. Her argument had been unanswerable; that was what he got for dating a damned lawyer. He could hardly complain. But he could worry.

Pen's van appeared about twenty minutes later, and he pulled out onto the busy street behind her. He gave her plenty of room on Century and then on the 405. Pen had learned some extra vigilance in the course of taking on corporate saboteurs, crooked politicians, Russian hackers, and . . . who was it this time? What was the malevolent force behind billionaire Paul Landrum?

Pen had talked very little about the logistics of her operation —she wasn't supposed to talk about it at all—but it sounded as though she didn't have a lot of protection or backup. She seemed to be doing reasonably well, but Carter wondered if her employer—the US attorney or the FBI or whoever—knew how fragile she was. He and Pen had been through the nightmares and anxiety attacks together, but now she was on her own. He wasn't supposed to know where Pen was staying—didn't really want to know. But now he was going to damn well make sure she got there safely. He could do that much.

He followed Pen south on Highway 55 and then onto the Coast Highway. At Superior, across from the entrance to Balboa Peninsula, Pen took a right, up the hill, past a large open area. Carter followed, hanging well back. She turned left into a condo complex. *Nice digs*, he thought. He paused at the entrance to the complex, scanning the buildings in front of him, until he saw Pen getting out of her van. She struggled with her overnight bag, and he had to suppress the urge to go and help her. Carter pulled over into an inconspicuous space in the back of the lot and waited until she got into the apartment with her bag. When he saw the lights go on, and Pen's form moving behind the curtains, he reluctantly left.

He knew he shouldn't have followed her. Now he'd be tempted to come back, to make sure she was okay. And if he did that, he might be spotted.

He wasn't sure he could resist the temptation.

*   *   *

Viktor Kamensky was tired. It had been a long drive from the mountain cabin back to LAX Airport. But it hadn't been a fruitless trip; Desiree Walker had reclaimed her van in mid-afternoon. And she had been alone. Disappointing, but that told him something, too. He was hot on the trail now. PACIFIC had called him yesterday with some disturbing news.

"Mother found no records of a flight by Desiree Walker anywhere. What does that tell you, Viktor?"

"Two options. She could have left the airport via another ground mode, intending to give us the slip."

"Or?"

"Or she flew out under another name. Maybe her real name."

"Bingo. Either way, the alarm is shrieking pretty loudly. Find out who she is, Viktor."

Now he followed her down the 405 toward Orange County. Presumably she was going home. That was fine; he'd found three observation points in the parking lot of an adjacent complex where he could inconspicuously watch Walker's building through the trees. It would be interesting to see who else might show up—Wendy Nomura, for instance. He'd never actually seen Nomura here, but he would have bet this was where she went when she eluded Kamensky in the evenings.

He drove on ahead of the target, keeping an eye on her position with his GPS tracker, and stationed himself at Walker's complex. Dez appeared about five minutes later, and as she got out of the van, he saw a silver BMW enter the lot, moving to a parking space along the back row. Dez got herself into the building, and the Beamer left. Kamensky started his own vehicle. He had a feeling this car had been following Walker, maybe in a protective mode. Or it might have nothing to do with Dez. But Kamensky had a feeling.

The silver car took a left on Pacific Coast Highway, then proceeded south. It took a right on Jamboree, then turned south on Bayside. A half-mile or so later, the BMW pulled into the parking lot of a small marina. Kamensky drove past, then looped around and found a spot on the street. He pulled out his binoculars, watching a confident-looking black man walk through the gate and down a walkway to Dock D, and from there down to a good-sized boat. Kamensky peered at the name on the side: the *Alicia C.* And on the dock next to the boat stood . . . a wheelchair lift.

The guy reappeared a few minutes later, returning to his car. Kamensky noted the Beamer's license number. He could trace the owner later. But for now, he stayed in place. It was the handicap lift that interested him. The BMW left.

Kamensky waited the better part of an hour, watching the boat, as the twilight descended on Newport Harbor. He glanced at his watch. He needed to get back to make sure Dez didn't go anywhere, as she apparently had over the weekend. But he would check out the boat and the wheelchair lift. He'd be back. Soon.

Chapter 38

I took a long shower, washing off the travel grime and sweat, and rolled out to the living room to call Nomura.

"Hi," she said. "Did you enjoy your weekend?"

"It was very nice." I wouldn't, of course, tell her about meeting Diane Landrum or Courtney Stapleton. "I had a thought, though, during the flight."

"What's that?"

"I think it would be worth checking out where Landrum got the startup capital to finance his hedge fund. What if he got some help, maybe from the Russians?"

"That would take us back more than twenty years."

"I guess it would, yes."

A short silence. Then, "You didn't by any chance stumble on some information up in Minneapolis, did you?"

"It's just a thought," I said.

"Right." She didn't believe it. "I'll look through the files to see if that was ever checked out."

"Thanks."

"In the meantime, I checked with my superiors about your situation. They agreed that additional surveillance for you is appropriate. Starting early this afternoon, your apartment has been under twenty-four-hour video surveillance. A team in Washington, which doesn't know the particulars of the case, will be monitoring it continuously."

It wasn't quite the twenty-four-seven protection I'd hoped for, but I'd take it. I wondered why Landrum and his people hadn't put a tracker on my van.

Maybe they had, and Nomura either didn't know or wasn't going to tell me.

"What if I'm being watched?"

"That would be terrific. We'll find out who it is."

"You're using me as bait."

She didn't respond.

"How about back and forth to work?" I asked.

"We still don't believe that following you would be wise. That's when our tail would be most likely to be noticed. Remember, you've still got the panic button and your phone location tracking. You haven't noticed anybody else following you after that one day, have you?"

"No." To shadow me during my commute, I noted to myself, the FBI would mostly likely have to assign additional surveillance personnel, something they seemed keen to avoid. It was true that I hadn't noticed a tail since I thought I'd seen a blue pickup truck following me home. But that might be because they now knew where I lived. Of course, Hornsby and Landrum already knew.

"Obviously," Nomura said, "we won't have you covered during the workday. You're in no danger there."

I hoped she was right. What could they do to me out in full view at DSI headquarters?

"I checked out that attorney, Steve Li," she said. "He looks legit. He was born in Taipei, immigrated as a child, and is now a US citizen. Has his own small practice. Went to law school at Berkeley. Specializes in clients doing business in China and Taiwan. No criminal or disciplinary record."

Fine, I thought. But why would Pat Dalton hire a solo practitioner rather than a white shoe law firm? And why would the guy turn up at Dalton's house unannounced?

"It's the home stretch," Nomura said. "Barely a week left before the closing."

"I really want to get these bastards, Wendy."

"Good luck."

Chapter 39

Week 5

Monday

Maybe it was my imagination, but I thought people at work were looking at me a little differently, a little warily, when I returned on Monday morning. I tried to keep my mind on my work, but my thoughts kept returning to the problems of how to find out what Landrum was up to and what had happened to Keri. The two puzzles, I figured, were probably one and the same.

During a trip to the bathroom in mid-afternoon, I went by the door to Keri's office, which was still vacant. I'd tried the doorknob on several occasions during the past few weeks and always found it locked. After glancing discreetly up and down the hallway, I now tried the doorknob again. This time it was unlocked, which probably meant that Lieutenant Howard and his people were finished with the room and had found nothing interesting inside. But Howard hadn't shared anything with me. It was worth a look.

I worked late, watching the floor gradually empty out. It was nearly seven when I decided to make my move. I rolled toward Keri's office. Most of the floor was dark, but there was an occasional light on. With barely a week to go, some people were undoubtedly working hard on the Hulbert closing. I continued to glance around; the coast seemed clear. If I encountered somebody, I could just continue on to the bathroom.

But I reached Keri's door without meeting anyone. I took one last look around, then opened the door, flipped on the light, and rolled inside. I spun around and closed the door gently behind me, then got my bearings, taking in a faintly musty smell. I imagined Keri sitting in here, working hard—until she had discovered something about Paul Landrum. Windows on one side of the room looked out over the darkened parking lot. On the opposite wall, somebody had stacked half a dozen boxes of office supplies; they were using the room for storage.

The credenza was clear, except for a phone and a monitor. I couldn't find a computer; I imagined the police might still have it. On top of the desk was a cardboard file box with a sticky note on top that said, "Returned from police." I pulled the box onto my lap and looked inside. There were time records, project lists, to-do lists, and paper correspondence. About halfway down I found half a dozen sheets bound by a rubber band, with hand-written notes containing what appeared to be dates, numbers, and abbreviations. On top was a yellow sticky note on which somebody had written, "What is this?" I didn't see an answer anywhere. I pulled out my phone to take pictures of the documents. Then I gasped as I saw feet underneath the door to the office. I quickly stuffed the notes into my purse and returned the box to the desktop.

The door slowly opened, and Clay Ritchie stood in the doorway. He took in the scene, and a smile slowly formed on his face. "Well, well. Who are you, Dez?"

Chapter 40

Ritchie didn't call Security. He didn't turn me over to Hornsby. Instead, he invited me out for a drink. That sounded pretty good compared to the alternatives, and so half an hour later we sat across from each other at a bar in a strip center a few miles from the office. Nomura wanted to escort me whenever I went someplace outside my normal commute, but this was an excursion best kept to myself.

Although Ritchie seemed to have no interest in reporting my little trespass, he had great interest in who I was and what I was doing. And by now, I wanted to know the same about him. We found a table toward the back and ordered drinks, a white wine for me and beer for him. "On me," he said.

"Are you trying to bribe me?"

"Maybe a little. Looks like we've both got secrets, things we'd get into a lot of trouble disclosing to anybody."

I couldn't disagree.

"But I also think," he said, "that we'll probably need to bend the rules on that just a bit if we're going to accomplish our objectives."

"What do you propose?"

"First of all, are your people, whoever they might be, watching us right now?"

"Almost certainly not."

"Good. Same from my end. If we should be spotted and have to explain, this is just a social chat."

"Fine."

"Let's start with the basics. Is Dez Walker your real name?"

"No."

"And so, your real name would be . . ."

I didn't answer.

"Pen?" he asked.

"No comment."

"All right, put that aside for now. As an act of good faith, I'll tell you Ritchie is my real name. Now, how about our respective affiliations?"

This was the moment of truth. To this point, I hadn't crossed any lines. Now I had a decision to make. Was this guy the real deal? Or was he a weasel, planted by Landrum to find out what I was up to?

"I can't do this," I said.

His eyes flashed with frustration. He looked away, then back at me. "Look, we're not going to find out what's going on by fighting each other. All right, then, I'll get the process started. I work for the Pentagon, for Air Force OSI. Office of Special Investigations. I was placed at DSI because military technology has been leaking out of here for two years."

This surprised me; my chief concern had been the risk of a future leak, maybe related to Hulbert. "Have you found out who's leaking it?" I asked.

"If I knew that, would I be risking my career by telling you these things and trying to work with you? Come on, I'm trying to meet you halfway here. More than halfway."

I hesitated. If I guessed wrong about Ritchie, the consequences could be catastrophic. But at this point, what choice did I have? I wasn't going to get the job done by playing it safe. I glanced around the bar; a group of younger men across the bar was starting to get loud. A TV set suspended above our table displayed some kind of karate or martial arts match, featuring a couple of scrawny punks kicking the hell out of each other.

I took a good, long drink from my wineglass. "I was put here by the FBI."

He nodded. "It's about time. Where has the Bureau been for the past two years?"

"I'm not sure. But I think they have internal problems."

His face wrinkled up, then relaxed in comprehension. "Internal security problems. That's what I always suspected. A bad apple. Not incompetence."

I nodded.

"So, are you a special agent?"

I chuckled. "Hardly."

"Okay, a CI."

"And my career as a Cooperating Individual will last another week and a half."

"Until the Hulbert deal closes. What's the significance of the Hulbert acquisition?"

"I have no idea. In fact, I've made basically no progress."

"Who's the focus of your investigation?"

"Landrum."

He looked a little surprised. "He can't steal technology directly. He's just a shareholder."

"I know. But for the Bureau, this isn't necessarily about stealing technology."

"Okay, I'll bite. What is it about?"

"You first."

His fingers drummed against his beer glass as he deliberated, trying to decide how much to tell me. He glanced around the bar; nobody was paying any attention to us. "I've been here for a year, but I haven't made any more progress than you have. We've had DSI's anti-ship missile guidance software show up in Iran. Close copies of their latest antitank rockets have appeared in Syria. We've heard intercepts suggesting that some newer anti-aircraft technology might be showing up in North Korea."

"Rogue states. Our enemies."

"Right. Recent quality technology that's not generally available on world markets. But not as advanced as what Hulbert has. They have sci-fi stuff you wouldn't believe. If these countries get their hands on it . . ."

"Who do you suspect of stealing it from DSI?"

"Normally you'd suspect the Chinese—they have the most active espionage efforts against our defense industries. But my superiors at the Pentagon tell me the Chinese have basically caught up to us in the areas where these leaks have occurred."

"What about the Russians?"

"They have even less need for it. Wait a minute—do you know something about the Russians?"

Now it was my turn to glance discreetly around the bar. "We think Landrum may have a Russian connection."

He gave me an astonished look. "How on Earth—" He stopped and thought for a moment. "Something to do with Keri?"

"Yes, and I'd rather not say anything more about it, at least not yet. We actually don't know a lot."

"The Russians are out there, and we know very little about what they're doing. Some years ago, we closed the Russian consulate in San Francisco. The place was lousy with spies, and they were all over our West Coast defense industries. We kicked them all out of the country."

"And so—what? They're just relying on cyber hacking to do their snooping now?"

Ritchie sighed, looked away, and then back at me. "We've both disclosed way too much. But I'll need more from you before I go any further. Tell me about Keri."

I finished my wine and glanced around. The group of young guys continued to make a lot of noise, but they were all the way on the other side of the bar. "All right." For better or worse, I was staking it all on Ritchie. I told him about Keri's phone call to the FBI before she was killed, and the possibility of a Russian connection to the murder.

"What did Keri know about Landrum?" Ritchie asked.

"We don't know. Just that he wasn't what he appeared to be."

He frowned. "There has to be more than that."

"I'm still looking." I wasn't about to tell him about Kamensky. "Okay, your turn."

"We believe there's still a human Russian spy presence on the West Coast."

"Why do they need a human presence? Why not just rely on hacking?"

He gave me a skeptical look, as though reluctant to believe that someone spying for the FBI could be so ignorant in the ways of espionage. "Intelligence services still need human sources. Corporations and governments have hardened their information systems against hacking. Humans are needed to steal information and to help make sense out of it. And human sources need to be recruited and serviced. They need somebody to meet personally with them, encourage them, reassure them, tutor them on what to steal and how. Then they need to get the information out of the country."

"Why can't they send it to Moscow electronically?"

"They could, but it's risky. The CIA and NSA are listening at both ends. It's much safer to send it out in person, in a diplomatic pouch."

"That's what they did from the San Francisco consulate," I guessed.

"Yes. We don't know how they're doing it now. But we believe there are human spies here, and that their leader is a person code-named PACIFIC. And that's basically all we know."

I sat for a moment, trying to take this all in, realizing that Nomura likely knew all this and hadn't told me. But for me, a Landrum-Russia connection, possibly involving an entire espionage operation, now took on much greater significance. Had Keri discovered the connection? The stakes had been raised again.

"Wow," I said. "Just wow."

Ritchie smiled and nodded.

"Have you checked out Landrum's wife?" I asked.

"Thoroughly. We haven't found the slightest bit of evidence that Irina is anything other than what she seems: a bimbo who doesn't know diddley."

That squared with what the Bureau had concluded. I said, "Hornsby has been on my case from the beginning. I'm afraid there might have been a leak out of the FBI."

"Possible, but I wouldn't necessarily conclude that," Ritchie said. "Look, the guy is a professional paranoid. He's just a savant at spotting phonies. You're right to be wary of him, but don't assume he knows anything specific."

We were silent for a long moment.

"This really changes things for both of us," he said. "Just by having this conversation, we've made more progress than either of us had made separately, and I've been here a year. You take away all the rivalries between agencies, all the compartmentalization, and amazing things can happen. If our intel agencies had done this in 2001, 9/11 wouldn't have happened."

"This conversation never happened," I said. "I don't feel like going to prison."

"Agreed. I served my country in Iraq. I'd hate to have the same government put me in the slammer."

"You must have a genuine finance background."

"I do. I worked for the Defense Department doing fraud investigations. White-collar stuff. Eventually I got more serious about it. Took field agent training. This isn't my first undercover assignment."

A trained agent. I felt better about having him on my side. "I'm just a lawyer," I said.

"A lawyer with a knack for finding typos."

I gave him a sheepish smile. "That didn't work out too well. But I still have a job to do, and you've given me a lot of information to process."

"Likewise. I'll have to do some thinking about Landrum, especially with the Hulbert closing coming up."

"But as you pointed out, Landrum won't be able to just waltz in there and scoop up top-secret intel. He'd have to have collaborators inside the company."

Ritchie nodded. "Serious collaborators. Even with the highest clearances, you'd have to overcome checks and balances to get access to the systems, as well as covering your tracks. But there have been dozens of DSI people over at Hulbert for weeks, preparing for the merger. All kinds of people gaining access, and many more to come. Hard to tell who might be involved."

"We need to stay in touch," I said. "Work together. It's our only hope of digging out the truth in a week."

He stood up. "We'd better get going."

He walked out behind me. As we headed for the front door, I could see the rowdy group of guys approaching from the other side of the bar, also headed out. There was a door leading to a little entryway; Ritchie held it open for me, and I rolled forward. Then I pressed the big round button to activate the automatic door leading outside. As the door opened, one of the rowdy guys walked ahead of me through the door, forcing me to stop abruptly to avoid hitting him.

"Hey, watch it!" Ritchie called from behind me, but the guy was gone.

I resumed. But then a second guy tried to squeeze in front of me through the door. This time I wasn't able to stop, and I hit him in the leg with one of my footrests.

"Ouch!" the guy yelled. He staggered and hopped through the door ahead of me.

I finished going through. The second guy, equipped with a beer belly, Budweiser cap, and scraggly beard, was not an agreeable drunk. He squared on me. I dug frantically in my purse for my can of pepper spray, but it was too late.

He stepped forward. "Stay the fuck out of the way, you retarded cripple." He put a foot on my chair and shoved me.

I hit the wall next to the door. "Hey!" I yelled.

I rolled forward, now with the pepper spray canister in my hand, but Ritchie took over. He came through the door, stepped in front of the guy, and cocked his arm as if to punch him. The guy held his hands up reflexively, at which point Ritchie kicked him in the groin.

The guy doubled over in agony, sinking to one knee, gasping. "Oh shit oh shit oh shit."

By now, the first guy had turned around and come back to help his buddy. He rushed forward—into Ritchie's fist. His head snapped backward, and blood trickled from his nose as he slumped back against the wall.

"Let's get out of here," I said, thoroughly spooked.

"Come on," Ritchie said. He pushed me to my van. I glanced back; the guys were gradually getting to their feet.

We stopped beside the van. "You didn't have to do that," I said.

"I shouldn't have. It was stupid to draw attention to us like that. And we should have left separately." He shook his right hand, holding it gingerly.

"Nice work, anyway. Did they cover street fighting on the CPA exam?"

He said nothing but gave me a little smile as I rolled into the van.

I drove home, my head spinning. At a stoplight on PCH, I felt my chest contract, and I was seized with panic. I pulled over to the side of the road, trying to breathe, my hands shaking uncontrollably. I was gripped by the fear that I had just spilled everything to a man I barely knew and who might be my enemy, and that the conversation could land me in prison for a long time. I fumbled in my purse for the bottle of pills I kept for these occasions; I hadn't had to take one in months. But now, with shaking hands, I shook a pill into my hand and dry swallowed it.

Eventually I calmed down and resumed my drive home, thinking about Ritchie. If he wasn't for real, I'd made the worst decision of my life. I'm basically an instinctive decision-maker. Sometimes it paid dividends. But sometimes, as with my decision to blow the whistle on Landrum's "typo," it didn't. How, I wondered, would it work out this time?

Chapter 41

Tuesday

I passed the next day uneasily at the office, trying to focus on my work. But my work didn't require a lot of focus, so a sizable part of my brain was still free to think about Ritchie and Landrum and Keri.

Ritchie and I acknowledged each other perfunctorily at lunch. After eating, I rolled out of the cafeteria, with Ritchie carrying my tray for me. I noticed his right hand was red and puffy. He deposited our trays and said quietly, "Check your purse when you get back to your office. Talk to you later."

I took the elevator up to the seventh floor, and as I got off, I nearly bumped into Marisa Costas. "Hi," I said.

She looked at me with an expression that bordered on alarm, then quickly forced an awkward smile. "Oh, hi."

And that was the extent of our conversation. As she walked away, I wondered how I might have approached her differently. She had been my best prospect for learning what had happened to Keri, and I had let her slip away.

When I got back to my cube, I looked in my purse and found a small burner phone, which Ritchie had slipped inside. I checked the speed dial directory; a single number had been programmed in, with the label "R." It was an addition to my phone collection, which included Pen's cell, Dez's cell, Nomura's burner, and now the dedicated cell for contacting Ritchie. I returned the new phone to my purse, hoping to God that Ritchie was for real.

I was packing up to leave in late afternoon when a call came in to my Dez phone. I didn't recognize the number, but I answered it anyway. "Hello?"

"Hello, Dez?" A young male voice.

"Yes?"

"This is Tim Dalton."

"Oh . . . Hi, Tim."

"How are you?" Awkward.

"I'm fine, thanks."

"Okay. Good. Uh, listen, I'm down in OC, and I'm wondering if you'd like to catch a bite to eat?"

The invitation caught me off guard, and I wasn't sure what to say. Was this self-described don't-give-a-shit screwup, a dozen years my junior, asking me out? Unlikely. Then what did he want? I decided I'd better find out. "That would be nice," I said.

Chapter 42

Special Agent Ward Gilbertson sat at his desk in early evening, staring at a picture on his screen. He knew he should be home with his wife and children. He knew he presumed upon their understanding, their acceptance that an FBI agent was forced to work long and irregular hours. Gilbertson loved his family. But now, he felt compelled to give his attention not to the objects of his love, but to the object of his obsession.

He returned his attention to the screen, to the picture of Special Agent Wendy Nomura. God, she was beautiful, staring at him with that look of seriousness—even severity—that made her flat-out hot. He'd just spent an hour scouring her communications, her activities, her reports, her schedule. Imagining her as she sat at her desk, interviewed witnesses, met with corporate executives.

And plotted to bring him down.

He'd been in denial about it, but PACIFIC had made clear that she was the enemy and had Gilbertson in her sights. She might be working with the inspector general's office, or the top management of the LA field office, or maybe even the leadership of the Counterintelligence or National Security divisions of the FBI in Washington. How did PACIFIC know this? The same way, he imagined, as he himself should have known it, as any objective boss would know it: by looking at the facts that stared him in the face.

Where did she disappear to every night after work? Why had she met with Lieutenant Howard of the Newport Beach police, if not to look further into the mysterious call from murdered attorney Keri Wylie? Why had she seemingly retained an interest in the Bureau's relationship with DSI, a company at which PACIFIC clearly expected to have a free hand to operate? Of course she was working against him.

He mentally went down the list of other agents who might be helping Wendy, but he suspected she was working alone. And he was forced to agree with PACIFIC's conclusion that she wasn't just keeping an eye on him or waiting to trip him up or asking questions about him, but was running an operation. And that op might well involve DSI, to which PACIFIC seemed closely connected.

It was true that he worked for PACIFIC under duress, facing the threat of exposure, disgrace, and prosecution. It was his weakness for women—that was how he'd gotten into this fix in the first place. That girl in Moscow—God, she was hot. And he'd been a long way from home in a cold city, and . . .

The Russians had done it right, setting up the honeypot trap with video, sound, and professionally rendered copies, all ready for delivery to his wife and superiors. As an intelligence professional, he had a grudging admiration for his adversary's skill.

But, blackmail or no, he had to admit that he'd never had a huge problem with working for PACIFIC. In his stint in Counterintelligence before Moscow, Gilbertson had diligently performed his official duties, trying to ferret out and thwart the activities of foreign intelligence agencies and related assets as they attempted to infiltrate the defense industries in southern California. But he'd had no illusions about it. Foreign students and businesspeople would continue to enter the country freely, and he couldn't keep track of all of them. Foreign hackers, working beyond his reach, were going to do their thing. No one forced unhappy or financially squeezed employees of defense contractors to betray their companies—their country—nor could the Bureau easily prevent them from doing so with the resources at hand.

He knew the FBI had been forced by public opinion and Congressional mandate to give priority to the perceived threats of terrorism, specifically Islamic terrorism. And so hundreds of agents had been assigned to combat the threats posed by blowhard imams and disgruntled knuckleheads with Muslim names and their boneheaded loose talk about bombing a church or a public building. Meanwhile, the Russians, Chinese, and North Koreans continued to pick the pockets of the defense establishment. No, Gilbertson's conscience hadn't been unduly troubled by working for PACIFIC.

He returned his gaze to Wendy Nomura, remembering the electric excitement he'd felt from touching her, massaging her shoulders. He imagined touching her all over. Was there no hope with her? Had she totally eluded his grasp? Was there nothing that could bring her around, even for a short time, before his inevitable professional and personal collapse? He felt his rage building as he watched her expression on the screen—placid, judgmental, superior. Who the hell did she think she was? She worked for him, damnit.

He collected himself and looked again at her reports and schedules, hoping to absorb some essence of her. His time was short. PACIFIC had big plans, probably involving DSI in some way. He wondered if more people would have to die to make the plans become a reality. In any event, when the scheme came to fruition, he suspected he would be of little further use to PACIFIC.

Gilbertson had idly considered turning himself in, offering to work against and expose PACIFIC. But it was too late for that, and the danger to his family too great. No, there was no way to redeem himself from the failures, the betrayals. He just had to plow ahead and finish it up.

Chapter 43

Tim Dalton waited for me on the patio at a bar and grill just off Jamboree and PCH in Newport Beach. He hastily got up and moved a chair away so I could roll up to the table. "Thanks," I said.

"Drink?" Tim asked.

"Sure." He signaled a waiter, and I ordered a glass of Chardonnay.

We looked at each other awkwardly for a moment. Then he said, "I suppose you wonder why I invited you."

I gave him a little smile and shrugged.

"Lots of people want to be my friend," he said. "It has nothing to do with me. They know my dad's a CEO. They want a job, or an internship, or a loan, or a contract, or something."

I nodded.

"You did something good for my dad. And you don't seem to want anything from him."

"I guess I don't. It was nice of him to invite me to dinner."

"He wants everybody to like him, and mostly, people do. Anyway, after what you did—with Landrum—you seem like a straight shooter. I—well, I liked talking to you."

"Thanks. I enjoyed it, too."

"I mean, the world is so full of bullshitters. People who try to be something they're not."

I sensed a sharp internal pang that felt a lot like guilt. "You seem like a pretty genuine guy."

He looked embarrassed. "I don't know. I just hate phonies."

I changed the subject. "I imagine your dad is pretty busy with the merger."

Tim nodded. "He's a little stressed. And he has to watch his back, with Landrum scheming against him."

"Has he thought about retiring?"

He shook his head. "I've asked him, and he doesn't seem at all interested in hanging it up. It's almost like he has something important yet to accomplish."

"The Hulbert merger?"

"No, beyond that. He's determined to keep going. I'm not sure why."

"Is he a workaholic?" I asked. "The type who needs to keep busy?"

"Not really. He doesn't live to work. He likes to relax—go sailing or golfing. He always liked just hanging out with Mikayla and me."

It looked as though Tim had just now seen the obvious contradiction. A man with plenty of money and way too much hassle, who liked to live the good life, but who seemed driven to stay at his job.

We ordered burgers. I pulled my sweater around me to ward off the March chill, wishing I was sitting here with James. I still wasn't sure what I was doing here, or why Tim seemed inclined to open up to me. I didn't have any agenda here. But maybe he did.

There's a look that men give women, a look I didn't receive so often anymore. But I could still recognize it, and, improbable as it seemed, I was getting it from Tim. I thought I had noticed it when I'd had dinner with his family; now I was sure.

I tried to lighten the tone. "Well, if Landrum prevails, I guess I'll be unemployed."

He smiled as he chewed his cheeseburger. "I suppose. I don't pay a lot of attention to Dad's business, but I know enough to understand that Landrum's a scumbag who doesn't care about anything except money and power. My dad cares about people."

"About his family," I ventured.

His response was slow and grudging. "Yeah, I guess. More than my mom does, anyway."

"They've been divorced for a while?"

"Eight years. I was never completely sure what their problem was. Mom is more of a quiet type, I guess. She just wanted to stay at home, while Dad was always flying off here and there, for meetings, interviews, speeches. She felt uncomfortable. She and Dad actually got along pretty well for the first few years after the divorce, but then . . ."

"Mikayla," I guessed.

"Yeah." He looked surprised, even though I thought the scenario was pretty obvious. "She blames him for Mikayla's death. And I guess he feels guilty about it, even though I can't see how it was his fault."

"How serious is their rift?" I asked.

"It isn't just them. I haven't seen Mom since Mikayla's memorial service two years ago. She said she just couldn't handle seeing us."

I was shocked. She had abandoned Tim.

"I told you Mikayla and I were close," he said. "That's not really true. I resented her. She was the golden girl. Top grades, great career out of college, tons of friends. Now I feel like shit for resenting her. I always wanted to be closer to her. If only she hadn't been so damn perfect."

"That might have changed over time."

"Mikayla? Nah."

"You never know. Life has a way of turning things around in a hurry."

He nodded, took a bite of his burger, then stopped, turning slowly back toward me, understanding.

"I was Mikayla," I said.

He glanced at the wheelchair. "An accident?"

"A car accident, yes."

He looked at me expectantly. I didn't really want to talk about this. I seldom did. But I had raised the comparison with Mikayla myself.

"I was an achiever," I said. "Strong and athletic and confident."

"Wow. And—"

"And insufferable."

He was silent.

"I had it all. Everything, except character. And that always comes the hard way."

He looked at the wheelchair again. "Pretty hard."

"Yeah."

"And Mikayla?"

"I didn't know her, Tim. Who can tell what might have happened? All I can say is that I'm really, really sorry."

He turned away suddenly, and I saw him brush a tear from his eye with the heel of his hand. I hadn't related to Tim the entire story of my accident. I hadn't told him that the crash had killed my six-year-old niece, Tracy, and that I was partly to blame. Telling him would have breached security, disclosing identifying details about Pen. But more than that, telling him would have meant reliving something that had occupied my consciousness far too much over the years.

Tim walked me to the parking lot after dinner. We hadn't said much of anything after our exchange about Mikayla and my accident. I clicked my key fob, lowering the van's profile, opening up the side door, and extending the ramp. We looked at each other awkwardly.

"Well, thanks," I said.

"Sure. Maybe, well, we could do it again sometime."

I stuffed my guilt a little deeper. "That would be fine."

We weren't sure whether to shake, hug, or whatever, so we settled for little waves. I rolled into the van, maneuvered into place behind the steering wheel, and clamped my wheelchair securely to the floor. Then I waved again and drove away, unsure of exactly what had just happened.

Chapter 44

Wednesday

I was at the sink in the ladies' room at work when Marisa Costas walked in.

"Hi," I said.

"Hi, Dez." She glanced around; we were the room's only occupants. "I saw you come in here."

I reached for a towel from the dispenser, but came up just short, as I often did. Marisa pulled out a towel for me.

"Thanks."

She nodded. "You asked a couple of weeks back if I wanted to talk about Keri."

"I just imagined talking might help you feel better."

"I wasn't sure why you offered to listen," she said. "I'm still not. But after the incident with the typo, I could tell you were no friend of Landrum. I was thinking maybe you might be someone I could trust."

"I'd like to think so."

"Could we get together? Maybe tonight?"

I hesitated, trying to think of a way we could meet without being followed or spotted. "Do you know the Publix store on PCH?" I asked.

"Sure."

"There's a deli area in the back, with tables and chairs."

"Right."

"Tonight at eight?"

"Fine." She left, and I followed a couple of minutes later.

Back at my desk, I found it hard to concentrate. Was this a breakthrough? I tried not to get my hopes up. I thought

186

about calling Ritchie but decided to hear what Marisa had to say first.

My Dez phone buzzed. I pulled it out of my purse and glanced at the screen. I didn't recognize the number.

"Hello?"

"Hi, Dez. This is Jackie Soares."

I hesitated, trying to place the name and the slight accent.

"Pat Dalton's friend," she prompted.

"Oh, sure. How are you?"

"I'm great, thanks. Listen, I just wanted to tell you again how much we enjoyed having you over the other night."

"I enjoyed it, too."

"I talked to Pat, and we're wondering if you'd like to come down on Friday and spend the weekend with us?"

"That's really kind of you," I said, wondering why on earth they would want me. I suspected it was Tim's doing. It might be fun, but having fun wasn't my primary goal as my project wound down. Still, when the request came from your company's CEO, it was as much a summons as an invitation.

"Sure," I said.

*   *   *

I headed for the elevator at five-thirty, anxious to get home and leave myself plenty of time to prepare for tonight's clandestine meeting. I hoped Marisa had something useful to tell me. If not, I'd be nothing more than a disappointed grief counselor, at a virtual dead end. I was almost to the elevator when I saw a vaguely familiar figure approaching from the opposite direction.

I froze. It was Laura Dixon.

I swerved into a little hallway to the right of the elevator alcove, which led to the stairwell and nothing else. There was no plausible reason for me to be there, and of course I couldn't get away via the stairs. My heart was beating out of control as I watched Laura, who was talking to another woman, wait for the elevator. I prayed she wouldn't turn in my direction. I glanced back quickly—she hadn't noticed me. I grabbed the wheels of my chair tightly.

The bell for the elevator rang. I glanced back again, and when Laura got on, I shot around the corner before she turned around toward the closing door. She might have gotten a glimpse of me. But maybe not. Either way, there was nothing to be done about it now.

I hid in the bathroom for ten minutes, then slowly, carefully, made my way out of the building and headed for home.

Chapter 45

Viktor Kamensky was getting edgy. Something was going on with Dez Walker, but he couldn't figure it out. First, she'd disappeared for a weekend. Then she'd come back, and two evenings later had gone out for dinner with a man who had to be ten years her junior. He'd taken a picture of the young man and sent it to PACIFIC for identification. And then there was the man who may or may not have followed Walker home to her apartment, a man who had a boat equipped with a wheelchair lift. That was really too much. Somebody was messing with him, making him look like an ass. Again.

Kamensky pulled in at the parking lot of the marina on Bayside Drive. He took out his binoculars and focused them on the *Alicia C,* the boat with the lift. The vessel didn't appear to be occupied, although he wouldn't necessarily have expected anybody to be there on a weekday. He looked around and thought he saw movement on the boat at the next slip, a similar vessel called the *Kirsten D.* He settled back to wait.

He idly pulled out his phone and looked at the picture of Vanya, wondering if he'd ever see the boy again. Sometimes he wondered if he belonged back in Moscow, with a family—with Vanya—doing what normal people did. Would it be better than sitting in cars, watching people? Better than stalking people?

Killing people?

A pointless question, he decided. He was here, and he wasn't going anywhere.

The marina wasn't a big one, and no one arrived or left during the next hour. Kamensky felt his gaze wandering over to Balboa Island, just a short distance across Newport Bay. A wealthy, peaceful place. He really did love LA.

After about an hour, he again spotted movement aboard the *Kirsten D.* A couple of minutes later, someone disembarked and began walking down the dock toward the parking lot.

Kamensky left the car and intercepted the guy as he came through the security gate to the lot. "Excuse me, sir?"

A fit-looking man in his early fifties, with thinning gray hair and glasses, looked up. "Yes?"

The Russian produced phony credentials identifying him as an Orange County sheriff's deputy. "Just a few routine questions."

"About what?"

"About the owner of the boat next to yours."

"The *Alicia C.*?"

"Yes. What's the owner's name?"

"James Carter."

"How well do you know him?"

"Reasonably well," the guy said. "We've been neighbors for a number of years."

"What does he do for a living?"

"James runs his own venture capital business."

"I notice he has a handicap lift on the dock next to his boat."

They guy gave him a puzzled look, then, "Oh, right."

"How long has it been there?"

The man shrugged. "A few years, I guess. I'm not sure exactly."

"Why does he have it?"

"It doesn't get a lot of use. His elderly mother is in a wheelchair. She visits maybe a time or two a year."

"Does anyone else use it?"

"Not that I know of."

"What is Mr. Carter's domestic situation? Is he married?"

"Divorced."

"Is he dating anyone?"

"No one regularly, as far as I know."

"Does he see anyone at an apartment up on Superior?"

"Could be. I don't know."

Frustrated, Kamensky closed his notebook. "All right. Thank you." He stalked off.

*   *   *

Hal Dwyer watched the deputy's car disappear down the street. Dwyer had snapped a picture and noted the guy's license number. He had little doubt the man was a phony; the would-be "deputy" hadn't even asked Dwyer's name or left a card. He'd been interested in James, and ultimately, in Pen. That couldn't be a good thing. Dwyer had recommended Pen for an undercover assignment, and now it looked as though security on the project might have been breached. He pulled out his phone to call Wendy Nomura.

Chapter 46

I left for the supermarket at 7:30. I usually did my grocery shopping in the evening, when the traffic and crowds had died down, and sometimes the employees had time to help me. As Pen, I had largely switched to online ordering with home delivery. But Dez needed to get out occasionally, especially tonight. I pulled out onto Superior, hoping nobody was following me. But I knew I wouldn't be able to tell; I wasn't a trained field agent, and I didn't have Nomura covering me. I wanted to keep the meeting with Marisa to myself for now. I didn't want Nomura all over me with questions and second-guessing. I'd have to assume I was being watched, or that my vehicle was being tracked.

I'd talked briefly to Ritchie on the burner phone he'd given me. "You didn't have to punch those guys out at the bar," I'd said. "I had it all under control."

"I knew you wouldn't be grateful. All I got for my troubles was a sore hand. Just to be sure, I ran the plates on those knuckleheads' vehicles. It wasn't a setup; they were just garden variety ornery drunks."

I'd never considered the possibility that the encounter had been staged. I was just glad nobody had called the police.

"Encouraging news about Marisa," he'd said. "Let me know what she says."

"I will."

There were still quite a few customers at the supermarket. I rolled inside and began a cumbersome procedure I'd given some thought to on the way over. First, I managed to grab a cart inside the entrance and drag it with me into the store. The idea was to move it to a safe place, where I could use it as a collection point. I was pulling the cart when an older man approached. "Can I help you with that?" he asked.

"Thanks," I said. "Could you put it over there by the organic vegetables?"

The man complied, placing the cart where it could be seen through the big front windows. I nodded my thanks, then picked out a head of lettuce and put it in the cart. I didn't really want the lettuce, but it would deter an employee from returning an abandoned cart. I went back to the entrance and picked up a basket, which I placed on my lap. As I left with the basket, I glanced out into the parking lot, hoping nobody was watching me but assuming someone might be. I made my way to the back of the store, picking out a couple of items and putting them into the basket. Since I have long legs, my knees stick up, allowing things to sit fairly securely on my lap without the threat of sliding off. I returned to the produce area and transferred the items to the cart, then left again for the interior of the store.

I didn't really shop this way. I seldom bought more than a single basket of groceries on one trip. But the procedure seemed plausible, and I hoped it might buy me some time if anybody was watching me.

*   *   *

In the parking lot, Kamensky watched as Dez Walker dragged her cart into the store, then came back to the entrance for a basket. Then she took the basket deeper into the store, out of sight. Presumably she'd return to the cart after collecting some items. He waited; she was taking a long time. But eventually she returned, depositing several items, before disappearing again. He didn't expect that she'd be holding a secret meeting in the store, but in truth, he'd nearly given up trying to figure what the hell she was up to.

*   *   *

I took the basket and headed directly for the back of the store, where Marisa Costas sat at one of the deli tables. We were the only people in the seating area.

"Hi," I said.

"Hi."

"Let's sit at that table." I pointed to a location behind a tall cooler, where we wouldn't easily be seen by anyone who wasn't in the deli.

I rolled up to the table, and Marisa helped me move a chair to one side as I rolled up to sit across from her. She looked as striking as ever, but she had, I thought, yet to develop the kind of mature, refined beauty that Wendy Nomura had. "Thanks for coming," I said. "I'm afraid I don't have a lot of time."

"I'm sorry about unloading on you. I'd like to talk to somebody about Keri, and I just don't know who I can trust."

"What did you tell the police?"

"Nothing. They never interviewed me."

I was stunned. "Why not?"

"I guess they didn't think I would know anything useful."

"They talked to other people she worked with, didn't they?"

"Yes, but I didn't work with her."

"You were her friend."

"I'm not sure how many people actually knew that. I was only administrative staff—maybe it never occurred to them that we'd be very close. They talked to a few attorneys and managers, but that was it. I'd known Keri a little bit in high school. She had been a friend of my older sister. But when we started working at the same company, on the same floor, we became closer. She knew I didn't want anything from her. I wasn't a rival. I wanted her to succeed. And she mentored me, wanted me to go back to school, to finish my degree. I was making plans to do that when she died."

"What would you have told the police?"

"First, I need to know I can trust you."

"Trust me to do what?"

"Not to tell anybody."

I studied her. "Marisa, if you have information that's relevant to Keri's death, withholding it is not an option."

"I don't know if it's relevant. I thought—well, you have some legal training, right? Maybe you'd know if I need to tell the police?"

"I'm not a lawyer. The police should decide whether it's relevant or not."

"But . . ."

I waited.

"But I'm scared."

I wanted to tell her we'd get to the bottom of it, that I wouldn't rest until we found out who'd killed her friend. But I was just a paralegal named Dez. "All I can say is that I'll listen and help you in any way I can."

She bit her lower lip.

"You'll have to excuse me for a minute," I said. "I'll be right back."

*   *   *

Kamensky was about ready to go into the store. Dez hadn't returned to the cart in the organic produce area by the entrance. What was she doing in there? He doubted she was holding a clandestine meeting. But his employer was paying him to be thorough, and if he had to risk being spotted by Dez or by a surveillance camera, so be it. He got out of his vehicle and started walking toward the store. He was about to enter through the automatic doors when Dez appeared around a corner, basket in her lap. He ducked to the side, behind a pillar. The paralegal placed the items from the basket into the cart, then disappeared back around a corner. Kamensky returned to his car.

*   *   *

195

I wheeled through the store, throwing random items into my basket, then returned to my cart and transferred the basket's contents. I felt silly, acting so paranoid. But I thought of Keri, who hadn't been paranoid enough.

Marisa waited patiently for me back in the deli. "Sorry," I said. "Now, what do you think might be relevant about Keri?"

"She was suspicious of Paul Landrum."

"Why?"

"She seemed to think he was living a double life somehow, that he wasn't what he seemed to be."

"In what way?"

"She told me once — and this was after a couple of margaritas — that she thought Landrum was connected to the Russians."

"When was this?"

"Only a few days before she died."

"What made her suspect a Russian connection?"

"She wouldn't say. She always thought Landrum was a little strange."

"Why?"

"For one thing, he has a weird relationship with his wife. Keri said it's common knowledge that Landrum lives in the guest house whenever he's at home. Meanwhile, Irina has plenty of, um, visitors. Apparently, Landrum knows this and doesn't care."

"An open marriage or arrangement of some kind?"

"It would be a one-sided arrangement. If Landrum is seeing other women, no one knows about it."

All this was suspicious, I thought, but it was far short of conclusive, damning evidence and provided no motive for murder. I pulled several sheets of paper out of my purse and handed them to Marisa. "These were found in Keri's office."

Marisa examined the pages of notes I had found. "This is Keri's handwriting, but I can't make any sense of them."

I returned the notes to my purse. "I don't know, Marisa."

"I know," she said. "I mean, it's not evidence of anything, is it?"

Even less was it proof that Landrum was "not who he appeared to be," I thought.

"Wait," she said. "There's something else I was going to show you."

I glanced out into the store. I was taking longer than I should have. "Go ahead."

"The legal department has a little library. It's hardly ever used anymore, because everything's online. But Keri liked to work in there; it was quiet and private. A couple of days after she died, I happened to be walking by the library, and I decided, just on impulse, to go in. There were a couple of books on the table that hadn't been reshelved."

"What were the books?"

"I don't remember, but there was a sheet of scratch paper lying next to them. I don't know if it had anything to do with the books or not." Marisa dug through her purse, pulled out a crumpled notebook page, and handed it to me. "This is Keri's handwriting."

The sheet contained the handwritten notation: "17 180.1." Below the notation was a name: "Elena."

"Who's Elena?" I asked. "And what are these numbers?"

"I don't know."

"It looks like there's a space between the '17' and the '180.1.'"

"Yes, but I don't know what that means. I almost threw this away. I'm not sure why I kept it, or even why I went into the library that day—just to be in Keri's space a little bit, I guess."

"You'll have to talk to the police about this, Marisa."

She looked scornfully at me. "Haven't I just been doing that? You have to be a cop, or an investigator of some kind."

I shook my head. "Marisa, why on earth didn't the police question you?"

"Why? *Why?* Because I'm a nobody. A secretary. Just a bimbo who doesn't understand a lot of big words. If the cops don't think I'm worth their time, if they expect me to go crawling in there and try to convince them I'm worth listening to, they can go to hell."

We looked at each other, stunned. I didn't know which of us was more surprised. She had issues, I realized. As a younger woman considered pretty, I'd been ignored and disrespected plenty of times and weathered my share of blonde jokes. My law degree helped to some extent. But mostly, I was fortunate to be self-assured enough to shake them off, and assertive enough to demand the respect I deserved. Marisa wasn't there yet.

She sobbed silently, wiping her eyes with a tissue. "Marisa," I said quietly, taking her hand across the table, "I know the detective in charge of the investigation. You'll be treated with respect and taken seriously, I promise you."

She nodded, tears still streaming down. "Nail Landrum," she said. "For what he did to Keri. For being a pig. For being a rich bastard. Just nail him." She stood up and stalked out of the store.

"Wait," I said. But she was gone.

*   *   *

It was time, Kamensky decided. Walker had been in the store forever. He walked briskly toward the building and approached the produce department. The cart was gone. He headed cautiously for the checkout counter, and in one of the only two open aisles, he saw Dez placing her groceries on the belt. He glanced around.

"Excuse me." A hot-looking young blonde brushed past him on her way out the door. His gaze followed her as she walked out to the parking lot and disappeared to the right. He glanced back toward Dez, who hadn't spotted him and continued checking out. Then it hit him: The blonde had not bought anything. Had she been meeting with Dez?

He would have bet on it.

He hurried out the door, but the attractive young woman was nowhere to be seen. *Damn* it. Had he just been had? He continued walking, scanning the lot. *There.* A Kia sedan was making its way toward the exit. It had to be her. He was just close enough to make out her license plate.

He returned to his car, preparing to follow Dez home.

*   *   *

The clerk finished bagging up my groceries, nearly eighty dollars' worth. I wouldn't need most of it, but maybe the information from Marisa would be worth the cost. About the only solid lead she'd given me, however, was the note she'd found in the legal department's library. And that might easily be nothing. I followed another clerk as he took my groceries out to the van, my mind swirling.

I found it hard to believe that the police had never talked to Marisa, but her explanation had been plausible. They had gone into the office and talked to the attorneys, managers and people in Keri's department. And Marisa's name hadn't come up. How else would they have known Marisa was a friend? At some point, I'd have to break my word and tell Howard about her, but Marisa didn't really have that much to tell. She'd confirmed that Keri suspected a Russia-Landrum connection. Otherwise, the meeting with her had been a bust; there was nothing conclusive on Landrum. True, I now had the note from the library to follow up. I just hoped I had enough time.

Chapter 47

Kamensky was sitting in his car, watching Dez Walker's apartment, when PACIFIC called. "We identified the man Dez went to dinner with," the handler said. "His name is Tim Dalton."

"Dalton . . ."

"His father is Pat Dalton. The CEO of DSI."

"What the hell was she doing, meeting with him?"

"We don't know, but it's obviously a huge red flag."

"Do you think Dalton planted her in her job?"

"I doubt it," PACIFIC answered. "If spying was really Dalton's objective, he would have planted somebody at Techinvest."

"So then, what?" Kamensky asked. "He's rewarding her?"

"Could be. But we need to know. This woman is a phony. Find out who she is and what she wants."

"I will."

"Anything new on her?"

"As a matter of fact, yes. There's a plate number I need you to check out."

*   *   *

"Is there any doubt it was Kamensky?" ADC Kirk Hendricks asked.

Wendy Nomura produced a blowup of a grainy cell phone picture of a man in a car, taken by Hal Dwyer at the marina on Bayside Drive. She swiveled the laptop on the conference table for the ADC to look at.

Hendricks peered at the photo. "It's him."

Wendy nodded.

Hendricks leaned back in his chair in the windowless conference room. "So he asked about Carter, the wheelchair lift, who Carter was dating, and the building on Superior Drive."

"Yes. Hal's response—"

"I'm sure he covered it well. But there are too many points of connection. We have to consider her blown."

She said nothing.

"Wendy, your efforts have been heroic. You've done it on your own. But in any op, you have to know when it's time to go home."

She stared at him, stunned. "Where do we go from here?"

"We still have a crisis on our hands. I'm counting on you to keep at it, to think of something."

"But Pen—"

He stood up. "She's done."

Chapter 48

Thursday

I left work at my normal time. As I went out the main gate, I took a different route home, west toward Bolsa Chica, Warner, and ultimately PCH. My route included a couple of detours. Following the instructions Nomura had given me, I made a right turn, into a parking lot belonging to a funeral home. A high wall of shrubbery screened the lot from the street. A tan sedan pulled in beside me.

Wendy Nomura got out of the car, came over, and got into the van's passenger seat. "You're clean," she said. "Nobody suspicious behind you."

"All right."

"We should still make it quick." She kept glancing toward the road, and I wondered if she knew something I didn't.

"Has the surveillance cam spotted anything?"

"No. But of course, it's focused on the building itself, not the periphery. We have to assume they're watching."

"I guess."

"What do you have for me?" she asked.

I told her about Keri's vague suspicions about a Landrum-Russia connection. Predictably, she was unimpressed. "That takes us a bit further. But we need to know *how* she saw a connection—what the actual connection is."

"I know."

"Look, Pen, there are half a dozen ways Marisa's story could be wrong. But even if it's right, I just don't see how it makes Landrum 'not who he appears to be,' nor would it provide a reason to kill her."

I said nothing. She was right.

"And," she added, "Marisa said he doesn't get along with his current wife—well, he apparently didn't get along with the first one, either."

Right again.

"Do you have anything else we should consider?" she asked.

"Just the question I asked the other day: Who financed Landrum's hedge fund when it was started?"

"I'm doing a discreet search on the files. So far, I've seen no evidence of any Russian connection over the years."

"Maybe that was the idea."

She studied me, and I imagined her wondering if I'd come across some information independently, which of course I had, from Courtney Stapleton. "I don't know, Pen. The search isn't complete yet. But without subpoenas and document production —without the involvement and knowledge of Landrum—it would be really hard. And sensitive."

"I understand." A normal inquiry could alert people in the FBI who couldn't be trusted.

"Pen, I need to know where you got this information, on the capital for the hedge fund."

"It's just a hunch."

"I think you learned something in Minnesota. Out with it."

"How about this: You tell me about your backup for this operation, and I'll tell you my source."

"The two issues are different."

"Yes, they are. Your withholding of information affects my safety. Mine doesn't."

We eyed each other. I was playing with fire; if Nomura reported to O'Shea that I was being uncooperative, he could make my life a living hell.

"I told you I'd look into it," she said at last.

"Thank you."

"Anything else?"

I shook my head.

She paused, adopting a serious look. I had a feeling she was about to get to the real purpose of our meeting. "Pen, what did you tell James about the project?"

"Just that it was secret, and that I was undercover and wouldn't be in contact until next week." I had told him that Paul Landrum was the target, but I wasn't going to admit that to Nomura. I'd be in trouble if I told her, but I also wanted to avoid any trouble for James.

"It has to be something about that trip to Minnesota," she said. "Somehow, they know about James."

I tried to harness my breathing. "What do you mean, they 'know about him'?"

"Viktor Kamensky showed up at the marina where James docks his boat. He asked about James, his boat, and the handicap lift. He also asked if James knew anyone who lived up the hill, off Superior."

My stomach convulsed, and for a moment I feared I might lose it.

"Fortunately," she continued, "he talked to Hal, who apparently succeeded at throwing him off the track, at least for now. But where did Kamensky get the lead? How did he make the connection?"

I gripped the steering wheel with both hands. "I don't know. I really have no idea, Wendy. You followed us to the airport. I suppose he might have been waiting for me when I got back, but James drove separately. We separated at the gate. You know that."

Nomura nodded. "I know. But I'm afraid this is the end of the line, Pen. Security has been breached. We're pulling you out."

"You're pulling—what?"

"The project is over, effective as of this moment."

I couldn't speak.

"Nobody is angry or dissatisfied with you. In fact, we were impressed with your efforts. But having you continue is too big a risk; when you set foot outside the office, we can't protect you."

"Wendy, you can't do this."

"It's done." She opened her door. "There will be paperwork. We'll ask you to write a complete report. We've rented the condo for another two weeks, but you need to get out as soon as possible and stay away. I think it's safe to say there'll be a sizable financial bonus for you. We'll be in touch in a couple of days to clean up the details."

I just stared at her, feeling as though a massive weight was crushing me.

"One more thing," she said. "I'll need your phone."

I pulled the Dez phone from my purse as the full impact of her request hit me. She wouldn't be tracking my phone anymore. She wouldn't be on speed dial. There wouldn't be a panic button. Our connection was being cut, physically as well as legally.

I handed the phone over.

She started to get out, then looked back. "I'm sorry, Pen."

*   *   *

Two blocks down the street, sitting in a newly rented sedan, Viktor Kamensky craned his neck, peering down the road, confirming that he had seen what he had seen. Wendy Nomura was good—very good. She'd eluded him for a long time. But nobody was perfect all the time, and Kamensky had never given up. Following the tracker on Dez's van, he had seen the vehicle come to a stop. As always, he'd approached slowly. And just as he'd arrived at the scene, he'd spotted a familiar tan car pulling back onto the road. She'd met with Dez and waited an instant too long to leave. Now, here was the connection he and his superiors had sought for so long: Special Agent Wendy Nomura meeting with paralegal Desiree Walker. He grinned. He could now report to

PACIFIC that he hadn't gone soft in LaLa Land. He'd done his job. It would be up to his boss to decide what happened next.

*   *   *

Nomura left, and I sat in the van by myself, trying to empty my mind of racing thoughts, hoping that the panic attack I felt coming on would subside. I did my breathing and relaxation exercises, and eventually I regained my equilibrium. It took every ounce of willpower I possessed to keep from calling James and telling him to get out of town—get out of the *country*—and hide, that a murderous Russian thug was on to him. But I knew it was futile. You couldn't really hide from the Russians, as the murders of their own dissidents outside Russia had proven. And any rash actions by James would merely confirm the Russians' suspicions. I hoped that maybe Hal Dwyer had discreetly told James to be careful. I would have given anything to know how they'd found James.

I sat and thought for a while longer, letting the incredible truth sink in: I was done, just like that. I went back over my conversation with Nomura. I'd wanted to tell her I was close to a breakthrough. But I wasn't.

There had to be some important things Nomura wasn't telling me. But the reverse was also true. Most importantly, of course, I hadn't told her about my cooperation with Clay Ritchie. I'd also withheld a couple of longshot clues that could be pursued—the notes from Keri's office and the paper Marisa had found in the law library. I didn't regret withholding these things from Nomura. I trusted her, but I also had a nagging fear that the FBI had a serious security problem. If my leads got passed along prematurely or to the wrong person . . . I didn't want Marisa to end up like Keri.

But none of that mattered now.

I drove back to Newport Beach, up the hill, and into the parking lot of Dez's building. But Dez didn't exist anymore. I wasn't really supposed to be here. I wasn't even sure the video feed was still being monitored. And whatever protection Nomura had been giving me had ended. I was on my own.

Inside, I sat with my trusty wine bottle, looking out over Balboa Peninsula, trying to think about my future. But I still needed to process my present—my failure; my deception; the things undone; the questions unanswered. I needed to just let it all go.

I drank some more. And thought some more. And considered the risks. And thought about Keri.

And decided I was not done.

Chapter 49

Dez lived, at least for now. I went into work knowing there was a good chance I'd been discovered. I kept waiting for Les Hornsby to show up at my cube and unmask me or arrest me or something. When I somehow managed to stop worrying about that, I worried about James. And when I managed to leave that subject behind, I worried about all the trouble I could be in for defying the FBI and continuing to work under-cover. Of course, whatever time I spent worrying, I didn't spend figuring out the mysterious notes Keri had left behind in her office.

Unable to keep my mind on work, I discreetly pulled out the notes and looked at them again. There were two photocopied sheets; the police presumably still had the originals. The words and numbers were jumbled and didn't seem to make any sense. I tried to concentrate.

Eventually, I noted thirteen numbers that might have been dates. All started with a 9, 10, 11, or 12—presumably September, October, November, and December. Each date—if it was a date —was followed by several numbers that didn't make any sense to me. There were other notes, and for nearly all of them, I either couldn't make sense of the abbreviations they apparently repre-sented or couldn't read the handwriting. I went back to the first possible date I'd seen: 9/7. There was no indication of a year. I looked at my calendar for last year and saw that 9/7 was a Friday. I squinted further at the notes underneath and thought I could make out the letters "Teter," a word or abbreviation that meant nothing to me.

I moved to the next date on the list: 9/19. A Wednesday. Not a weekend. And no "Teter," or any other letters, following. The next date was 10/5. Another Friday. Again, a series of numbers followed, but no indication of a possible location. I moved down the list. The sixth date, 10/25, had a notation that could have been "Exec KPWK." The very next date, 11/2, was a Friday. It was followed by numbers, along with "Teter." That word again.

The ninth date, 11/20, was followed by the letters "Oak." The next date, Friday, 11/30, once again indicated "Tet." The remaining two dates were in the first half of December. I studied the notes for a while longer, trying unsuccessfully to pick out a pattern, or some indication of what the additional symbols, numbers, and notations were.

"Dez?"

I looked up suddenly, thrusting the notes to one side. Bart Crosby stood behind me. He'd been watching as I studied the notes. Now I looked guilty as hell. I composed myself and smiled. "Can I help you with something, Bart?"

He studied me without expression for a few seconds, then walked away.

I waited for a couple of minutes while my heart rate returned to normal. I'd been working on the notes for a long time and had lost awareness of my surroundings. I looked back at the notes; I had no idea what Bart thought about my studying them. That depended, I thought, on whether he'd somehow been involved in Keri's murder. If he hadn't, he might be mildly annoyed at me for goofing off on company time. But if he had . . . I was dead.

I didn't spend much time worrying about Bart. I needed results, and with only a few days left until closing, I decided to press my luck. I dug out the handwritten sheet Marisa had found in the law library. I spent only a few seconds comparing it to the notes I had been studying; they looked to be written by the same person, but the numbers didn't appear to match up. As far as I could tell, the two items didn't have anything to do with each other.

I looked at the notations on the crumpled sheet again: "17 180.1," and "Elena." I still didn't have a clue who Elena was. But I wondered if the numbers found in the law library might be a legal citation of some kind. I rolled out of my cubicle and down the corridor, glancing around and keeping, as always, a wary eye out for Laura Dixon. But nobody saw me enter the little library.

I flipped on the light and got my bearings. There were four shelves, stretching to the ceiling, and a small work table and chair. I studied the shelves, looking for anything that might give me a clue to Keri's thought process when she had written the note. Or maybe she had written the note before coming here and had brought it along as a guide to looking something up. The shelves contained a legal encyclopedia, along with reference books and dictionaries. There were several legal periodicals, with current editions sitting on display shelves and back copies underneath. Taking up another block of shelves was the US Code, an entire set of federal laws.

I looked back at the numbers on Keri's note, which began with a "17." I noted again that the "17" seemed to be separate from the "180.1." and wondered if it could be referring to Title 17 of the US Code. I looked for the volume containing Title 17 and saw to my dismay that it was on an upper shelf, out of my reach. I thought of asking Marisa or Ritchie to come and help me, but I didn't want to be seen in here with either of them. Keri might have preferred the dusty old books, but I'd have to check out the citation the new-fashioned way. I pulled out my phone and did a Google search on 17 USC 180.1.

The search results were curious. They showed not a US code citation, but a section of the Code of Federal Regulations. The CFR consisted of regulations put out by federal agencies to flesh out the laws enacted by Congress. Chapter 17 started with rules put out by the Commodity Futures Trading Commission. I recalled that Paul Landrum had made much of his fortune through commodity trading and still produced significant income from it.

Ding, ding, ding.

The section at 17 CFR 180.1 was entitled, "Prohibition on the employment, or attempted employment, of manipulative and deceptive devices." The regulation contained broad anti-fraud language, similar to that found in Rule 10b (5) of the Securities and Exchange Commission, which outlawed fraudulent dealings in the stock market. Unfortunately, the language was broad enough that I couldn't tell what Landrum might have done to run afoul of the law. Employing a manipulative or deceptive device wouldn't exactly make him a freakish outlier in the investment business.

I opened the library door, glanced down the corridor, and eased my way out, my heart pounding. Back at my desk, I thought about what I'd learned. I realized I was making some rash assumptions. It was a big leap to assume that Keri had discovered some type of commodities trading fraud by Landrum.

But of course she had. Some things you just know.

Chapter 50

I sat at the window in my apartment at 5:30 PM. My ride to the Daltons' wouldn't arrive for another half hour. I would rather have driven myself, to avoid being stuck there without any independent means of leaving. But being transported by professionals in a secure vehicle sounded good, so I'd accepted Jackie's offer of a ride. Despite all the huge worries and unanswered questions churning through my consciousness, I found myself relaxing a little, looking forward to being in a place where I'd be safe for a couple of days.

The invitation was something new for me; I didn't do a lot of weekending at the Hamptons or Nantucket or San Clemente. I suspected the Daltons simply wanted me to hang out with Tim, and I supposed wealthy people could do that—just order up people to be brought to them, like room service. I had no reason to believe Pat Dalton wanted anything more than for me to be a friend to his son. But for all I knew, maybe Dalton, like Landrum, wasn't what he seemed, either.

While I waited, I used my Pen phone to call Lieutenant Howard. "Pen," he said. "I heard they pulled the plug on you."

"That's right," I said. "I'm done at DSI. But I'm wondering if you might have time to get together."

"Why?"

"I'd like to see a list of Keri's phone calls."

"Because . . ."

"Because I've met a number of people over the past few weeks. I might recognize a name or two that you didn't."

"I don't know, Pen . . ."

"I'd also like to see the pictures of people coming off the Peninsula after the murder, for the same reason. I might recognize a face."

"I don't think it's a great idea."

"Lieutenant, you're not prolonging a terminated operation. I'm just a witness you should interview. Why not see if I learned something that might help you?"

Silence.

"And I'm more than just a Joe Blow CI. I was a prosecutor, trained in sifting and evaluating evidence. You need a break; what do you have to lose?"

He was silent for another long moment. "All right. It will probably have to be Monday."

"I'll talk to you then."

My next call was the result of a difficult decision. I didn't want to deceive Clay Ritchie but was crossing a very dangerous line by continuing to work undercover at DSI. If Ritchie knew about it, he could be deemed complicit. He might be in almost as much trouble as I would be. I'd warn him but wouldn't tell him the op had ended, at least not yet.

I pulled out my Ritchie phone and punched in the single speed dial number. "Dez," he answered. "Any big breakthroughs?"

"I wish. But the only big news is that I might be blown." I told him, without mentioning James's name or going into any details, that Kamensky had somehow made a connection between my two identities.

"But you say he's been diverted?" Ritchie asked.

"For now. But they could identify me at any time, if they haven't already."

"So we'll have to watch our backs even more carefully. Did you find out anything from Marisa?"

I didn't want to tell him about the note from the law library —not yet. "I just have some thoughts I need to pull together."

"Come on, Dez. Why the mystery?"

"No mystery. I'll touch base with you over the weekend."

"All right. Call me if you come up with anything."

"I will."

*   *   *

The SUV arrived promptly at six, brought by the same guy who'd driven me last time. He apparently did have the power of speech after all, and I finally got a name out of him (it was Neil).

And I was still Dez. Even though the Daltons' invitation was a social one, I planned on going back to work at DSI on Monday, and this weekend, I considered myself very much on the job.

"How long have you worked for Mr. Dalton?" I asked Neil.

"About four years."

"Were you in law enforcement?"

"Military. Served in army intel in Afghanistan. Three deployments."

"What made you go into private security work?"

His smile, which I spotted in his rearview mirror, was faint and a little sheepish. "I got tired of the financial struggle. We had a toddler and another kid on the way."

Neil returned to silent mode—vigilant and professional—for the rest of the ride. We crept along through the Friday afternoon rush-hour traffic, and I saw him checking his rearview mirror frequently. It was nearly 7:00 when we finally pulled in at the circle drive, and another security guy came over and helped Neil lift me out of the vehicle into my chair.

A maid came out and took my overnight bag into the house, and I rolled along the breezeway to the rear patio. The huge terrace was subtly and tastefully illuminated by lamps, seen and unseen. The night had grown cool, but heating towers solved that problem. Money could solve a lot of problems, I reflected. But usually not the important ones.

Jackie Soares appeared almost immediately, greeting me warmly. "So nice of you to come, Dez."

"I appreciate the invitation."

She gestured to a little desk off to the far side of the terrace, where Pat Dalton sat in front of a laptop, talking on the phone. "You'll have to forgive Pat this weekend. He'll be working quite a bit, with people coming and going. The closing is only five days away."

"Of course," I said, but the words hit me like a two-by-four. Five days to try to figure this situation out. I was about to spend two of them doing nothing, and I might be caught at any time, by either the bad guys or the FBI.

Jackie excused herself to see to dinner and gestured toward Tim, who was sitting across the terrace in the same spot where we'd talked before, scrolling on his phone. I approached him. "Hi," I said.

He looked up suddenly and stashed the phone. "Oh, hi." He rose briefly and awkwardly shook my hand, then sat down again, as if recovering himself and realizing he was supposed to be cool, surly and detached. I suppressed a laugh.

We made small talk about the traffic and the weather and the idiot customers at the coffee shop where he worked and one of his pain-in-the-ass roommates. I mostly just listened; what else could I do? My past was phony, and my present was secret. Eventually Gloria, the maid, called us to dinner.

Tonight's meal was held inside in a huge dining room, decorated in Newport style with bleached colors and a nautical theme. The three of us sat at one end of the long table, and we were soon joined by Pat Dalton, who'd changed to khakis and a polo shirt. He gave me a distracted greeting and said little as we began the meal. We began with a shrimp salad and eventually moved on to grilled swordfish. I enjoyed the same Portuguese wine I'd had during my first visit and had to be careful not to drink too much. Tim drank beer.

The small talk continued. Jackie, it turned out, was an artist of some local notoriety, and she talked about the opening of a show she was putting on in a gallery in Laguna Beach next weekend. "We'd love to have you come, Dez," she said.

"Sure. I'd love to." Except that next weekend I'd no longer be Dez Walker. I'd be Pen Wilkinson, living in Long Beach, unemployed, and licking my wounds from the failure of my assignment.

Pat Dalton excused himself before the sorbet and coffee was served, and after dessert Tim and I went back outside. The evening chill and the breeze carrying the smell of the sea woke me up, counteracting the meal and the wine. We sat for a few minutes in silence, just listening to the wind and the crashing of the surf. I was almost able to relax.

"I can't think of anything to talk about," Tim said at last. "I know I'm boring."

"Don't say that," I scolded.

"It's true."

"No, it's not true. Tim, listen to me: There are plenty of people in the world who are ready to run you down. Don't join them. You don't have to be able to make small talk with somebody you barely know in order to be an interesting and worthwhile person."

He managed a weak smile. "You sound like a self-help guru or something."

"No, I'm just speaking from experience, that's all."

"Anyway," he said, "I'm getting to know you a little bit, right? We have the rest of the weekend. Maybe it will get a little easier."

I gave him an uneasy smile, wondering just how well he wanted to know me.

The guest room I was shown to turned out to be a palatial suite bigger than my entire apartment, either the actual version or the phony one. Its accessibility wasn't ideal, but that was made up for by its sheer spaciousness. I got ready for bed, then rolled over to a set of French doors leading out to a balcony. I opened the door and spent a couple of minutes just taking in the dark infinity of the Pacific. Then I closed the door, leaving it open just a bit to let in the sound of the surf.

I laid out stuff from my overnight bag and took my phone out of my purse for charging. Glancing at my screen, I saw that I'd received a text. The sender of the text wasn't identified; the address consisted of a five-digit number. I opened the message, which consisted of two words:

They're flights.

What on earth . . .

I looked at the address again; I still couldn't tell who'd sent the message. And then it all came to me. The message referred to the notes from Keri's office. And the text, I would have bet but might never know for sure, had come from Bart Crosby.

I pulled out Keri's notes again, with the numbers that might have been dates, and letters or abbreviations I didn't understand. Then it hit me: I'd failed to take an incredibly obvious step. I Googled the word "teter." The first result that came up was Teterboro Airport, a private airport in New Jersey. I looked at the Wikipedia entry. Teterboro, located in New Jersey, was the leading airport for private jet traffic in the New York area.

Of course. Next, I Googled the letters "KPWK." That, I discovered, was the code for Chicago Executive Airport, which served a similar function for flights to the Chicago area. I didn't need to Google OAK, which I now recalled as the code for Oakland International Airport.

Of course they were flights. And the person who had taken these trips? How about a secretive man—Paul Landrum, say—who, according to Courtney Stapleton, owned his own plane?

I needed to check out the flights, but obviously I couldn't ask the FBI to do it. Clay Ritchie, employed by the Air Force, might have connections for researching something aviation-related. I called him.

"Hey," he said. "Enjoying the high life down in San Clemente?"

"It just got a little more enjoyable. But I have a confession to make."

"Let me guess. You found something in Keri's office."

"How did you know?"

"Just had the feeling."

"Look, I'm sorry—"

"It's all right. You had no way of knowing if I was for real. But we're a team now, okay?"

"Okay." I described the notes.

"Have you figured them out?" he asked.

"Partly. I think they're flights." I explained about the airport codes.

"So, what are the rest of the notes?" he asked.

"Some of the numbers look like dates."

"Right."

"And the rest of them—I don't know. Maybe registration numbers, or flight plan numbers, or vectors, or fuel invoice numbers, or something. But we've got dates and destinations. Paul Landrum has his own plane. You must have sources—how'd you like to check out the whereabouts of the plane on those dates?"

"I guess I can do that. It's the weekend, but I'll roust somebody."

"I'll take pictures of the notes and send them to you."

"It could take a day or two, Dez."

"The closing is Wednesday. You might want to hurry."

Chapter 51

Saturday

Saturday was a cool, breezy, sunny day. After breakfast, Jackie, Tim, and I went to hang out and watch some TV in a small sunroom. I told both of my hosts that they didn't need to babysit me and that I could easily fend for myself, but they assured me there was nothing they'd rather do than hang out with me. I found I liked relaxing with people around. I'd had too many boring evenings and weekends at home alone during the past month and a half. In late morning we ventured out to the terrace. It was still cool, but it felt good to smell the salt breeze, listen to the surf, and watch the boats out on the Pacific. Then Jackie came out and asked if we'd like to join those boats.

We got into one of the SUVs and drove down to the Dana Point marina, just a short distance away. I shuddered as we wound down the hill toward the docks. I had once been abducted at this very location and hauled off to be killed. But I had put in the work with therapy and taking my meds and doing my relaxation exercises, which had made this and other traumatic experiences gradually fade into the background of my memories. Our destination proved to be a yacht named the *National Defense*, which looked big enough to land small aircraft on the deck. The vessel was staffed by a three-man crew, who greeted Jackie and Tim and carried me and my wheelchair up on deck.

It seemed to take a long time for the boat to pull out of the dock and cruise out of the harbor, past the breakwater toward the open ocean. Despite the breeze, our boat was big enough to handle the waves well and give us a fairly smooth ride. I wore a jacket as well as a sweater, and I needed both. The sunlight was intense. Jackie came over and sat down next to me while Tim wandered the deck, apparently lost in his thoughts.

Jackie sat back and gazed out at the receding shoreline. "Isn't it beautiful?" she exclaimed.

"Absolutely. It's all amazing." Pen had seen this shoreline and this ocean view many times from the *Alicia C*, but I had to remember that Dez had not.

"I don't paint landscapes," she said, "but I love coming out here and taking in the colors and the distances and even the movement."

"How about Mr. Dalton? Does he enjoy it out here?"

She nodded. "This is Pat's favorite way to decompress. He likes the golf course, too, but there's nothing quite like this. I'm anxious to get this closing behind us so he can come out here and relax. I haven't seen him this stressed since Mikayla died."

"Tim still seems to be taking her death hard."

She gazed out toward Catalina. "I'm afraid so. They were close. Of course, there wasn't a lot of closure, without a proper funeral or burial. Just a memorial service a couple of months later."

"Why was it done that way?"

"I guess you wouldn't be familiar with the circumstances of Mikayla's death. She was surfing too close to the rocks. She fell and hit her head. And then she was washed out to sea. Her body was never recovered. Pat watched the whole thing from shore, totally unable to help her."

"Good heavens. Did you and Tim see it happen, too?"

"No. Thankfully, we'd gone back to the house we'd rented. It was late in the afternoon, and the beach was nearly deserted by that time. What a helpless feeling it must have been, watching her disappear. We were there for another three days, working with the local authorities on the search and rescue. But Mikayla was never found."

"That's awful."

"The worst. And Pat blames himself, even though he'd warned her about surfing too close to the rocks. Even Tim feels guilty—he feels as though he should have been there and somehow prevented it." We were silent, and I thought about the horror everyone must have experienced. I gazed out across the ocean and imagined someone being swallowed up by its vastness.

Back at the house, the day had warmed up, and I sat by the pool, reading a magazine, while Tim paced around fitfully. Jackie remained in the house but came out a couple of times to check on me and see if I wanted anything. Pat Dalton was also inside, working.

I tried going back to my magazine but couldn't concentrate. I was sitting here, idle, as the time ticked away relentlessly toward Wednesday. Tim continued to wander aimlessly in and out of the house, and I wondered why he was staying down here for the weekend.

But I knew. It was because of me.

It was nearly six when a familiar figure appeared along the breezeway, headed toward the house. It was Steve Li, Dalton's attorney. He carried a briefcase and wore a weekend casual outfit. He gave me a smile but said nothing as he strode past.

My magazine now became a prop, something I was using to look occupied. I tried to figure out why Dalton's personal attorney would be here now. Dalton was swamped with last-minute work on the merger, and the two men didn't seem to be friends or intimates.

After about half an hour, Li emerged from the house. Instead of leaving, he walked over to the outdoor desk Dalton had been using yesterday. He sat down behind the desk, pulled out his phone, and punched in a number. Then he began a conversation I couldn't hear. I decided a trip to the bathroom was in order.

I rolled over to the door closest to Li, which led into the house. As I approached the door, I had already activated the voice recorder on my phone and wedged it in between my leg and the side of the chair. I ignored Li, who was leaning back in his chair, chatting in a language I didn't understand, but which I assumed to be Chinese of some kind. When I got to the French door, I had a hard time opening it, propping it open and rolling through.

Actually, I didn't. But I took my time, feigning difficulty. Hopefully I'd pick up a usable snippet of his conversation. I went inside and used the bathroom. When I returned to the terrace, Li was finishing up his conversation. He hung up, grabbed the folder he had brought, and started for the breezeway. His path took him past me, and as he approached, he slowed down, giving me a once-over with little subtlety. I felt my heartbeat ramping up; had he noticed me recording him? He stopped for just a few seconds, then gave me a phony little smile and disappeared.

Dinner was less formal tonight. This time the cook had set up a lavish taco bar, complemented by plenty of tasty sides and supplemented by Coronas. Pat Dalton seemed to make a genuine effort to relax and join the conversation, but I wasn't fooled. His mind was a long distance away, and I wasn't sure his distraction was all about the closing. But if not the merger, then what?

After dinner, Tim and I went to the great room, a place that more than lived up to its name. It was huge, dominated by windows that overlooked the ocean. I rolled up to a long sofa, and Tim asked, "Would you like to sit on the couch?"

"Okay." He helped me transfer and then sat down next to me. He sat very close, and I began to regret the lack of an exit strategy. I decided to try to divert him.

"Jackie is really nice," I said.

He nodded. "She's propped us up, held us together. I'm really glad Dad met her."

We were silent for another minute. "I saw Mr. Li again today," I said.

"He seems to wander in whenever he feels like it. Acts like he owns the place."

So it isn't just me, I thought. "How long has he represented your dad?"

"A couple of years, I guess."

Tim sat in silence for a minute, then said, "I could use another Corona. How about you?"

"Go ahead," I said. "I think I'll pass."

It looked to me as if Tim was working up his nerve.

When he returned with his bottle of beer, complete with a lime wedge in the top, I tried diverting him again. "Have you been in touch with any of Mikayla's friends since her death?" I asked.

"Somewhat, but less often as time has gone by. Everybody has moved on. Except me."

"How about your dad?"

"I'm not sure. He seems to have put most of his energy into his job. Not as much travel or leisure time as before."

We sat silently for a minute. Then, "I like you, Dez."

"And I like you."

"No. I mean, I like you. Do you understand?"

He leaned forward to kiss me, but I held up my hand. "I'm sorry, Tim. I'm very flattered, though. I like you, but—"

"But 'not that way.' I know. Is it because I'm a lot younger?"

"Not really. I work for your dad's company. I feel the need to keep it friendly."

"What if Dad was cool with it?"

"That's kind of hypothetical, Tim. Why don't we just enjoy the evening?"

He nodded. He felt a little embarrassed, undoubtedly, but didn't seem to be angry. He seemed to have expected rejection. "Do you mind my asking a question?" he said.

"Go ahead."

"Do you have a boyfriend?"

"No, I don't. I did until recently."

"Still on the rebound?"

"Right." I hated to flat-out lie to him, but the "rebound" observation left both of us with a face-saving way out of the awkwardness.

Surprisingly, resolving our romantic status, or lack of it, seemed to relax Tim. "You've hardly talked about yourself at all," he said.

"My life isn't very interesting."

"Come on, I'll bet it is." In the conversation that followed, he was full of questions: Why had I moved out here? Why hadn't I gone to law school? What was being a paraplegic like? What were the details of my accident? Were my parents still living? Did I have brothers or sisters? I was forced to draw on my legend, which fortunately I still recalled in detail. Surprisingly, he seemed genuinely interested in me, in a just-friends sort of way.

We eventually said goodnight, and I accepted a peck on the cheek. Back in my room, I suddenly felt exhausted, both from trying to read the situation in the Dalton household and from answering a slew of Dez questions. But I knew I needed to check in with Ritchie.

"Nothing on those flights yet," he said when I called. "We should have something tomorrow."

"Good. Now, here's something to chew on." I told him about Steve Li.

He was unimpressed. "So what, Dez? He's close to the family—"

"No. Only to Dalton himself. Even then, I didn't detect warmth or familiarity between them. And I think he gives Jackie and Tim the creeps, just as he does me."

"So how do we check him out?"

"Open up the voice recorder on your phone. I'm going to play you a clip." I played the recording of Steve Li's conversation.

"That's Li?" Ritchie asked.

"Yes. I don't know for certain what language he's speaking, but since he grew up in Taiwan, I assume it's Mandarin or Taiwanese or some other Chinese dialect."

"I'll check that out, too."

"Thanks, Clay."

A pause. "Are you okay there, Dez? Things sound a little weird."

"I think I'll be all right," I said. I felt better since my conversation with Tim. "I'm headed back tomorrow afternoon."

"Gotta get back to work on Monday. Earn your pay." I could imagine his grin over the phone.

"Goodnight, Clay."

I tossed and turned in bed for a long time as my thoughts churned, refusing to assemble in any kind of order. I needed them to fall into place soon.

Chapter 52

Sunday

Sunday proceeded uneventfully. We enjoyed a huge brunch a little before noon, and I chatted with Tim and Jackie until it was time to leave at three. I rolled out of my room, struggling with my overnight bag, and Jackie rushed forward. "Good heavens, we'll take care of that," she exclaimed.

"Thanks."

"Dez, I just wanted to tell you how much we've enjoyed having you."

"I've enjoyed it, too. Thank you so much."

"And Tim—it looks like you two got things sorted out?" She obviously hadn't been an idle observer of our interaction.

I smiled. "Yes. I hope it sorted to Tim's satisfaction."

"It certainly seems so. He's still trying to find his way, and having a friend—a real friend—makes all the difference."

"He's a good guy. I'm sure everything will turn out well for him."

"You'll have to come again."

"Absolutely."

We rolled out to the terrace, and I tried to suppress my shame. All weekend long, the lies had come rolling out of my mouth with little effort or hesitation. True, I was a lawyer. But I was relieved to still feel ashamed.

I accepted a hug from Jackie; Pat Dalton was away, probably at the office. Jackie discreetly retreated, leaving Tim to push me down the breezeway to the parking area. "I really enjoyed the weekend, Dez."

"So did I."

"I'm sorry for the, uh, approach I took last night."

"No problem at all. As I said, I'm really flattered, and under different circumstances, who knows?" Yesterday, I thought, this response would have been BS. Now, it felt right.

Fortunately, Tim didn't press me on making plans to get together again. He helped Neil load me into the SUV and stash my chair, then came back around to the open door. "Well, thanks again." He started with a handshake and finished with a cheek-peck. The car pulled away.

At home, I went into the bedroom and lay down; I figured I'd take a quick nap before returning to my work.

*   *   *

The phone woke me up. I fumbled for it and glanced at the time. Two hours had passed.

"Hey, Dez."

"Clay?"

"Did I wake you up?"

"No. Yes."

"The weekend must have been exhausting."

"More than I realized."

"I've got some news on Landrum's flights."

"Great." I pushed myself up to a sitting position.

"First of all, Landrum does have a private plane, which he flies out of Van Nuys Airport. The dates and destinations do represent flights attributable to him. The other numbers are a mishmash and not really important."

"What about the dates that don't have any destinations noted?"

"Ah, but they do. You noticed that for the flights with no destinations, in the approximate spot of where the airport is listed for the ones that do, you see what looks like the number eleven?"

"Right. I noticed that."

"They're not elevens. They're quotation marks."

"Meaning that flight's destination was the same as the one listed before it."

"Exactly," Ritchie said. "All thirteen of the flights went to either New York, Chicago, or the Bay Area."

"Probably places where Landrum has business," I said. "Why was Keri interested in the flights?"

"I don't know. But there's more, and my guy didn't pick this up right away. You have to look at the *return* flights. In four cases, Landrum filed a flight plan for a return to LA. But on those four trips, he diverted to Minneapolis."

"Which four trips?" I asked.

"September 7th, October 5th, November 2nd, and November 30th."

"The four Fridays."

"Right. And in each case, he stayed in Minneapolis overnight and returned on Saturday. Now you're on a roll. Tell me what he did in Minneapolis."

"He visited somebody. Maybe a business associate or an ex-flame. Or a current flame. Maybe even Diane."

"Plausible. But if he did visit a woman, why did he keep it a secret?"

"Embarrassment?"

"Maybe."

"He's only been married to Irina for four years. Didn't take long for the relationship to go south."

"I guess not. I just don't know what any of this means, Clay. It's basically another complication. We're further from the solution than we were before learning this."

"On that cheery note," Ritchie said, "I checked out that snippet of Steve Li's conversation you recorded."

"And?"

"To begin with, he was apparently chatting with his girlfriend."

"That's weird enough," I said. "How is it that you wander into a client's house—a Fortune 100 CEO, no less—and then sit down, put your feet up, and call your girlfriend?"

"There's more. He wasn't speaking Chinese. It was Korean."

"Really?"

"Look, I checked this guy out, but I didn't find out much more than the Bureau did. No criminal record. Has a legitimate-looking practice with mostly clients involved in trading with China. But it's interesting—in one of the early documents I came across, his name was spelled Lee. L-e-e."

"So?"

"That's the traditional Korean spelling. Some Chinese spell it that way, too, but more often, the Chinese spelling is 'L-i.'"

"What does that tell us?" I asked.

"Damned if I know. We have absolutely no reason to suspect the guy of anything, except that he is apparently Chinese and speaks Korean, and that he shows more familiarity in his client's home than you'd expect."

"I guess we'll have to put that on the back burner," I said. "We need to concentrate on Landrum."

"Agreed."

Neither of us spoke for a moment. "So," I said, "we've learned a couple of new things, which seem only to complicate things further. And we have only two working days to solve the mystery of Paul Landrum."

"Sums it up nicely."

I clicked off, hesitated, and then made another call, to Diane Landrum.

She answered right away. "This is Diane."

"Hi, Diane. It's Pen Wilkinson."

"Well, hello. It's nice to hear from you."

"I'm wondering if you could answer a quick question for me."

"Of course, if I can," she said.

"I'm afraid it's about your ex."

"Ah, yes. Is your friend James still going to meet with him?"

"He is. And I thought that if they met in Minnesota, I could tag along. I'm always looking for an excuse to see Simone and Alicia. Do you happen to know if Paul ever gets back to Minnesota?"

"Once in a while, I guess, mostly for holidays and for Meghan's birthday."

"But nothing on a regular basis?"

"Not really, although I suppose he could slip in and out of town without my knowing about it."

"Oh, well. It was worth a try," I said. "Thanks anyway."

"I do hope you find a reason to come back," she said. "Stop in and say hello."

"I will, thanks."

I hung up. My pretext for calling had been nearly as flimsy as the one for my in-person visit to Diane in Minnesota. The call had been worthwhile; I now knew that Landrum was keeping his visits to Minnesota a secret—from whom, I didn't know. And, as with so many other mysteries related to Landrum, I had no idea why.

Chapter 53

Monday

"Where do we start?" asked PACIFIC.

"Dez," said Landrum.

Viktor Kamensky didn't want to talk about Dez. He knew he was missing something about her, something basic, and it didn't reflect well on his work. On the plus side, he had finally caught her meeting with Wendy Nomura. A lot of things had fallen into place after that, but not everything, which was why the trio had assembled at the mountain cabin safe house early in the afternoon. PACIFIC and Landrum sat on the couch, while Kamensky fidgeted in a side chair, nursing a Diet Coke and wishing he had vodka. The group spoke Russian.

"Who is Dez working for?" Landrum said.

"The obvious answer is the FBI," said Kamensky. "She's met with Nomura."

"But she's also met with Dalton," PACIFIC pointed out.

"Let's start with the Bureau," said Landrum. "Viktor spotted Dez meeting with Nomura. The obvious inference is that the Feds planted her in the company."

"Why would they do that?" asked PACIFIC.

"I think it must have come from Keri and her phone call. They put her on my case."

PACIFIC said, "If they're investigating you, then why not plant somebody in Techinvest? That would have put them a lot closer to you."

"It could have been opportunistic. Maybe Dez happened to fit an opening they had in Keri's department, down the hall from me. I asked Griffin, and Dez actually knows that software they have her working on."

"But she's just a paralegal. What did they expect her to learn? What *has* she learned, for that matter?"

"They're desperate," Kamensky asserted, trying to put a positive spin on the situation. "They did what they were able to do, even though it wasn't ideal. They couldn't take that call from Keri and do nothing, not with Hulbert at stake."

PACIFIC chuckled. "'Not ideal.' That's one way of putting it. As far as we can tell, Nomura has been running the op basically by herself. They need to keep Gilbertson out of the loop."

"Which they pretty much have. She's kept it secret from us, too. Kind of impressive, actually."

"It is," PACIFIC conceded. "I've checked with my sources in Washington, and they haven't caught a whiff of it. But that means Nomura's not getting much help."

"Do you suppose the real objective of the op is to trap Gilbertson somehow?" Landrum asked.

"Oh, they'll deal with Ward, but that will be after the merger."

"We'll need to deal with him before they do," Kamensky said.

"Of course. We can't just feed him to the Bureau, even though there's not much he can tell them. You'll have to bring him up here and have a chat. After that, whatever."

"Where are they at in terms of investigating our operation?" Landrum asked.

"They have to know we exist," PACIFIC said. "They'd have to be incredibly dense not to have figured that out. And I'm afraid they must know Gilbertson's been supporting us. But the only thing linking us to the operation—"

"Is Keri," Landrum cut in. "And that's where Dez comes in. We need to know if they've got anything other than Keri's phone call."

"I doubt it, but Viktor will have to bring her up here and find out for sure."

"Of all the rotten luck, that Keri should happen to have the connection with Elena."

"Well, we took care of that," PACIFIC said. "But we'll have to find out if she learned anything from that secretary who works for the COO. Maria—no, Marisa."

"I'd bet anything she didn't," Kamensky said. "But I'll question Marisa thoroughly."

"I'll bet you will," said PACIFIC with a wry smile. "I've seen her picture."

"What do we do about Nomura?" Landrum asked.

"I think we leave her," PACIFIC said. "It would be nice to find out what she knows, but it wouldn't be like Gilbertson. We'll be doing them a favor when we take him out. But Nomura—if we took her, we'd have the whole Bureau on our case. We don't need that. Dez should be able to tell us about the op."

Kamensky toyed with his soda can. "What's the deal with Dez and Dalton? If Dalton is working with the FBI, we could have problems."

Landrum shrugged. "I've seen no evidence of that. My sources tell me he was just being nice to Dez after she found the typo. After that, she and Dalton's kid hit it off. Kind of pathetic, really—Pat is eager to take care of whatever friends he can find." He leaned back on the sofa, shaking his head. "That goddamned typo. I knew she was sharper than she let on. But apart from the typo, I can't see that she's learned anything at all."

"She's probably trying to pick up Keri's trail," PACIFIC said.

"And what is the trail?" Kamensky asked.

Landrum sat up again and leaned forward, forearms resting on his knees. "Elena, obviously. But we shut down that trail, quickly. Keri didn't tell them about Elena—didn't want to endanger her, I suppose—and I just can't see what else Keri would have been able to tell them. She said I'm 'not what I seem to be.'

That's meaningless and doesn't point toward Elena at all. And I know for a fact that both DOD and FBI have had me under the microscope—hell, anybody with a connection to the Hulbert deal."

"They've had their antennae out ever since the consulate was closed," PACIFIC said. "They've had their suspicions."

"And what has their response been?" Kamensky asked. "To plant a paralegal down the hall. Pretty pathetic. So when do we pull the plug on her?"

"I'd say anytime," PACIFIC said. "We're two days away from the closing. If there's any chance she could do something to gum that up, we don't need to take the risk. Have you thought about the extraction?"

"Sure. It shouldn't be a problem. Hell, she's a cripple in a wheelchair."

PACIFIC sat up a little straighter. "What did you say?"

"She's a paraplegic. Didn't you know that?"

PACIFIC shot an irritated glance at Landrum, who had never shared this fact. "Let's see a picture."

Kamensky reached for his laptop, hit some keys, and brought up a photograph. He turned the screen around on the coffee table to show his boss.

A faint smile worked its way across PACIFIC's face. "Oh, my. Mystery solved. Her name is Pen."

Chapter 54

I rolled out of Dez's condo the next morning, wondering who might be watching. Was somebody in Washington observing me over a video feed? Was Wendy Nomura waiting down the road to intercept me, to make sure I had quit? Or maybe Viktor Kamensky had decided to pay a call, his employers having decided they'd had enough of my prying and interference. But, as I got into the van and started it up, dressed as Dez, the depressing truth sank in: it was entirely possible that nobody cared what I did.

I reached DSI without incident, logged in on the ground floor, and rolled over to the elevator. It was just another day at the office for Desiree Walker, the woman who was no longer supposed to exist, on an assignment that had been terminated. I worked listlessly through the morning, keeping an eye out for Hornsby, Laura Dixon, Landrum, and . . . the list was long and depressing. Ritchie didn't appear for lunch, so in early afternoon, I texted him on the burner phone and asked him if he could take a break, go outside, and look under my car for trackers.

About half an hour later I got a return text:
It's a big yes. What do you want me to do?
I responded: *Pull it off but don't disable. Put it on front seat.*
OK.

Now I was left to wonder who had placed the device. I was pretty sure it was Landrum & company, since Nomura had been tracking me via my phone. But what if the Bureau had decided to keep tabs on me, phone or no phone? In any event, Nomura had probably known about it. She'd left it on for valid reasons—to avoid tipping the bad guys, and to preserve the option of using the van as a decoy or setup. But she had not told me, and she hadn't taken it off after terminating my assignment.

I finished the day without any trouble, which was nice. But why was I still here? I'd accomplished nothing to further my now-defunct assignment. Why was I assuming the risk?

It was nearly six by the time I pulled into the parking lot at the Newport Beach Police Department, having stopped at home and left the tracker there. I checked in and was shown to a conference room. Dan Howard sat at the table, armed with a grim expression. And so was the person seated next to him.

Wendy Nomura.

I managed to avoid an audible groan, but my face must have conveyed the nonverbal version. And it was enough to cause Howard to smile. And then to laugh. And then he was joined by Nomura. I couldn't remember actually hearing her laugh before. Finally, I joined them.

"Yeah, you're busted," Howard said.

I held out my wrists for cuffs. "Take me away."

"I knew you weren't going to stop," Nomura said.

"So where does that leave us?"

"I'm interested in anything you might have," Howard said.

I looked at Nomura. "So am I," she said. "But you're dealing with me, not the FBI."

I was flabbergasted. "You're—"

"My interest is personal," she said. It was a delicate way of saying she was going rogue, just as I was.

"You're not going to turn me in?"

"No. But I also can't offer you any support from the Bureau. I'll do what I can—personally." She handed my Dez phone back. "I can still track it," she said, "but no panic button. Just the speed dial with my number. And the video feed at the condo is off."

I took the phone, relieved to have it back. What if somebody from DSI tried to call me? "Why are you doing this?" I asked.

"I'm doing what the Bureau would do if it could. But it's ham-strung by rules, procedures, and most of all by internal security problems. This is about PACIFIC, Pen. Russian spies in southern

California. I don't know how it will all be resolved, but I'm convinced things will come to a head soon, and we need your help."

I spread the notes from Keri's office out on the conference table.

Howard squinted at the notes. "I don't remember seeing these. They were in Keri's office?"

"Yes," I replied.

"Then presumably we looked at them."

"They represent flights, by Landrum's plane. Unless you happen to hit on the flight angle, and to link it with Landrum, there's really nothing here to interest you." I explained about the flights' dates and destinations, concluding with the return stopovers in Minnesota. "Your people probably looked at this but concluded it was something work-related and irrelevant."

"Right," Howard said, but I could tell he felt embarrassed. "Let me track down our copy, and we'll take another look. If he was stopping secretly in Minneapolis, that's interesting, but hard to see how it fits with the murder."

"How did you figure out these represented flights?" Nomura asked.

"I made some calls." I hoped the vague response would suffice. I couldn't tell her about Ritchie.

"Here's another thing," I said, pulling out the note from the law library. "This is also in Keri's handwriting."

Howard nodded. "What are the numbers?"

"They're a citation for federal regulations prohibiting commodity trading fraud."

"I'm assuming Landrum trades commodities."

"Yes."

"Who's Elena?"

"I don't know."

He put the note aside. "Anything else?"

"Not right now," I said. "But as I told you on the phone, I'd like to look at the names and pictures of people coming off the

Peninsula after the murder, and at the names on Keri's cell phone records."

Howard pulled up a file on a laptop and slid it over to me. "Here's a list of the vehicles we checked, along with their owners. The murder happened around one or two. To be on the safe side, we ran everybody who came off before 6:00 AM, although I don't know where they would have been from the time of the murder until then."

There were dozens of names on the list. I scrolled through them deliberately. After about five minutes, I came across a name, Lila Rayfield, that I couldn't quite place but that seemed familiar, linked with a Toyota Land Cruiser. In a split-second decision, I decided not to call attention to it.

Nomura and Howard, being professional law enforcement types, spotted the hesitation. "What did you see?" Nomura asked.

"Unfortunately, nothing," I lied. "A name that looked vaguely familiar, but it isn't the person I thought it might be." I spent another ten minutes reviewing the remaining names.

I looked up from the list. "I don't recognize any of them."

Howard gave us an I'm-not-surprised look.

"Now," I said, "could I see the ones you got pictures of?"

The detective pulled up the pictures. There were only a couple dozen of these. The seventh picture was a man of about forty, with short, blond hair, a tough, vigilant look, and protruding eyes. He was leaning forward, looking up.

"Kamensky," I said.

Howard nodded.

"He's looking for cameras?"

"And that's what did him in. He found one."

I looked through the remainder of the pictures but didn't see the vehicle I'd spotted on the list. Finally, I looked up. "Sorry," I said. "I thought it was worth a look."

"There was no 'Elena' on the list," Nomura observed.

"We can look for her in the cell phone records."

We did. And we found her.

Howard produced a list of Keri's calls, obtained from the cell provider, with handwritten notes next to each number identifying the caller or recipient of a call. I went down the list, with Howard and Nomura looking over my shoulder. Two calls, spaced about a week apart, carried the notation "Marisa – secretary." They had identified her as a work-related contact, not a friend. I continued the search.

"Here it is," I said. Five days before Keri's murder, a number with a 703 area code had been listed as making a seventeen-minute call to Keri's number. There was a handwritten notation next to the listing: "Elena - friend."

Howard immediately picked up a phone. "Run down this number," he said without preamble. "Now." He read off the number.

The response came a couple of minutes later. The lieutenant scribbled down the information, then looked up at us. "It's a mobile number, belongs to Elena Morton of Arlington, Virginia."

"Apparently she was a friend of Keri's?" Nomura asked.

"We need to find out for sure. This is Kozlowski's handwriting." He picked up the phone and called Detective Mary Kozlowski. I was familiar with the name; she had worked with Howard when he'd arrested James Carter for the murder of his ex-girlfriend.

Howard reached Kozlowski at home and asked about the notation next to Elena Morton's name. "Uh-huh... Okay... And then—All right . . . All right. Thanks, Mary." He hung up and looked at us. "Kozlowski says Elena Morton is an old law school friend of Keri's who lives in northern Virginia. Kozlowski called her a couple of times but got voicemail. She talked to Keri's parents, who confirmed that Elena was a friend and that they talked every month or two."

We waited for the rest of it, but there wasn't anything. Howard just shook his head, indicating that Kozlowski had never connected with Elena. Her decision was frustrating, but hard to second guess. What were the odds that a call from an old law school friend from across the country might have something to do with the murder?

Come to think of it, what were the odds now?

While Nomura and Howard were discussing Kozlowski's lack of follow-up, I decided to do the obvious thing, the step I'd overlooked in researching Keri's notes on the flights. I pulled out my phone and Googled the phrase "Elena Morton Virginia." I looked at the first result, and after reading for only a few seconds, I gasped. Howard and Nomura looked at me, and I held up my phone, which displayed a Google news entry featuring a picture of a dark-haired, pleasant-looking woman in her thirties. Three days before Keri's death, Elena Morton, an attorney for the Commodity Futures Trading Commission in Washington, DC, had been murdered.

Chapter 55

PACIFIC chuckled. "Her name is Pen. Pen Wilkinson. She was a federal prosecutor."

"*Prosecutor?*" said Landrum, alarmed. "They've reached the point of trying to make a case against me?"

"I don't think so. She's not a prosecutor anymore. The US attorney wouldn't be running an undercover operation. She seems to be working for the FBI."

"Why would they send a paraplegic?" Kamensky asked.

PACIFIC shrugged. "Maybe they figured nobody would suspect a cripple. Just another mystery, which you can solve in the course of your exit interview with her."

"She's got nothing on me as far as we know," said Landrum. "But we can't take the chance that she's somehow found something, either on me or on our operation."

"Of course not," PACIFIC said. "She has to go—the sooner, the better."

"What if she's already learned something?"

"Nothing we can do about that. All we can do is find out about it and respond." To Kamensky: "How soon can you get her?"

"Pretty much any time. I'll need about a day to evaluate her protection—although she hasn't really had much of anything so far—and to set things up."

"Do it. Before the closing, for sure. And after that, be ready to move on the next phase. To drop the deadfall on DSI."

Kamensky's features tightened. "I'll be ready."

Landrum said, "Get everything ready for Dez, Viktor, but don't move until I give you the word."

"What's the hang-up?" PACIFIC asked.

"I've got an idea that might get us some quick information, assuming she shows up for work tomorrow. I need to talk to Les."

"Fine."

"Are we done here?" Landrum asked.

"I guess so," said the woman next to him on the couch. And with that, Paul Landrum leaned over and kissed PACIFIC, also known as Diane Landrum.

Chapter 56

"What can I say?" Lieutenant Dan Howard asked. "We should have followed up on it. Obviously, if we'd known this woman had been murdered—"

"Which is undoubtedly why she didn't return Kozlowski's calls," Nomura cut in.

"—we would have been more aggressive. There has to be some connection here, and we'll get to the bottom of it. We're due for a break on this case."

I thought Howard was being a little hard on himself. Following up more aggressively on a phone call from Keri's out-of-state old friend, especially without knowing about the note Marisa had found, seemed like an extreme measure, or at the least, a borderline judgment call. Keri had talked to dozens—maybe hundreds —of people in the weeks leading up to her murder. No police agency had the resources to thoroughly check out every single person, much less to understand all the nuances of each relationship.

While Nomura and I waited, Howard called the Washington, DC police, finally reaching the detective who'd handled the Elena Morton murder, a man named Guzman. The detective described the killing, which had taken place in the Columbia Heights neighborhood, as a mugging gone bad.

Elena had been shot while walking to her car late at night. The neighborhood was not considered a bad one; it was a trendy, recently gentrified area, and Elena had been walking back to her car after a work-related party at a friend's house. Surveillance footage from a nearby convenience store showed a male suspect in a hoodie fleeing the area, but no further evidence and no suspects. Guzman had talked to Elena's supervisor at the CFTC, who knew of nothing controversial Elena had been working on, and no one at work or elsewhere who disliked her.

"We'd like to talk to the husband," Howard told Guzman.

"Be my guest. Just let me know if he tells you anything. He wasn't able to give me any help."

"Will do. It's late tonight, but we'll try to connect with him tomorrow."

"Fine." Guzman gave Howard the husband's number.

Howard hung up and looked across the table at us. "DC never looked at this case as a targeted assassination. Why would they?"

Nomura, a/k/a Special Agent Wet Blanket, said, "Let's not get ahead of ourselves. Granted, it's quite a coincidence, the two of them being murdered. But all we've got is a phone call."

"I'll talk to Elena's supervisor at CFTC tomorrow," Howard said. "See if Landrum's name rings a bell."

"Speaking of Landrum," I said, "Keri looked up his flights from a four-month period last year. We don't know why she used that time period. But it seems to me we should take another look, see where he—or his plane—might have gone around the time of Elena's murder."

"I'll do that, too," Howard said.

"Dan," Nomura said, "if you don't mind, we'd like to be in on the call to the husband."

He hesitated and glanced at me.

"Pen, too," she said, to her credit.

"Fair enough," he said. "Pen brought me the lead."

"Can we make it late tomorrow afternoon?" I asked. "Tomorrow is the last day before the closing, and I'd like to be at the office until quitting time."

"Tomorrow has to be your last day," Nomura said. "There's no reason to hang around after the closing."

"All right." I wasn't going to argue.

"Let's make the call at six," Howard said. "I'll patch you in remotely."

"One last thing," Nomura said. "Why did you go to Minnesota? Don't tell me it was just for a fun weekend break."

"I was pursuing some angles," I admitted.

"Did you learn anything important?"

"I'm sure I did. I just don't know what it is yet."

Howard walked us out to the parking lot. We paused outside the door, and he said to me, "Why is it that every time I screw something up, you're involved?"

"I don't see this as a screwup."

"Nice of you to say, but what else would you call it? And last time . . ." He shook his head. "Arresting James Carter was the worst mistake of my career. I won't survive another one like that."

I didn't say anything, even though I knew the decision to charge James had been the district attorney's, not Howard's. But Howard was a loyal team player.

"Let's hope we can salvage this one," the detective said.

Nomura and I murmured our assent and started for our vehicles. We paused next to my van. "They might know you're here," she said. "I'll follow you home."

"They don't know I'm here."

She looked uncomfortable.

"I had the tracker taken off the van," I said, "and tonight I left it at home."

Now she appeared embarrassed, a new look for her. "Look, Pen, I—"

"It's all right. I'm assuming it was theirs, not yours."

"Yes."

"Fine. If you want me to put it back in for any reason, let me know."

She started to walk off, then turned back. "You deserve to know. We do have a security problem in my department. My boss, Ward Gilbertson, is under suspicion. That's why we've had to be so secretive, and why I've had to do this alone."

I wanted to know a lot more than that, but I just nodded.

"This might be it, Pen. This might tell us why Keri was killed. Nice work."

"We'll see. Nothing like waiting until the last minute."

Nomura left. I got into the van, got myself situated, then pulled from my purse a homemade booklet I'd been given when I'd joined the DSI legal department. The booklet contained the name, birthday, spouse's name, and cell number for everybody in the department. Nancy Griffin's assistant, who had compiled the little directory, had presented it to me on my first day of work. I found the cell number I was looking for and placed a call.

"This is Dez," I said when the person answered. "We need to meet. Right now."

Chapter 57

McCartney Williamson was already seated at a rear table at the McDonald's on Pacific Coast Highway in Newport Beach, waiting with a cup of coffee. It was strange seeing him in an open-necked shirt and jeans; at work, he was always dressed like a guy who explains funeral options to bereaved families. He nodded to me when I rolled up across the table from him.

Williamson seemed ill at ease, lacking his usual quiet confidence. "You certainly piqued my curiosity, Dez. What's the urgent matter about Keri that you'd like to discuss?"

"Let's talk about your whereabouts on the night she was killed."

"And you would be interested in this because . . ."

I didn't respond.

"I've always sensed that you were more than just a paralegal with a friendly interest in your fellow workers," he said. "Who are you?"

"I'm working with the FBI."

His eyes widened. "How about that? I had imagined a reporter, or a private detective perhaps. And you're an FBI agent?"

"Not an agent. I'm just cooperating with the Bureau."

"I see. And you're investigating Keri's murder?"

"In an indirect way. I'm interested in Landrum."

"Indeed."

"Could we return to my question about the night of the murder?" I asked.

"Is this an official interrogation?"

"No."

"Then forgive me, Dez, but is there a compelling reason why I should answer your questions?"

"I might be more agreeable about it than the Newport Beach Police. They know that the Toyota Land Cruiser that was spotted near the murder scene that night is registered to Lila Rayfield. They don't know that Lila Rayfield is the wife of McCartney Williamson, a friend and co-worker of the murder victim."

"But you do."

"And I'm giving you a chance to explain it to me first. I'm giving you the benefit of the doubt because you've been kind to me, and I haven't been honest with you."

"Will you report what I tell you to the police or the FBI?"

"Only if I have to, if it's directly relevant to the murder or to the Bureau's investigation."

"I'd like to be able to believe that."

"Consider this: I haven't told anybody yet. You could be in an interrogation room at Newport Beach police headquarters at this moment."

He spent a minute pondering his options, then came to a decision. "I guess it's time. I was a fool to think it wouldn't come out. Yes, I visited Keri that night."

"Why were you there?"

"I was forced to go."

"Forced by whom?"

"I don't know. It was a distorted voice over the phone."

"Male or female?"

"I couldn't tell."

"What were you supposed to do when you got there?"

"Talk to Keri until another person got there. Then let the person in."

My heartbeat accelerated. This was it. He had set Keri up. "Why would they need somebody to let the person in?" I said. "Why couldn't they just talk or force their way in?"

"Keri was terrified. She stuck close to home, watched for followers, wouldn't go out at night. There's no way she would have opened the door to a stranger. She had very strong locks on the door. I knew she had a gun, too." He looked up at me. "As you've probably surmised, Keri and I were much closer friends than I've let on. I'd been to her house on other occasions."

"What was she terrified about?"

"She'd been troubled during the last few weeks of her life. She told me she had crossed Landrum somehow and was afraid of the blowback. I assured her that her career would be fine, even if she had to take a new job somewhere else. She said it might be worse than that."

"What else did she say when you went there that night?"

"She said she was still afraid of Landrum, and that he might have been responsible for a friend of hers being killed. She admitted she wasn't a hundred percent sure and didn't have any proof. I told her she should tell the police, and she was dead set against it. She didn't want to risk any more trouble with Landrum."

"What happened next?"

He paused, steeling himself. "There was a knock on the door. I'd remained standing, and I let the person in."

"Can you identify the person?"

"No. He was masked."

"A man?"

"I assume so, because of the build. I could see his eyes through the mask's eyeholes, and they seemed to protrude a bit."

"Was he armed?"

"I couldn't tell."

"What did you do?"

"I—I left," he said, struggling to control his emotions. "God help me, I left her to be killed." His head sank into his hands as he sobbed. Tears oozed between his fingers. Finally, he composed himself, wiping his face with a McDonald's napkin.

"Did you realize at the time what was going to happen?" I asked.

He nodded. "The caller said they just wanted to talk to her, to reason with her. But I knew."

"Why, Mac? Why on earth would you do that to your friend?"

"I didn't have any choice. The voice on the phone said they'd have Lila's parents deported."

"Deported, as in—"

"As in shipped back to Jamaica, after forty years. They're not in this country legally, Dez."

"You're a US citizen, right?"

"And so is Lila," he said. "Her parents started the naturalization process, all those years ago, but the authorities kept raising one objection after another, and it wasn't looking good. Finally, when they moved with us to the West Coast, they said screw it. They never completed the process. They live with us, Dez. They're part of our household. Our kids adore them. They're in poor health—they wouldn't last a year in the old country. I couldn't let them be deported."

"And a voice on the phone threatened to do just that?"

"I don't know how they knew, but I guess it wouldn't have been hard for somebody with a few dollars and access to databases to do some investigating."

"Who are 'they,' Mac?"

"Landrum, I suppose."

"Mac, a few days before her death, Keri made an anonymous call to the FBI. She said that Paul Landrum was 'not who he appeared to be,' and that it was critical to expose him before the Hulbert closing. Do you have any idea what she might have been talking about?"

He thought about it. "No. As I said, I was aware that she'd had some conflict with Landrum, but I didn't hear anything like that."

I looked around the deserted McDonald's, trying to process everything I'd heard. "I guess you know what happens next," I said.

He nodded. "I get a lawyer and turn myself in, try to make a deal, hope by some miracle they don't pursue my in-laws' deportation."

"That will be up to Lieutenant Howard and the DA."

He stared across the room, toward the statue of Ronald McDonald. "Was it utterly stupid not to pressure my in-laws to get legal?" he said. "Of course it was. I'm a lawyer—I should have known. But sometimes . . . sometimes the whole system just wears you down. It was the biggest mistake of my life." He looked down into his coffee cup. "Until it wasn't."

Chapter 58

Marisa Costas pulled her aging Kia up in front of her apartment, located in a marginal area of Santa Ana. Her plan had failed. She had hoped that by getting Dez off her back, she might be able to avoid talking to the police. But Dez, apparently working with, if not for, some kind of law enforcement agency, had acted very concerned, arranging cloak-and-dagger meetings and telling her that what she knew was critical.

Really? A crumpled handwritten note was a big deal? And Keri communicating with somebody named Elena might be important in solving her murder? Yet she had always sensed that something very serious was going on at DSI, at a level far above her lowly pay grade. And now she'd do her duty, to tell the police what she knew, unlikely as it seemed to be relevant. It was all she could do now for Keri, the friend who had treated her as a friend.

She let herself into the apartment. Before the door had entirely swung shut, the intruder had clamped his hand over her mouth. Within seconds, she was on the floor, gagged, with zip ties on her wrists. She looked up, terrified, into the cruel, protruding eyes of a man who hadn't bothered masking himself, and she knew with certainty that this person had killed Keri.

He leaned forward. "I need some answers, Marisa. Now, I've got a place up in the mountains where I could take you, and you'd discover a few things about pain you never knew before. But it would be inconvenient and time-consuming to drive all the way back up there, and so I'm thinking you might just make it easy for me. Can you do that?"

Chapter 59

Tuesday

I rolled into the office on my last day of work, keeping, as usual, a vigilant eye out for Laura Dixon. Thankfully, I'd been able to stay out of her way since our near-encounter by the elevator. The Hulbert closing was scheduled to take place at a downtown law office at 9:00 AM tomorrow. All we'd be able to do is hope the dire, unspecified events Keri had warned of wouldn't come to pass. We knew now that Kamensky, with Mac Williamson's help, had killed Keri. We also had some important leads on nefarious activities by Landrum, including the murder of Elena Morton. But none of that was sufficient to actually implicate Landrum, or to stop the closing.

After the meeting at McDonald's, I had called Howard, who had come over with a uniformed cop to take Williamson in for questioning. The lieutenant had told me he had no interest in having Lila Rayfield's parents deported, and that given the lack of direct, knowing involvement by Williamson, he expected a deal would be made for little or no jail time. "Not that I like that outcome," he'd added.

Now I sat in my cube, looking at the screen. I was up to date on my work, leaving me little to do except try to make sense of the strange things I'd uncovered during my time here. I assumed Clay Ritchie would stay beyond tomorrow; he still hadn't found the source of technology theft from DSI. He also wasn't, as far as we knew, under suspicion.

At lunch, the talk was all about the merger, and who would be moving where and in charge of what. People noticed Williamson's absence, and I didn't enlighten them. I realized I was enjoying the company of these people for probably the last time. I'd miss them. I'd deceived them, but I thought our friendship had been genuine. I liked the camaraderie of a regular job and realized how much I'd missed it since leaving the US attorney's office. Still, it was hard to imagine going back to work for a large organization.

* * *

I was back at my desk around two when my Ritchie phone buzzed. I answered.

"Get out," he said without preamble.

"What?"

"Get out. They're coming for you right now. Leave the building. *Now.*"

"Okay." I grabbed my purse and blazer.

"Listen," Ritchie said. "Do exactly as I tell you." I quickly stuck a headphone in my ear so I could propel myself while listening.

"Go to Pat Dalton's office," Ritchie said.

"What the hell—"

"He's not there. Just go."

Obediently, I headed across the floor toward executive row, my heart pounding.

As I approached the office, I saw Dalton's assistant through the door to the outer office. "What next?" I asked Ritchie.

"Go in."

"But his assistant is there."

"*Go in*, damnit. Ignore her."

I didn't have time to think about it. I looked back. Three men were headed toward my cube from the elevator: Les Hornsby, his assistant, Royce, and a guy I didn't recognize. I plowed ahead, rolling past Dalton's assistant, meeting her bewildered expression with my nicest fake smile.

I entered the cavernous office. "What now?" I asked Ritchie.

"Go out the door at the back. It's on your left."

Sure enough, there was an inconspicuous door to the left of Dalton's massive desk. I went up to the door, pushed it open, and rolled through. I found myself in a little hallway.

"What do I do now?" I asked Ritchie.

"Go left. There's an elevator two doors down. Take it."

I moved down the little hallway, the existence of which I'd been unaware. I found the elevator, which I assumed was for the private use of the executives, and pushed the Down button. The door opened without a chime. "I'm getting on," I said. "I might lose you."

"Go to the ground floor. *Not* the parking garage. Ground. You'll come out by a loading dock. I'll meet you there."

I followed his instructions. The elevator seemed to take forever to get to the ground floor. There were no buttons for the floors in between. I wiped my slick hands on my pants, wondering how long it would take Dalton's assistant to report my intrusion to Hornsby, who was already on the seventh floor.

The elevator stopped, and the door opened onto a little alcove, empty except for a single door. It was a heavy door; I pushed the bar and struggled to get through it. Finally, I made it outside, finding myself next to a single-bay loading dock, serviced by a stairway and a ramp. I proceeded down the ramp.

I heard a vehicle approaching. Glancing down the roadway behind the building, I saw, incredibly, my van approaching. The engine was revving irregularly, and the van's progress was slow and jerky. Finally, it stopped at the foot of the ramp. I had my keychain out, and I pushed the button to lower the profile, open the side door, and extend the ramp.

"Get in here and drive," Ritchie yelled. "I don't know how to work this thing."

He moved over to the passenger seat, holding a baseball cap over his face. I slid in behind the wheel and clamped my chair into place as the ramp retracted and the door closed. Then I took off.

"Where to?" I asked.

"Out. Anyplace. Just get off the premises."

I headed for the employee exit. As I rounded a corner for the main aisle, I saw flashing lights across the lot.

"Shit," Ritchie said. "Floor it. They're trying to cut us off."

I sped up, heading for the exit. There was a gate at the exit, a bar that lifted automatically when a vehicle approached. You had to pull right up to it, trigger a sensor, and wait for it to go up. During peak exit times, you could go out right behind another vehicle without stopping. But now there was no other vehicle. I'd have to come to a near-complete stop and wait for the gate to go up.

"They might deactivate the gate," Ritchie said. "In fact, they probably have. You'll have to crash it."

"*What?*"

"It'll be okay."

I watched the stationary bar ahead of me. "I can't."

"Just *do it!*" he barked.

The lights were gaining. I sped up a bit. "Hang on," I said. Ritchie had already fastened his seat belt. I sped up some more.

I managed to keep my eyes open as we crashed the gate, which gave way with a loud, sharp crack, but the impact did little to slow us down.

"Go, go, go!" Ritchie yelled. "Toward the freeway!" The flashing lights were in my rearview. I made the turn onto Bolsa and headed for the 405. I approached a red light up ahead. Cars waited in all three of the lanes going our way. Fortunately, there were clear lines of sight in both directions of the cross street. I saw one car approaching from the left, nothing from the right. The light was still red, the cars ahead of me still stopped. And the flashing lights gaining.

I swerved into the left turn lane and drove through the red light, slowed down slightly to miss the one car from the left, then jammed down on the hand accelerator. Half a block later, I dared to look in my mirror. The flashing lights had stopped in the intersection, blocked by cars making left turns.

"Turn," Ritchie said. I made a right, then several other turns on side streets. Eventually we came to Westminster, a major street leading to the 405. We had lost them.

We relaxed a little. "Gutsy," Ritchie said. "Great driving."

"Once you talked me into crashing that gate, I was on my way."

"Those hand controls were baffling. How do you drive this thing, anyway?"

"It's probably easier than starting it without a key." I nodded toward the screwdriver sticking out of the ignition lock. A busted plastic panel from the steering column lay on the floor.

"Sorry about that," he said. "I'll get it fixed."

"How did you know they were coming for me?"

"Royce gave me a heads-up."

"Why would he do that?"

"When you're investigating a security breach, you need sources. I've got Royce. I don't think he likes Les, anyway."

"What were they going to do once they got me?"

"They were going to question you for a while, then have you arrested for criminal fraud—lying on your job application and using a false identity."

"I would have been out of jail in an hour."

"They know that. But they were really interested in seeing who showed up to bail you out."

"I suppose. Even so . . ."

"Dez, Royce says he didn't know what they were going to do after the arrest, but that wouldn't have been the end of it. They had plans for you. Something they couldn't do at headquarters."

I felt my hands tremble against the steering wheel as my imagination went into overdrive. "I see. Where are we going, by the way?"

"My place. I can't think of any better location for you right now. In the meantime, you'd better talk to your friends at the Bureau about some protection."

"I guess so."

Ritchie lived in an apartment complex on the west side of the 405, across from the massive South Coast Plaza shopping area. The complex consisted of about a dozen three-story buildings, which appeared to be accessed by exterior stairways.

"I'm on the first floor," he said. There was half a flight of steps leading up to that level.

"Uh-oh," I said.

"There's an elevator down at the end. Park over there." I parked next to what looked like a service door.

I rolled down the ramp, feeling wrung-out. The freeway was only a block away, and its noise would have made it hard to hold a conversation in the parking lot. Ritchie opened the door for me, admitting us to a stinky alcove with a garbage chute and a scratched-up elevator for the ride up to the first floor.

The spotless apartment was, like the one I occupied as Dez, perfunctorily furnished with rental items. "You should be okay here," Ritchie said.

"Won't they find out you helped me?"

"I don't see how. We're not known to be friends. Even our agencies don't know we're working together. Look—I need to get back. I'm planning to stay awhile after the merger and continue my futile quest." He pulled out his phone, presumably to order an Uber, and put it away after a few clicks. "Sorry to bail on you."

I grabbed his hand. "Are you kidding? Without getting too melodramatic, you might have saved my life, Clay. And think of all the fun I would have missed out on: a narrow escape; a car chase."

He pulled something out of his jacket pocket. I recoiled.

"Ever fire one of these?" he asked, handing me the pistol.

I hesitated, then nodded. Apart from an hour once at a shooting range, I had fired a gun twice in my life. Neither experience was one I wanted to repeat.

"Just keep it handy," he said. "You never know."

I stared at the gun as he placed it on a side table in the kitchen. "No," I said. "You never do."

Ritchie left, and I looked around the apartment. The bathroom was barely accessible. There was a bed in a spare room, but it would be tough getting in and out of it. If I stayed here tonight, I'd also need my paraplegic supplies, but I wouldn't be able to go home to get them. My computer was also at home—I'd have to get by with my phone.

I called Nomura. "It's official," I said. "I'm blown. I got out."

"Where are you? Are you safe?"

"I think so. I'm at an apartment that belongs to a guy from DSI, Clay Ritchie. He works in Finance, and I've gotten to know him." I omitted, of course, the fact that my host worked undercover for a rival agency, had helped me make a hair-raising escape, and was good at hot-wiring vehicles and serving knuckle sandwiches to belligerent punks.

"All right—I can see where you are," Nomura said, apparently tracking my cell phone. "I've got no place to put you and nobody to watch you right now. I'll try to figure out something."

"Okay."

"We've set up the call to Elena Morton's husband for seven tonight. Any reason you can't do it from right where you are?"

"That should be fine."

"Pen, you should know . . ."

"Yes?"

"Marisa Costas is in the hospital."

"Why?"

"She was found, traumatized and speechless, in her apartment. They're still not sure what was done to her."

"My God."

"I have to ask you what she knows."

"Wendy, please."

"I know you're upset, but it's critical to assess the damage. We have to assume they now know everything she knows."

"Give me a minute." I took deep breaths, trying to hold it together and sort out my thoughts. "She knows Keri had a friend named Elena," I said, "but claimed not to know who she was. She might know more, but that's the main thing she's told us."

"That makes tonight's call to Elena's husband all the more important."

"I want to go to the hospital to see Marisa."

"Nice thought, but we need to stay away until she's able to receive visitors. One other thing: Howard found out that Landrum's plane took a trip to Washington the night Elena was killed. We're not sure who was on it, but we know Landrum wasn't."

"My money is on Kamensky."

"Makes sense."

"It reeks of panic," I said.

"It certainly does. Anyway, it will help build a case against Landrum."

We signed off. I thought about Marisa, and how my amateurish attempts to foil surveillance at the supermarket must have failed, exposing her to capture and mistreatment. Poor Marisa, who'd wanted so badly to be taken seriously. Sometimes, I thought, it was better to be invisible.

*   *   *

Kamensky stood at the door of the condo rented by Desiree Walker, or as he now knew her, Pen Wilkinson. He took one more look around before pulling out his lock picks and going to work on the door.

Over the past few days he had systematically and discreetly searched the area around the complex and had found, perched on a light pole, a video camera trained on the front of the building. The camera didn't appear to be active, but he had re-aimed it away from the building anyway. Four minutes later, he was inside the condo.

The place looked clean overall, but within a few minutes he'd turned up a brunette wig and a burner phone.

He felt like a fool. This cripple had been playing him, playing PACIFIC, for weeks. A session up at the cabin was definitely in order. He still felt the buzz from questioning Marisa—that had been good. Pen would be better—a lot better.

Chapter 60

At seven that night, I dialed in to a conference number Nomura had given me. Ritchie had not yet returned home, and I sat in the spare bedroom. Nomura and Howard were already on the call. I put the phone on speaker and set in on the bed next to me.

"Pen, are you there?" Howard asked. He was taking the lead on the call.

"I'm here."

"Pen, as you know, we have Special Agent Nomura on the line. We also have Detective Artie Guzman from the DC police."

We exchanged hellos.

"Finally," Howard said, "we have with us from Arlington, Virginia, Mr. Cole Harker, Elena Morton's husband."

"Hi," I said. "I'm sorry for your loss, Mr. Harker."

"Thank you," said an exhausted-sounding voice.

"Mr. Harker," Howard said, "let's start with some basics." For the next few minutes we went through vital statistics on Harker and Elena—full names, address, length of marriage (seven years), education (both had law degrees), and children (none). Harker gave concise, almost robotic responses.

"Thank you," Howard said. "Detective Guzman, could you briefly fill us in on the murder?"

The detective described the shooting, three days before Keri's murder, at approximately 12:30 AM, giving the address and re-iterating that the neighborhood was no longer considered a dangerous one. The DC police had done extensive canvassing of the area and closely checked out all the people at the party Elena had attended but had come up empty. They had talked to supervisors and co-workers at the CFTC but found nothing about her work that was unduly contentious or controversial. Elena seemed to get along fine with her co-workers.

Brian Lutterman

"Let's talk about Elena's friends," said Howard.

Guzman answered: "We talked to several of Elena's closest friends here in the DC area, and one in Boston. All told us that they knew of no enemies Elena might have made, or unusual stressors in her life, or financial or addiction problems."

"That's correct," Harker confirmed.

"Then let's talk about Keri Wylie," Howard said.

"I've met Keri several times over the years," the grieving husband said. "She was a pretty close friend of Elena's when they were in law school on the West Coast."

"When was the first time you met her?"

"A year or two before we were married. We were on vacation in San Diego, and we drove up to see Keri."

"How about after that?"

"Probably at our wedding."

"Was Keri a bridesmaid?" Nomura asked.

"No. Elena considered asking her but just felt they didn't see a lot of each other anymore, and that was likely to continue. Keri got married just before us and didn't ask Elena."

"What was the nature of their contacts after that?" Howard asked.

"They saw each other a couple of times. They talked quite often on the phone after Keri got divorced a few years ago. Lately, they seemed to have talked every month or so."

As I listened, I would have bet that Howard already knew exactly how many times they had talked. It also occurred to me that the DC cop had undoubtedly seen Keri turn up in Elena's phone records but apparently hadn't followed up. And based upon what the DC police knew, I'm not sure I would have faulted them. There was no evidence pointing to a targeted killing as opposed to a street crime.

"Do you recall their most recent conversation?" Howard asked.

"No. I didn't realize they had talked. But Elena had told me that they would."

My felt my heart rate climb. This was it.

He continued: "Elena was going through some papers one night, working at home, and said something like, 'I think I might give Keri a call on this.'"

"Why was that?"

"She said, 'I've got a pattern here on oil futures. Looks like somebody might be trading ahead of announcements by the Russian state oil company. It might go back for years. The name of this outfit sounds familiar; Keri might know something about them, in a general way. They're on the West Coast.'"

"Did she say who the suspected trader was?"

"No. She had to be careful—there are rules about confidentiality of an ongoing investigation."

I looked up suddenly and nearly had a heart attack. Clay Ritchie was standing in the doorway. I was jumpy to begin with, and I hadn't heard him come home. I wasn't sure how long he'd been listening. He turned as if to go, but I motioned for him to stay.

"Detective Guzman and I talked to Elena's boss earlier today," Howard said, "but he said there was no record of such an investigation by Elena, or by anyone in the office."

Guzman added, "The killer took Elena's purse, which had her cell phone in it. He also took her briefcase, which was in her car, apparently accessing the vehicle with her keys, which were also in the purse. With Mr. Harker's permission and cooperation, we searched Cole and Elena's residence for anything related to the investigation and came up empty."

Howard said, "Mr. Harker, I'm going to run a couple of names past you. The first is Techinvest Partners."

"I've heard of them, but only in the news. I never heard Elena mention them."

"The other is Paul Landrum."

Harker hesitated. "I may have heard the name. I'm not sure. If I did, it was probably from the news as well. Elena never mentioned him."

After a few more follow-up questions, Harker dropped off the call. Guzman and Howard agreed to talk tomorrow, and Guzman hung up. That left Howard, Nomura, and me.

"What do you think?" Howard asked.

"The Russian connection rings a big-time bell," Nomura said. "It would solidify Landrum's connection to them." Across the room, I saw Ritchie nodding.

"But," Howard said, "all we have is the husband's word. If there was an investigation, it must have been very preliminary—so much so that Elena didn't even have a chance to open a file."

"I wouldn't jump to that conclusion," I said. "I'd ask Elena's boss tomorrow if they've had any recent data breaches."

I could feel Nomura's skepticism over the phone. Howard said, "I'll ask," but it was clear that he didn't expect to find anything on that score, either.

Now Howard said, "Wendy, can you explain what Harker meant by 'trading ahead of' announcements by the Russian state oil company?"

"I think so," Nomura said. "Statements by the Russian state-owned oil company, which is one of the largest in the world, could have an impact on world oil prices. If they report that their production for the previous quarter was lower than expected, that could cause prices to rise. If they announce that they've discovered a big new oil field, that could cause prices to fall. Are you with me?"

"Yes," Howard and I said in unison.

"Good. So, if the Russians tipped somebody—say, Landrum—ahead of the announcement, he'd be able to get in on the action before the price changed. His profits would be magnified by leverage and by using futures contracts. It's like insider trading in the stock market."

"How much money could he make by doing that?" Howard asked.

"That depends on how long he's been doing it. If he was careful, he'd be selective about it so as not to attract attention. Potentially, the profits could be huge."

"Landrum isn't a stats geek," I pointed out. "It makes sense that he might be relying on inside information instead of brilliant analysis."

"Where does this leave us?" Howard asked.

"The merger will go on," Nomura said. "We can't stop it."

"Couldn't it be delayed, even a little?" I asked.

"No. I talked to the ADC this afternoon. He says it's been delayed three times already, and there's too much momentum to close the deal tomorrow—too much money and political influence. Did you know that Pat Dalton plays golf with the President?"

"All right, I get the message." I now knew what I'd long suspected, that Nomura was working directly with Assistant Director in Charge Kirk Hendricks. That made me uneasy, since Hendricks was a friend of Dave O'Shea. But the ADC obviously didn't know Nomura was still working the DSI operation on the sly.

"So, you understand why we can't delay the closing," Nomura said. "But I'm certain that we're on to something here. Let's sleep on it and reconvene tomorrow."

"Anything new on Marisa?" I asked.

"No. She still can't tell us anything." I suppressed the waves of guilt that were churning up nausea in my gut.

We talked for a few minutes longer. Howard wanted to hear the details of my escape from DSI headquarters. "I'd expect some negative feedback on your next job performance review," he cracked.

Nomura asked, "Pen, are you able to stay where you are tonight?"

"Yes."

"Do you feel secure there?"

I glanced up and gave Ritchie a mock-skeptical look. "Yes, I'm okay."

"Good. Don't go back to your condo for any reason."

"I won't."

"I'm working on finding you a place to stay, informally."

"Informal?"

"A friend of my brother's."

"I see." One of the problems of going rogue, I thought. No FBI safe house.

"I'll call in the morning with a plan for relocating you."

"Thanks."

"Goodnight, everybody," Howard said.

I clicked off and turned to Ritchie. "That's it," he said flatly. "That's why Keri was killed. The question is whether you'll ever be able to prove it."

"The CFTC can pick up where Elena left off," I said. "Unravel what Landrum has been up to."

"Unless they can prove an actual link, a transfer of information from the Russians to Landrum, it will be hard to nail him."

"We know one thing for certain: they're concerned about us finding the channel for the transfer of information. Look what they did to Marisa." I told him about my meetings with her and about the assault she had suffered last night. "Right after meeting with me," I concluded. "She was reluctant to get involved. With good reason, it turned out."

"I wouldn't assume it was your meeting," he said. "It could have been general suspicion. For now, we have to figure out what the rest of Landrum's plan is and keep anything from happening to you."

I nodded. "You shouldn't get too comfortable, either. They may have their suspicions about you."

"They probably do. We'll see." He held up a paper bag. "I got the stuff you asked for."

"Thanks." I'd asked him to buy me some paraplegic supplies, which I couldn't retrieve from Dez's apartment.

I got ready for bed, struggling in the apartment's undersized bathroom. I'd have to settle for a sponge bath in the morning, since a shower was out of the question. But I'd done that plenty of times over the years.

When I was settled back in the spare bedroom, Ritchie knocked on the door.

"Come in."

Ritchie stuck his head into the room. "You doing okay?"

"I don't know. That escape cost me about a gallon of adrenaline and a few whole-life flashbacks." In truth, I was mildly surprised and very relieved that I hadn't had any PTSD symptoms. "I'm starting to come down from the buzz, I think."

He came in and sat down.

"Thanks for hosting me," I said.

"My pleasure. And you can be my driver anytime. Your van is fixed, by the way. The ignition, I mean. You still need some body work."

"That was quick."

"No problem. Sorry I had to mess it up. But it was for a good cause."

"Thanks, Clay, for bailing me out today. They may have been planning to have me arrested, but who knows? Look what they did to Marisa."

"True. And you're not out of the woods yet." He leaned closer. "Thanks for trusting me. By telling me about your op, you put yourself in the center of a huge federal bullseye. You're probably looking at jail time if they find out."

"I was looking at Landrum and Hornsby if I didn't."

"Hell of a dilemma."

"I can't believe we've come this far, gotten this close, and we're too late."

"Too late to stop the merger," he agreed. "It will happen at nine. And then people will start going over to Hulbert, and everybody will get logins, and it will be open season on all of Hulbert's products."

We looked at each other. The silence was heavy and awkward. "You're blonde," he observed.

I realized he'd never seen me sans wig and glasses. "No jokes, please."

"Not a chance. And your name is . . . Pen?"

"Yes. That woman who recognized me used to work at my old office."

"I figured. When this is over, maybe we can tell each other our stories."

"Might be fun."

More awkward silence. "You have somebody, don't you?" he said.

"Yes."

"I could tell. Too bad. Who knows what might have happened with us?"

I smiled but didn't say anything.

"Good night—Pen."

Chapter 61

I woke up and checked my phone—nine o'clock. I had slept nearly twelve hours. I dragged myself out of bed, negotiated the cramped bathroom, and got dressed. In the kitchen, Ritchie had thoughtfully taken the coffee out of the cabinet and left it on the counter where I could reach it and filled the coffeemaker with water. He'd also moved the toaster over to the kitchen table, leaving out a bag of bagels, along with a plate and knife. I found the cream cheese in the refrigerator.

I was done at DSI. It would have been nice to quietly resign and say goodbye to my co-workers, but that was out of the question now. Hornsby and his people were after me, and everybody had to know it. I wondered what slanderous story they were putting out about my sudden flight. I glanced at my phone again: 9:40. The Hulbert closing was happening as I ate. Keri's warning had been in vain; I had fallen short in my efforts to learn the truth.

Fortified with food and caffeine, I found a notepad and pen on a desk in the living room and began to think, to sort out what it all meant. At the top of the notepad, I wrote down the first topic that came to mind. I felt the story had probably begun with Landrum's Russian-backed commodity trading scheme, with Elena and Keri finding out and then being killed. I wasn't sure covering up the scheme was really a reason for committing murder, much less bringing in a professional assassin to do the job. Didn't Wall Street offenders often get off with a slap on the wrist, or a short stint in Club Fed?

What, then, was the reason for Landrum's concern? I felt sure it was the Russian connection, which must have gone deeper than the trading scheme and involved more serious crimes. I wondered how far back the connection went, recalling that the Russians not only might have supported Landrum's trading scheme but provided some of the seed capital to get his hedge fund started. Nomura was supposedly looking into this possibility, but actually finding records that old and piecing together actions from that long ago seemed like the longest of long shots. I wondered if Landrum's former associate, Stewart Kyler, had discovered the Russian support and paid the price for his discovery with a fatal car accident.

Topic number two: What was the current nature of the Landrum-Russian connection? Was it the West Coast spy ring, headed by somebody code-named PACIFIC?

My next topic was entitled "Landrum's Flights." Landrum had been flying off to Minnesota and had made at least some effort to conceal the trips. Why? I also wondered why Keri had zeroed in on the flights for only a limited period.

I sat back and tossed the pen and pad onto the kitchen table, utterly frustrated. There were all kinds of fishy things going on, but every path toward an answer seemed to peter out, leading nowhere. And yet, we must be getting close; Landrum and his people were doing all kinds of things to cover their tracks.

And to silence the investigators.

Chapter 62

Les Hornsby shut the door behind him after entering Paul Landrum's office. "Make it good," Landrum said. "I just spent two hours at a closing. Trapped in a conference room with about eighty lawyers. That's enough to put anybody in a shitty mood. Do you know where she is?"

"We might. We should know shortly."

"How the hell did she get away?"

"She was tipped. And she had help making her exit."

"Who helped her escape? One of Dalton's people?"

"Nope." Hornsby sat down, uninvited. "It's a guy we've had some doubts about, but not serious doubts. Clay Ritchie."

"That young guy in Finance? I've met him, I guess. Are you sure?"

The security man nodded and placed an electronic tablet in front of Landrum.

"Here's the loading dock," he said, pulling up a video. "This is Dez's van, coming up the back driveway."

"She wouldn't have had access to that loading dock area," Landrum pointed out.

"She used the executive elevator. Went right through Dalton's office to get there."

Landrum's eyebrows lifted. "Brazen."

"Okay, so somebody is driving the van up to the dock. You see the door opening and the ramp come out. Now she's going in. Meanwhile, the driver has shifted to the shotgun seat."

"Holding his hat to shield his face from the cameras. No dummy."

"Now, by this time, we've alerted our people in the lobby and at the parking lot exit. We switched the exit gate to manual. Okay, they're driving away. She's behind the wheel."

The scene on the tablet switched to an exterior view of the parking lot. He pointed to one corner. "There—you can see her headed for the exit. And there's our security car, chasing her. Now she crashes the gate and turns onto Bolsa."

"And then you lost her."

"She ran a red light. It was a fluke. We weren't able to—"

"*And then you lost her,*" Landrum repeated, his voice rising slightly, menacingly.

"Yes," Hornsby said calmly. "Then we lost her."

"What are you doing to find her?"

"We'll find her through Ritchie."

"He hid his face. How do you know it was him?"

"He checked in at the employee entrance an hour later. Turns out he had never checked out. I looked at the lobby cam footage—he arrived by Uber."

"Now he's got her stashed somewhere?"

"Probably at his own apartment. We're doing preliminary surveillance right now."

"Do you think you can get her out of there—and him, for that matter—without making too big a mess?"

"I'm sure we can. We'll do it tonight."

"Because I've got other people who can do the job."

"I'm sure we can handle it."

"That's good, Les, because you don't seem to have handled things all that well so far. This woman sat fifty feet from my office for a month and a half, and you didn't have a clue. I had to find out who she was myself."

"But—"

"And then she sneaks out of here, right under your nose. And we haven't even begun discussing Ritchie yet. How long has he been with DSI?"

"I don't know offhand. A while."

"And who does he work for? What's the relationship between him and this Pen?"

It was clear that Landrum didn't expect an answer. He continued: "I want an extraction plan for tonight in place in two hours. You'll work with my people on it."

As Hornsby walked out, Landrum added, "You'd better find out who the hell tipped her — Ritchie, or whoever it was. And my guy will get some damn answers out of them."

Chapter 63

I was pondering a trip to the hospital to see Marisa when my Dez phone buzzed in my hand. I glanced at the screen: Tim Dalton.

"Hi, Tim."

"Hi, Dez. I'm down in OC today and wondered if you'd like to do happy hour with me."

I thought fast. With everything going on, it seemed crazy to go out drinking. I'd planned on returning quickly after a brief trip to the hospital. On the other hand, I was starting to feel like a stationary target, a sitting duck, here at Ritchie's place. And I needed a break badly. "Sure, Tim."

*   *   *

I needed to go to the hospital. I didn't want to go, and Nomura had told me to stay away. But I couldn't not go. I parked in a handicap spot in the ramp and made my way to the reception desk in the lobby, giving my name, receiving a badge, and obtaining Marisa's room number. On the eighth floor, I got off and looked up at the sign; Room 824 was on my left. I didn't know whether Marisa would be able to talk or, if she was, whether she would want to talk to me, but I plunged ahead.

Halfway down the hallway there was a waiting area. I slowed down. A middle-aged couple sat together, watching CNN with the sound turned down. I glanced over and studied them, trying not to be obvious about it. The woman was definitely Marisa's mother, with the same blonde hair, green eyes, and sculpted face. I couldn't see any resemblance between Marisa and the man, and I wondered if he was a stepfather, or other friend or family member.

The couple seemed settled in, so I deemed it safe to proceed to 824. I arrived, glanced up and down the hall, and listened at the door. Nothing. I slowly pushed the door open and adjusted my eyes to the dim light. The room contained two beds with a curtain in between. The bed closest to the door was unoccupied. I slowly rolled toward the other bed. At the edge of the curtain, I paused, collected myself, and moved ahead the last couple of feet.

I thought I had prepared myself for the worst. I hadn't. The woman who stared at me from the bed was a haunted, grotesque version of the person I'd met with at a supermarket a few nights ago. Her skin was gray, her unkempt hair matted. But the eyes . . .

I knew I would never forget the eyes. They conveyed horror and resignation, a forced detachment from the monster—from a world—that had violated and betrayed her. They reflected, involuntarily, the unimaginable sickness and depravity of the alleged humans who had done this to her. But there was one more feature in those eyes, in the gaze that looked somehow both intense and unfocused as they stared at me.

They were accusing.

I heard myself gasping, emitting little shrieks, as I fled from the room. I can't run, of course, but I did the wheelchair equivalent, and in this case, the running wasn't mostly about physical movement. It was about escape—the illusion of escape.

*   *   *

It was a little after five when I arrived at the waterfront bar in Newport Beach. I wasn't going back to DSI, and I wondered if it was time to officially retire Dez Walker. But it would have been complicated and possibly premature to explain everything to Tim. So I donned wig and glasses again, at least for this occasion.

Tim had already claimed a table and stood up when I rolled in. "You made good time," he said. "Did you get off work early?"

"Um, yes."

"You look a little upset. Everything okay?"

I managed to nod.

"I hope you don't mind sitting outside again. It's warmer today."

"It's fine." I found myself scanning the bar for people with malevolent intent, although I wasn't sure what they would look like. I hadn't noticed anybody watching or following when I'd left Ritchie's place. If Landrum was on to Ritchie, we were both in deep trouble. Nomura was supposed to have a safe house ready by seven. I took comfort in the fact that she was able to track my phone, and I was poised to hit the phone's speed dial button.

"Have you talked to your dad?" I asked as the waitress brought our drinks. "He must be feeling pretty good right now."

"He should be," Tim agreed. "I haven't talked to him today, though. I just hope that with the merger complete, he'll be able to slow down and relax a little. Maybe play some golf and do some traveling again. That's what he likes to do—at least he used to."

"You might not want to get your hopes up too much," I said. "There will be a lot of work, integrating Hulbert into DSI."

"I suppose." He sipped from his craft beer. "I honestly don't understand why he feels the need to keep going. He's got plenty of money. Why doesn't he just hang it up while he's still young enough to enjoy retirement?"

"He probably feels a responsibility to see the merger through for a while," I said. "And he undoubtedly wants to make sure Landrum doesn't get his hands on the company."

"There you go," he said. "He'd stay until he's ninety to prevent that."

"Kind of strange that Landrum supported the merger, too."

"Yeah. A bigger prize for him to take over."

I'd never thought of it that way, but Tim might have been right. "Tim," I said, "has your dad ever expressed concern about security at DSI? About spying or leakage of technology?"

"Not specifically. I'm sure he's concerned about those things, but he's never mentioned it when I've been around."

"Does your father have any ties to Russia? Business dealings or friends?"

He gave me a curious look. "Why are you asking these questions?"

I tried my winning smile. "I'm just a curious busybody, Tim. I've hung around your family a bit, and I work on the executive floor, so I hear some interesting stuff. I got grilled for a long time about my personal life by that creepy security director, so I can only imagine the kind of security checks your dad has to go through."

He seemed to accept this. "I don't hear anything about Russians, really. I mean, I'm sure he's been there at some point and knows people who are from Russia, but I never hear him talk about it."

I shifted the conversation to other subjects, asking about his job and his roommates. He answered my questions but didn't seem interested in the topics. As usual, he seemed more interested in me.

"So how do you like it at DSI?" he asked.

I didn't think the time was right to tell him I was done there. That would have meant explaining why, which I wasn't yet in a position to do. "It's fine, Tim. To be honest, the work is a little tedious, but the people are good, for the most part."

He grinned. "But not the security guy? I've heard about him."

I returned the smile. "He's a piece of work, like somebody out of the Cold War or *Dr. Strangelove* or something."

"And you got questioned by him?"

"Yep." I looked at myself and the wheelchair. "Don't I look like a foreign spy to you?"

He gave me a mock critical look. "You do ask a lot of questions."

We chatted for a while longer about innocuous things. I tried to go easy on the wine; I had a lot to do yet tonight. When our conversation reached a pause, Tim leaned back, drained his beer, and said, "I really like talking to you, Dez. It's like—it's like talking to Mikayla."

"I'm really flattered, Tim."

"I mean it."

"Jackie told me that Mikayla wasn't found after the accident."

His mood instantly soured. "That's right."

"That's really too bad. Makes it tough to get closure."

"I guess."

"Your dad just came back and told you what had happened?"

It was one question too many. "You really are inquisitive."

"Sorry. Just not too smooth in making conversation."

"I mean, these things are—why are you so interested?"

I abandoned my attempts to smooth things over. He wasn't about to be mollified. And he'd been drinking, which may not have helped.

"I've had this feeling," he said, "that you're more than just a paralegal working on my dad's floor. Do you have some other agenda?" He was getting worked up.

"I'm just trying to be a friend."

"Sometimes I believe that. But you know what? It's probably bullshit."

I decided to keep my mouth shut, which I'm able to do every now and then.

"Jesus," he said. "I just can't figure you out." He stood up abruptly, tossed some bills on the table, and started to leave.

I caught his arm. "Tim, what really happened in Thailand?"

He walked away.

*   *   *

Ritchie called just as I was leaving the parking lot a few minutes later. "Everything okay?" he asked.

"So far. I've been out for a while, and I'm headed back to your place now. I should be hearing soon about my relocation."

"I'll be leaving for home shortly."

"I'm not sure where we go from here," I said. "I'll get a better sense when I hear from Nomura."

"I've got to report in, too. Let's compare notes later tonight. See you back at the ranch."

"See you then."

*   *   *

Ritchie hung up and straightened the papers on his desk. So Dez/Pen was blown, which meant he couldn't be far behind. He had the feeling they were close to a major break in solving the leaks of classified material from DSI, and maybe to cracking the Russian spy operation on the West Coast. They just needed a bit more time.

First things first, he thought. Time to get Pen to a place of safety. He'd have to move, too, in case he was blown as well. Tonight, he'd have to explain to his handlers why he'd helped Pen escape and then taken her in, jeopardizing his own cover. It wouldn't be a fun conversation.

He shut his light off, closed his door, and headed for the elevator. The floor was eerily deserted; most of the administrative staff had already gone home, and he suspected that those executives and attorneys who weren't over at Hulbert were out celebrating.

He never reached the elevator. From an alcove in the hallway, Les Hornsby stepped out in front of him. Holding a gun.

Chapter 64

Nomura called shortly after I got back to Ritchie's. "Are you ready to go?" she asked.

"Any time." *And the sooner the better*, I thought.

"My brother has a friend who's in China. You can stay at his place up in LA."

"Fine."

"Howard followed up with the CFTC today," she said. "They've thoroughly searched Elena's office, files, and hard drives, and they can't find any record of an investigation of those Russian trading patterns. But—and I hate to admit you were right—they did have a data breach, right around the time of Elena's murder."

I wasn't sure why anyone would have been surprised, given all the sophisticated and destructive hacking the Russians had done against the United States over the past few years. "The breach is certainly suggestive," I said. "But unless we turn somebody and get them to talk, we may never know exactly what Elena found."

"I'm afraid you're right again. Meanwhile, the Hulbert deal has closed. There was a nice ceremony, with Dalton and Landrum standing side by side, all smiles."

"At least one of them can't be too happy."

"The closing went ahead. The world didn't end. Nobody turned into a pumpkin."

"Right." We both knew the real fallout, whatever it was, had yet to occur.

"I made some discreet inquiries about Techinvest Partners," she said, "and was able to quietly access our files on them from around the time they acquired an interest in DSI. Landrum was asked at the time about the original sources of capital for his hedge fund, MinnFund Partners. He was vague about it. He said there'd been 'loans and investors,' and admitted some of them might have been foreign. He pleaded memory failure for the most part."

"What was the follow-up?"

"There really wasn't any. The whole thing was just deemed too remote in time from the purchase of the DSI stake, which of course was made by Techinvest Partners, not its predecessor, MinnFund. The investigators didn't see any red flags, and so they left it at that."

"So that's it?"

"No. As soon as we resolve our internal problem, which I expect to be soon, there will be a full investigation."

"You should check out his ex-wife, too. She might know something."

"Why do you say that?"

"No specific reason. She was there at the time, that's all."

"You're right. I was looking back through all this old stuff, and I saw that her parents had an FBI file."

Diane's father had been a factory worker from Wichita, I recalled. I wondered what possible interest the FBI could have had in him.

"What's in the file?"

"I don't know. I've ordered a copy."

"Wendy, I think I've figured some things out, about Landrum and about some other subjects."

"Good. We need to talk, to spend some time. Then we can figure out how to approach your official debriefing."

"Sounds good."

"Just sit tight. I need to make a quick stop at home, and then I'll be right over. See you in an hour."

Sitting at the kitchen table, I looked at my notes some more. And thought some more. And a mental light went on. I picked up my phone and called Nomura back. The call went to voicemail.

Then I pulled out my burner phone and tried Ritchie. Same result.

I was feeling uneasy and a little lightheaded, and it had nothing to do with the wine. I glanced over my notes again. I thought about Keri some more.

I tried Nomura again. More voicemail. The same with Ritchie. Damnit, I needed to get going. Finally, some things were becoming clear.

Chapter 65

Wendy Nomura turned onto her street in the quiet neighborhood in Fountain Valley. She'd gotten this modest house after her divorce three years earlier, and at times it didn't seem like much of a prize. The palms needed trimming, the garden was overgrown, and she could see that another tile had come off the roof. Maybe she'd have time to deal with it all now that the DSI operation was ending.

Pen claimed to have some things worked out. She'd made similar claims before and had usually been right. But they had been little things, and after a month and a half, Pen had actually learned very little. It wasn't Pen's fault, for the most part, although it couldn't have helped that she'd freelanced the typo incident, antagonizing Landrum. Wendy tried to think positive. The Elena Morton angle might yet prove fruitful. With a little more time, Pen might well have figured it all out.

But even if Pen hadn't worked out the big picture yet, there was every reason to believe Landrum would be concerned about her. The attempt to detain her at DSI headquarters confirmed that, as if the murders of Elena Morton and Keri Wylie weren't enough. So Wendy had taken no chances; she'd called Dan Howard and arranged for somebody from Costa Mesa PD to keep an eye on Pen until she could be taken to the safe house. Pen was probably safe while staying with a guy from work named Ritchie, but Wendy didn't know him. No reason to take chances.

Meanwhile, Wendy's role in the case was nearing an end. The focus now would shift to Newport Beach, where Howard would be taking the lead in trying to tie Keri Wylie's murder to a cover-up of Landrum's commodity trading scheme. Wendy would stay involved, monitor the Russian angle, and keep trying to get a handle on the Russian spy operation, headed by a person named PACIFIC.

She parked in the carport, walked around to the door leading to the house, and pulled the keys out of her purse. She unlocked the door and was about to go in when a voice stopped her.

"Hold it, Wendy."

Ward Gilbertson.

She turned around. "What the—"

"Put your purse down." Her boss covered her with his Glock. Wendy complied. She glanced around. Thanks to her neglect of the landscaping, the encroaching shrubbery left only a narrow sight line to the street.

"Now put your piece on the ground."

She obeyed, pulling the weapon from its belt holster beneath her blazer and dropping it to the carport floor. "Ward, have you lost your mind? Put that gun away."

"Go into the house. Slowly. And keep your hands up."

She studied him. His face was a mask of quiet madness. He'd snapped.

They stepped into the kitchen. "Now enter the alarm code," Gilbertson said. "Put in the distress code if you want, but I wouldn't. Everything will just end sooner."

Now thoroughly spooked, Wendy entered the distress code. She wasn't sure how long it would take the alarm company to respond.

"Into the living room," her captor ordered.

Wendy walked through the kitchen with her hands raised.

"Sit down." Reluctantly, she sat on the highest, hardest chair in the room.

"No. On the floor."

As she lowered her tall frame onto the floor, a sound came from the carport. Her cell phone. In her purse. On the floor. The alarm company.

Gilbertson, his tie loosened and hair disheveled, looked exhausted and disappointed. "Why did you have to enter the distress code, Wendy?"

The phone rang again.

"Killing me won't solve anything," she said. "The IG is onto you."

He waved off her statement. "You think that's what this is about?"

Ring.

"Then what *is* it about? Landrum?"

"For God's sake, Wendy. This isn't about Landrum or PACIFIC. This is about you. About us."

Wendy had been feeling serious fear. Now she felt terror.

The fourth ring. Now the call would go to voicemail.

"My life is over," Gilbertson said. "It's been over since Moscow."

"What about your family?"

"I've lost my family. I've disgraced myself. I threw them away." He moved closer, a catch in his voice. "And I'd do it again. For you."

Wendy slid away from him. "Oh, no. You can't be serious."

"Ah, you don't take me seriously. Don't you think I know that?"

For Wendy, it had been the wrong thing to say. But what was the right thing? She had to *think*.

He went on. "My family doesn't have a father or a husband anymore. They only have a traitor and a stranger, who loves another woman."

She tried to dial it down. "Ward, we can talk about this."

"No, we can't. It's too late. I don't care about the Bureau or my country or my family. I care about you. I can't have you rejecting me. I can't live with that."

Wendy, at a time when quick thinking might be the only way to save her life, found her brain seizing up. What should she say?

"I can't have you with anyone else. I can't have you look at me with that look that says you don't respect me, don't love me, don't take me seriously. It has to stop." He raised the gun.

"No!"

She watched his gun hand, watched the muscles contract, watched as he squeezed the trigger.

The gun fired. Wendy Nomura, bleeding from the abdomen, fell over unconscious.

Chapter 66

Officer Calvin Torres sat in the unmarked, scanning the apartment complex's parking lot and then returning his gaze to the entrance to the first-floor apartment. People had mostly returned home from work now, but there was a steady flow of residents coming and going in the early-evening darkness. This wasn't how he'd planned on spending his evening, but he didn't mind the overtime.

They'd told him the request had come from Newport Beach, that there'd been a threat to a person in 114A. They didn't tell him the nature of the threat, but he assumed it came from an ex-husband or boyfriend. The use of the unmarked was a little unusual, dictated by Newport's request to keep the surveillance "low-key." Often, you'd want to use a squad for a show of force, to deter the bad guy. As his gaze wandered over the parking lot yet again, he wondered why Newport Beach had specified an unmarked.

He supposed the protectee could be a celeb or VIP, but he doubted such a person would be staying in a modest place like this. Then an unsettling thought occurred to Torres: maybe they were using anonymity to try to protect *him*.

*　　　*　　　*

I had everything packed and was ready to go. I hoped Nomura had some time blocked out tonight, because she was about to hear a hell of a story. But she wasn't answering her phone, and I was starting to worry. True, Landrum might not even know of Nomura's involvement in the DSI operation. But Ward Gilbertson might. In any event, her lack of response was strange. I was also getting a little concerned about Ritchie, who should have been back by now. At least the delay would prevent an awkward encounter with Nomura.

Screw it, I thought. Wendy Nomura was in the midst of a critical operation. She would not be out of touch now, forgetting to charge her phone or to turn the ringer back on after a meeting. This was not right. I called the Newport Beach Police Department and asked for Lieutenant Howard. Somebody needed to do a welfare check on Special Agent Wendy Nomura.

*   *   *

Officer Calvin Torres felt uneasy. It wasn't just the unmarked; his cop's sixth sense had been activated. He surveyed the scene again; something was off. He wondered where the vibe was coming from. There was a vestibule down the hallway from 114A; maybe he should check it out on foot. He debated getting out of the car, but it was a move he never got to make. A hole appeared in the windshield. A millisecond later, a bullet embedded itself in his head.

*   *   *

Viktor Kamensky, peering through the rifle scope, confirmed the kill. The shot had been an easy one—decent visibility in the darkness, minimal wind, and the range short. The dumbass cop never had a chance. No clue. Kamensky tossed the rifle into the back of his van, got into the driver's seat, and immediately drove across the road to the parking lot. Someone might have heard the shot or seen the cop go down—there was no time to be lost.

He didn't expect problems from Dez, or Pen, or whatever her name was. True, she wouldn't be able to walk under her own power. He'd have to throw her over his shoulder and carry her to the van. And she might have had agent training of some kind —she obviously wasn't a pro but might be a little more inclined to attempt some resistance. Or maybe she'd be like Marisa and fold instantly—you never knew. At any rate, unlike Marisa, Dez rated the full treatment. She'd be going up to the safe house.

He circled the lot once, confirmed that the cop had brought no backup, and pulled into a parking spot next to the stairwell. He'd already satisfied himself that no surveillance cameras covered 114A or the steps leading to it. He got out, activated the cell signal jammer clipped to his belt, checked his lock-picking tools, and walked briskly up the half-flight of stairs. He checked the door, confirming that it was solid, secured with a deadbolt. He'd have to pick the lock. He pulled out his tools.

*　　*　　*

I heard the clicking and scratching at the door. I stifled the urge to call out and ask who was there. After a few seconds, it became clear that it wasn't Ritchie. I'd heard enough. I pulled out my phone and punched in 911.

Nothing happened. I checked the signal. Zero bars. What on earth? I repeated the procedure. Same result, or lack of result. The clicking continued. I looked around for a landline but couldn't find one. Now I had nothing to lose. "Who is it?" I yelled.

No response.

Oh, God.

*　　*　　*

The lock was a decent one, but Kamensky picked it in a little over two minutes. He pulled out his gun but had been told not to use it. We want her alive, they'd said. He checked that he had his little bag containing the duct tape and syringe, then turned the knob and slowly pushed the door open a crack. Dark. He was about to enter when he heard a male voice behind him.

"Hey, what are you doing?"

Kamensky swiveled, leveling the gun at the source of the voice.

* * *

I quickly shut the living room light off. There was still some illumination coming from the hallway—I rolled over and shut that light off as well. The apartment was now in near-total darkness. I debated hiding in the bedroom or bathroom, but I'd be cornering myself, and probably delaying the inevitable. I decided my only chance was to try to catch the intruder by surprise. I positioned myself in the living room, over to the side of the doorway, out of the direct line of fire. As my eyes adjusted to the dark, I saw the door open a crack, then a little further. A shadow filled the crack, and I couldn't clearly see where the wall ended and the intruder began. With two shaking hands, I raised the pistol Ritchie had given me. But I still couldn't clearly locate the person.

Then I heard a voice: "Hey, what are you doing?" The door opened a little further, and the shadow turned in the doorway. I aimed carefully, using the technique I'd been taught when an FBI friend had once taken me to a range. Then I fired twice at the movement.

* * *

Kamensky was hit by the second shot. He yelped, spun, and went down, shot in the thigh. *Shit*. He'd been distracted just enough by the mystery man behind the pillar to allow himself to be silhouetted in the doorway. And the shooter hadn't missed. He looked down at his leg; apparently the bullet had missed the artery, but he was still losing blood at a dismaying clip. He'd never be able to carry Dez to the van. And it hurt like absolute hell. *Damn* it. He'd have to retreat and come up with a different plan. He limped to the van, managed to work the gas pedal with his left leg, and started for the exit.

Goddamnit, this bitch was going to pay. And pay.

*   *   *

I quickly moved sideways right after firing the shots, keeping the gun aimed at the door. I was pretty sure I'd hit the intruder, and his yelp confirmed it. There was silence. Then I heard a vehicle start up and drive away. I really, really hoped it was the intruder.

"Dez? Don't shoot—it's Tim!"

"Tim?"

"The guy left. I'm coming in."

"Okay."

He appeared in the doorway, reached in, and turned the light on. I shaded my eyes. "What on earth are you doing here?"

"I followed you," he admitted. "I—well, I behaved like a dick. I wanted to apologize." He looked at me and at the gun, wide-eyed. "You *shot* that guy."

"And you distracted him. Thanks."

"Is this where you live?"

"No," I said, "and I'm getting out of here, right now." This place was blown, and there were probably more goons where this guy had come from.

"I'm going with you."

"No, no . . ."

"Look, you can take me with you, or I'll follow you."

I sighed. "Let's go." I grabbed my purse, stashing the gun inside it and leaving everything else behind. We went outside, and I could see dark droplets on the ground leading over to the steps. We proceeded quickly down the hallway. "Try 911 again when we get to the van," I told Tim as we got onto the elevator. "He might have been blocking the cell signal."

A couple of minutes later I was in the van and clamping myself behind the driver's seat. Tim opened the passenger door. Then, in a blur, another figure stepped in behind him and slugged him over the head. I screamed. Before I could do anything, a second figure appeared at my door, holding a gun to my head.

Diane Landrum.

Chapter 67

Paul Landrum, it turned out, was the figure who had hit Tim. Now he dragged Tim up the ramp, through the side door, and heaved him onto the floor in the back. "Get his phone," said Diane. Landrum dug the phone out of Tim's pocket, and in my mirror, I saw him jam it under the back wheel of the van. Diane next made me hand over my purse. She dug through it, collecting Ritchie's burner, my Pen phone, and my Dez phone, along with my gun. She tossed all three phones to Landrum, who placed them under the other back wheel. Then she took my purse and threw it into the bushes.

"Ready," Landrum reported. "Viktor checked for trackers. None on the vehicle—not even ours."

"Close up the side door," Diane said. I complied. Diane went around to the passenger seat and got in next to me. Then Landrum got into the back.

"Let's go," said Diane. As I backed the van out, I could hear the cell phones crunch as we rolled over them. Diane directed me out of the complex and then along a series of side streets. In my rearview I could see Landrum holding a gun on me. Diane, using her phone's flashlight, searched the inside of the van, quickly coming across my knife. She tossed the knife onto the floor in back, then settled in the passenger seat.

"Is Tim still alive?" I finally asked.

"He should be okay," Landrum said. "A concussion, probably."

"Was that Kamensky who broke into the apartment?"

Diane answered. "Yes, the idiot. We told him to take Hornsby along. But he was full of macho bullshit as always, insisted he could handle a cripple in a wheelchair by himself. We figured we'd better back him up. Good thing we did." After I'd driven a

294

few minutes longer, she said, "Here's the deal, Pen: You're going to tell me everything. And I mean everything. If you're talkative enough, you get a bullet in the head. If I think you're holding back on me, I turn you over to Viktor."

"Why should I believe you?"

"What choice do you have?"

Good point, I thought. I figured I better start talking. I really didn't want to get questioned—and probably tortured—by Kamensky. More than that, I hoped that the more I told them, the likelier it would seem that I'd told somebody else. But I was dismayed at the thought of how little I'd told Nomura and Ritchie.

"Do you know who I am?" Diane asked.

"PACIFIC."

"A-plus. How did you figure it out? You didn't reach that conclusion from a little chat in Simone's kitchen. Turn right up ahead."

"Keri researched Paul's flights last fall. I don't know how she got interested in them. She left behind some notes. When I deciphered them and checked the flights out, I saw that on four occasions, he'd secretly stopped over in Minneapolis on the way home—presumably to see you. There might have been some other reason, but I couldn't think of one."

"Who did you tell about the flights?"

"Nomura." They obviously had linked me to the FBI somehow, not even bothering to ask who I worked for.

"Not a chance. Gilbertson may be a little dim, but if Nomura had found out, he'd know. We had him flag all flight inquiries. Any inquiries about Paul at all, basically. Even if you'd gone through Washington, we would have found out. Don't lie to me again Pen. If you do, the deal is off. Now what did the flights tell you?"

"It told me you must have been involved, although at the time I didn't see how. A spy network needs in-person servicing—recruiting, questioning, assigning, paying, collecting product. Since the Russian consulate in San Francisco closed and the spies who worked there got kicked out of the country, I'm thinking you're the one who does these things. You're not well-known and you're from out of state—none of the spies would have any idea who you are. And if anybody did check you out, you've got a hell of a cover: a divorcée from the Midwest. I bet you're good at holding their hands and encouraging them. I suppose most of them work for defense contractors and are either disgruntled or broke or both."

I glanced over at Diane; she confirmed my statement with a slight nod.

"It looks like you go out there on a monthly schedule," I said. "But you're very security-conscious. The FBI has always assumed other spies have replaced the ones who were expelled. Last fall, when your daughter was out of the country on a semester abroad in Australia, you had no ready excuse to fly to LA for a couple of days every month, and you decided not to risk it. So Paul, who's well-known in the defense industry and couldn't risk meeting with your sources in person, could still pick up their materials at dead drops and do the deliveries. Where do I turn?"

We had reached a "T" intersection. We had crossed the I-5 freeway, and I thought we were probably in eastern Irvine. I gripped the wheel to keep my damp hands from shaking, taking deep breaths. I tried to keep functioning despite the terror that gripped me, figuring that concentrating on questions and answers was my best coping mechanism.

"Left," Diane said. "Keep talking."

I took the left turn. "You told me you also go to New York regularly. You'd use those trips to deliver the product to your people at the Russian UN mission so it can go out of the country in diplomatic pouches. You must do the decoding and processing, otherwise Paul would have just delivered the materials to New York himself when he flew there, to Teterboro."

"Keep going." Diane had been texting with somebody—maybe Kamensky—while I drove. I risked a glance in the rearview and saw that Landrum was still holding the gun on me. He looked fascinated by my narrative.

"I'd guess your trips to the West Coast—and Paul's replacement trips to Minneapolis—probably served another purpose: it allowed you and Paul to see each other. Your divorce looks like a sham. Paul's move to the West Coast must have been ordered by the Russians. He married Irina, but they don't seem close, to put it mildly." Pretty ironic, I thought. Paul Landrum was a cheat, a crook, and a traitor. But it was love that had exposed him.

Landrum couldn't take it anymore. "How on earth do you *know* all this shit?" he demanded. "You were a damn paralegal sitting in a cube for a few weeks."

Diane answered, none too patiently. "I told you, Paul. She's more than that. She's a former federal prosecutor. She's worked on several major investigations, like the murder of Simone's husband."

"Even so," Landrum grumbled.

"Who at the FBI knows about us besides Nomura?"

"More people than you would think. Hendricks for sure."

"Well, well, the big man himself. Even if he knows about the op in a general way—even if he knows about us—there's no way he's got proof. He can't know about the flights. Even if he did, it's all conjecture."

"Kamensky isn't conjecture."

"He'll be out of the country as soon as he finishes the project and his leg heals. You didn't hurt him too badly, it turns out."

That was a shame, I thought. But if the flights were only conjecture, the commodity fraud investigation was not. It would go ahead, and it might tie Landrum to the murders.

"Keri shouldn't have made that call to the FBI," Landrum said defensively.

"Right. She's one of those really annoying people who insist on getting themselves murdered."

"Shut up," he snapped.

"Knock it off, both of you," Diane ordered. She clearly seemed to be the one in charge. "Pen, keep talking. You look horrid in that wig, by the way."

"I still sort of wonder why you two do this," I said. "But I guess you have a few billion reasons."

"For the money?" Diane scoffed. "You may be sharp in general, but still a little clueless about us, Pen."

"You don't like being billionaires?"

"We won't deny that it's a lot of fun."

"Especially when it's so easy. Just cash in on a Russian oil tip here and there."

There was a tense silence. They didn't know that particular secret was out, and it changed everything.

"Tell me what you know about that," Diane said.

"Elena Morton. Another one of those irritating people who forced you to murder them. The police linked Keri's murder to Elena's."

"Jesus," Landrum muttered. "How?"

I explained. The couple reacted with more silence.

"You think you two will get out of the country?" I said. "I'll bet you weren't even planning on leaving. Yes, the Newport Beach police know, the Washington, DC police know, and the FBI knows."

"Bullshit," Landrum said. "They may have some suspicions, but it's all supposition."

"They're very methodical," I said. "They'll check the trading records again—pick up where Elena left off."

"No way. We buried the trades, obscured them."

"I don't know everything about how these schemes work, but you were concerned enough to send Kamensky out to Washington on your plane to kill Elena. Then you had him kill Keri, and then you had Russian hackers erase Elena's investigation. Maybe not so obscure anymore." And then I understood. "You used the trading profits to finance the spy operation, didn't you?

That would have saved the trouble of getting funds into the country."

More silence.

"But I bet the scheme goes way back," I said. "We know the Russians provided the seed capital for your business—using carefully laundered funds, of course. This whole scheme smacks of a very long time frame. All the way back to Stew Kyler." I looked for a reaction and thought I saw a slight flinch from Landrum. "So that brings me to the question, why? If not for the money, why are you doing this?"

"Right at the stop sign," Diane answered. It seemed as though we'd been driving aimlessly. I thought I knew roughly where we were; we were crossing Jamboree, somewhere north of Irvine. Now the city was thinning out, and we were climbing. I kept trying to focus on my conversation with Diane. If I didn't, I'd think about Kamensky and what he'd done to Marisa.

Diane still hadn't answered the "why" question. I didn't say anything. "I guess you'd have to ask my grandparents," she said at last. "They emigrated to the United States from Germany after the war."

"East Germany," I guessed.

"From the eastern zone," she corrected. "The German Democratic Republic—East Germany—hadn't been formed yet. Anyway, they came with a mission."

"This goes back to your grandparents?"

"Oh, yes. Franz and Teresa Mueller—Miller in English—were dedicated Communists. Their children, including my father, were thoroughly indoctrinated. It was almost seventy years ago."

Which might explain, I thought, why those long-ago Millers had an FBI file. "But I thought your father was a factory worker in Wichita," I said.

"And a very productive one. Wichita was home to plants that manufactured military aircraft. Herb Miller found ways of stealing all types of plans and technology."

"And after college you moved to Minneapolis and worked for Honeywell," I said. "A defense contractor. I'd guess you might have infiltrated other companies in Minnesota's defense industry. Contractors like Sperry, Honeywell, Control Data, FMC, Alliant, Cray."

"They were all great sources of intelligence. When Moscow asked us to take over the West Coast, we were experienced and ready to go."

"Your parents had indoctrinated you?"

"Sort of. By then, nobody was really a believing Communist, least of all the people who ruled Russia. But they were patriotic Russians. And, despite being German originally, so were we. I was brought up with sympathy for the underdog, for a country that had undergone unimaginable suffering during the war, while the overfed Americans sat back and let them do the fighting. And over the years my contempt for this country has only increased. Americans are the most self-righteous, hypocritical, spoiled, arrogant people on earth."

"And your Russia is led by a bunch of thieves and thugs. You may not be in it for the money, but the Kremlin's rulers sure as hell are."

"They've never had a chance to be a normal country. But they will, if we can keep the Americans off their backs."

I wasn't about to argue politics with these two. It wasn't an argument I could win, and I thought it was basically a crock, anyway. The Russians had set the Landrums up in business, made them billionaires, and now owned them. The rest was so much self-delusion.

But I didn't want to think about the end game, either my quick demise or the slow, painful version, and as we began our ascent into the Santa Ana Mountains, I tried to keep the conversation going.

"When you get your hands on DSI, it will be quite a prize for you, especially with Hulbert included," I said.

"That's true," Diane replied. "Even though the Russians don't really need their technology."

"You'll get a lot more than technology. You'll have all of the political and policy influence DSI has in Washington. They own half of Congress and the Pentagon, not to mention the National Security Council. All that clout will be yours. You'll learn about developments in the defense industry and keep abreast of counterintelligence techniques. And you might be able to help your allies out."

"All true," Landrum said. "We came close to getting control a couple of years ago. We'll get our chance again—very soon."

"You took a shot when you planted that 'typo,'" I said.

"It was worth a try. It was just a fluke that you found it."

That was true enough, I thought.

"Controlling DSI will be a tremendous coup," Landrum said. "Just the opportunities to bid on contracts will give us access that's really unique."

"And Hulbert will make it even better for you," I said.

"Sure," Landrum agreed. "The acquisition was an unexpected benefit. We can control and monitor Hulbert's technology for anything that might be useful. We've supported the merger, but I've let Dalton do the heavy lifting on it. I'm not sure why he was so gung-ho about it, but we'll take it."

I barely heard the words. My mind was focused on a decision I'd made almost as soon as we'd left Ritchie's apartment. As I drove higher into the mountains, on roads that had become steep and winding, I began to look for a place to drive over the edge.

Chapter 68

It was the same type of decision I'd had to make last year, and I was at peace with it. Then, as now, I was going to be taken away and killed, and I'd decided not to cooperate. I obviously hadn't been killed on the prior occasion. But the experience had taught me a lesson, about my fears and about what I valued. I'd found that ending my life on my own terms was important to me. And now, taking these two treasonous slugs with me would provide an added bonus.

"I need to know what you know about Keri," Diane said.

"Not much. She got a call from Elena. I'm thinking Keri must have confronted Paul about Elena's suspicions. Worst decision she ever made."

"She was naive. How did you identify Kamensky?"

"Gilbertson didn't tell you?"

"He doesn't know," she said, sounding disgusted.

"Nomura never really let me in on that. Obviously, she couldn't have used facial recognition, since Gilbertson fiddled with that. She probably just passed the picture around the office and somebody recognized him."

"You're lying," she said.

Unfortunately, I wasn't. And now, I saw up ahead, after a long descent, a sharp turn to the left. There was a guard rail, but it looked flimsy. A hard right, taken just before the curve and the guard rail began, should do the trick. My van, already dented from crashing the exit gate at DSI, wouldn't be stopped. At the top of the rise, with the mountain rising steeply up to my left, and steeply down to the right, I began to inconspicuously pick up speed.

"Tell us about Clay Ritchie," Diane demanded.

"A good-looking guy."

"I'm losing patience, Pen."

"You know what? So am I. I don't feel like answering any more questions, Diane. In fact, fuck you." I pushed down on the accelerator lever.

There it was. I'd committed. As I had in a similar spot last year, I now saw scenes from my life as they replayed swiftly in my mind. Of good times, of friends, of family, and of James. Most of all, of James.

I'm sorry, James. You were right.

"What the hell—" It took Diane a moment to realize what I was doing. Landrum reached up into the front seat and yanked my arm off the accelerator. But we'd already picked up a lot of speed and were going downhill.

"How do you push the brake on this thing?" Landrum yelled.

I wasn't about to help him out. I still steered with my left hand.

"You need to push on that lever," Diane said, correctly.

Landrum leaned further forward, grabbing my right arm and trying to reach the brake/accelerator lever. I took a quick glance backward and rammed my elbow into his face. "Shit!" he yelled, blood spurting from his nose, all over me. He continued to fumble for the lever. Diane tried to get a bead on me with her gun, but then seemed to realize that shooting me wouldn't get them anywhere. Landrum, trying to stop the bleeding from his nose, dropped his gun to the floor in the back seat and let go of the brake lever.

Tim.

The thought flashed into my consciousness from nowhere. I'd forgotten all about him. He was still unconscious in the back, and he hadn't asked to die. Didn't deserve to. Maybe they would let him live. Reluctantly, I grabbed the brake lever and pushed down. But I wasn't sure I could stop the van in time.

I leaned into the brake, pressing it with everything I had. We skidded as we reached the edge, and I cut the wheel to the left.

The van shuddered, and we glanced off the guardrail with a deafening metallic scrape, but I managed to steer us, fishtailing, back onto the road.

Landrum was on me instantly, screaming in my face. "You stupid bitch! You could have killed us!" He lunged over the seat, slamming his fist into the side of my head. My head hit the window and snapped back. Dazed, my head pounding, I tried to hang onto the wheel with my left hand, but my right hand came off the gas.

He hit me again. This time, his fist caught me in the face, and my head hit the window again. I fought disorientation as my vision narrowed to a tunnel. My glasses were now askew. I could feel us slow down. My hand came off the wheel, and I knew we were drifting. I managed to focus my eyes and then reach for the accelerator/brake lever.

Then his hands were around my throat.

I gasped for breath as both my hands were now off the controls, trying desperately to pry Landrum's hands from my neck. And then I saw headlights, coming directly at us.

I didn't know where we were on the road—right, left, or center. I was powerless to do anything about it, anyway. A horn sounded.

I was fading out, my field of vision narrowing again. My chest felt ready to explode. We lurched suddenly to the right as we apparently missed the oncoming car.

"Paul!" Diane yelled. "Stop it, for God's sake! She has to drive this thing!"

I blacked out, but it must have been only for a moment, because when I came to, we were still in the same predicament, drifting on the road and slowing down. I found I could breathe again, at least a little. Landrum's hands weren't around my neck anymore. Diane had reached over and grabbed the wheel; she must have steered us out of the way of the oncoming car.

We were still slowing down. Diane reached over and slapped me. "Take the wheel," she said.

I sucked in air, reached for the wheel, and managed to grip it. Then I took the brake lever with my other hand and steered us to a stop on the side of the road. I looked in my rearview and saw Paul Landrum with wild eyes, breathing hard. The ultimate control freak had lost control, and as Courtney Stapleton had said, it wasn't pretty.

Now Diane started on me. "You fucking idiot! You could have gotten us killed!"

"That was the idea," I said in a husky voice, my heartbeat gradually slowing.

"Then why did you—" Then she got it. "The kid. What were you doing with Dalton's kid, anyway?"

"I'm actually not sure. But he's a nice guy, and he probably saved my life."

"Well, wasn't that big of him. You damn near killed us."

"Again, that was—"

"The idea, right. You try anything like that again and I'll—"

"What, kill me?"

"No. I'll turn you over to Viktor."

"Something tells me you're going to do that anyway," I said.

"All right, let's get going."

I tried to collect myself. I was still gasping and coughing; my throat felt partly closed. After a couple of deep breaths, I reached down, pushed the accelerator, and pulled out, steering with a shaky hand. We went for a couple of miles without incident.

"Turn here," Diane said. I took a right, just before reaching Silverado. The road got narrower and more winding. We were climbing toward my appointment with Kamensky. My hands shook.

"When are you going to leave the country?" I asked.

"We're not going anywhere. The FBI and police have nothing on us but their suspicions, and I don't think you've told them everything. We'll have to shut PACIFIC down for a while. They might have enough to look into the commodity investigation, but that will drag on for years and end up with a slap on the wrist. There's no link to the murders."

"If that's true, why did you have to kill Elena and Keri?"

"To protect the Hulbert merger. Their accusations would have gone away in time and will still go away. But they could have gummed up the closing."

Of course, I thought.

"We'll have to feed them Gilbertson," Diane continued, "but he knows enough not to implicate us. He knows we'd get his family and, ultimately, him. You and Ritchie will disappear, and Nomura will be preoccupied with wrapping up Gilbertson. Viktor will have to leave when he's finished with the project, but there won't be any link to us. He'll be tagged as the killer, unreachable in Russia, and the mystery of how he got into Keri's house will remain just that."

The terror I felt was now charged with despair. Diane was right; there was every chance that for this rotten bunch, life would go on as always. The identity of Keri's betrayer was no longer a mystery, as Diane still thought. But Williamson couldn't implicate her.

"You're going to kill Pat Dalton," I said. "That's why Kamensky can't leave just yet. And that's how you'll take control of DSI." It was a realization that seemed incredibly obvious in hindsight, but it hadn't dawned on me until I'd been going through my notes at Ritchie's, and I hadn't had a chance to share it with anybody.

She nodded. "It's a deadfall trap, and we're ready to drop it. Dalton blundered right into it, and with him out of the way, the shareholders will turn to us."

"Paul will take over as CEO?"

"Maybe. We may put our own person in charge."

"How will you kill Dalton?" I asked. "A heart attack?"

"An accident. Viktor has been planning it for weeks."

Our destination proved to be a small but well-kept cabin on the other side of Silverado. Neighbors could be seen on either side, but they were some distance away, shielded by trees and scrub. We weren't far from the city, and through breaks in the trees I could see the lit-up expanse of Orange County. "Park over there," Diane said. I put the van in a spot over to one side of the clearing. There was a parking area for about four vehicles, defined by a neat row of small painted rocks.

"Get out," she said. I opened the side door, extended the ramp, and released my chair. Landrum had revived Tim, who was staggering out into the clearing under his own power, while Diane covered my exit from the van. An exterior light on the cabin provided faint illumination, allowing me to make out Tim's unsteady figure across the clearing.

Diane looked at her phone. "Viktor will be here shortly." We waited silently for a moment while I tried to figure out some type of plan. Diane turned toward me. "We gave the typo a test run, you know."

"What?"

"We inserted it in the previous draft, then sent it over to DSI for proofreading. Nobody caught it, so we thought we were clear to do it in the final version. You just had to catch it, didn't you?"

I rolled over the uneven gravel and grass to where Tim leaned against a tree. Landrum raised his gun, but Diane said, "Let her go. She's clean."

"How are you doing?" I asked Tim.

"I think I'm going to be sick." He stepped away from the tree, leaned over, and retched, reappearing a minute later. "Sorry."

I put a hand on his arm. "You saved my life, back at the apartment."

I could see his faint smile in the dim light. "You mean I didn't screw up? I did something right for once? I'm losing my touch."

Diane and Landrum were conferring in low voices a short distance away. I suspected they were trying to decide what to do with Tim. They'd already decided my fate.

Kamensky arrived a couple of minutes later, driving a van. He got out of the vehicle, hobbled around to the rear, and opened up the back door. "Give me a hand, will you?" he called to the Landrums.

Paul walked over and shined a flashlight into the back. "Let's get him out." They combined to pull a figure out, dropping it onto the ground. Landrum used his flashlight again, and I gasped when the light revealed the bound and gagged figure of Clay Ritchie, who looked like he had bruises on his face.

"Good job," Diane said.

"Hornsby did most of the work," Kamensky admitted.

"How's your leg?"

"Hurts like hell, thanks to that bitch." He looked accusingly at me. "I can't wait to get her inside, to the room. It will be fun, questioning her." He, Diane, and Landrum then switched to Russian for further discussion. Diane and Landrum sounded fluent.

A strange noise stopped the conversation. All of us looked around. And then something flew over us: a helicopter. The three spies looked at each other, then resumed their conversation.

After a minute, Diane walked over. "Viktor will have to get creative with you guys, like he did with Marisa," she said. "No marks, but believe me, we'll make sure we know each and every thing you know. Pen, you and Ritchie will be a murder-suicide. Tim, we haven't decided on yet. He might just disappear—he's been an erratic guy, anyway."

The helicopter went over again, lower and more slowly. The spies froze, then Kamensky came hobbling over toward us as quickly as he could. Without a word, he shoved Tim to the ground, then leaned over and began searching him, feeling all over. Then he yanked something off Tim's body. "Shit!" he yelled.

"What is it?" Diane demanded.

Kamensky held up a tiny device. "GPS transmitter with a panic button, built into his belt buckle. Rich people equip their kids with them in case of kidnapping." With that, he exploded into a torrent of furious Russian, giving Tim a kick to the ribs.

We could hear the chopper again, but not overhead. It sounded nearby.

Diane managed to calm Kamensky down, and then their Russian-language discussion took on greater urgency. Finally, Diane came over to Tim. "Does that button bring the police?"

"I don't know," Tim said. "My dad's people gave it to me after Mikayla's death. It brings help—I don't know who from."

"When did you push the button?"

"In the van," he admitted. "I was conscious for a couple of minutes."

"You signed your death warrant, you little shit. We'll have to just leave your bodies here and get out. The cabin's ownership is untraceable."

"Too late for that," I said. "Howard knows how Keri's murder went down. He knows it was Williamson who got Keri to open the door."

Diane's mouth opened involuntarily. She stared at me, disbelieving. I was playing my final card, and it was having an effect. Kamensky and Landrum, presumably suspecting that the chopper had landed nearby and discharged rescuers, scanned the trees with flashlights, holding their guns out.

"Keri told Williamson all about Paul's trading scheme and his threats," I lied. "He's ready to testify."

Diane's composure finally gave way. "You're *lying*!" She slapped me across the face.

We heard the helicopter again, nearby but not directly overhead. Was it taking off again? Was it leaving? I hung one of my long arms down beside the chair, feeling on the ground for any kind of projectile.

Suddenly, the scene was illuminated. A powerful searchlight shone down from the helicopter onto the clearing. Kamensky wheeled around, gun still pointed toward the woods. He started for the cover of the jeep, then hesitated, unsure of which direction the threat came from. "Drop it!" somebody yelled as the light hit him squarely. Kamensky fired, and his shot was answered by a volley of shots from the woods. He went down.

The light swept across the clearing, now moving to Landrum. He was holding Tim around the neck, a gun to his head. "Come out of the woods and drop your guns!" Landrum yelled.

No one moved. "*You* drop it!" a male voice screamed from the woods. "Do it now!" The helicopter sounded louder, and the light seemed to widen out.

Landrum remained motionless with his gun to Tim's head. I decided to try to distract him. "Landrum!" I yelled and whipped one of the border rocks in his direction. He wheeled toward me and flinched. Tim elbowed him in the head, broke loose, and fled. Landrum turned toward him, but a shot rang out from the woods, and the billionaire hit the deck.

Next, inexplicably, the light swept over and illuminated Tim as he ran toward the woods. That allowed Diane, who had raised her gun, to draw a bead on him. I lurched forward, hitting her in the leg with my footrests. She staggered as she fired, apparently missing Tim, and turned toward me. I maneuvered around and grabbed her gun hand.

Diane yanked my chair back and forth as we struggled for the gun, her face contorted into a wild grimace. She let go with one hand and tried to hit me in the head. I managed to turn my head but still took a glancing blow. Somehow, I still held onto her gun hand, which she pushed downward, once again aided by her other hand, trying to point the weapon at me.

The light was right on us now. I heard another shot from the woods, but I paid no attention to what was going on. I was trying to keep from being shot in the face.

I twisted desperately with both hands, but I could see it was a battle I wasn't going to win. I'm not weak; I have strong arms from propelling myself in a wheelchair all day. And Diane wasn't a big woman. But standing over me, using her lower body, she had too much leverage.

Diane leaned forward, putting her weight into the effort, and the gun slowly moved to within inches of my face. I let go with my left hand, reached down and grabbed the left wheel of my chair, and yanked it sharply. Diane, leaning forward, lost her balance, firing the gun as she stumbled. I yanked on the wheel again as I pulled her forward. She tripped over the footrests, landing on her hands and knees, then rolled over, pointing the gun at me.

She had me, point blank.

"Now eat this," she said.

At that moment, a crouched figure darted from the shadows and put a gun to her head. "Drop it or I'll blow your brains out!" the figure hissed.

Diane dropped the gun. The light widened out, and my savior was revealed as Neil, Pat Dalton's security man. Air Dalton had come to the rescue.

Paul Landrum sat on the ground, his hands zip-tied behind him, watched by a second armed man. Neil hauled Diane over next to him.

Then a third man walked briskly into the clearing: Pat Dalton. He looked around, spotted Tim, and walked over. Tim awkwardly stepped forward, and father and son embraced.

"Mr. Dalton," I said, "we've got a man down—over there." I pointed toward Ritchie.

"Who is he?"

"Clay Ritchie."

It took him a moment to place the name. "The finance guy? What's he doing here?"

"He may be hurt."

Dalton yelled at one of his men to check on Ritchie. Then he hollered to Neil, "What about the guy you shot?"

"Dead."

"Jesus." Dalton turned back toward me. "And Dez—what the hell are *you* doing here?"

I looked around. "All this is really tricky to explain. Have you seen who the kidnappers are?"

He shook his head, walked over, and looked at the seated Landrums. "*Paul*? What in God's name—who's the woman?"

"Diane," I answered. "Landrum's ex-wife."

"His ex—Dez, who the hell are you, and what's going on?"

I ignored him and wheeled over to Ritchie, who was sitting up and conversing with Neil. His face was bruised, and he was wincing in pain.

"Dez," he said. "Holy shit, are you okay?"

"I'm fine." I realized I had Landrum's blood all over me.

"Who do we have to thank for bailing us out?" Ritchie asked.

"Tim Dalton."

His face showed serious surprise. "These guys work for Dalton?"

"Yes, they do," said Pat Dalton, who had walked over to join us. "I was at home when Tim's signal came in. My staff is instructed to respond instantly, and I went with them. The police are on the way."

"Well, thank you," Ritchie said.

"Are you okay?" Dalton asked.

"Just a little beaten up. Some bruised ribs." He winced, gasping, as Neil helped him carefully to his feet.

Neil said, "The sheriff will be here in a few minutes."

"There's a call I need to make," I said. "Could I borrow a phone?"

Dalton nodded, and Neil handed me his. It took several minutes, but I finally reached Lieutenant Dan Howard.

"Bad news," he said without preamble. "Wendy's been shot."

I gripped the phone with a sweaty hand. "Is she alive?"

"She's critical. Could go either way. I'm at the hospital now. Kirk Hendricks is on the way."

"Who shot her?"

"Special Agent Ward Gilbertson. Who then ate his gun."

I was speechless.

"It's a good thing you told me to have a welfare check done," Howard said. "It gave us a chance, maybe. And there's another thing."

I waited.

"Costa Mesa PD lost an officer, a fellow named Torres." A pause. "Wendy and I had him sent to keep an eye on you."

I gasped, dropping the phone, and my stomach convulsed. I leaned over but managed to avoid being sick.

"Pen?" I heard Howard's voice from the phone on the ground.

I took deep breaths.

"Pen? Are you all right?"

I picked up the phone. "Yes. Just give me a second. Let me catch my breath." I pulled myself together. "What happened?"

"He was shot to death. They're still investigating."

I exhaled. "You need to get involved here, pronto." I gave him a quick summary of what had happened.

After I'd finished, he paused, obviously hesitant to leave the hospital. "You got that bastard Kamensky? Good for you guys. I'll leave as soon as Hendricks gets here. They'll probably move you down to the station for questioning pretty soon. I'll meet you there. I'll also see if I can get hold of whatever deputy will be in charge."

I managed to thank Howard and hand the phone back to Neil.

Dalton said, "Will somebody tell me what's going on here?"

Ritchie and I gave him the five-minute version. When we'd finished, he just stood there, expressionless. I didn't know how much of it he believed—it was a lot to take in. At times, he seemed to be only half listening. He glanced at his watch a couple of times, pausing once to send a text. In all, he seemed less interested than he should have been in the presence of Russian spies in his company, and in the kidnapping of his son.

Finally, he stared at me. "Who are you, Dez?" Without waiting for a response, he said, "You ate at my table. You befriended my family. You took a salary from my company. Who do you work for?"

"The FBI."

"And they sent you to spy on me?"

"No, they sent me to spy on Landrum."

"You did your spying at *my* company," Dalton said.

"You had a Russian agent and murderer at *your* company."

"You think I wanted him there, for God's sake?" He shook his head, turned and walked away.

We could see the lights from sheriffs' cars working their way up the road, and I knew we were in for a long night of questioning. *Better than the questioning I would have gotten from Kamensky,* I thought.

I spotted Tim half-sitting on a car bumper and rolled over to him. He looked like he'd spent the day putting up "Lost Puppy" posters.

"How are you doing?" I asked.

He didn't answer.

"Thank you for saving my life."

"Yeah, right," he muttered. He looked up. "I trusted you. I told you some personal stuff. I thought I'd met somebody who didn't want anything from me or my father. I thought you were my friend."

"I'd like to think I still am."

"Really? I don't know who you are—is Dez even your real name?"

"I was doing my job."

"Your job didn't lie to me. You did." He walked away.

I gazed through the trees, out at the vast urban grid, trying to get my head around what was really going on. I'd lied. And I'd done my job. Both the bloodless bureaucrats who'd hired me to deceive, and the flesh-and-blood individuals who'd been on the receiving end, could agree on one thing, if for completely opposite reasons: They didn't care.

Chapter 69

We were at the scene for the next hour and a half while the deputies arrived in waves. First came the uniforms, then the homicide team—detectives, crime scene, and medical examiner. Crime scene personnel, working under portable lights, processed the exterior of the cabin. The homicide team was unhappy that Kamensky's body had been moved and that we had walked and rolled all over the yard after the shooting.

The paramedics checked me over, bandaging a small cut on my face and concluding that I didn't have a concussion. My voice was still husky, and my throat felt constricted from being throttled by Landrum. Inside the cabin, the deputies had discovered a room that appeared to have been outfitted as a torture chamber. I had stayed outside.

Around ten-thirty, everyone was taken to the sheriff's department headquarters in Santa Ana. I was allowed to drive my van, accompanied by a deputy. Everybody—Pat Dalton and his crew, the Landrums, Ritchie, Tim, and me—had been separated and questioned, and it would have been a miracle if the investigators, all new to the case, had been able to make any sense out of the answers. There were so many strands to the investigation, and so many gaps in the stories, that the situation must have seemed like a hopeless jumble.

Dan Howard's arrival did a lot to bring order to the chaos. He explained the circumstances to the deputies and vouched for Ritchie and me, steering the investigators toward a consensus that the Landrums and Kamensky were the culprits, and that Ritchie and I, as federal law enforcement employees, were on the side of the angels. Pat Dalton and his security team seemed to fall somewhere in between. I caught a couple of glimpses of

Dalton in between interviews, noting again that he seemed fidgety and preoccupied, checking his watch repeatedly.

One of the deputies' biggest problems was finding somebody to handle the federal espionage elements of the case. With Wendy Nomura down, Ward Gilbertson dead, and ADC Hendricks preoccupied, who would deal with the two suspected Russian agents? Eventually, Hendricks left Nomura's bedside long enough to request that the Landrums be held overnight. Meanwhile, he arranged for a team of agents to fly in from Washington to take over the investigation.

It was nearly 3:00 AM when I was released. Dan Howard, who met me in the corridor, told me Wendy Nomura had survived emergency surgery, but was still in critical condition. I wanted to get to the hospital to see her, but Howard urged me to wait until tomorrow. Wendy needed rest and I needed sleep, so I agreed. I hesitantly asked about Officer Torres.

"Don't beat yourself up, Pen. Wendy and I set up his assignment to watch you. I made the call—we'll all have to deal with the guilt. I listened in on your debriefing, and you have to look at it this way: It took Kamensky some time—we don't know how much—to spot Torres, get into position, and set up the shot. The extra time gave Tim a chance to get over there to disrupt Kamensky's attempt to break into the apartment. I'd say Officer Calvin Torres saved your life. He did his duty."

I lost it. Howard put an awkward hand on my shoulder as I sobbed. Eventually I got myself under control.

"You going to be okay?" he asked.

I nodded.

"You look a little alarming."

I glanced down at myself. I still had Landrum's blood all over my white blouse and beige jacket. "Just a play for sympathy," I said.

"I'll see you at the hospital tomorrow."

A minute later, I felt another hand on my shoulder. Clay Ritchie.

Ritchie had his arm in a sling, with some bandages on his face. He'd been checked out by paramedics at the scene, who'd bandaged his cuts and taped his ribs. I saw a bench down the hall; I rolled over and he sat down.

I'd managed to compose myself, and we spent a few minutes comparing notes on our questioning sessions.

"What's next for you?" I asked.

"Back to the Pentagon, I guess. Then, who knows? Maybe another undercover assignment. Maybe overseas. Maybe a desk job. We'll see what they want."

"A lot of uncertainty. Do you ever get the urge to settle down?"

"Sure, now and then. I get tired of living in short-term rentals, with leased government cars, in new places. And . . ."

He didn't finish the sentence. He didn't have to. The missing fragment was ". . . and being alone." And I was thankful that, with all the uncertainty I faced in resuming my life, I didn't have to worry about that.

We were silent for a minute. "How are you doing?" he asked at last.

"Okay, I think. The adrenaline will wear off soon, and then I'll crash. I might be tempted to help the process along with some wine. You?"

"Pretty shaken, to be honest."

"Have you ever had anything like this happen before?" I asked.

"Not really. I didn't see combat in Iraq. I've had field training, but I've been a desk warrior. Do you get over it?"

"Not easily."

"You've had experiences like this before?"

"More than once, unfortunately."

He smiled, shaking his head. "Man, I want to hear your stories someday."

"We'll see. Maybe. It's, well . . ."

"Not easy to talk about?"

"I guess not."

He stood up.

"Do you need a ride?" I asked.

"I've got a DOD guy picking me up. I'll call you in the next day or two. You've still got a few things over at my place."

"Sure. Thanks." I realized I'd been wearing the same clothes for two days. He leaned down and gave me a peck on the cheek. "Thanks. For everything."

"Thank you, too." We clasped hands briefly, and then he was gone.

I sat in the hallway for a couple of minutes, trying to work up the energy to go home. I figured I'd go back to Dez's condo for the rest of tonight. Tomorrow I'd recruit James to help me move my stuff back to Long Beach.

I spotted movement down the hall. Pat Dalton was walking toward the parking lot. He got to the door, then stopped, checked his phone, then hurried on. And then . . .

Time stopped.

Chapter 70

I rolled down the hallway as fast as I could, then out the door. Outside, I saw a black SUV's headlights flicker to life. I rolled as fast as I could toward my own vehicle, halfway down the lot. I spotted Dalton getting into the SUV. I kept rolling, pumping my arms, using every bit of my waning energy.

I saw it all now. The answers to all the questions my subconscious mind had been working through came to me in a flash, explaining all the things that didn't seem to make sense.

Dalton's reluctance to retire.

Mikayla's death.

A Chinese-American attorney speaking Korean.

The SUV backed out, heading for the exit. I approached my van, then stopped and fumbled in my purse for my key ring. The SUV drove past me. Dalton was driving, alone in the vehicle. He didn't appear to notice me.

I found my keys. It seemed to take forever to open the side door and extend the ramp. I scooted up the ramp and into place behind the wheel, clamping myself in. I risked a quick glance down the street and saw Dalton turning onto Flower Street. I started the van and waited for the ramp to retract. With the door still closing, I backed out, then yanked the car into drive and took off after Dalton.

I spotted him a couple of blocks ahead of me. With middle-of-the-night traffic sparse, it would be easier for me to follow, but also easier for Dalton to spot me. I followed him south on Flower to First Street, then east, probably toward the I-5. We cleared the lights easily on First. I risked letting a car get between us, but I wasn't going to let Dalton get too far ahead of me. The consequences of letting him succeed in what he was going to do were . . .

I couldn't afford to think about it. I had to focus on the task at hand. I needed to call somebody—Ritchie; Howard; the police—somebody—to get help. Dalton was about to do something unthinkable, and I couldn't stop him, not by myself. But my phone—all three of the phones I'd had—were in a hundred pieces on the ground in front of Ritchie's apartment. I didn't even have a purse—the Landrums had discarded it at Ritchie's.

We pulled onto the I-5 and headed south. Traffic was light, and I had to push up my speed to keep up with Dalton. Soon we were going eighty. I couldn't believe how slow I'd been to understand what Dalton was up to. He'd remained at his job at DSI despite personal tragedy, had used all his resources and credibility to push for a merger with Hulbert, and was planning to stay on even longer, after the merger. He was doing these things, all out of character for him, because he felt he had to.

We pushed on toward San Clemente. Dalton was apparently going home, but I doubted he would stay there long. I dropped back when we left the I-5 but managed to keep his tail lights in sight. We had slowed down considerably, but Dalton continued at a comparatively rapid pace, well above the speed limit. His son's kidnapping had delayed the urgent task that had been scheduled for earlier in the day, the day of the merger.

The gate was already closing, with Dalton inside, when I pulled up in front of his estate. I hung back, away from the entrance, and cut my lights, hoping I wouldn't be noticed by security cameras. I'd considered trying to go in after Dalton and confront him there. If nothing else, maybe I would have been able to convince Tim or Jackie to try to stop him. But they might well have sided with Dalton. And if so, they wouldn't have let me use a phone. I glanced up and down the street, looking for a phone, somewhere. It wasn't to be; the houses were sparse, secluded, and gated. And it was three in the morning.

I really, really needed a phone.

The gate opened again.

Dalton emerged less than two minutes later, driving the same vehicle. For the first few blocks, I managed to follow him with my headlights off. As we neared the I-5, picking up a bit of traffic, I turned them on again. Dalton turned north on the freeway, once again picking up speed until he was going eighty. In a few minutes, he switched to the Highway 73 toll road. I dropped back a bit further, but not too far. I had no idea where he was going and couldn't risk losing him.

It all made sense now. Technology—good stuff but not the crown jewels—had been leaking out of DSI for the past couple of years, showing up in the hands of questionable regimes around the world. Ritchie had been stymied in his efforts to discover the leak because he had never thought to investigate Pat Dalton. But DSI's chairman and CEO had in fact been the source of the thefts. He possessed unquestioned, unaccountable access to everything in the company, and with an IT background, he knew how to use it. And again, he had done it because he'd felt he had to.

Dalton turned south on Highway 55, a freeway leading down to the Balboa Peninsula, toward Dez's apartment. I still didn't know where he might be going. Where do you hold a clandestine meeting in the middle of the night? Where could you be assured of no police, no passersby, and no cameras? A parking lot? A deserted street? I glanced ahead again—and couldn't see Dalton.

Frantic, I sped up, passing the car ahead of me, but the freeway was clear for a long way ahead. What had happened to Dalton?

Panicky, I pushed down on the gas. He couldn't have gotten as far ahead as the next cars in front of me. Which meant he must have gotten off. An exit appeared on my right, but I'd already passed the ramp.

Or had I? I braked and yanked the wheel hard to the right. I was skidding straight toward the dividing barrels. *Oh, God.* I let up on the brake, tried turning again, and just missed the barrels, fishtailing on the exit ramp. I got the van under control and saw, down at the bottom of the ramp, a black SUV making a right turn.

I followed, hoping Dalton hadn't seen me in his mirror, and hoping I wouldn't have a heart attack. I'd been awake for so long, with so much stress, that I'd lost concentration.

We were now on a more westerly course, heading toward Huntington Beach. I still had no plan, no way of stopping Dalton. But I had to try. After a few more miles and a couple of turns, Dalton pulled over on a deserted street, which led down toward a huge tank farm. He parked the SUV and killed his lights.

I slowed to a crawl. Dalton hadn't gotten out of the car. I wondered what to do next. I could wait and see who he would be meeting with. But I already knew. And by then it would be too late. I pulled ahead, swung out beside the SUV, then pulled in front of it at an angle, blocking it in.

Dalton got out of his vehicle. By then, my side door was already opening, and I'd unclamped my wheelchair. He came around to my driver's window, but I wasn't there—I had turned and was waiting for my ramp to extend. I had no plan beyond stalling, and hoping that somehow, events would intervene to prevent the disaster. Delay and pray.

"Hey, what are you doing?" he yelled. Then he saw me through the window. "Dez? Aw, shit."

He walked around the van and waited for me as I wheeled down to the curb. "What the hell are you doing here?" he demanded. "You have to go away, and I mean now!"

I clicked the button on my keychain to close up the van. "Mr. Dalton, I know what happened with Mikayla, and I'm really sorry about it. But you need to do the right thing, now."

"Dez, you cannot screw this up. You don't know what's going on."

"Maybe not every detail. But I know that North Korea has a long and sordid history of kidnapping foreigners in Asian countries and using them for all kinds of evil purposes. They've done it dozens—maybe hundreds—of times. And that's what they did on a beach in Thailand two years ago. Does Tim know?"

Dalton hesitated, then shook his head. "He knows something strange happened, probably knows that it didn't happen the way I represented it. He doesn't know she disappeared while on land instead of surfing. And he doesn't know she's alive."

"Are you sure she's alive?"

"I talked to her this morning. Li sometimes lets me talk to her."

"Is there any doubt it's her?"

"No. I recognize my daughter's voice, and they sometimes provide a video feed."

"What happened on that beach?"

He glanced down the empty street, looked back at me, and sighed. "She was surfing. I was sitting on the beach. Jackie and Tim had gone back to the house. Mikayla went from the beach up to the bathroom and never came back. I was starting to worry when I got a call from the kidnappers. They told me I had to cooperate if I ever wanted to see her again. I followed their instructions—reported her drifting out to sea after a surfing accident. After the search was over, we went home and waited for more instructions."

"You've been stealing tech from your own company," I said. "That's why Ritchie and the FBI haven't been able to trace the leakage. It never occurred to them that you could be the source. You've been giving it to Steve Li."

"We can't mess with Li. And he'll be here any time."

"Why didn't he just meet you at home?"

"This meeting is the ballgame. The final exchange. He's not taking any chances it might be monitored. Do you know who he is?"

"He's not a Chinese-American attorney. He's a North Korean agent. He began 'representing' you right around the time of Mikayla's disappearance. Does Jackie know?"

"I had to tell her. Li has been pressuring and bullying me, appearing at the house unannounced at all hours to keep us on edge and afraid."

"Does anybody else know?"

"Neil. He couldn't handle Li showing up all the time and behaving like an asshole. I had to tell him."

"What have you given them from DSI?" I asked.

He gestured vaguely. "Different stuff."

"But Hulbert has the good stuff—the missile countermeasures. That's what the North Koreans want, isn't it? The Hulbert acquisition was their idea—they made you do it."

He hesitated, then nodded.

"They can use it to defeat our defenses. They'll probably sell it to other hostile regimes, too, like the Iranians."

"I can't be concerned with that."

"You have to be. You have to tell him you can't do it."

"That's out of the question," Dalton said. "The delivery has to be made. Mikayla's life is at stake."

"I don't know about that. But I do know our national security is at risk."

"I can't abandon her. I have to give them what they want. After that, you can tell the FBI everything—whatever you want. I don't care what happens to me."

"You can't open us to attack by the North Koreans."

Dalton turned to me with the face of a desperate man. "You don't understand. I don't have a choice. She's alive, as of this morning. I'll be flying to China next week to collect her. They'll be sending her across the border."

"That's a fantasy. You can't count on them to keep their word. They'll just keep demanding more. And even if you could trust them, this cannot happen. You can't commit treason."

"You're not a parent. You don't get it. What am I supposed to do? Write off my daughter? Abandon her to a bunch of murderous thugs?"

"Let the State Department handle it. They negotiate releases of foreign hostages all the time. You've got proof she's alive."

"The diplomats aren't always successful. Sometimes the hostages die. I can't take that chance."

"Mr. Dalton, you know this is wrong. Even if by some miracle you got Mikayla back on your own, you wouldn't be able to avoid going to prison, probably for life. Would you want her to live with that?"

He didn't answer.

A vehicle appeared from around the corner. It moved down the street toward us, then made a Y-turn, coming around to face us until its headlights flooded us. Dalton and I shielded our eyes. The vehicle was a plain sedan; the driver watched us for a long moment before getting out. We turned sideways to avoid looking directly into the headlights.

"Dalton, what is this shit?" Steve Li demanded. "What is this cripple doing here?"

"She followed me."

"She—who the hell is she?"

"I work for the FBI," I said. "They're tracking my moves, and they're listening to this conversation." I was making it up as I went along. Delay and pray.

Li looked at Dalton, who said, "I doubt that. I've got what you asked for."

"Then hand it over, and let's get going."

Dalton turned toward the SUV. I grabbed his arm. "You can't do this."

He shook me off. "I have to." He reached in and grabbed a briefcase.

In desperation, I turned to Li. "You won't make it out of the country. The Bureau is on to you."

"Shut up," he snapped. To Dalton: "Just hand it over."

I tried to block Dalton, but the CEO shoved me aside, walked forward, and handed Li the briefcase. Then Li leveled him with a sucker punch.

Dalton lay on the ground, moaning.

Li gave him a vicious kick to the ribs. "That's for keeping me waiting, and for bringing her along. As for that slut daughter of yours, I'll let you know when we decide whether to let her live." He turned toward his car.

"Hold it," I said.

I rolled forward, and he turned back. "You're cornered," I said. "If you stop now, maybe you can avoid anybody else getting hurt."

"Shut up. You're full of shit."

I pulled my knife, retrieved from the back of the van, from my jacket pocket. It was the only weapon I had. I didn't know what else to do.

Li gave me an exasperated look and pulled a gun from his coat pocket, pointing it at me. "You're an idiot, in addition to being a pain in the ass."

I retreated. It had been a stupid idea to begin with. I'd literally brought a knife to a gunfight, and now I was powerless to stop a catastrophic theft. My delay and pray strategy hadn't worked. At least he hadn't shot me.

Li got into his car, started it up, and began to pull away.

Boiling over with frustration and fury, I whipped the knife toward his open driver's window. Miraculously, it sailed through the window, hit the inside of his windshield, and clattered around.

The car screeched to a stop, and Li, furious, got out of the car, gun drawn.

I rolled backward toward the van. "Mr. Dalton!" I yelled. "Call 911!"

Dalton wouldn't do it.

Li came forward. "I've had about enough of you, goddamnit."

I sensed motion in my peripheral vision.

So did Li. "Who's there?" he demanded, scanning the side of the road behind the SUV and my van.

I tried to distract him. "Give it up," I said.

Li looked back at me, and at that moment a figure emerged from behind the front of the SUV, holding a gun. "Drop it!" he yelled.

Li pointed his gun toward the figure. Neither man fired.

The new arrival moved slowly into the road, the gun still trained on Li. I now recognized him as Neil, Dalton's security man.

"Neil," Dalton gasped, pulling himself to a sitting position. "I've got this. Stand down."

Neil didn't move.

"Dad." We wheeled around; Tim stood behind us.

"Tim, get back!" Neil yelled.

Li was furious. "You fucked this up, Dalton! You're an idiot. You want your daughter to die? All I have to do is make the call."

"Don't try it," Neil warned.

"Dad," Tim said, "Is it true? She's really alive?"

The elder Dalton, still on the ground, nodded. Tim turned abruptly to one side, brushing tears away. After a long moment, he said, "We have to get her back. We have to. But this . . . isn't right. You shouldn't be giving this guy things from work."

The elder Dalton was now on his feet. He leaned over, hands on thighs. "Tim, I've got this. I will handle it."

"Please, Dad. We'll get her back. But this isn't the way."

"It's done," Pat Dalton said, then slumped to the ground.

Tim rushed forward, leaning over his father. Then he looked at Li. "You son of a bitch!" He rushed toward the Korean.

Li fired. Tim yelped and spun away. Then Neil fired three shots. Li went down instantly.

Neil approached Li, kicking the Korean's gun away and checking him briefly. Then he ran over to Tim, who'd apparently been hit in the shoulder.

Pat Dalton held his phone out to me. I called 911.

Neil went to the SUV and returned with a first aid kit. He knelt down and began working on Tim.

"I'm sorry, Mr. Dalton," Neil said as he bandaged Tim. "I know I work for you. And I was fond of Mikayla. But before any of that, I served my country. I couldn't let this happen."

Dalton, sitting up again, looked dazed.

"It was Tim," Neil continued. "He said he'd seen Dez's van follow you to the house. When you came in and got the briefcase and left right away, he demanded to know what was going on. I told him. He said he was going after you, and of course we have tracking on all our vehicles. I told him if he was going, I was going with him."

Tim was still conscious. "I'm sorry, Dad. But . . . but you've taught me to do what's right."

Dalton watched his son, shaking his head. "Yes. Yes, I suppose I did," he muttered.

Tim turned to me and managed a weak smile. "I didn't fuck up. Again."

Epilogue

They wouldn't let us stay long. Lieutenant Dan Howard and I stood on either side of Wendy Nomura, who lay in her hospital bed, tethered to IVs and monitors. She was, the doctors had reported, out of danger, the surgeons having repaired extensive internal damage. She didn't look good but was mentally sharp and able to converse.

"Who gets the Landrums?" Nomura asked, her voice sounding cracked and raspy.

"The FBI," I said, "at least to start. Eventually, Dave O'Shea and his superiors in Washington will get to prosecute them for espionage and related charges."

"But they're not talking?" Nomura asked.

"Not a word. They know better than to cross the Russians. Their best hope is to be traded to Moscow for somebody we want to get back." I imagined the Russians would soon arrest some luckless American tourist or businessperson in Moscow for the trade.

"The Landrums can now be linked to a notorious Russian assassin," Nomura said.

"True," Howard said. "But I'm dubious about getting them for Keri's murder, or Elena Morton's, for that matter."

"And Pat Dalton is lawyered up and free," I said.

Howard shrugged. "That's the FBI's problem, not mine. I wish them and the US attorney well in trying to figure out what to do with him."

"You said Dalton gave away national security secrets," Nomura noted. We'd learned that he had on several occasions given the North Koreans passwords, codes and back doors that had enabled their hackers to access the plans for DSI's weapons systems. The briefcase he'd tried to give Li contained more of the same for Hulbert's ultra-secret missile countermeasures system.

"Dalton gave away those secrets under duress," I pointed out. "I don't know what should be done about that."

Nobody else seemed to, either. I couldn't begin to imagine how I would have reacted in his place. I suspected a deal would be struck, especially if Dalton came clean about everything. And it made sense that nothing would be announced publicly as long as Dalton's daughter was being held by the North Koreans.

Nomura shifted slightly in her bed, trying not to tangle all the IV lines and tubes. "Is anything being done for Ward Gilbertson's family?"

"I've heard they're being treated as any family of an agent killed in the line of duty would be," Howard said. "Hendricks has been to visit them."

She shook her head. "I should have seen it coming. It's just that . . ." *I get hit on a lot and he seemed like just another pig*, she didn't have to add.

In situations like this, where nobody quite knew what to say, it might have been useful to have the plain-spoken James Carter present. "So the guy blew his brains out," he'd commented when I'd told him what had happened. "He saved the taxpayers the cost of locking him up and feeding him."

Thank you, Mr. Sensitive. But, as Nomura had pointed out, Gilbertson had had a family.

Nomura hadn't talked about her own future. In a fair world, she'd be in line for Ward Gilbertson's job. But in the FBI world, there was full awareness that I had ignored instructions to shut down my undercover operation, aided and abetted by Nomura. Things had turned out reasonably well, but in my experience, that didn't count for much. I hoped she would keep her job. As for me, Dave O'Shea had made no move to carry out his threat to have me thrown in jail if I refused to be a team player, even though I had clearly failed on that score.

"We'd better get going before they kick us out of here," Howard said.

"You rescued me from the gang out there," Nomura said, gesturing toward the hallway, where family members were taking a break from their vigil. A steady stream of her fellow FBI agents had also appeared. Howard and I had been among the few visitors allowed into the room.

Each of us grasped her hand, careful to avoid pulling out her IV, and then we started for the door.

"Pen?" I returned to her bedside. Howard gestured that he'd meet me outside.

"I'm really sorry—" she began, her voice now sounding weaker.

"You have nothing to be sorry for. I volunteered. I'm an adult."

"It's more than that," she said. "I should have told you more, and I shouldn't have been fighting you all along. I should have let you do your thing. That's what Hal told me to do, and I didn't listen. You were even right about the damn typo."

I smiled and took her hand again. "Don't worry about it. Get well."

I met Howard outside. We nodded to Nomura's parents, who sat in the hallway, then went down to the elevators.

"You looked good on TV," I said. "Crisp, no-nonsense—all cop."

He shook his head. "I hate doing interviews. Normally the chief is glad to handle it. But this case is so complex, I think he was concerned about being tripped up by a question."

Howard's interviews were only a drop in the wave of media coverage, for which there was ample fodder: the arrest of a billionaire and his ex-wife for espionage; the kidnapping of a CEO's son. And yet there was much more to come; the media still hadn't tied these events to the murders of Keri Wylie or Elena Morton, or the deaths of Steve Li and Viktor Kamensky. And the abduction of Mikayla Dalton was still unknown to the public.

"I heard Marisa got out of the hospital," I said.

Howard nodded. "We haven't even interviewed her yet. I hear she's got a good therapist, and eventually she should be able to tell us what Kamensky did to her."

My breathing still grew shallow when I thought about it.

We took the elevator down and went out toward the parking lot.

"What's going to happen with our pal Les Hornsby?" I asked Howard as we waited to cross the drop-off lane.

"Orange County has him in custody on charges of beating Ritchie up and kidnapping him." I would have bet that the fall-out at DSI hadn't ended. Nancy Griffin had resigned as general counsel, but she vehemently denied inserting the typo into the Techinvest-DSI shareholder agreement. The culprit would probably prove to be an attorney at one of the law firms handling the transaction. Pat Dalton had announced his retirement from the company, effective immediately, and had declined to provide any reasons to the media or shareholders, except to say that with the Hulbert merger complete, his work was done. We had no knowledge of what the State Department might be doing to get Mikayla back.

Tim Dalton also faced new realities. Now recovering at home from a non-life-threatening shoulder wound, he had decided to return to school and to move back to his father's house for the time being. I'd tried calling him, but he had ignored the attempts. And who could blame him? He'd been looking for something real, and with Dez—with *me*—he hadn't found it.

We reached the parking lot. "What about the other killings?" I asked.

"The good news is, they took a rifle from the back of Kamensky's van. He'd probably planned to bury it or ditch it up at the cabin. Anyway, they matched the ballistics on it to the bullet that killed Officer Calvin Torres. No surprise, of course, but nice to have it wrapped up."

"That's the good news?"

"Yes. There's bad news, too. The handguns that Kamensky and the Landrums used the night they got you and Ritchie can't be linked to Keri's murder. Handguns are cheap and easy to get rid of, so I doubt we'll ever find the right one. All we have on Kamensky for Keri's murder is the picture of him coming off the island."

"The DA has to try," I said. "The Landrums can't get away with killing Keri and Elena."

Howard put a hand on my shoulder. "Don't worry about it. You did good. And . . . thanks." He walked away.

*   *   *

That evening, James and I sat on the deck of the *Alicia C*, looking out over the harbor, enjoying the excellent bottle of pinot grigio Hal Dwyer had brought over that afternoon.

"Glad to be you again?" James asked.

"I guess. Dez was kind of a bore." I was getting used to being Pen again, but I wasn't thrilled with her, either. In yet another misguided effort to prove my toughness and independence, I had slipped all too easily into a role that embraced falsity and deception.

James gestured toward the wine bottle Dwyer had brought. "Hal feels guilty for getting you into this."

"He had no way of knowing it would turn out like this. Nobody did."

We were silent for a couple of minutes.

"You've been sleeping well," he observed. "No nightmares. And no panic attacks, unless you've been hiding them again."

"I've been doing okay." We both knew the PTSD symptoms could return. But nearly as frightening as that prospect was the thought that I was getting used to violence and danger, that for me, the awful was becoming normal. And yet, I now feared neither of these outcomes as much as I dreaded the days and weeks ahead, with nothing to fill them except the gnawing, relentless guilt. How could I keep from reviewing the trail of human wreckage I'd left behind me? How could I erase the images of Marisa? Of Officer Torres? And worst of all, I knew that as long as I lived, regardless of what happened, I'd be haunted by the thought of Mikayla Dalton in a North Korean prison, knowing I might be responsible for keeping her there.

"You dug out the truth," James said. "Again."

"But the cost . . ."

He sighed. "I suppose it's pointless to tell you not to beat yourself up. But you're not to blame for any of it. It's all the fault of the people who weren't truthful." He looked up at me abruptly, having realized what he'd said. Then he took a drink from his glass, looked out over the harbor, and then returned his gaze to me. "Look," he said, "it's—"

"It's different. I know. I worked for the good guys. With official sanction. But it's not different for the people I lied to. Deception is always personal."

"And we encounter it every day," he said. He pulled his chair closer to mine and embraced me. "Makes you want to hang onto what's real. Hang on tight."

And we did.

Acknowledgments

The author gratefully acknowledges the assistance of all those who helped with the writing and preparation of *Deadfall*. Special thanks to LuAnn Svendsen, Robert Junghans, and John Baird Rogers for their comprehensive and insightful comments on early drafts. I also received invaluable feedback from my old friend, mystery author Fredrick Huebner, who tragically passed away before the publication of *Deadfall*. And a shout-out to the following people, who assisted in reviewing and critiquing early versions of the manuscript: Dawn Albrecht, Charlotte Babler, Trisha Fussy, Dennis Johnston, Kandi Kult, Kelly Langdon, Leslie Nielsen, Carl Schwanbeck, Judy Van Derhule, and Marveen Villarreal. Thanks as always to my editor, Jennifer Adkins, and to Christopher Valen and Jenifer LeClair, the principals of Conquill Press.

THANK YOU FOR READING

Thank you for reading *Deadfall*. I hope you'll take a moment to leave a quick review online. Reviews are an author's lifeblood. To read more about me and my books, and to receive notice of future publications, sign up for my email list at www.brianlutterman.com, where you'll also find news about my appearances and other features related to my books.

AN INVITATION TO READING GROUPS/ BOOK CLUBS

I would like to extend an invitation to reading groups/book clubs across the country. Invite me to your group and I'll be happy to participate in your discussion. I'm available to join your discussion either in person or via the telephone. (Reading groups should have a speakerphone.) You can arrange a date and time by e-mailing me at brian@brianlutterman.com. I look forward to hearing from you.

Not Sure What to Read Next?
Try these authors from Conquill Press

Jenifer LeClair
The Windjammer Mystery Series
Rigged for Murder
Danger Sector
Cold Coast
Apparition Island
Dead Astern
Death in the Blood Moon
www.windjammermyseries.com

Chuck Logan
Fallen Angel
Broker
www.chucklogan.org

Brian Lutterman
The Pen Wilkinson Mystery Series
Downfall
Windfall
Freefall
Nightfall
www.brianlutterman.com

Steve Thayer
Ithaca Falls
The Wheat Field
The Leper
www.stevethayer.com

Christopher Valen
The John Santana Mystery Series
White Tombs
The Black Minute
Bad Weeds Never Die
Bone Shadows
Death's Way
The Darkness Hunter
Speak for the Dead
Other titles by Christopher Valen
All the Fields
City of Stones (with Dan Cohen)
www.christophervalen.com

For more information on all these titles go to:
www.conquillpress.com